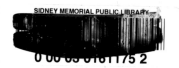
SIDNEY BOOKF
De Lint, Charles,
The mystery of Grace /

The Mystery of Grace

By Charles de Lint from Tom Doherty Associates

The Mystery of Grace

Charles de Lint

TOR®

A Tom Doherty Associates Book
New York

This is a work of fiction. All the characters, organizations, and events portrayed in this novel are either products of the author's imagination or are used fictitiously.

THE MYSTERY OF GRACE

Copyright © 2009 by Charles de Lint

A Tor Book
Published by Tom Doherty Associates, LLC
175 Fifth Avenue
New York, NY 10010

www.tor-forge.com

Tor® is a registered trademark of Tom Doherty Associates, LLC.

Library of Congress Cataloging-in-Publication Data

De Lint, Charles, 1951–
    The mystery of grace / Charles de Lint.—1st ed.
        p.   cm.
    "A Tom Doherty Associates book."
    ISBN-13: 978-0-7653-1756-8
    ISBN-10: 0-7653-1756-7
    1. Magic—Fiction.   I.   Title.
PR9199.3.D357M97   2009
813'.54—dc22

                                     2008046436

First Edition: March 2009

Printed in the United States of America

0   9   8   7   6   5   4   3   2   1

for

Paddy & Jim

(still hot-rodders at heart)

Acknowledgments

I'd like to thank Stu Jenks and Wilf Clarke for making my reference work go so much easier, and also Stu's friend Patricia for helping me name the city properly. Stu provided me with lots of wonderful reference photos and support (check out his exquisite art at www.stujenks .com), while Wilf (who works for H. B. Fenn, my Canadian distributor) sent me a stack of hot rod and custom books that were not only indispensable, but also vastly entertaining.

And speaking of hot rods, I'd also like to thank the editors and contributors of *Kustoms Illustrated, American Rodder, Traditional Rod & Kulture Illustrated, Ol' Skool Rodz,* and *Car Kulture DeLuxe.* These magazines not only helped inform me about the nitty-gritty of rebuilding old cars, but also kept me in the right mood while writing.

That mood was also helped by the stream of rockabilly and surf guitar I had playing while I worked. I've always loved this stuff, but didn't know nearly as much about it as I do now (and I'm still no expert), and that's only thanks to blogs by people with improbable user names such as rideyourpony, Boppelsag, EekTheCat, Yesterdays Gold, Fat City Guitar Lounge, Rock Is Dead/R.I.P., RedondoRoundUp, Uncle Gil's Rockin' Archives, Rocker Stomp, and Frisian's Other Favorites. They're chock-full of miniessays illustrated with classic album art.

I could fill pages of this book listing the artists I listened to while writing this novel. So let me just say that for contemporary music in this style, a few of the artists I enjoyed included The Reverb Syndicate, The Mermen, The Torquays, Los Straitjackets, HorrorPops, the Creepshow, The Langhorns, and Southern Culture on the Skids. For the classics, where do you start? Try Duane Eddy, Link Wray, Dick Dale, Davie Allen, The Deuce Coupes, The Super Shocks, Eddie Cochran, and The Ventures, and go on from there.

Acknowledgments

The blogs mentioned above are a good source for more information on all the above and more. As is *Blue Suede News: The House Organ of the Church of Rock 'n' Roll,* which sadly only comes out a few times a year.

Thanks are also due to you, the readers—I'd still write these stories if I wasn't being published, but because of you I get to make my living doing so; to Rodger Turner, friend and first reader, and also Web master for my website (www.charlesdelint.com) and the indispensable www.sfsite.com; to my agent, Russ Galen, who made sure that I would have the time to write this properly; to my editor, Patrick Nielsen Hayden, who, besides being a great guitarist, is also a most patient man; to my publisher, Tom Doherty, for his ongoing support of my career; to Irene Gallo, the art director at Tor, who book after book has designed some of the best covers in the field—I'm so lucky that some of those books are mine; and to the folks in the publicity department at Tor who never fail in their enthusiasm to get my books out to my readers.

Last, but not least, there aren't enough thanks for MaryAnn, who not only helps make all of this possible (the least of which is her reading and editing the manuscripts before anyone else sees them), but also completes my life.

OTTAWA
Winter 2008

I do not understand the mystery of grace—
only that it meets us where we are, but does
not leave us where it found us.
   —ANNE LAMOTT, from *Traveling Mercies*

We stand always on the edge of wonder . . . and
need only to be pointed in the right direction
to see it.
     — ROBERT J. HOWE, from his
introduction to *Coney Island Wonder Stories*

When we die . . . it will different for each of us.
     — TORI AMOS, from an interview
in *Mojo*, October 2006

The way to love anything is to realize that it
might be lost.
     — G. K. CHESTERTON

The Mystery of Grace

She woke up when he got out of bed. As she lay there, listening to him pee, it occurred to her that she'd actually been sleeping. She couldn't remember the last time she'd had a real sleep. She stretched languorously, appreciating the pull on her muscles and how the sheets slid across her skin. When the toilet flushed, she sat up to watch him return to bed, but he didn't climb back in. Instead, he sat at the end, pulling up his feet to sit cross-legged on the comforter.

"I killed my brother," he said.

"You *what*?"

He lifted a hand. "Oh, I don't mean literally. I killed him by neglect."

She leaned back against the headboard, pulling the sheets up over her breasts. A moment ago, she'd been comfortable with her nudity. Now she felt uneasy and goose bumps marched up her arms. She realized that for all their earlier intimacy, this was still a stranger's room. *He* was still a stranger, and she wasn't sure she liked the turn the evening had suddenly taken. No, scratch "evening." Make that late, late night. Almost morning.

If she couldn't remember the last time she'd had a real sleep, she *really* couldn't remember the last time she'd gone home from a club with a stranger. But he'd seemed so nice. He still seemed nice. Except right at this moment she didn't trust that he actually *was* what he seemed.

"Why are you telling me this?" she asked.

"I don't know. It's the anniversary of his death—he's always on my mind at Halloween. And I find that any time I'm really, really happy, I think of him and how it's one more thing he'll never get to experience."

"That's messed up."

"No kidding."

"You're still not saying why you're telling me this."

He shrugged. Those dark brown eyes of his settled their gaze on hers and she found it hard not to melt into their warmth.

"I know we've just met," he said, "but I felt this real connection with you, right from the first moment."

She smiled, and relaxed a little.

"You don't need a pickup line anymore," she said. "I'm already in your bed."

He smiled back. "I know. I guess I just wanted to share an . . . I don't know . . . intimacy with you."

She let the sheets fall and scooted over the bed until she was sitting right in front of him, cross-legged as well, their knees bumping. She took his hands.

"Tell me what happened," she said.

It wasn't a long story, but it was long enough. His bedroom windows faced west, so neither of them saw the dawn pinking the city's skyline. She wanted to tell him what happened wasn't really his fault, but she knew that wasn't the way this kind of guilt worked. Intellectually, he already knew that. It was his emotions that were tripping him up. The tangle of love and memory and what might have been.

She wanted to make love to him again, but a pressure in her bladder told her that first she needed to use the toilet herself. She leaned forward and they shared a lingering kiss.

"Hold that thought," she said as his hand rose to her breast. "I just need to pee."

He stayed on the bed when she got up, listening to her use the toilet as she'd listened to him use it earlier. He waited, but there was no sound of flushing. There was no sound at all. After another few moments, he turned around.

"Are you okay in there?" he asked.

There was no response.

"Grace?"

He got up and walked barefoot across the hardwood floor. The sun was up now. When he reached the bathroom door, he could see that the small room was empty. He stepped over to the bathtub and pushed the shower curtain aside. She wasn't there either.

He'd had his back to the bathroom, but surely he would have heard her leave the bedroom. So where did she go? She hadn't come through the bedroom. The only other way out was through the bathroom window, but it was too small to crawl out of and he would have heard the squeak of it opening because it always got stuck halfway up.

He backed out of the bathroom and looked around his bedroom. That was when he noticed the scatter of his clothes on the floor by the bed. His clothes. Hers weren't there.

Had he fallen asleep and she'd slipped out without him noticing?

He knew he hadn't, so she couldn't have.

Had she even been here in the first place?

That was an odd thought, except suddenly he wasn't sure of the answer. Real people didn't vanish into thin air.

He could remember her every detail. All the tattoos. The smell of her hair. The silky touch of her skin contrasting against the rougher texture of her hands—a mechanic's hands, she'd told him. He could remember her enthusiastic participation in their lovemaking, and his penis still had a touch of postcoital thickness.

He'd definitely had sex with someone—unless he'd just been jerking off in his sleep.

He sat on the bed and stared out the window for a long moment before he went through the apartment, turning on lights.

There was no one here.

It didn't look like there'd ever been anyone else here.

Great. He'd just fallen in love with a dream. Or a hallucination.

And surprising as that was, falling in love was exactly what had happened. He'd fallen for a woman he'd only just met, and fallen hard. Except it appeared that she was imaginary.

He rubbed his face with his hands. Halloween was always bad. It had been ever since the night Tim died. He'd always been able to bear the pain of the anniversary with a certain stoicism, hiding it from the world at large, staying busy, making sure he was around people so that he didn't have time to brood. But no matter how much he tried to distract himself, eventually he had to come back to the apartment, where the memories lay in wait.

Tonight had been different. He'd met Grace. She'd come home with him. They'd talked for hours, made love, fallen asleep in each other's arms.

Except he'd only imagined her. He'd imagined all of it. The sex. Feeling this incredible, immediate bond with her. Even sharing the story of Tim's death, which he never did with strangers . . .

Then his gaze rested on the two wineglasses standing on the coffee table. He remembered opening the bottle when they got back from the club. They'd each had a glass. There was still residue at the bottom of the glasses and the wine bottle on the table beside them was half full. More to the point, there was lipstick on the rim of one glass.

He looked back into the bedroom.

So she *had* been here.

But if that was true, if he hadn't just imagined her, then how the hell had she disappeared?

He waited until the hour was vaguely reasonable—staring at the clock until the digital numbers finally changed to seven—before he picked up the phone and called Danny. It rang a half dozen times before Danny finally picked up.

"Man," he said, his voice thick with sleep, "if you're selling something, it better be good."

"What could anyone sell you? You've already got everything you need."

"My point exactly." Danny paused for a moment, then added, "Jesus, John. It's seven o'clock in the morning."

"Yeah, I know. Sorry about that. I just need you to answer a question for me."

"The answer is: yeah, you're a dipstick. Now can I go back to sleep?"

"At the club last night," John said. "Was I with a woman?"

"Are you kidding me?"

John's heart sank. He knew it had been too good to be true. Except then Danny went on.

"She was awesome, man. I mean, not cover girl pretty, but a genuine looker. And seriously hot. Kat Von D hot, what with the tats and all."

"Who?"

"Come on. Didn't you ever watch *L.A. Ink?*"

"I don't have a TV."

"And that's something we need to have a serious conversation about. Who doesn't have a TV? What happened to you, man? You used to be just as much of a media geek as the rest of us."

"I've got a computer."

Danny laughed. "That's like saying you've got a cell phone. These days, everybody's got both. Hell, my grandfather's got a BlackBerry and I can remember having to set the time on his VCR whenever I went over to visit because he couldn't figure even that out. Forget taping a show. But now? He's like this tech pro, downloading game scores and weather forecasts, sending text messages to my mom and dad. You totally need to get back into the game."

John didn't bother to argue the point. He was too high on the swell of possibilities filling his head and his heart to even really pay much attention.

She *was* real.

He still had no idea how she'd left his apartment without him seeing her go, but that was completely overshadowed by Danny's confirmation.

"So why were you asking about that woman you left with last night?" Danny asked.

He laughed when John finished explaining.

"What?" Danny said. "You think you're such a loser that you made her up? Get real, Burns. Everywhere we go, women are always giving you the eye. It's like I was saying last night. You're this total chick magnet."

"Oh, come on."

"And I guess what's so appealing to them is that you're oblivious to it."

"I think you're—"

"She went home with you, didn't she? Do you think she'd just go home with anybody?"

"I hope not."

"Anyway, I wouldn't worry about it. If you guys got on as well as you say you did, she'll probably be calling you soon. Or you can always ask Nina to find out who she is. I think she knew everybody at the Solona Music Hall last night."

"She didn't know her."

"Well, someone must."

"I guess. That was a quite a crowd there last night."

"Tell me about it. And some of those Wicca girls are totally hot. Who knew? I thought they'd be all, you know, not so much."

John didn't bother to ask why. Danny was a sweet guy, but sometimes he just got too focused on women and their hotness factor.

"And Helen," Danny went on. "That girl you saw me talking to? I didn't get lucky like you, but she totally wants to get together again." He paused a moment, then added, "Unless she gave me a bogus number. Aw, man, what if she gave me a bogus number?"

"I'm sure she didn't."

"Says the guy who calls to confirm that he even met someone last night."

John laughed. "I should go. Sorry about getting you up so early."

"That's okay. You owe me a favor now, right?"

"I suppose . . ."

"And we totally need some new concept drawings for the Addison DVD. They want something edgier for when we come out of that intro clip into the main menu."

John sighed. "And when do you need them by?"

"Yesterday?"

"I'll see what I can do."

But when he went to his drawing board after he hung up the phone and picked up a piece of charcoal, he found himself sketching Grace's features on the paper tacked to the board instead.

The need to see her again was like an ache in his chest.

Altagracia "Grace" Quintero

Abuelo—my grandfather on my father's side—always liked to say, if you're going to do something, do it the best you can. Do it like it's the last thing you'll ever get to do, the one thing by which you'll be remembered when you're gone. It doesn't matter if it's pulling somebody out of the river or replacing a set of spark plugs. What's important is that you make it count.

I remember when my father first left us, Mama didn't want anything more to do with Abuelo. She got a divorce and became a Convertino again. My brother Tony took her maiden name, too, but I stayed a Quintero—not out of any loyalty to Papa, but out of respect for Abuelo. He was such a sweet old man, as loving and loyal as Papa hadn't proved to be. Tony never warmed to him—he saw too much of Papa in him, I suppose—but though she came to regret it, Mama let me visit with him whenever I wanted.

Abuelo was seventy-eight when Papa left us. He lived another ten years, and he lived those years well. I never met another person so present in the moment, giving whatever occupied him his undivided attention. You could think it was because he was old, but I don't think that was it. It was just how he lived his life—how he'd always lived it.

I wasn't so good with giving the present moment my best, that first winter after Papa was gone.

I was in my final year of high school, wishing I was a cheerleader, but for all the wrong reasons. I wasn't exactly brimming with school spirit, and I didn't really care to stand on the sidelines when it came to sports. I just wanted to be popular, or at least accepted, but it was my curse to be average. Not fat, not thin. Not pretty, not ugly. Just . . . average. The kind of person who always fades into the background of any social gathering. I remember thinking that even being stupendously grotesque would be an improvement, because at least I'd be noticed.

It was only when I stopped trying so hard that things changed for me, and Abuelo had his hand in that, too.

He lived and breathed cars. Abuela had died years ago—so long ago that I barely remembered her—and after Abuelo retired, he devoted his time to rebuilding a junked 1929 Model A Ford in his garage. I can't tell you how many hours I spent working on that car with him. I think we did everything but the engine build, window glass cutting, and the front seat upholstery.

It's such a sweet ride, painted a classic hot rod primer red. It's got the bigger '32 Ford Flathead V-8, '46 Ford truck brakes, and we had to do a two-and-a-half-inch chop and shortening of the rear to accommodate a '32 Ford rear gas tank, but otherwise we went the traditional route from front to back. I hate it when gearheads mix styles too much. What's the point of a custom restore if you can't still see the original lines? Because that's what it's all about. You find the line.

You take something Detroit built and you make it better. Trim it, stretch it, get rid of all the unnecessary stuff.

Find the line.

That's why Abuelo's Model A is so sweet. He found the line. *We* did. And when I understood—when we were done and we stood there looking at this beautiful thing that we'd made from an old junker—there was nothing else I wanted to do after that.

Working on the Ford in Abuelo's garage led me to taking shop at school, and that was where Mama started to have her regrets. She realized I wasn't her good little Catholic daughter anymore, meeting the world in a pretty dress with perfect hair the way I had at my confirmation.

"Gracie," she'd say, "girls don't work in a garage. No boy's ever going to want a girl who knows more about cars than he does."

She was wrong about that. I was the only girl in shop, and I'm the only girl mechanic at Sanchez Motorworks where Abuelo got me a job. The boys like it that I'm not a pretender. I'm my abuelo's grand-daughter. I live and breathe classic cars and the whole hot rod culture that goes with it. The rockabilly music, the lowriders, the tattoos and all. My mother gave up on ever marrying me off to a lawyer or a doc-tor after I got my first tattoo, on my left shoulder. It's of my namesake, Our Lady of Altagracia, and we're talking a serious tat here—none of your butterflies or Chinese ideographs that could say any damn thing and you wouldn't know. No, this is a full shoulder, color portrait of the saint.

Abuelo smiled when he saw it. Back in his day, only the real tough chicas got tattoos. Now anybody with a few dollars and the time can get one done. But I don't care. I don't care how trendy it is, I just like skin art, even if it is a little like crack. Getting them becomes addictive. These days I forget how tattooed I am until I see myself naked.

"Tattoos," Abuelo once said, "are the stories in your heart, writ-ten on your skin."

He should know. He had a half dozen of his own, including a por-trait of Abuela on his chest, right above his heart.

Abuelo's funeral was three weeks ago, which is what's got me to thinking about all of this. I've been going through old pictures of him, looking for one that I can have put on my skin the way I got a portrait of Mama after she died. The one of her is on the left side of my chest, just under my collarbone so that she and Our Lady of Altagracia can look at each other and keep each other company.

Abuelo was eighty-eight when he died. He still lived on the East Side in that little house of his with the big garage on the side, and he still worked on cars. The latest project was a '50 Ford coupe—Abuelo always had a fondness for the Ford Motor Company, and I can still re-member his big grin when I got FoMoCo tattooed down my right leg. It's in a loose, loopy red script, with a stick of lipstick in a flourish at the end as though it had been written with the lipstick. I'd been help-ing him out on weekends, and we'd just finished chopping the top on the way to giving it that killer fastback stance those old Fords carry so

well. We had plans to head over to a swap meet on the weekend, hoping to trade for a grille and front bumper—the ones on Abuelo's coupe
were trashed. Knowing he wasn't such an early riser anymore, I called
him on the Friday night to find out what time he wanted to leave.

I got worried when there was no answer. I'd bought him a cell a
few months ago, and made him promise to keep it charged and clipped
to his belt, so I knew that he'd answer if he could.

I don't think I ever made such good time crossing the city as I did
that night. I'm just surprised I didn't get pulled over. I pushed that old
Fairlane of mine to the limit, changing lanes, jumping lights, doing
anything I could to get out to his house on time.

But I was too late.

I found him in the garage, under the Ford coupe, a wrench in his
hand.

Next to holding court in a corner booth at Chico's, a shot of
tequila in hand and his compadres gathered around, this is how he'd
have wanted to go out. Though he'd probably be pissed that he wasn't
going to see the coupe up and running again.

I sat there on the concrete floor and cried for a long time before I
was finally able to call 911.

There was no one else to make all the arrangements. I had no idea
where my father was—if he was even still alive—and there was no
other family around. Maybe there were some cousins back in Mexico,
but I didn't know any of them and Abuelo never talked about the
people in his old life before he immigrated here. Abuela was long
gone. Tony lived in Italy now, working for some architect. He didn't
even come home for the funeral. When I called to tell him that Abuelo
had died, he actually said, "I didn't know he was still alive."

I know they'd never been close, but still. That was harsh.

The long and short of it was that Rodrigo Quintero was laid to
rest on a cool, overcast autumn day with only one member of his immediate family in attendance, which would be me. Though I don't
mean to imply that I was the only person there. It might have been the
middle of the week, with the weather offering up a grey day to suit
my mood, but San Miguel Cemetery was filled with people for his
funeral.

My best friend Vida Ortiz stood beside me at the graveside—

looking gorgeous in a tight black dress, her dyed blond hair subdued by a veil. My boss, Shorty, and the rest of the guys from Sanchez Motors were there, along with the gang from Chico's, members of the local hot rod club, and all kinds of people who normally I'd only see at car shows and rallies and swap meets. Outside the cemetery, Mission Street was lined with vintage cars for blocks in either direction. Getting here, we'd been like a parade following the hearse—it didn't hurt that the hearse itself was a rebuilt 1930 Nash 480 Special Six that a friend of Shorty's had lent us for the day.

Abuelo would have loved it, though he'd probably have preferred the hearse to be a Ford.

After the ceremony, we all went back to Chico's, filling the parking lot and the streets around the taquería with customs and classics. Vida organized all of this. She might play the part of the dumb blonde when she's posing for photographers at the car shows in her vintage outfits, but she's been running a successful tattoo shop for ten years and you don't stay in business that long being dumb. She's the most organized person I know.

As often happens at Chico's, after a couple of hours an impromptu jam started up in one corner featuring a mix of mariachi and rockabilly. At one point, Shorty got up and sang one of Abuelo's favorite songs: Big Boy Groves's version of "I Gotta New Car" with its litany of the problems that buying a new Caddy caused him. And of course it's got that classic last line about how the next time he gets a new car, it's going to be one that he can "afford," and when he says afford, he means "a Ford."

It didn't matter how many times Abuelo heard that line. He'd always laugh and bellow it out along with whoever was singing the song. I usually did, too, but that day it just made the tears well up in my eyes. I remember Vida grabbing my hand before I could smear the mascara she'd so carefully applied hours earlier and dabbing the tears away with a Kleenex.

"This is going to be so hard," I told her when I could trust my voice not to break. "I don't know what I'm going to do without him."

"You'll do what he'd want you to do," she said. "You'll carry on, like he did after your abuela passed. Like you did with your mother."

I nodded, but I knew it wasn't the same. Mama and I hadn't always gotten along as well as we should, so besides the sadness, I also had to carry around all this guilt. I don't think Abuelo and I ever had a cross word for each other. I mean, *ever*.

"Are you still going to get a portrait of him?" she asked.

"Oh yeah. But I have to find the right picture."

She nodded. "Come by the shop whenever you're ready."

Vida was my tattoo artist as well as my friend. Her brother had done my first tat of Our Lady of Altagracia, but as soon as Vida started working for him, she was the one I went to for my ink. When she opened her own shop, my business followed her.

"You should say something," Vida told me.

She nodded to the makeshift stage where Shorty was trying to get my attention.

I wished I hadn't looked. There were a thousand things I had to say, but I wasn't sure I'd get through any of it without breaking down.

Vida knew me too well. She could see that all I wanted to do was escape into the parking lot. She put a hand on my arm. I wasn't sure if she was comforting me, or stopping me from taking off.

"You have to go up there," she said.

"I know. I'm just . . . I don't know if I can get through it."

"These are all his friends, Grace. They're all your friends, too. If you can't finish, they'll understand."

I knew she was right and finally I got up on the stage.

For one long moment I stood there looking out at all these people who had been so much a part of Abuelo's life. Who were still a part of mine. I cleared my throat, and gathering my courage, I started to speak. My voice cracked more than a few times, and I kept having to blow my nose and dab at my eyes, making a mess of my mascara. But I got through it.

Other people got up after me, sharing stories, talking about how they'd first met him, how he'd helped them. I'd known he was well liked in the local hot rod and custom community, but I guess I never realized before that day what an impact he had, not just on me, but on so many other lives.

I think about that, and it's comforting, but then I always start thinking about how maybe I could have prevented his death. If I'd gone out to his place right after work instead of going home first. If I'd made sure he was getting regular check-ups. If, if, if . . .

I'd been worrying at the memory of my abuelo like a dog with a bone, filling my head with what-ifs and should-haves and if-I-could-do-it-over-agains, which is pretty ironic, considering that advice of his. Here he was gone, and what do I do instead of living in the moment and doing the best I can? Pretty much the exact opposite. I even took up smoking after having quit for eighteen months.

Vida was so pissed off at me. I tried to make like it was no big deal, but it's scary how quickly *that* little addiction takes over your life again.

I convinced myself during the first week that it was just to get through this serious rough patch, what with Abuelo gone and Tony being a jerk and me having to handle everything. I'd let the cigs get me through and then I'd just go cold turkey again. It wouldn't be so hard, this time around. I'd already done it once, right?

By the second week, I knew I wasn't kidding anyone, least of all myself. By that second week, I was already rearranging my life to accommodate the habit, because you know the smoker's motto: smoking comes first. Someone invites you to do something—go out for dinner, stop by their apartment for a visit—and your first thought isn't whether or not you'd like to do it. No, the first thing you wonder is, can I smoke there?

By the third week I knew I had to get real about this. Shorty was ragging me about all the smoke breaks I was taking. I was already rediscovering my old smoker's cough, and started to get a little out of breath walking up the two flights to my apartment. So I threw my half pack of cigarettes in the trash at the garage before I went home and you know, I was doing really well there for a while—at least an hour and forty-five minutes—until I realized that, yes, I was going to quit, I really was, but not tonight. I'd get serious about it tomorrow. Tomorrow was Saturday and I could go to the garage and distract myself with work.

Normally, I did all the custom jobs, working on the classics. Old Fords, 'Vettes, Monte Carlos, DeSotos, Chryslers, Tuckers, Caddys. If it was slow, I'd help out in other areas of the shop, but I can't remember the last time I didn't have three or four jobs lined up to come into my bay. I don't want to sound like I'm bragging, but Sanchez Motor-works has got a serious rep as the go-to place for hardcore gearheads and hot-rodders, and I'm part of the reason. Not the biggest. That'd be Shorty, who's been customizing and rebuilding cars since I was still in diapers and tats were just pretty pictures on my abuelo's skin.

Right now I'm working on a killer '56 two-seat T-Bird. It's not a big job. I'm just replacing the porthole and rear windows on the re-movable hardtop, then giving the whole vehicle a new paint job.

But the real reason I was going in is that I'd promised to help Shorty's nephew Tito work on his car. Tito's a good kid, but he got into some trouble recently. He was starting to run with some gang-bangers and got busted trying to boost a car. It was only a first of-fense, but the D.A.'s office doesn't see much beyond the brown skin when it comes to people like us. Tito was looking at county time, ex-cept he got lucky and pulled Andy Hoffman as his public defender. Hoffman's got a reputation of being a bulldog and the D.A.'s office knows it, so they played fair and Tito got a sentence deserving of the crime: community service, a fine, and a stern warning.

To keep him out of trouble, Shorty lets him hang around the garage where he's been helping us all out. When you're under a car, you can always use an extra set of hands to pass you a wrench, or that Phillips that's just out of reach.

Last week, Shorty gave him a junked '72 Monte Carlo and even promised to help him out with the insurance once it's up and running. All Tito has to do is keep his nose clean and do the work on the car. No charge for parts.

He's supposed to do it on his own, but we've all been helping him out. We don't do the actual work. We just show him what he needs to do whenever he isn't sure about how to tackle the next problem. Well, mostly. Sometimes it's easier to do than it is to show, and it's a big job for anyone to do all on their own. But like I said, he's a good kid. We all like him. So putting a few hours in here and there to help him out isn't a hardship. And I know that if I get deep into working on a car, I won't even think about having a smoke.

But that's tomorrow.

Tonight there's just me, alone in my apartment with no distrac-tions and too many thoughts.

So I put on a jacket that I don't really need over my sleeveless T and leave my apartment, walking down the street to Luna's—the local corner grocery, which is actually in the middle of the next block. It's a warm night but there's a cool breeze blowing in from the desert. I can't see the mountains because of a cloud cover. The sky's been teasing us with October rains for days but it never quite delivers more than a few minutes of misting rain—just enough to bring the smell of creosote into the air.

If Solona was a town, instead of just one small part of Santo del Vado Viejo, 26th Street would be its downtown main street. Most of the area is made up of single-story adobe houses with dirt yards, cacti, scraggly palo verde trees, and mesquite, but the buildings lining 26th are two-story brick and wood, except for where I live. The Alverson Arms rises to a towering five stories of grey stone that some enterprising builder hauled all the way down from the mountains back in the early part of the last century. I'm guessing it was a showpiece in its time, but now it's just as run-down and shabby as the rest of the neighborhood, except taller and grey.

The rest of the buildings on the street are small businesses with apartments overhead. For the most part, name-brand businesses and affluent yuppies have yet to take over this part of Solona, and everything's a little scruffy-looking—Vida likes to say it's "genteel." That's not to say we don't get the touristas from the 'burbs or downtown coming here to shop, to try some barrio food, or just to check out the bands playing at the Solona Music Hall. But if you live in this neighborhood, it doesn't matter if you're Mexican, Indian, black, or white, the one thing we all have in common is that we don't exactly have a lot of disposable income. It's month-to-month for most of us down here.

On the plus side, at least we know pretty much everybody—to nod to, or say hi, if nothing else. It's possible to be a woman and walk around these streets in the early evening without needing some burly boyfriend to keep the wolves at bay, and I like that. I'd never do it downtown, and I don't scare easily. I may look like a tough chica, but I'm all about being safe.

I love walking into Luna's. As soon as you come in the door your nose fills with the redolent smells of chiles, shredded beef and pork tamales, salsas, cilantro, and corn tortillas, fresh off the press. Estefan and Dolores Luna, the owners, are invariably behind the counter, no matter what time of day you come. If they're not, it's one of their kids. Joe, who's studying to be a lawyer. Rosie, who's going to be a chartered accountant. Or Mateo, the youngest, who's still in high school.

Ranchera or norteño music is usually playing on the sound system, or they're watching telenovelas on an ancient fourteen-inch color TV—an old set with a line of static running along the top of the screen. The counter is laden with CDs and cassettes of Mexican music, jars of salsa, cans of spiced fruit, thick guayaba and membrillo jam, plastic bags of wheat-flour tortillas, and there's always a small metal tray lined with wax paper on which are laid out rows of fresh empanadas. Dolores makes the fruit turnovers herself, just as she makes all their salsas and tamales.

Behind the counter are all the cigarettes. Above them, on a long shelf that runs the length of the wall, is a row of votive candles from which Jesus, the Virgin, and various saints look down upon the store.

The Lunas always have a smile for me when I come in, though they were wary the first time. I could see it in their eyes: What kind of trouble is this tattooed girl going to cause? It's something I get all the time from people who can't see past the skin. The flip side are the people who can focus only on the skin—like my tats are all I want to talk about. With all my ink, and the grease I can never completely get from under my nails, I guess the only place I really fit in is with my own people—the hot-rodding crowd. Or with folks like the Lunas who know all about snap judgments made on how a person looks.

I knew I was going to get a lecture tonight from Estefan about buying cigarettes. He might sell them, but he wasn't happy about it. Still, he knew the demand was there and if people had to go to the 7-Eleven for their cigarettes, one block farther down the street, across from the park, then they might also do the rest of their shopping there: picking up their beer, pop, chips, and all the other sundries for which people don't feel like making a special trip to one of the big grocery stores.

Not everybody's in love with the homemade Mexican specialties that you can only get in a small family-run shop like Luna's.

I can see the bright lights of the 7-Eleven as I linger outside the grocery store for a moment, not quite ready to go in. Both Estefan and

Dolores had been happy when I told them I'd quit smoking. I was so not looking forward to breaking the news to them by buying a pack of cigarettes, but I didn't even think of going to the 7-Eleven. That just felt like it would be disloyal.

But finally—because after all, "smoking comes first"—I push open the door and go in. Estefan and his daughter Rosie are behind the counter, watching TV. Smiles light up their faces when they recognize me.

"Hola, Grace!" Estefan says, speaking Spanish as he always does with me. "<What did you forget tonight? Some of Dolores's salsa?>"

I had dropped in on the way home from work and bought a bag of fresh flour tortillas. I usually have it with salsa, rice, and beans, but tonight I'd felt like making rolled up peanut butter and sprout sandwiches.

"<No, I just wanted to get a can of, um, beans,>" I reply.

I don't know why I said that. I suppose it seems easier to pick something else up first and then, when I get to the cash register to pay, to casually ask for some cigarettes as well. How pathetic is that?

"<You know where they are?>" Estefan asks. I nod, but before I can go down the aisle, he adds, "<Here it is, Friday night. A pretty girl like you . . . why aren't you out with some nice boy?>"

I don't know who's more embarrassed, his daughter Rosie or me.

"Pop!" she says. "You don't ask things like that."

But he just shrugs and smiles, unrepentant. "<I was only saying.>"

"It's okay," I tell them, switching to English. "I wanted an evening in by myself—that's all."

I know they can read the lie. Ever since Abuelo's funeral, I've been holing up in my apartment when I'm not at work. I don't want to party. I don't want to go out for drinks or a concert, which is driving Vida crazy. And as for "nice boys" . . . I've never been good with relationships. Friends who happen to be male? Sure, lots of them. Lovers? Not so much. I think that's Papa's legacy to me. I don't trust anyone to stay.

And now Abuelo's death has once again reinforced the fact that life is transitory. Nothing withstands the cruel march of time, especially not relationships.

"I'll just get those beans," I say.

I hear the front door open as I head down the aisle—followed by Estefan greeting whoever's come in, the way he does with everybody. I don't think anything of it until an unfamiliar male voice tells him to empty his till. I stop in the middle of the aisle, and turn around to see a young white guy—just a kid, really—standing at the counter with an evil-looking pistol in his hand. He has his back to me. His hand is shaking and he keeps looking from the front door to where Estefan is slowly opening the till.

I hate guns. I hate the people who use them even more.

I don't think the kid even knows I'm here, and I want to keep it that way. But all he has to do is glance down the aisle and he'll see me. He's obviously a junkie, and the one thing you don't want to do with a junkie holding a gun, is startle him.

I start to back away, out of his line of sight. Instead, I trip over a box filled with packages of rice that's sitting on the floor. I lose my balance and start to fall backward. Trying to compensate against the backward momentum, I'm too successful. Just as the kid turns in my direction, I'm lunging forward, arms flailing the air.

I know what it looks like. I know what he sees.

It's one of those awful moments like a car wreck when time stretches, but no matter how much time you seem to have, you're actually rushing forward with the speed and force of an eighteen-wheeler to an inevitable conclusion.

I want to shout, No! I'm not trying to take you down.

But all he sees through his junkie paranoia is some crazy, tattooed woman, waving her hands as she charges toward him.

I see the muzzle of his gun flash before I hear the sound.

I hear the loud thunder of the shots, booming in the confines of the store, before I feel the impact of the bullets.

They punch me in the chest.

Once.

Twice.

The force of the impact spins me around. It sends me crashing into the displays of canned and dried goods. I claw at the shelves. Cans and packages of beans and rice come crashing down all around me as I fall.

Falling . . . falling . . .

Then the shock of the pain hits me.

I try to suck in air as I tumble to the floor, but there's no air to breathe.

I can't hear anything for the roar in my ears.

I can't feel anything except the screaming pain.

I can't see anything.

No, that's not true.

I see a light.

The overhead fluorescents.

And somehow, I'm falling into them.

Falling . . . falling . . .

I sit up with a gasp, my pulse drumming. My T-shirt is soaked with sweat, front and back, and I'm making this weird gulping sound as I try to take in air.

My dislocation is total.

For long moments I'm in two places at once: dying in Luna's Food Market and safe here in my own bedroom.

Safe.

I manage to focus on my surroundings. My gaze goes to the familiar mess on top of my dresser. Makeup and jewelry and a little stack of folded-up panties that are clean. I just haven't gotten around to putting them in a drawer yet. I look at my desk with the scatter of paperwork beside my laptop, which is standing open, the screen blank. Morning light is creeping in around the edges of my curtains.

I'm safe.

Mary, Mother of God, thank you, thank you.

It was just a dream.

I've fallen asleep in the jeans and T-shirt I was wearing last night and the nightmare isn't real.

My pulse hasn't slowed yet and I'm still sitting straight upright in my bed, hands clutching fistfuls of bedding. But the panic is ebbing.

Until I hear a sound in the hall outside my bedroom.

I usually keep a baseball bat leaning against the wall between my bed and the night table, but I'd moved it when I was cleaning my apartment the other day. I can see it leaning against the wall, under the bay window, a shaft of light from the bottom of the curtains cutting across the black tape wrapped around its handle. It's so close, but there's no time to get it.

A large figure fills the doorway and my pulse, which had just started on its way back to normal, jumps back into overdrive.

I'm stronger than a lot of girls, but not more than most guys. I've learned to fight dirty, when I've had to. But I'm not wearing my boots, so I can't give him a kick where it hurts. I'm not even standing up.

The phone, I think. If I can just dial 911.

"So, you're finally awake," the figure in the doorway says.

It's a warm, friendly voice, and it stops my hand from inching toward the handset. The figure steps out of the hallway shadows into the room where I can see her better, but I still don't know her. Or why she's here in my bedroom.

She's a tall, overweight black woman in a loose print dress. Her smile is as welcoming as her voice, her broad face creased with laugh lines. The vibe I get from her reminds me of Lia Giuliani, the owner of Mama Lia's, an Italian restaurant just off Alamos Street. It used to be my mother's favorite place to eat out. Mama Lia would bustle out of the kitchen whenever we arrived and personally see us to our table. We never ordered from the menu. Mama Lia would just start to bring out food, working her way from antipastas up to the main course.

But that was back before the freeway accident that, if you don't count our deadbeat father, left Tony and me orphans. Before Tony moved to Italy. I haven't been to the restaurant in years, though I did see Mama Lia at Abuelo's funeral. I didn't get the chance to talk to her but I'm guessing she was there for me, because I doubt she knew Abuelo.

But just because the stranger reminds me of Mama Lia doesn't mean I'm happy to have her in my bedroom.

"Who the hell are you?" I ask.

"Where are my manners?" she says. "I'm Edna Browning, from one-ten. I've been here a long time now."

Here, where? I wonder. In this city, this apartment building, my room?

She looks around with open curiosity, her gaze pausing on the laptop on my desk in the corner, the phone, my clock radio.

"Things sure have changed," she says. She points to my laptop. "What's that? Some kind of newfangled typewriter? I'm telling you, girl, you have things in your kitchen I have *no* idea what they're for." She shakes her head. "And—no offense—you've got so many tattoos I was thinking that maybe you used to work in a circus sideshow."

I can't seem to speak. How long has she been prowling around in my apartment?

Normally, I don't take a lot of crap from anybody, but as she comes closer to the bed, I find myself shrinking back against the headboard and I'm actually thinking I should own a gun like Shorty's always telling me I should.

"Don't you worry," she says. "This isn't the kind of thing that makes sense all at once. You just take your time with it."

I clear my throat.

"What are you doing here?" I ask.

She shrugs. "I just thought I'd check in to see if you were coming around yet. We brought you up from that store three days ago and you were past due to wake up." She looks around my room again. "I haven't seen this before," she goes on. "Usually, the only place that comes along is where you died, but you brought your whole apartment with you, too. Must be because you lived here in the Alverson Arms, just like I do. Other folks, they aren't so lucky. They lose all their stuff when they cross over."

"What the hell are you talking about?"

She gives a sorrowful shake of her head.

"You died, girl," she says. "I guess I could ease into telling you, but there's no other way to put it."

"That's not funny."

"I didn't say it was. But it's true."

I shake my head. "I'm not dead. I think I'd know if I was dead."

But the dream comes back to me, the junkie's skittering eyes as he turns his gun in my direction and fires. The shock of the bullets hitting me and driving me back into the display shelf. The cans tumbling around me as I fall. The pain. The light above, pulling me up.

The light . . .

And then I realize that I'm still dreaming. No wonder I can be so calm about all of this.

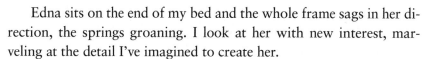

Edna sits on the end of my bed and the whole frame sags in her direction, the springs groaning. I look at her with new interest, marveling at the detail I've imagined to create her.

"So, we're both dead?" I ask.

I'm willing to go with the flow of the dream now, to see where it will take me.

Edna nods. "You, me, and maybe, oh I don't know how many others who died somewhere in the few blocks around this building—the Alverson Arms, I mean."

"And you found me in Luna's Food Market and brought me back here."

She nods again.

"How'd you know where I live?"

"I'm not stupid, girl. You had a wallet in your jacket pocket. All I had to do was look at your driver's license."

"Okay, but *why* did you bring me here?"

"I thought you'd be more comfortable waking up in familiar surroundings than on the floor of the grocery where you died." She cocks that broad head of hers and adds, "You're taking this well. My guess is you've decided you're dreaming."

"Are you saying I'm not?"

"If it keeps you calm," she says, "you can think whatever you want."

"So," I say, "the afterlife turns out to be exactly like things were before we died, except for the lack of privacy."

Edna shakes her head. "This is what people 'round here have figured out: anybody dies around the Alverson Arms, they show up here. It doesn't take in a big area. Maybe a block or two in each direction. You go to the edge of that, and there's nothing."

"Nothing."

"That's right. Now the funny thing is, when you die, the place where you died comes with you, so we've got us stores and apartments and buildings that are from all different parts of the past fifty years or so. Like the grocery store where I found you. Up until three days ago, that was a soda shop.

"The only difference between you and me and everybody else is, we lived here in the Arms, so our apartments are like they were when we died instead of whatever they were like before that. Though the difference between you and me is that I died in my apartment, so it makes sense that it would come with me—or at least as much as anything here makes sense."

I should have been writing scripts for the movies, if I can come up with this kind of crap.

"What, no Heaven, no Hell?" I ask.

"Well, now," she says. "You want to get religious—and let me tell you, I lost that urge about thirty years ago—you could consider this to be some kind of Limbo, I suppose. Everything's the same, day after day. Nothing changes until someone else dies and comes over."

"And you're okay with that?"

"I don't know. I don't really care anymore. There's nothing I can do to change it."

"How can you not care?"

Edna shrugs. "I see being here as a respite. All my life I had to scrabble for every penny I earned. To keep my family fed. To keep a roof over our heads. Here, I don't. Here, I can just rest. I can do nothing and not feel guilty. Sure, it gets old some days, but mostly I'm content."

Well, I'm not. I want this dream to end. And maybe the best way to do that is to stop buying into what Edna is telling me. Because it's easy to get lost in it. Her voice is so warm, her eyes kind and sympathetic. But she's only a figment of my dreaming mind.

"This is bullshit," I tell her. "And no offense," I add, throwing back at her the phony apology she used when she was talking about my tats, "I think you're a crazy woman and I need you to leave."

Edna smiles. She gets to her feet and the bed frame gives a groan of release.

"That's all right," she says. "I don't take offense. What's the point? We're all here together. I'll see you around later."

Not if I can help it, I think. I guess the words are written on my face.

She smiles again. "It's not like you're going anywhere."

"So you think I'm your prisoner," I say.

That'll last just as long as it takes me to get to my feet and have my baseball bat in my hands.

"Honey," she says, "you're nothing to me but another dead, brown-skinned girl who needs to adjust to the fact that she's not going back to the life she once had. That's the sorry truth and there's nothing either of us can do about it. You can be as mad at me as you like, but I had nothing to do with you getting here, and I sure can't get you out."

She turns before I can reply and leaves the bedroom.

I sit there in my bed, leaning against the headboard as I listen to her progress through the apartment. I don't move until I hear the front door close. Then I get up and walk into my living room. I engage the deadbolt before I turn to look around. The light's dim in here like it was in my bedroom. I push aside the curtains and the bright light that's been creeping in around their edges bursts into the room.

The Alverson Arms fronts onto 26th Street, facing south. My apartment's on the third floor, on the south side. From its windows I can see the domed roof of the Solona Public Library, one block over, and then the mountains, off in the distant desert. The sun's bright today, but there's a low mist or fog just on the other side of the library and I can't see past it the way I normally can.

You go to the edge . . . and there's nothing . . .

I open the window and take a deep, steadying breath of fresh autumn air. For a long moment I hang out of the window. It strikes me that the air really *is* fresh. It doesn't hold the usual brew of exhaust and dust with a faint underlay of garbage. This is like desert air, when you're standing at the foot of the mountains and you can look out forever. The kind of air coming in the window when you drive down some back road on the way to a swap meet or some classic car rally.

And it's so quiet. I don't see anybody on the streets—I mean, *anybody*—and there's no traffic. I can see a few cars, parked here and there along the curb, but the thing is they're not the rice burners and beat-up old American cars I usually see in this neighborhood. We're talking a gearhead's wet dream here. A '57 Imperial with those classic fins. A two-tone '56 Bel Air with a ragtop. A '72 Monte Carlo with its reverse curved rear window to give it that convertible look. Not one, but two hardtop '67 Camaros.

They're up and down the street, one classic vehicle after another, all of them in great shape. Even the bus at the intersection down the street is at least thirty years old. I remember that style from the seventies, square and bulky, the windows smaller than they are now.

I look across the street and I feel as if I'm looking at the sound-stage for a movie, or a photo from some old issue of *Life* magazine. The view is a trick—it has to be. The shapes of the buildings are the way they're supposed to be, but none of the businesses are the same. All the storefronts have an old-fashioned, almost quaint appearance.

I pull my head back inside.

I am so done with this dream. I want to wake up. I need to wake up. If I don't . . . I'm afraid I'll end up believing in this place because everything seems so damn real.

I'm starting to get the shakes and my legs feel all rubbery. I bang the heel of my hand against the windowsill as if that will wake me up.

But nothing changes.

So I put on my boots, pick my jacket up from the back of the sofa, and leave the apartment.

There's something different about the hallway and stairwell, but it's not until I get down to the first floor that I realize what it is. It doesn't smell as bad and the walls are covered with wallpaper in a flowered design. I don't remember there ever being wallpaper in the Alverson Arms. I suppose they could have put some up in the last week or so and I just never noticed it, except it's obviously been around for a while. When I examine it more closely I see a few stains and places where it's been scuffed through to the bare wall.

I'm still thinking about this as I walk down the front hall to the foyer. I notice an open doorway ahead and I can hear music—some kind of old R & B playing on small speakers so it sounds a little tinny. When I pause at the doorway and look in, I see the woman who was in my room earlier. She's in a kitchen at the end of a short hallway, sitting at a Formica-topped table with another black woman who's as tall as Edna, but she's all bones and angles. They're playing cards, feet tapping to the music. Edna looks up before I can turn away.

"Grace!" she calls. "Come in and meet my friend Ruth."

She's smiling. Ruth, when she turns to look at me, smiles as well. It's all so normal. I think of how carefully I locked my apartment door behind me—just as I always do—but here they have their door open wide. Sure, they're at home, but I still keep my door closed and locked when I'm at home, and I can take care of myself a little better than most.

"Grace . . . ?" Edna asks.

I back away from the doorway without speaking and escape out the front of the apartment building. But I don't get any farther than the stoop.

I know. I've already seen all of this from the window of my living room. But the sheer strangeness of the view hits me all over again. Now I feel as if I'm standing in the middle of that movie soundstage and they're about to film something from the fifties or sixties.

It's my street, but it's not.

The first thing I notice is how much room there is without a line of cars parked bumper to bumper along the curb. There's *so* much space it's disorienting, like when you drive from downtown into the 'burbs where they've got all the room in the world for yards and wider streets.

I go over to the two-tone Bel Air I spied from my window upstairs. I walk all around it, trailing my hand across the hood, the chrome trim, the smooth curve of the fins. The paint gleams—turquoise and white, front to back, with a white ragtop and whitewalls set off by the turquoise hubs. I peer into the window, then step back to take the whole of it in again.

This hasn't been rebuilt. I can tell. This car is in its original condition. It's obviously been driven, but it still looks like it only just came out of the factory a year or two ago, not decades.

I straighten up and my gaze goes to the steel railway ties running down the middle of the street. I've never seen them here before, but I know what they're for. Though it's been gone since the sixties, there used to be an east-west streetcar line that went down 26th Street. I look up and find the electric wires that would have powered the cars. I start to shiver as I try to figure out what it means.

Except then I start to pay attention to the buildings across the street. This part of 26th Street around the Alverson Arms is a mix of residential and commercial, and that's still the case here. But while I recognize the profiles of the buildings themselves, the stores aren't familiar. QuikClean Laundromat. The 26th Street Diner. Vallance

Records & Tapes. There's a grocertia. A pawnshop. Marshall's Vacuums & Electronics. Carilla's Nearly New Clothes. On the far corner, Perez Billiards.

They're not new; they look like they've been there for years. There's a thick patina of dust and grime on the pawnshop's window. The grocery has a tattered handmade sign saying "Bananas on Special" that's curling off the glass at one corner. In the record store window there's a poster for a band I've never heard of that's playing at the Alona Cruz downtown.

They weren't there yesterday. And they weren't there when I went to Luna's last night.

The only place that looks familiar is in the middle of the next block: the Solona Music Hall. Or at least the marquee and façade look familiar from this angle. I know it as a club featuring live bands a couple of nights a week, but in the past it's housed everything from burlesque revues to a theater company and film retrospectives.

I pull my gaze from the Solona Music Hall's marquee and look back at the stores directly across the street from me. My shivering turns to dizziness and I have to hold on to the stoop's railing to keep my balance. I don't know what's going on here and I almost go back inside to Edna's apartment to see if she or her friend can help me understand.

Almost.

But they're a part of this . . . this . . . whatever's happening to me.

And then I remember that I'm dreaming. It might be a very linear dream, playing out in real time instead of jumping from scene to scene the way my dreams usually do, but it's still just a dream.

I turn away from the confusing view of unfamiliar stores on a street I know so well and make my way to the end of the block, turn right on El Encanto, then right again into the dirt alley that runs behind the Alverson Arms.

I stand in the mouth of the alley and stare down its length. There's the usual crap you'd expect to find in a Solona alley: some bald tires, a few garbage bins, a junked Toyota missing its wheels and doors. Shrubs and prickly pear grow along the sides of the building.

But my street car's not there.

The Ford Fairlane I baby the way Vida's mother babies her yappy little Chihuahua.

I know that I should be freaking—normally, I *would* be freaking. I mean, some asshole stole my car. But instead I retrace my steps to 26th Street and start down the block to Luna's Food Market, ignoring everything except what's directly in front of me. I can see Luna's sign ahead. I reach for the calm that the familiarity of the sign should bring me, but all I can feel inside is a sense of impending doom that gets stronger with every step I take.

And then I'm there, in front of the store. My hand trembles as I push the door open. I step over the threshold, but that's as far as I can go in. My heart's drumming way too fast in my chest and I have the shakes again.

It's just a dream, I remind myself. A long, weird, and freaky dream, but that's all.

I take a few steadying breaths.

I can do this.

On legs that feel like jelly, I edge my way inside. The door bangs shut behind me. Everything looks the way it's supposed to—the shelves are stocked, there are empanadas on their tray by the cash register, the row of votive candles on the shelf behind the counter. I can smell the spices and tamales and all, but their scent isn't as strong as I remember. It's silent in the store, and I'm alone. There's no sign of the Lunas or any of their children.

I move deeper into the store, past the cash counter, past the display of tamales and salsas behind glass, until I'm looking down the aisle where earlier in my dream I . . . where I . . . where the junkie aimed his gun . . .

I see cans of vegetables and fruit, packages of dried beans and rice, everything scattered all over the floor. And there, by the box of rice packages that tripped me . . . there, where I fell when the bullets punched my chest . . .

I stare with morbid fascination at the large, dark pool of congealed blood.

My hand goes under my T-shirt without my even being aware of having lifted it. The skin is smooth, I'm unhurt.

There are no holes in my T-shirt. It's not stained with dried blood. But I remember the shots.

The shock of their impact.

The flood of pain.

My gaze goes up to the overhead fluorescents. I turn away and stumble back as a wave of dizziness sets my head to spinning again. Grabbing the counter, I let it take my weight as I half shuffle, half pull myself along its length, back to the front door. I don't think I take even one breath until I'm finally back outside.

I lean with my back against the front window and slide down until I'm sitting on the pavement. I pull my knees to my chest and press my face against them.

I want this to be done.

I just want to wake up. To be home again and safe in my own bed without some big crazy woman standing there in the doorway of my bedroom telling me I'm dead.

I'm *not* dead.

I'm *not*.

I don't know how long I sit there having my meltdown before I realize I'm no longer alone. I never heard anyone approach, but somewhere in the welter of emotion I become aware of another person nearby. I lift my head from my knees to find a scruffy street kid sitting cross-legged on the pavement in front of me.

She's wearing faded jeans, torn at one knee, with a black hoodie overtop, the hood thrown back. Her hair's an unruly mess, short and dark, and her brown features are attractive—interesting rather than magazine-cover pretty. White earbud wires connect her to the iPod she holds in her hand and I can hear the faint rhythm of whatever it is that she's listening to. Her eyes are large and brown, their gaze fixed on me.

I'm not quite sure how old she is—I'd guess mid- to late teens—and I have the oddest feeling that I know her, or at least that I've seen her somewhere before.

She smiles and takes the earbuds out.

"Hey," she says.

"Do I know you?" I ask.

"Not unless I've become posthumously famous."

I give her a blank look.

"You know," she says. "When you become famous after you've died."

"I know what 'posthumous' means," I begin, but then what she said actually sinks in.

Here we go again.

"I'm Conchita Rodríguez," she says. She points to the building behind me and adds, "Is that where you died?"

"Why would you say that?"

She shrugs. "Because I've never seen you before, and that store wasn't here a few days ago, and you're sitting in front of it looking like most of us do the first time we see the place we died."

"I'm not dead."

"Of course you're not. You're just resting."

"No, I'm—"

"Dreaming," she breaks in. "Yeah, yeah. You think you're the first person to come up with that explanation?"

"Do you have a better one?"

"You mean, like, where are we and why are we here?"

I nod.

"Haven't a clue," she says. "All I know is that if you die close enough to that big old greystone down the street—you know, the Alverson Arms—this is where you end up. A couple of blocks farther in any direction, and your guess is as good as mine. Maybe those people get to go to Heaven or Hell. Maybe they get on the reincarnation wheel. Who knows? But for you and me, and everybody else here? This is what we get."

Just like Edna was in my bedroom, she's so persuasive.

"Why should I believe you?" I ask.

"You mean because I'm only a figment of your dreaming imagination?"

I give a slow nod.

She smiles, but there's sympathy in her eyes.

"It doesn't matter what you believe," she says, echoing what Edna told me earlier. "This is *still* all you're going to get."

I look past her, across the street, down the block. Everything's so different, but with a hint of familiarity underlying it all. It's the shapes of the buildings, not the businesses in them.

When my gaze returns to her, I remember where I know her from. I'd never met her personally, but a few years ago her face was staring out at me from every newspaper and TV news broadcast. She'd been murdered in the cacti garden behind the library. Stabbed to death, by person or persons unknown, as the police jargon would have it.

It must have been a slow week for her to have spent a couple of days as a lead story. Violent crime is hardly a novelty in certain parts of Santo del Vado Viejo, and she was just another brown-skinned street kid. Normally, her story would have been buried in the City section.

She gives me a quizzical look. "What?"

"I remember you now," I say. "You were—"

"Knifed. I know. I was there."

"How can you be so offhand about it?"

"It was a long time ago." She sighs. "And yeah, it was horrible and traumatic. No question. But I had a shitty life and it's different here. Boring as hell, most of the time, if you want to know the truth, but it's kind of restful, too. And safe."

She's been looking at the ground. Now her gaze lifts to meet mine.

"I never had that before," she says.

I hear Edna's voice in my mind. *I see being here as a respite.*

"So I'm . . . I'm really dead . . ." I find myself saying.

I don't truly believe it. It's more as if I'm trying on the words to see if they fit. But there's something calming about the idea—once you get past the part where you're dead. Oddly enough, that seems to be less and less important. Or rather, it's getting easier to not obsess on the fact.

Conchita lifts a hand and points at the tattoos peeking out of the top of my T.

"That looks like serious ink," she says.

I actually find myself smiling.

"Well, at least there's a lot of it," I tell her.

I pull down the shoulders of my jacket so she can see Mama and the saint looking at each other. I tell her who they are.

"I never had a saint looking out for me," she says.

"If what you're telling me is true, she wasn't doing such a great job for me the other night."

Saying that gives me a bit of a queasy feeling.

"Yeah, there's that," Conchita says. She gets to her feet and adds, "Do you have a place to stay? There's not a lot of people here—I mean, compared to how much real estate's available. I've got an apartment above the record store that no one was using and there's a couple of others in the building that are empty."

I think my legs will be too jelly-weak to stand, but I manage to get up all the same. I guess I'm more resilient than I give myself credit for.

"I lived—*live* in Alverson Arms," I tell her.

"That's cool."

I give her a considering look. That's the first thing she's said that makes her sound her age.

"How old are you?" I ask.

"I was seventeen when I died."

"You sound a lot older."

She shrugs. "I grew up fast, living on the street. And like I said, I've been here for a few years. There's not much to do so I go to the library and I read a lot."

"The library . . ." I repeat.

It's not visible from here, but I look in its direction anyway.

"Yeah, it's nice in there. I used to go there all the time when I was alive because it was, you know, a safe place to hang out. Here, you have to put up with Henry, but he usually has his nose buried in a book, so it works out okay."

"Henry?"

"Henry Parker. He's just this guy who spends all of his time in there, trying to figure out what this place is all about. He'll bore you to tears, if you give him half a chance, and he's kind of creepy."

"Creepy . . . how?"

I'm thinking pervert and I guess it shows on my face because Conchita laughs.

"Not like you're thinking," she says. "It's just, you know how the place you died comes over with you?"

I don't really, but I nod anyway. Both she and Edna have mentioned it, but I'm still not clear on how it works.

"Well, Henry lives in hope of somebody dying in the library soon so that the building will get a serious upgrade. Right now, it's exactly the way it was when this old librarian named Bernardo Alvarez died back in nineteen sixty something. But if somebody dies now—"

"The library will change to reflect how it is at the time of their death?" I try.

She nods. "Exactly. New books. New magazines. Hell, CDs and DVDs and computers and all the good stuff it doesn't have right now." She holds up her iPod. "I had this when I died, so it came with me, but it's a bitch getting new tunes to put on it. Have you been to the record store yet?"

I shake my head.

"Vinyl and cassettes only. It's so lame. And it seems that libraries back in the sixties—or at least the Solona library—didn't carry records or tapes except for a bunch of spoken word stuff. Let's face it. Even if I could get any of it on my iPod, why would I want to? Bor-ing."

"I suppose."

I actually enjoy the audio books I have on my own iPod.

"Anyway," Conchita goes on, "Henry'll be happy to see you. He likes to debrief every new arrival."

"Was he in the military?" I ask.

"Not that he's ever said. Why do you ask?"

"It's just that term, 'debrief' . . ."

"Oh, I'm sure he picked it up from some spy book."

"So why would he want to . . . debrief me?"

"He's always looking to add to—how does he put it? Our body of knowledge about this place, which, by the way, he calls the Alverson Arms world. If you ask me, it's a lame name and trying to figure this place out is a waste of time."

"I don't know," I tell her. "I wouldn't mind knowing what's going on."

"Sure, but where does it get you? We know that anyone who dies around that old greystone ends up here, but knowing that doesn't change anything."

"I suppose not."

I look up and down the deserted street.

"How many people *are* here?" I ask.

Conchita shrugs. "Who knows? I think thirty to forty. Henry says

it's closer to seventy. It's hard to tell because some people just find themselves an apartment where they hole up and then kind of shut down. So
if you walk into some place and you see somebody laid out like a
corpse—you know, arms folded across their chest and everything—
don't freak out. They've just gone away somewhere in their head."

I nod as though I understand.

"Anyway," Conchita goes on, "it's not like anyone's done a census, though I'm sure Henry would love to. I do know I'm the youngest,
except for a baby that Edna found in a Dumpster in the alley that runs
behind the 26th Street Diner."

"Oh my God."

"Yeah, horrible, isn't it? A woman who lives in the apartments
above the Laundromat across from your building took the kid in. I
think she used to be a schoolteacher. She wanted to take me under her
wing, too—you know, 'show me all the things a young lady should
know,' but I set her straight before she could get too far into her spiel.
I mean, I didn't do school while I was alive, so why would I start now?
Anything I need to learn, I can figure it out for myself, and I sure as
hell don't need some Anglo telling me how I should live."

She cocks her head and studies me for a moment.

"So are you doing okay?" she asks.

"It's a lot to take in."

She nods. "Yeah, I suppose it is."

"And I can't help but feel that I'm . . . you know . . ."

"Dreaming. I get that. Everybody goes through that. I think the
weirdest thing for me is that it's just so damn quiet all the time. Which
is why I walk around with my tunes."

She holds up her iPod, the earbud wires looped a couple of times
around her hand, the earbuds themselves dangling.

I nod in response. It *is* quiet.

"There aren't any animals," I say. "No birds . . ."

She shakes her head. "Could you imagine if every pigeon and rat
and bug that died around the Alverson ended up here? We'd be over-
run." Then she smiles. "But we do have a dog—or at least Jonesy
does. They died at the same time when they got hit by a bus. Lucy's a
beautiful golden retriever."

I nod again because I don't know what to say. I've been relaxing more and more through my conversation with Conchita. I like her. I suppose I'll like Edna and Ruth, too, if I give them a chance. But every time Conchita mentions somebody dying, so casually, like she's talking about their nationality, or where they work, I feel like the world shifts underfoot and this wave of loss washes over me.

"I . . . I enjoyed meeting you," I tell Conchita, "but I think I need to go lie down for a while to just, I don't know, digest everything."

"Sure. I understand. You want me to walk you back to the Alverson?"

"No, I think I'll be okay."

There's an understatement if I ever made one. I don't know that I'll ever feel okay again.

"Well, if you're looking for company," she says, "I'm always around. I told you where I live, right?"

I nod. "Above the record store."

"Second floor, apartment number three. The door's never locked, so if I'm not there, you can just leave a message or whatever."

"I'm in apartment three-oh-two," I tell her.

She touches my arm, her eyes filled with sympathy.

"It gets better," she tells me.

How? I want to ask. If I'm not dreaming, I'm dead. Where does the better come in?

But all I do is nod and start back to the Alverson Arms.

Edna's door is still open when I come into the lobby, but although the radio's on, I don't see anybody when I glance in. It's probably just as well. The way I'm feeling, I'm in no shape to have a meaningful conversation with anybody. When I get to my own apartment, I wander aimlessly from room to room. I feel completely shut down inside. I don't know what's happening to me.

I remember dying, but I don't feel dead.

I could be dreaming, but if I am, this is unlike any dream I've ever had. It plays out in real time, just going on and on with no jumps to the interesting parts.

It suddenly occurs to me that I haven't had the urge for a cigarette since I first woke to find Edna in my apartment. I still don't. Which is funny, considering the jones for a cigarette is what brought me here in the first place. They aren't kidding when they say that smoking can kill you.

I'm not hungry, and I've always been a girl with a good appetite.

I think of lying down, but I'm not tired either. At least not tired in a go-to-sleep sense. Deep inside me there's a vast weariness. A hole. A sense of loss. A darkness that I can't penetrate. I don't know exactly *what* it is, just that it's there. Distant, but present.

I sigh.

I find I'm standing in the middle of my bedroom. The laptop on my desk catches my gaze. I walk over to the desk, sit down, and switch the laptop on. It goes through the motions of waking up. Once my desktop is open, a little icon pops up in the bottom right-hand corner to tell me that—surprise, surprise—my wireless card can't find a connection.

I stare at the screen for a long time. The desktop image is a picture that Shorty took of Abuelo and me standing beside another of the old Fords we'd fixed up, a burgundy '40 sedan with a two-piece rear window. It was taken a few years ago at the local annual Rod & Kustom Show in the parking lot of the old Mountain View Motel just off the I-10. It's been a popular gearhead hangout for ages because a couple of miles farther down the dirt road that runs behind it is an old dried lake bed where rodders have been racing their machines since the sixties. Behind the clapboard front of the motel you can see the Hierro Madera Mountains rising tall and blue-green in the distance.

I'm never going to do that again. I'm never going to race in the lake beds, or go to any more shows at the Mountain View. I'll never see the Maderas, except like this. In a picture.

And Abuelo . . .

I'm pretty much a lapsed Catholic, but I always thought that if there was an afterlife, I'd meet up with Mama and Abuelo there. I'd finally get to know Abuela, my grandmother. I could make my peace with Mama. Maybe there'd be a racetrack, or at least a garage with a decent set of tools and a couple of old Fords that Abuelo and I could work on into eternity.

I'm not sure why I drifted away from the Church. Could be because Mama was so wired into it. Could be because Abuelo wasn't. It

didn't have anything to do with the news reports you'd see about pe-
dophile priests because the priests around here weren't like that. You
could be cynical and say they just weren't caught yet, but you don't
need a reporter pointing these things out to know what's true and
what isn't. Our priests are part of the community—they work and live
right alongside of us. Father Alejandro, South Solona's parish priest,
even comes to some of the vintage car shows.

I shut off the computer and pick up my phone receiver. The line's
dead. I dig my cell out of my purse, but I can't get a dial tone on it either. I close my cell and push away from the desk to go back to wan-
dering through my apartment. Eventually, I sit down in an armchair
and watch the night outside my front-room window. I close my eyes. I
don't really sleep—it's more like a switch has been flicked and I'm
turned off—but the next thing I know it's morning and I'm still sitting
there in the chair.

Something Conchita said yesterday returns to me.

*Some people just find themselves an apartment where they hole
up and then kind of shut down. So if you walk into some place and
you see somebody laid out like a corpse—you know, arms folded
across their chest and everything—don't freak out. They've just gone
away somewhere in their head.*

Now I think I understand what she meant. It's such an easier way
to deal with the whole thing. And oblivion is more what I expected to
follow death.

But I'm not ready to fall into it yet.

I get up from the chair. I don't feel at all stiff from a night spent
sitting up in a chair. I'm still not hungry either, and that's weird because I usually wake up hungry. I think about having coffee and a cigarette. I still don't need a smoke, but the idea of holding a warm mug
in my hand appeals to me, so I go into the kitchen and make myself a
cup.

I drink my coffee back in the chair by the window where I can
continue to watch the street. More than the unfamiliar stores, it's the
complete lack of traffic or people that seems the most eerie. I only see
one person in the half hour or so that I'm sitting there—an older man
walking a golden retriever. Conchita told me about them yesterday but
all I can remember is that the dog's name is Lucy.

I watch them pass, tracking them all the way down the street until they turn a corner and are lost from sight. I get up and put my mug in the sink. I look around my apartment, not quite sure what to do. Then I remember that eerie sensation of turning myself off last night and I go into the bathroom to take a long shower, as though the water can wash all of this way.

It doesn't, of course. When I've dried off and I'm dressed again, everything's the same as it was before except that now I'm clean. But I can't stay inside any longer. Weird as the empty streets are, the way my apartment's unchanged is even more disturbing.

I decide to go to the library.

Edna's door is still open when I go by. I hear the sounds of someone in the kitchen rattling dishes and hurry out the front door. It no longer seems so strange that she was in my apartment when I woke up yesterday. By her account, she brought me from Luna's back to the apartment so that I could wake up in my own bed. It was a kindness and I'm embarrassed now at how I spoke to her. I don't take crap from people, but I also try to meet kindness with kindness. In fact, I make a point of initiating those kindnesses.

You catch a lot more flies with honey, Abuelo used to say.

I'm half a block away from the Alverson Arms, heading west on Kelly Street, when I stop dead in my tracks. I shuffle over to the steps leading up to the building beside me and sit down, using the railing to lower myself. Suddenly I have no strength because I just realized that I've really and truly bought into all of this business about being dead.

No. If I'm going to be honest, what I've done is accepted it. Accepted that this situation I'm in is real. And that means . . . that means . . .

There's no way to pretty it up.

It means I really did get shot in Luna's.

It means I'm really dead.

I stare down at the pavement, hugging my knees to stop from shaking. I can feel that dark place inside me rising up, big and black, ready to suck me back into last night's oblivion. I can't feel my arms, or my legs. There's a lightness in my head, a tightness in my chest.

But just before I'm gone, a voice pulls me out of the void. An angry voice.

I lift my head to see a man standing on the far sidewalk. He's around twenty and looks like one of those juvenile delinquents you'd see in some old black-and-white movie: tight jeans with the cuff rolled up over black pointy boots. A white T-shirt and a black leather jacket. His face is long and narrow, his longish hair slicked back into a ducktail. Actually, you still see a lot of these guys at the car shows—rockabilly holdovers with vintage coupes, looking tough, though they're usually teddy bears at heart.

But I think you'd have to look deep and hard to find a teddy bear in this guy. Something about his eyes doesn't look quite right.

"Yeah, you!" he's saying. He points at me. "Stop following me."

I'm still a little light-headed, but I know that's not why this isn't making any sense.

"You think I don't know?" he yells.

He starts across the street toward me, fists balled at his sides.

"Who're you with? Are you a narc?"

A funny thing happens as he closes in on me. I don't see him. I see that junkie who turned from the counter in Luna's and shot me. And for what? A few bills in the cash drawer to feed his habit for another half day. *That's* enough reason to shoot somebody? *That's* a good enough reason to end their life?

I stand up before he reaches me.

"I don't have to tell you a damn thing I don't want to," he shouts. "You hear me? Where's your badge, anyway? What're you going to do, shoot me?"

He fires the questions, spit spraying, talking too fast for me to answer even if I could. He's so angry, but I'm angry, too.

I can see he's not going to stop. He's coming right up on me, planning I don't know what. But I'm not a victim today. Truth is, ever since this started, I've just been looking for someone to hit. As soon as he gets close enough, I slip to one side and give him a push, throwing him off balance.

He catches himself on the railing and whips around.

"Did you see that?" he yells. "Police brutality!"

I have no idea who he's talking to.

I'm about to give him another shove as he clings there to the railing, but before I can, another voice cries out.

"Frankie! Stop it!"

I look up and he turns around. We see Conchita running across the street toward us.

"She's not a cop, Frankie," she tells him. She mouths a quick "Sorry" to me and returns her attention to the crazy guy. "Did you hear me? She's just new here, that's all. You need to leave her alone."

Frankie blinks in confusion. He looks at me for a long moment.

"How do you know she's not a narc?" he asks Conchita.

"I just do, okay?"

He shakes his head. "I don't know, man. What if you're wrong?"

"I'm not."

She steps closer to him and herds him away from the railing and me.

"Go on," she says. "Take a walk. You need to cool off."

"I guess."

He gives me another look. The anger's all gone now. All that's left is the bewilderment. But my pulse is still racing.

"It's all good, Frankie," Conchita says. "Really. But you need to go."

He nods finally and shuffles off. A moment ago he was so scary. Now he's just pathetic.

I remind myself to breathe again.

"What was all that about?" I ask.

"I'm sorry," Conchita says. "I should have warned you. Not everybody who died around here was necessarily nice. Or even all there. Frankie lives in a cloud of paranoia. He died from an overdose back in the early sixties and in his head he's pretty much stuck in those last few hours of his life. Hiding from the police, shooting up in the alley behind the Alverson."

"Is he dangerous?"

He didn't look it now, scuffling off down the street, chin on his chest and shoulders drooping. But he'd sure seemed capable of hurting someone when he first started yelling at me.

"Honestly, I don't know," Conchita says. "He's never actually hurt anybody yet, but who knows with a guy like that, forever caught up in some weird paranoid daze the way he is?" She cocks her head and adds, "But you looked like you could take care of yourself."

I don't bother answering. If I could really take care of myself, would I be dead?

"Are there more like him?" I ask.

"Well, we don't have any serial killers—at least not that I know of."

"That's not funny."

"You're right. So let me put it this way. There are a few people walking around with a chip on their shoulder, but they're as obvious here as they were back when we were alive. You just need to avoid them."

I nod. "Thanks for helping me with, um . . ."

"Frankie—Frankie Reid. No problem. I was standing at my window and noticed him crossing the street. If I could have gotten out a little quicker, I would have cut him off before he got to you."

"Is there anything else I should know?"

"Probably a million things, but let's see. There's a kind of mist at the boundaries of the blocks surrounding the Alverson. If you walk into it, you might get dizzy for a moment, but then you'll end up coming out of it from the opposite direction."

She points one way down the street as she starts to explain, the other way when she finishes.

"What else?" she says. "We get the same weather that the Alverson back in our old world does, and, oh, I know. Did you know that we get a couple of free rides back?"

"What do you mean?"

"Halloween and May Eve."

"I don't get it."

"Those are the days we can cross back over to the world of the living. October thirty-first and April thirtieth. Henry says this goes way back to before people even wrote down history. It's the time when the veils between the worlds are thinnest and all the fairies, ghosts, and goblins can cross over."

"You're joking."

"No way. I mean, I haven't seen any fairies or goblins, but we *can* go back. The deal is, you have to be at the place you died at moonrise.

Right at the moment the moon comes up, you get to go back and you stay until the sun comes up."

"Really?"

She nods. "But let me tell you up front, don't go looking for people you know. You can interact with the living and do everything they can do—eat, drink, make out, get high. Whatever. But the people who knew you before you died can't seem to see you. No, that's not right. They can see you, but they don't recognize you. I guess what I'm trying to say is that there's no point obsessing about your life before you died. If you go over, just appreciate the experience for what it is. It's like a, you know, a get-out-of-jail-free card that only works a couple of times a year."

"Have you done it?"

She nods again. "For three years now. I missed the first time I could have gone because no one had told me about it. You're kind of lucky, actually. Halloween's, like, a week away."

"What's it like—going back?"

"Weird at first. But then really good. I know a lot of people won't do it—it freaks them out because no one remembers them, or they miss their old lives too much and stuff—but I didn't have anybody to remember me, and my life wasn't exactly all that great, so . . ."

She shrugs.

"How do you find out exactly when the moon rises?" I ask.

"I don't. I just spend the day at the place where I died until, poof, I'm back. It's not like I've got anything better to do." She smiles. "So, do you think you'll try it?"

"I don't know. Maybe."

She does that thing again, when she's trying to figure out what a person is thinking: cocks her head, big brown eyes focused and serious.

"You didn't look too good," she says. "Just before Frankie started yelling at you."

She doesn't actually come out and ask me what's wrong, but the unspoken questions hangs there between us for a long moment. I look away down the street, then sigh and turn back to her.

"I was heading over to the library," I say, "and then it just hit me that I'm really dead. When Edna and you first told me it seemed impossible, like I had to be dreaming, but now I know it's true. I guess what makes it so hard to grasp . . ."

I'm not sure how to explain what I'm feeling, but she nods in understanding.

"Is how it all seems so ordinary," she says.

"Exactly. I guess you went through the same thing."

"Pretty much. But like I told you, for me it was an improvement."

That makes me incredibly sad for the life she had before she was murdered.

"Do you want to come with me to the library?" I ask.

She shakes her head. "Not today. I've still got a couple of books I haven't finished yet and Irwin—he's this guy who's taken over the record store—said he found some cool old vinyl in the back room that I could help him catalogue today."

I look across the street to the dingy storefront under the Vallance Records & Tapes sign.

"Who does he even sell them to?" I ask.

Conchita laughs. "Are you kidding me? None of his inventory goes out the door. All he does is organize it and play it. Anybody's welcome to come listen, but it's strictly hands off the merchandise."

"Weird."

"No, it keeps him busy so that he doesn't have to think. Some people can't bear to remember what they lost and he's definitely one of them."

"I guess I understand."

She reaches over and gives my forearm a squeeze.

"I'll see you later," she says. "Don't let Henry browbeat you. If you don't feel like talking, just tell him. And drop by the store later if you're not doing anything. We'll be there all day."

She gives me a wave and a grin. I watch her cross the street, then head off for the library.

When I turn down El Encanto Street, I see someone sitting on a lawn chair halfway down the block. I almost turn right around again. I don't have the wherewithal, the *energy,* to talk to anybody else just now, but I don't really feel like hiking the extra few blocks either.

I've never been much of a one for walking. I've had wheels for as long as I can remember—a pedal bike until I was finally old enough to get my license. Abuelo used to take me driving out in the desert back roads, teaching me everything I needed to know. By the time I took my driver's test I think I had more time behind the wheel than the guy giving me the test did.

Anyway, the point is, walking's never been a big priority for me—and that's a big ditto for public transport, too—so I bite the bullet and keep going down the street, taking the shorter route.

As I get closer the distant figure resolves into an older white woman, a little overweight, hair greying. She's wearing a pink tracksuit and running shoes—high-end, serious running shoes, but with the weight she's carrying, I doubt she's a runner, or even a jogger. Maybe she power walks. Maybe she just likes to be comfortable. In the end, it's not my business.

She has an empty lawn chair beside her with a closed hardcover book on the seat. There's a coffee mug balanced on the arm of her chair and a thermos on the pavement by her feet. I wonder if she lives in the adobe-and-wood building behind her. A flower box by the lowest window holds a half dozen geraniums that are gamely hanging on to their bright red and white blossoms. The tiny front has a good crop of prickly pear cactus and some patches of tall dead grass, but not much else.

She watches me approach with a welcoming smile, so I feel it's safe to assume that at least she's not going to start yelling at me like Frankie.

"Hello," I say when I'm close enough.

"Hello, yourself." She gives me a sympathetic smile. "You have the look of a recent arrival. I hope your passing wasn't hard."

It takes me a moment to realize what she's saying.

"Actually, it was," I tell her. "I got shot during a botched robbery. I don't mean that I was robbing anyone," I quickly add.

"I didn't think you had, dear. You don't look the type."

I have to smile. To most people, my ink makes me look like *exactly* the type.

"I was lucky," she goes on. "I died peacefully in my sleep. I can't imagine what it must feel like to carry around the memory of a violent end."

I think of Frankie, so deep into his paranoia that he thought *I* was a cop.

"Well, maybe some of us can deal with it better than others," I say.

She nods. "I'm Kathleen O'Brian, but my friends call me Kit."

"I'm Grace."

"That's a lovely name. I had a great aunt named Grace." She picks up her book from the other chair. "Would you like to sit?"

"Maybe later. I'm just on my way to the library."

"Ah yes. Checking in with Henry, are you?"

"I suppose."

It occurs to me that I haven't had this many conversations with people I don't really know since Abuelo's funeral. These past few weeks it's only been Vida on the phone, the guys at work, the Lunas, and occasionally people I might meet in the halls of my building. Otherwise, I've just kept to myself. I haven't been going out. I made Shorty talk to my customers so that I didn't have to.

"Well, I'm only halfway through this new book of mine," Kit says, "so I can put off another visit until at least tomorrow." She smiles. "That Henry's a lovely man, but I don't need to spend my every waking moment the way he does, worrying away at the puzzle of why we all ended up here. Still, I expect we all cope in our way."

"I guess we do. Nice to meet you Ms. O'Brian."

"Just Kit will do, dear."

I nod. "I'll see you later, Kit."

"I'm always around."

"Then I'm sure I will."

When I reach the end of El Encanto, I stand and stare at the wall of mist on the far side of 24th Street. Up close, it's impenetrable and creepy—a vast barrier that stretches up from the asphalt and as far as I can see down either side of the street. I can't imagine stepping into it the way Conchita says she does. I don't even want to look at it. So I turn down 24th, keeping my gaze on the tall saguaro that grow in the open space on this side of the library until I reach the steps. People talk about the desert as if nothing grows in it, but under the saguaros you'll find palo verde and mesquite trees, creosote bushes, prickly pear, and cholla. Even some scrubby grasses. And come March, there's a riot of wildflowers after the spring rains.

I didn't go to the Solona Public Library once in the six years I lived in this neighborhood, but I drove by it often enough. It doesn't look very different from what I remember and seems as out of place as the Alverson Arms—a huge stone building in the middle of all this adobe, wide steps leading up to the massive wooden doors, a pair of lions guarding the entrance. I always thought it looked a bit like the odd combination of an observatory and the inner keep of some old castle. It even has a small tower and ramparts all along the edges of the roof. But the big dome is just for aesthetics and the tall leaded windows on all sides wouldn't be much good for defense. Luckily, it's a library and doesn't need to defend itself from anything more dire than budget cuts—at least it had to before. Here? Not so much, I'd think.

I climb the steps. The lions are huge, this close up, and covered with graffiti tags. The door opens easily for all its obvious weight and I step inside.

Here's a funny thing. There's so little ambient noise outside that the inside of the library doesn't have the same hushed quality I usually associate with this sort of a building: libraries, galleries, museums. But the smell is right: paper and leather and wood. The leather heels of my boots on the marble floor are loud as I cross to the big central desk. All around me, bookcases are fat with rows and rows of books. They go off in all directions, orderly as soldiers on parade, and rise high from their bottom shelves, though not nearly as high as the vaulted ceiling with the big dome at the top.

A wide staircase leads up to the second floor with brass railings running from either side at the top making a complete circuit of the mezzanine. A little legend displayed on a sign by the central desk tells me that the nonfiction, rare, and local history books are all kept up there.

It feels strange to be in this big place on my own and I'm not sure why I came. I suppose I expected this Henry to be at the desk and he'd be able to tell me what's going on, and what I should do. But he doesn't seem to be around today. Maybe he comes in later, except I got the impression from Conchita that he basically lives here.

"Hello?" I call. My voice echoes in the cavernous space. "Is anybody around? Yo!"

There's no response and I wonder if I should just go and come back some other time. I call a last hello, then begin to retrace my steps to the front door. I'm about to push it open when I hear a faint humming sound coming from the mezzanine and then a voice.

"Who's there?"

I turn and see a black man peering down at me from over the railing. I can't tell much about him except that his hair is cropped so close to his skull that it's too short to curl. I walk back to the stairs and start to climb. I think he seems awfully short, until I realize he's in a wheelchair. That's the source of the humming sound that I heard: the wheels of his chair on the floor.

"Are you Henry?" I ask.

He nods. "And you are . . . ?"

"Grace Quintero." I wait a beat, then add, "Sorry I didn't die in the library."

He smiles. "You've been talking to either Conchita or David."

"Conchita," I tell him.

I'm at the top of the stairs now, looking down at him. He's wearing a white T-shirt that shows off a strong upper body. No ink that I can see. His jeans droop over legs that are withered and thin. I lift my gaze quickly, but he's already lost his smile.

"I can't tell you how sick I am of that pitying look," he says.

"It's not pitying," I say, though that's only partially a lie. Yes, I'm feeling sympathetic, but seeing the wheelchair brings another question to mind. "It's just," I add, "I'm trying to figure out why you're in that wheelchair." I lay a flat palm on the front of my T-shirt. "I was shot twice in the chest but I don't have even a trace of a scar."

The bitterness in his eyes clears a little.

"Oh, right," he says. "I can see why you'd wonder, but it's not a big mystery. I was in the chair before I died."

"Bummer."

He holds my gaze for a long moment, then the smile comes back.

"Yeah, no kidding," he says. "So what did Conchita tell you?"

"That you're going to debrief me."

That gets me an actual laugh and I guess the momentary awkwardness that lay between us is now forgotten.

"She is *never* going to let me forget that," he says. "It seemed like the perfect term until it came out of my mouth and she started grinning. But I *would* like to talk to you about your experience—if you're up for it."

"That's why I'm here."

He nods. "I'm using the local history room as my office. Why don't we go there and get more comfortable."

As he wheels away, I look at the stairs again before I follow.

"So how do you get up and down?" I ask.

"There's an ancient elevator on the other side of the mezzanine. But I don't go out that much."

I think I'd go crazy, but then I'm not much of a reader. Books-on-tape—or rather, their digital equivalent—sure, because then I can be doing something else. Waxing the car. Working in Abuelo's yard. And they're great on roadtrips when I'm not in the mood for tunes. But just sitting still and reading a book? Not so much. Never leaving a place like this library would drive me nuts.

But all I say is, "So you sleep and eat here?"

Because if he doesn't go out, someone must bring him his food.

He stops his chair and turns to me.

"I don't need to do either," he says. "And neither do you."

"What?"

"We're dead. Ghosts. Why would we need to sleep or eat?"

I suppose he's right. I think about the blank place I went last night, how it felt as though I'd just shut myself off. I know time vanishes when you sleep, but that was different. It was as though I didn't exist anymore. And then there's the fact that I'm *still* not hungry.

The whole thing is creepy.

"I had a coffee this morning," I tell him.

"I didn't mean that we *can't* eat or drink. Just that we don't need to."

"Oh."

"And as for sleeping," he goes on, "we don't so much sleep as . . . I don't know quite how to put it. We just go away. It's like falling into a coma."

I nod. "That happened to me last night."

"And it's a horrible feeling, isn't it?"

I don't know if I'd call it horrible, but it was weird, and not particularly restful.

I nod again.

"But here's the weird thing," he says. "Some people welcome it."

He starts to wheel his chair ahead again, aiming for a pair of double doors that stand open. As I follow behind him, I try to take stock of what I'm feeling. I seem to be breathing. There's a heartbeat in my chest. The floor seems very firm and solid against the soles of my boots and I don't seem to be able to walk through walls.

I don't feel like a ghost, but I guess that's what I am all the same.

The local history room looks like it took its design from some turn-of-the-century gentleman's club with all its wood paneling, big bay windows, and club chairs. A long oak table runs down the middle. The walls are pretty much all bookcases, of course, but there are also long glass-and-oak display cabinets with everything from arrowheads to weird bits of machinery displayed on the velvet spread out inside them.

Henry wheels to the long table with papers scattered all over its surface. The first thing that grabs my gaze is a large, hand-drawn map of the blocks surrounding the Alverson Arms building. There are dozens and dozens of little stars all over it, some blue, some red. I approach the table to get a closer look. Each of the stars has a name in it. I find Edna, Ruth, Kit, and Conchita. On the library there's a blue star with "Bernardo Alvarez" written inside it. That, I remember from what Conchita told me, is the name of the librarian who died here in the sixties.

"Those are all the people I've found so far," Henry says when he sees what I'm looking at. "Some I found on my own, but mostly I rely on what the people who come here for books can tell me. I know there are more."

"How many, do you think?"

"There's no way to get a true census. I've got notations on around seventy, but I've only definitely confirmed a little over half that number. Who knows how many others are lying in self-induced comas in some little bedroom? It's not like I can go door-to-door to check and no one else seems interested enough to help me."

He gives me a hopeful look, but I shake my head. There's no way I'm going to intrude on other people's privacy like that. If they've let themselves drop into the void, they had good reason to do so. It's not my place to bring them back just to add their names to Henry's map.

Henry has parked his wheelchair at the end of the table. I grab one of the club chairs and drag it over.

"So what's going on?" I ask him after I settle into the chair's deep cushions. "Why are we here?"

"I don't know. I think it's got something to do with the Alverson Arms building, but that's only because it's at the very center of this little world. I could be way off base. I've been researching the building—the architect, the various residents, the land it's built on—and everything about it seems completely normal."

"Except for its being here."

"Except for its being here," he agrees. "There was a little bribery with the city zoning commission when it was built, and Bud Echols, who had connections to the Las Vegas mobs, had an apartment there during the forties. If you dig into the history of any older buildings, you'll find a few skeletons like that. But nothing to explain what's happening to us."

He falls silent. My gaze goes to the map before returning to his face.

"This sure isn't what I thought the afterlife would be like," I say.

He nods. "I know."

"And it's funny, really," I go on. "If we can cross back on Halloween and May Eve, how come no one talks about it on the other side? You'd think people would have."

"Maybe people did. Would you have believed them without coming here yourself first?"

I shake my head. "Except I don't believe in vampires or fairies, but I still know what they are. You know, I've heard *about* them. And if this world's been here for—what? Fifty years?"

"Something like that. The longest resident I've found died in the mid-sixties."

"You'd just think that someone in the neighborhood would have had something to say about it by now."

"That's just one more thing I can't explain."

"I live in the Alverson," I go on, "and I've never seen or heard anything weird about it—at least not until I got here. Now there's wallpaper that wasn't there before, different light fixtures, that sort of thing. But until I came here, it was just a cool old building where I was lucky enough to find a reasonably priced apartment."

"Did you die in your apartment?"

"No. I got shot in Luna's."

"What's that?" he asks.

"A little Mexican grocery store on the same side of Twenty-sixth as the Alverson, but a block east. Edna said there used to be a soda shop there."

Henry nods. "Pike's Soda Shop & Lunch Counter. It had been there forever, apparently."

He pulls the map over to his side of the table. With a Magic Marker, he puts a blue star at the spot where I died, then prints my name on it with a black pen.

"And then when you went back to the Alverson," he says, "everything was changed?"

"I didn't go back. Edna, and I guess her friend Ruth or someone, brought me back to my apartment. I woke up in my own bed and nothing was different about my apartment until Edna showed up in the door of my bedroom."

"Wait a minute," Henry says. "The grocery store *and* your apartment came over with you?"

I nod. "Edna thinks it's because I lived in the Alverson."

"Well, this is new."

He makes a note on the foolscap pad in front of him.

"Does it mean something?" I ask.

"It must, though I have no idea what. That's what drives me crazy. I can't make *any* real connection to *anything*. I just make all these damned lists."

I can see the frustration in his face. He puts the pen down and sighs.

"So we don't eat, we don't sleep," I say. "What do we do?"

"Anything we want, pretty much. But it's hard to keep busy. You can try to take a Zen approach like Conchita does—just live in the moment, taking each day as it comes—but for most people that's easy to say, harder to do. Mostly you'll find yourself going back over your memories, cataloguing and filing them, searching for meaning and connections. But I do know this: if you don't keep yourself busy, it all goes away. First your memories, then the desire to do anything, finally whatever it is that makes you who you are."

He looks away, across the room, but I can tell his gaze is turned inward.

"And that's when you fall into the void forever," he says when he turns back to me. "Though some people choose to go before any of that happens to them."

I shiver.

"It's easy to treat it like sleep," he tells me, "because that's what it seems like at first. But I worry that every time we do it, we lose some little piece of ourselves. And we keep losing something until there's nothing of us left to come back."

"I'll remember that."

He nods. "And one more word of caution," he adds. "It's not a good idea to take that free ride back to the world of the living. Going back leaves you with a deep, aching discontent that only the void can alleviate."

"It doesn't seem to bother Conchita."

"Then she's the exception to the rule," he says. "Trust me. I've been here almost six years now and I've seen it happen to people over and over again."

"So you've never been back."

"I went once and it still hurts. My mother was there at the curb where I died. She was laying flowers—to mark the anniversary of my death, I assume—just standing there, crying without making a sound. I wanted to comfort her, to tell her that it wasn't so bad being dead, but she couldn't see me. Or rather she couldn't recognize me. She just saw another black man in a wheelchair and all it did was make the loss of her dead son hurt more."

"That sounds awful."

"It was. If we could choose the memories we lose, that would be on the top of my list." He taps his pen on the desk, then adds, "You should also stay out of the boundaries—you know, the misty area where the Alverson Arms world ends. I know that Conchita and some of the others use them for shortcuts, but I think it messes us up, too. I think it's like the void," he adds when I raise my eyebrows. "It steals away your memories, piece by piece."

"Maybe that's what we're supposed to do," I say. "Maybe we're supposed to let them go, and then when they're all gone, we move on."

"Maybe," he says. "But if that's true, why do the bodies stay behind, deep in comas?"

I give a slow nod. "There's no more answer here than there was when we were alive, is there?"

"Doesn't seem to be." He sits up a little straighter. "Anyway, why don't you tell me what you remember from crossing over."

I find it exhausting going over it all again and I'm happy when I can finally leave Henry scribbling notes on his foolscap and make my way out of the library. I stand there between the guardian lions for a long moment, looking out at the grey wall of mist across the street. It's easy to imagine it does everything Henry says it does, but I still find myself going down the stairs and crossing the street until I'm standing right in front of it.

I have this urge to touch it—to step right in and see what happens—because I've never liked to be told what I can or can't do. But I don't like the idea of losing my memories. They're all I have left of Abuelo and the whole life that's lost to me now. I miss it all. My family. The shop and my cars. Vida. The guys at Sanchez's: Shorty and Pedro, D.K. and Tito. Even Norman Morago, the homeless guy who hangs around the garage because I let him do odd jobs in my bay and keep giving him money.

And then I start thinking of all the things I won't be able to do now.

There's the tattoo portrait of Abuelo I wanted to get, but that's only the tip of the iceberg.

I've never been to Europe. I'm a Ford Motor Company girl, all the way, but I'd still like to see some of those European cars in their natural habitat. Porsche, Jaguar, Aston Martin, Alfa Romeo, Ferrari, Mercedes.

I wouldn't own one, or even want to work on one, but you can't deny their classic lines.

I've never followed Route 66 from start to finish—that's something Abuelo and I were always going to do in one of the cars we'd worked on. We'd talk about it as we worked side by side under the hood, or sitting on lawn chairs outside the garage, having a beer before we went back inside to see if we could finally get a fender skirt to fit, or if we wanted to take the easy way out and install a frame rail–mounted external fuel pump instead of an in-tank one since they work better, quieter, and aren't as prone to fall off.

I've never learned to play the guitar and I've always sort of wanted to. The sound track in the garage—when Shorty isn't playing his mariachi music—is all surf guitar and rockabilly, and I love those twangy guitars. Link Wray. Dick Dale. The Ventures. Duane Frankie. The Torquays.

I've never won a demolition derby. Hell, I've never even entered one. I don't really agree with smashing cars up just for the noise and fun of it, but I'd like to win one anyway just to wipe the smirk off the face of a guy like Shorty, who should know better than to say there's some things a girl just can't do as well as a guy.

I've never run a marathon. I'm not saying I want to, but I like the idea of pushing yourself to your limits, and then further again.

Okay, so maybe I'm only half-serious about the running, but here's a big one:

I've never been in love.

Lust? Sure. I've hooked up with guys. But knowing they're always just going to leave, sooner or later, I've never let myself open up enough to see if I can even love somebody that way.

I stare at the mist and I think of these things. Whether I remember them or not isn't going to make me a different person. What difference does it make whether I've never been the last car in a derby, or I can't remember if I ever was?

And I'm not sure I buy Henry's assumption, anyway. Conchita sure doesn't.

I decide Conchita's more my style, living "Mi Vida Loca" like the ink says on my back between my shoulder blades, rather than being like Henry, squirreled away in a library with his books and his theories and his lists.

So I take a breath, let it out, then step into the mist—

—and find myself with my back to it, staring at a row of adobe houses and dirt yards. It takes me a moment to realize I'm on 29th Street, five blocks north of 24th where I entered the mist. I turn to look back at the tall wall of grey. I'm on the other side of the Alverson Arms world.

I don't know if I'm missing any memories, but I do know that Conchita was right. The mists do work as a shortcut.

I study the face of the building in front of me and wonder how many people are lying in comas behind those windows. I'm not going to let that happen to me. I might be dead, but I'm going to live as full a life as I can make for myself here.

I turn from the buildings and walk east on 29th to Camino Vajilo, which will take me back to the Alverson Arms and the record store across the street. I want to ask Conchita more about this free ride back to the world our deaths stole from us.

It's Halloween and I'm sitting on the floor in the aisle of Luna's Food Market where I died, and how weird a thing is that to say?

Where I *died*.

But I'm getting used to it. Just as I made myself get used to coming into the store.

I've gone from having these huge stress attacks just thinking about crossing the threshold of Luna's, to where I am now, feeling only a little uneasy. Repetition did the trick.

On earlier visits to this empty store I turned into Ms. Homebody— if I was still alive and back in my own world, the guys at the garage would never have recognized me. The cars I used to work on were pristine by the time I was done, but my bay, and the girl herself, were always a total mess. My coveralls were invariably a Jackson Pollock canvas of fiberglass dust, plaster, paint, and grease. But here I've replaced all the cans and packages back on their shelves, mopped up all the blood, then washed the floors down again—and managed to stay tidy doing it. When you stand in the aisle now, it's like the robbery and my messy death never happened. There's only what I've got inside my head to remind me of what happened in this spot.

It's been an interesting week or so. I've kind of lost track of the days, so I'm not sure exactly how long I've been here, but I miss not talking to Vida. And I really miss my cars and the shop. I don't think it's ever been this long that I haven't been behind the wheel, or under the hood, fiddling with something. I could play around with the cars on the street, but what would be the point? It's not like I can drive them anywhere, though I suppose I could do a circuit around the limits of this world's borders like I was on a racetrack. But I've never been much of a racer. I'm more a cruising kind of a girl. That doesn't mean I don't like to go fast from time to time—really put one of those Flathead V-8s through its paces—but mostly I enjoy the feel of the car on the road, taking my time, enjoying the scenery and listening to that perfectly tuned engine purring under the hood. You can't get a better music than that. Give me a road trip over a race any day.

I've been pacing the aisle, but I make myself sit down. Pacing's not going to make the moment of passage come any quicker. I stare at the can and package labels on the shelves across from the aisle, and my mind starts to drift again.

Halloween was always an odd day in my family.

Mama was a good Catholic, but of the Italian variety. The pope's like God. Ditto the cardinals. She was respectful of nuns and, this is a little weird, flirty with the priests. Though she wasn't alone in that. All the neighborhood ladies were flirty with Father Calabria.

To her, Halloween, with its witches and ghosts and ghoulies, always seemed disrespectful of the teachings of the Church. But to make matters worse was that Halloween's also part of Los Dias de Los Muertes—the Days of the Dead—which Mom thought were holdovers from pagan times and a sure road to Hell. So there was no observation of it at home, nor was there trick or treating. But it was different at Abuelo's.

He didn't really celebrate Los Dias de Los Muertes the way they do in the barrios and over on the Kikimi rez, where they decorate their homes and the cemeteries, remembering the departed with a mix of reverence and revelry. They make the dead welcome in their homes and they party at their gravesides, embracing the fear of death so that it'll no longer have power over them.

But if he no longer celebrated the way he had as a kid, he still made sure Abuela's gravestone had a fresh coat of paint and put together an elaborate shrine for her every Halloween. His ofrenda would have a photo of her as a young woman, when they first started dating, and it would be surrounded by sugar skulls and candles, a vase of marigolds, her favorite biscuits and fruit, a cup of tea, her shawl, and a small portrait of the Virgin of Guadalupe. And there was always an old 45rpm copy of "Volver, Volver," which had been played at their wedding. It might seem odd that they would have used this song of a broken heart on their wedding day, but Abuelo said she loved the desperate romanticism of it, and after she had passed away, there was a poignancy to lines like "*Volver, volver, volver a tus brazos otra vez . . .*"

To return, to return, to return to your arms again . . .

If I had lived, I'd have made a shrine for Abuelo, and put that 45 under his picture. I miss him so much. Going back would be so much better if I could know he'd be there, waiting for me—though I suppose, if what Henry and Conchita told me is true, if he were still alive, he wouldn't recognize me anyway.

I don't suppose the Lunas will either when I show up in middle of their store. I just hope I don't give them a heart attack. I might have gotten used to the whole idea of ghosts and this weird little afterworld I find myself in, but it took me a while. Not just to get used to the idea, but to *accept* it. I know for a fact that, back before I got shot, if a dead person showed up at the shop or in my apartment, I'd have had a serious meltdown.

Funny how something so wildly impossible can now just seem so . . . mundane.

"This place takes all the mystery out of death," I said to Conchita one sunny afternoon while we were sitting on the steps of the Alverson Arms, appreciating the break from the October rains.

She grinned. "What do you know? Tattoo girl is a closet Goth."

"You know what I mean."

"I do," she said. "But the mystery's still there, isn't it? We're here, sure, but none of us have taken the last part of the journey yet. Nobody ever knows what's at the end until they get there themselves."

But back in the world where I died, nobody knows even as much as we do. Back there, the appearance of somebody you thought was dead is heart attack material, and I don't feel like sending any of the Lunas off to the hospital in an ambulance.

Given a choice, I'd return anywhere other than their store. A quiet alleyway sounds good. Or maybe behind some bushes in Guadalupe Park.

But that's not the way it works. I don't get a choice, and I just have to hope that the Lunas are more resilient than I'd ever have been.

While all of this is going through my head, I continue to sit cross-legged on the floor and wait.

And wait.

I make a list in my head of all the things I want to do when I get back. It's not very long. Mostly I just want to go back to the shop, see the guys, see Vida, maybe take a spin in my Fairlane for old time's sake.

And I wait some more.

I'm nervous and excited in a way I've not felt in years. It's like when you're a kid and it's the evening before your birthday or Christmas, but it's also like the night before a big exam, or when you have to tell a customer you can't do the custom the way they want it, where you're kind of dreading the coming of day.

When the passage over finally happens, it catches me by surprise. It happens fast, and feels like the color blue with a sharp static charge. I know, that doesn't make much sense. But I can't explain it any better.

One moment I'm sitting here in a deserted store, the next a woman almost trips over me. The air is filled with the smell of spices and fresh tamales and the sound of some norteño band.

"Oh, I'm so sorry," the woman says. "I didn't see you down there."

She's dressed in a business suit and heels. Her hair's that style women executives seem to favor—short with a few subtle colored highlights, feathered so that it doesn't look too harsh.

I barely get a chance to wonder what someone like her's doing in here, or register the look on her face as she takes in my tattoos and tries to figure out why I'm sitting on the floor. I'm still kind of stunned by the fact that it actually worked. We actually *do* get to come back to the world of the living.

"No problem," I tell her. "I'm just looking for some beans."

Right. Cross-legged on the floor, my jacket folded across my lap.

She gives me a small, polite smile. When she walks away, I stand up.

I feel different. Like I have more weight. My stomach growls and I realize I'm starving. I also have to pee something fierce.

I look to the front of the store and see Estefan's standing behind the cash register. I wait until he's finished serving the woman who almost tripped over me before I approach. I brace myself for the shock he's going to get when he sees me, but all he does is give me a mild, slightly wary look that I recognize from the very first time I came into the store. The look that says, while he's willing to give me the benefit of the doubt, he's ready if I start to cause any trouble.

But he doesn't recognize me. There's not even a flicker of recognition.

I suppose I was expecting it—both Henry and Conchita had already told me how it would be—but I didn't realize how much it would hurt until this moment.

"How can I help you, miss?" he asks.

"<Don't you remember me?>"

He smiles, and no doubt taking in my tats, he switches to Spanish to say, "<I think I would remember you.>" But I guess he sees something in my face because then he adds, "<Where did we meet?>"

God, this is so awful. I feel a tight pressure in my chest and my throat feels thick, but I manage to find my voice. I put on my jacket, though it's kind of late to hide my tats now.

"<No . . . um . . . you're right,>" I tell him. "<I just thought you looked familiar, but, you know. My mistake. Can I have a couple of tamales?>"

He nods. "<With pleasure.>"

No matter what I'd been told, I really thought it would be different for me. I thought, I'm too strong a personality to just vanish like that. My connections to people run deeper. I make an impression that sticks.

Wrong.

My gaze lifts to a framed picture on the shelf behind the counter, standing in among a display of sugar skulls and brightly colored paper flowers. It shows me leaning against my street car, that gorgeous '57 Ford Fairlane convertible I'd salvaged and put back to its factory original state using only stock parts. The best part of pretty much every year was when it finally warmed up enough in the spring so I could fold the hard top back into the trunk and go cruising out in the desert with the wind mussing my hair.

That photo was taken the day I finally finished the work on it and you can see the happy pride written all over my face. I'd given a copy of the photo to the Lunas last year when they'd expressed some curiosity about what I did for a living. Now, with small vases of fresh-cut flowers standing on either side of the frame, I assume it's a memorial.

"<That's a cool car,>" I say, pointing to the photo when Estefan comes back with my pastries. "<Who's the girl?>"

There's this awful moment when I think Estefan's going to cry. His eyes glisten and he has to turn away and clear his throat before he can answer.

"<She was a very good and kind customer of ours,>" he finally says. "<She was shot when a crazy man came into the store to steal from us. She died trying to stop him.>"

That's not what I was doing, I want to tell him. But all I say is, "<That's awful.>"

He nods. He runs a finger along the frame of my photo, then turns back to face me.

"<She was a good person,>" he says, "<but she should not have tried to stop him. Her life was worth much more than the little money I had in my till.>"

As he rings up my tamales, I study the picture. How can he look at it, then at me, and not know who I am?

"<I'm sorry to have reminded you,>" I say when he lifts his head.

He takes my money and makes change. Luckily, I had money. I'd almost forgotten to put my wallet in my jacket.

"<You've done nothing wrong,>" he says. "<I remember every moment of that day. How can I forget?>"

I nod. "<Did they catch the guy?>"

He shakes his head. "<He ran out of the store, but I didn't chase him. I was too busy trying to help Grace.>"

"<That was her name?>"

"<Yes. Grace Quintero.>"

I get a shiver when he says my name. Now I have an inkling of what it'd be like to show up at your own funeral, and it's totally creepy.

I don't know what to say, so I just nod and leave with my tamales.

The noise and smells when I step outside hit me like they never did when I was alive. It just wasn't something I ever paid attention to, but the contrast is huge—especially compared to the quiet of the Alverson Arms world. There's traffic, and people everywhere. The air's dusty and full of exhaust and the faint sweet smell of garbage. A guy with an armload of bags almost knocks me over in his rush to get to the bus and doesn't even bother to say he's sorry.

But you know what? I love it. Because this place is alive. Everybody here is alive.

I'm alive.

I stand there for long moments, just taking it all in, then finally I open the paper bag and take a bite from one of my tamales. It tastes like heaven melting in my mouth.

Now I just need to find a place to pee.

Two tamales, a coffee from the diner across the street, and a quick stop into their washroom later, and I'm a new woman. You forget how the little things can make such a difference. Like the way a loose heat shield can make the fanciest car sound like some crapped-out old jalopy, or a touch of lipstick can make you feel pretty, even though you're carrying a pound or two more than you'd like.

I pause in the washroom, staring at my reflection. I look exactly the way I always do, which makes me wonder who Estefan saw when he was looking at me.

With my basic human needs taken care of, I head to the alley behind the Alverson to get my car.

But of course it's not there.

I'm dead. I have an estate and the Fairlane was part of it.

I stare at the empty alley for a long moment before I finally turn away and head off to the shop to see if any of the guys are working late. Sure, my car's gone, and Estefan didn't recognize me, but it'll be different at the shop. It'll be different with the guys. Shorty and D.K.

and Pedro. Even if everybody else ends up seeing someone different when they look at me, the guys will still know me. All they'll have to do is talk to me. We worked side by side in the shop for years. We went to God knows how many swap meets and shows and bars together.

But when I finally get there, a long ten blocks' walk later, there aren't any lights on in Sanchez Motorworks. I stand across the street and look at the familiar dark building. I wonder if anybody finished that T-bird I was working on. I wonder where my own cars are.

I hadn't gotten around to changing my will after Abuelo had died, but I'd left provisions that if anything ever happened to the both of us, my cars and tools would go to Shorty; my jewelry, music, and clothes would go to Vida. Whatever else I was worth at the time would get divided up between my brother and a couple charities: the local soup kitchen and the animal shelter up on Presidio.

I cross the street and peer into the building's darkened interior to see if Shorty has brought any of my cars here, or if he's left them in the garage space I rented north of the city. It's too dark to make anything out. I can't even see if my Fairlane's in there.

I decide I want to go inside, one last time. Except for Abuelo's garage, I spent more of my life in here than anywhere else, and I guess I just need to say good-bye. I didn't exactly get the chance when that junkie shot me down in the Lunas' store.

I step away from the bay doors and head for the back. I know where Shorty keeps a spare key and unless he's changed the alarm code, I know that, too.

Behind the building it's like a miniature scrapyard—there are stacks of tires, big oil cans, old cars in various states, and car parts everywhere. You have to watch where you step, especially in this poor light, or you could break your neck. It's a gearhead's wet dream back here, and a real necessity for the business. Shorty and Pedro can build pretty much any part you need, but a lot of our customers come with production numbers in hand and only those vintage parts will do.

I'm about to reach above the back door to get the key when I hear a sound behind me. I turn to see a figure getting out of a junked car.

My eyes have adjusted enough to the poor light so that when he straightens, I recognize Norm by the distinctive stoop of his shoulders.

"Hey, Ms. Gracie," he says.

My heart lifts. Henry was wrong. People *can* recognize you when you come back.

"You can see me," I say.

"It's a blessing and a curse," he says, then adds, "So how's being dead treating you?"

And then I remember. Norm was always talking about seeing spirits.

While most people laughed off his claims, I tried to keep an open mind. Sure, it was hard to buy into the idea, but now that I know that ghosts are real, well, who's to say he can't see them? And he's certainly recognized me, where Estefan didn't.

Norm comes by his gift honestly. He's a distant cousin of Ramon Morago, a shaman up on the rez. In the Kikimi tribe, it's the women who form the council of elders, but even they, Norm told me, respect Morago's power.

Norm could have gone the shaman route, but all he ever wanted to be was an artist. Trouble was, the spirits wouldn't leave him alone. They were great for inspiration, he told me, but they made it impossible to concentrate enough to get any work done. Drugs and booze were the only things to shut them up, but those addictions only opened the door to a whole slew of other problems. The end result was that Norm found himself living under an interstate bridge on the east side, so messed up he couldn't function, never mind do his art.

He used to wake up there in the morning on a bed of flattened boxes and have no idea how he'd gotten there, or how long he'd slept.

I can't take credit for rescuing him.

That goes to Jenny Veda, one of the volunteers of the Milagros Outreach Program. She kept visiting him under the bridge, talking to him, bringing him sandwiches and coffee, until she finally convinced him to come to the walk-in clinic for a checkup. It turned out he had HIV. Jenny got him to clean himself up and back into his art. The program found him a place in a rooming house and paid for his meds.

That's where I came into the story.

I saw him panhandling in front of the coffee shop down the block from the shop. "For art supplies," he said. I remember thinking that was a new line, but we got to talking and when I realized he was on the level, I told him I'd pay him to help me out at the garage. Shorty and the others thought I was nuts, but the little salary I paid him came out of my own pocket, and it wasn't completely charity. With an extra set of hands, I got that much more work done, in less time.

When I didn't have anything for Norm to do, he sat in a corner of my bay, drawing, sometimes painting. Jenny—the volunteer who'd first helped him, and still came by to see him once a week or so—was also an artist. I thought she'd have the connections to get Norm a show at some gallery, but he didn't want to impose on her and wouldn't let me talk to her on his behalf. So I was going to set it up myself, except I went and died.

"What are you doing here?" I ask, because I realize he must have been sleeping in that car. "You didn't get kicked out of the rooming house, did you?"

I don't add "again." Norm's fallen off the wagon a couple of times since I've known him, and rent money's the first thing to get eaten up by his addictions. He can't dip into his meds money because that gets paid directly to the pharmacy where he gets his prescriptions.

"Not this Indian," he says. "I've been walking straight down the narrow path for six months now."

"That's great news. You're doing so well."

He shrugs, but I know he's pleased. It's that whole "little things" business again. Here, it's just an encouraging word that makes the difference.

"So what're you doing here?" he asks.

"I'm just looking around. Saying good-bye, I guess."

I didn't realize that's what I'm doing until I say the words aloud, but as soon as I do, I realize it's true.

He nods. "I get that. Back on the rez, old Ramon said that all the weight of our lives holds some spirits back when they die. Maybe they want to fly free and head off into the great wherever, but their unfinished business holds them back. Sometimes, he said, that business is just to say good-bye to the things that meant something to them."

"I guess. Being dead's not like what I thought it would be."

"Well, Ms. Gracie, that's why it's called the great unknown."

I laugh. God, it's good to talk to him again.

"Why are you sleeping in that car?" I ask.

"I'm just trying to clean up the sadness since you left. It lies so thick in this place that it gets hard to breathe sometimes."

"The sadness?"

"Oh, sure. What? You didn't think anybody'd miss you?"

"I . . . didn't really think about it." I look around at the mess of car parts that surrounds us, and add, "You're saying that sadness has a physical presence?"

Norm nods. "All the emotions do. The lighter ones—you know, when you're happy and everything's good—they tend to just float away. But sadness and anger pile up. So if you're feeling bad like Shorty and the boys have been, every time you come to work, that mess of old sorrow feels worse."

Before I found myself in the Alverson Arms world, I never would have said anything to Norm, but I sure would have thought that he was delusional. But now . . . I guess once you come to understand that the world's a lot bigger and stranger than you ever thought it might be, you can be a lot more accepting. Because really, lingering emotions aren't any weirder than ghosts.

"How do you make it go away?" I ask.

He pulls a half-burned smudge stick from his pocket.

"Prayers," he says. "And sacred smoke. I go all around the building once an hour and talk to the thunders—you know, asking for their help."

"All night long?"

"I can't do it during the day. Shorty'd just rag on me."

I nod. That he would.

"It's a good thing what you're doing here, Norm."

He grins. "Guess you don't think I'm so crazy now, talking to spirits and all."

"I never said—"

"You didn't have to, Ms. Gracie. But I'll give you this, no matter what you thought, you still treated me decent. I can't say that about most people. They look at me, and they just see some old drunk Indian.

And if I'd ever told them about the spiritworld, they'd just think I was crazy."

Except it took dying for me to really believe him, I think.

"How are the guys treating you since I've been gone?" I ask.

"Pretty darn good, considering what it was like before you died. Shorty buys me lunch and they keep me around to clean up all the bays now."

My gaze goes to the back of the building. I can't see inside from here any more than I could from the front.

"You wouldn't know what Shorty did with my cars, would you? Is my Fairlane in there?"

He doesn't answer me. Instead, he says, "I miss you just as much as the other guys, Ms. Gracie, really I do. And it's great to see you again. But either you need to go, or I do, because once I see one of you spirits, I start seeing you all. The only thing that can stop that is for me to start drinking again, and you know Ms. Jenny wouldn't like that."

"I don't understand," I say. "If I'd been able to see ghosts when I was alive, I'd think it was pretty cool."

He shakes his head. "There's just too many. And once one of them knows you can see and talk to them, they all start gathering 'round, thick as flies on roadkill. A shaman like Ramon, he can choose which he pays attention to, but when you're like me and you don't have a filter, all you can do is dull your brain until you can't see them anymore."

"So going on the wagon brought them all back?"

"No. But that's because I don't let on that I can see them. But if they see me talking to you like this . . ."

"I get it," I say. "I'm sorry. I'll go."

He touches my arm. "Don't think badly of me, Ms. Gracie."

I lean over and kiss his cheek.

"I'd never do that," I tell him.

I turn away, but before I can leave, he calls after me.

"Ms. Gracie!" When I stop and look back, he says, "You be careful walking this world. There's people around who'd like nothing better than to get hold of a spirit like you."

"What for?"

He shrugs. "The usual. Power. Spirit energy's like fuel, you know? If you've got the know-how, you can use it to do all kinds of things." He pauses, then adds, "You wouldn't like what they might do with what they take from you, Ms. Gracie. You wouldn't like it at all. Shamans who do that kind of thing, they're deep into dark magic."

Great. Now I've got that to worry about, too? I guess Norm sees that on my face.

"Just keeping moving," he says. "And go to places where there's a lot of people. You should be okay then, if you don't stick around too long."

"I've only got until sunrise," I tell him.

He smiles and looks more like the Norm I knew, the one who didn't talk so matter-of-factly about magic and spirits.

"Then you have yourself a good time, Ms. Gracie," he says. "You deserve that."

I nod, then walk away quickly with a lump in my throat. It's not easy leaving behind the one person who can recognize me. At this moment, the whole of my old life seems to be narrowed down into Norm and I'm beginning to wonder if maybe Henry's right. Maybe coming back isn't such a good idea.

When I return to the street, I pause for a moment, trying to decide what to do now. I was planning to hook up with Vida, but with the way things are, I don't think I can face the hurt I'll feel when she doesn't know who I am. Henry was definitely right about that. But I don't know what to do.

I remember when D.K.'s cousin Carlos got out of jail. He thought he was the happiest man in the world when he heard the big steel doors close behind him and he had his freedom again. But then he found that he just couldn't get comfortable. Nothing felt right outside the confines of his cell. It was too big and disorienting on the outside.

"In there," he told me, "there's always some screw or cholo telling you what to do, and if you don't want to get into trouble, you just do what they say. Man, I tell you, I used to hate it. But now? I miss it, you know? It's just so much easier when there's someone else telling you what to do."

"I can tell you what to do," D.K. put in. "Stay the hell out of trouble."

They both just laughed, but I saw the haunted look in Carlos's eyes, and I understand it now because nothing feels right to me either. Everything looks one way—welcoming and familiar—but feels another.

It didn't last for Carlos. He lost that feeling in a couple of weeks. But I only have the one night of freedom before I'm back in the jail that's the Alverson Arms world. I don't have time to adjust.

I know what I'd like to do. Get behind the wheel of my Fairlane and just drive until the Alverson Arms world pulls me back. Though I guess when I disappeared, the Fairlane'd get totaled with no one behind the wheel.

But I used to love to just go cruising. It was my favorite thing, especially before gas prices got so steep. I'd be coming back from Abuelo's, but instead of going home, I'd find myself driving the back streets for half the night. Or taking a long spin out in the desert, the asphalt humming under my tires, good tunes blasting on the stereo. A little HorrorPops, maybe. Some sweet harmonies from the Super Stocks. Or the growl of Link Wray's Les Paul.

I guess that's gone forever.

But if I can't go cruising, I can go walking, and that's exactly what I do. I give the old garage a last look and wave, then set off down the street, just going wherever my feet take me.

I've got the whole city to wander around in, so you'd think the last place I'd want to be is those few blocks from which the Alverson Arms world gets its cue. But here I am all the same, standing on the corner of 29th and Calle Escalante. It's different, of course. There are cars and people everywhere. A bus goes by, puffing diesel fumes. The buildings are all lit up, half the windows with the flickering blue-white light you get from a TV screen.

I can see the Arms from where I'm standing. Closer at hand is the Solona Music Hall, which is having a Halloween costume party by the look of the marquee and all the people standing around out front in costume.

I wait a long beat, then think, what the hell. I'll go in for a drink and check out the costumes. With any luck, the band'll be good. Maybe they'll take requests. Maybe I can get them to play a little Dick Dale. I just know that after the endless quiet of the Alverson Arms world, I need some noise. I need to be surrounded by people, dancing and having fun, with the music blasting from the stage, it doesn't much matter what it is so long as it's not disco.

And didn't Norm tell me to go someplace where there's a lot of people?

John Burns

Casa Canelo was busier than usual. The restaurant/bar invariably had a good after-work crowd, but combine people unwinding from their nine-to-five with those gearing up for an evening of Halloween celebrations, and it seemed as though everybody'd had the same idea today and stopped by for a drink. All the tables in the restaurant section were occupied, many with extra chairs pulled up. In the bar half of the room all the booths and tables were also full, and there were men and women crowded three deep around the bar, or standing in clusters to fill every other available space. Laughter and conversation almost drowned out the mariachi music playing on the house sound system.

John didn't mind either the noise or the crowd. He was a dedicated people-watcher and sitting at a corner table with his friends was the perfect opportunity to enjoy a beer and some conversation while watching the parade unfold. And it helped keep him from falling into the funk that always lay so close to the surface of his mind at this time of year.

At least half the crowd was in some sort of costume, although the men hadn't made much of an effort. John saw devil's horns, a few sleek Zorro masks, and one brave soul in full clown regalia—he wasn't going to pick up a woman tonight, unless she had a circus fetish. But the women more than made up for the men's halfhearted costume attempts. There were witches and vampires, schoolgirls and French maids, Playboy bunnies and cat women, all of them showing plenty of cleavage and skin.

He wondered when Halloween had become an excuse for women to turn out as hookers for the night.

Maybe he should ask their waitress, dressed in a Catholic school-girl outfit lifted straight from the video that first put Britney Spears on the musical map. She smiled at him as she approached their table, one arm holding the tray with their drinks above the crowd as she maneuvered her way from the bar.

After she'd served the drinks, John put a twenty and a five on her tray to cover their tab and a tip. The waitress touched the back of his hand and leaned a little closer to him.

"There's a Halloween party after the bar closes tonight," she said. "You should come."

She took a business card out of her change belt and gave it to him.

"Here's the address," she said. "It'll be fun." She waited a beat, then added, "Bring your friends."

She left to take another table's order before John could respond.

"See? That's what I mean," Danny said as the waitress sauntered away. His gaze was locked to the sway of her hips in her short plaid skirt. "Women are always doing that, and the thing I have to ask is, what do they see in him? He's not handsome, right? I mean, he's not movie-star handsome. He's just an ordinary-looking guy."

Wes grinned. "It's because he's a sensitive artiste."

Danny shook his head. "No, I'd get that if they talked to him first. But they've already made up their mind before he even opens his mouth."

"I'm sitting right here, guys," John said.

Danny held up a hand. "Hush. We're trying to work something out here."

"Maybe," Nina said, "it's because he doesn't sit there checking them out like he's alone in front of his computer screen." She reached over and plucked the card out of John's hand. "Her name's Shannon," she added. "Anybody want to bet she's planning a party just for two?"

John shook his head. "Now why would you say that?"

"I don't know. Because she makes eyes at you every time we come in here?"

"She said to bring my friends."

"We're getting off the point, people," Danny said. "The question is why John and not, oh say, me? And don't you start again, Nina," he added before she could speak. "Seriously. Because I've seen you checking out guys and you're not always exactly subtle."

"I *was* being serious," Nina said. "Women can read the difference between how John looks at them and how you do." She smiled. "And besides, you're not sensitive enough."

Danny was a horny nerd in a jock's body. It was as though someone had transplanted the brain and libido of a comic book and gaming fanatic into the physique of a blond linebacker with a face that had run a few times too often into the goalposts. Danny'd tried to excel at sports—mostly to please his dad—but his heart was never in it, and he was so clumsy that he'd trip over his own feet if there wasn't some other object close enough to stumble over.

And even if he did get talking to a woman, within the first few minutes of a conversation he was spouting off about the X-Men or his gaming stats, never noting the glazed look that filled her eyes.

"Hell, I'm sensitive," Danny said.

Wes laughed. "No, you're a hypochondriac who can't even stand the *idea* of pain. So yeah, you're sensitive, but it's not the same thing at all."

"Screw you, Porter."

Wes raised his eyebrows suggestively and Danny shook his head in mock disgust.

Wes had come out so long ago that they didn't even think about the fact that he was gay anymore, unless it was to tease Danny. He was slender to Danny's bulk, the lithe Siamese to Danny's bulldog.

The four of them had been friends since middle school, brought together by a love of comics, gaming, movies, and genre TV series. After university, Danny, Wes, and Nina had started up Wesdanina, a computer animation company. John, more interested in pursuing a career in fine art, had opted out of the company when it was being put together, though he did do contract work for them, mostly conceptual art and design. Nina was their resident programming expert, while Danny and Wes handled the hardware and day-to-day running of the office.

"So are you going to go to this party?" Wes asked John.

John shook his head. "Every year we promise Nina that we'll go with her to the Witches' Ball at the Solona Music Hall, and every year we cop out. So this is the Halloween we do it."

"But I'm not wearing a costume," Danny said.

Wes smiled. "Oh, I think Nina's got that covered for all of us."

Nina had poured her trim form into a white body stocking with a micro-short red dress over it. Completing the outfit was a pair of red lace-up boots, a long tail, which was currently draped across her lap, and white cat's ears that pushed out of her short black spiked hair, the one on the left decorated with a big red bow.

"Who are you supposed to be, anyway?" Danny asked. "Hooker Kitty?"

She punched him in the arm, then pulled a plastic shopping bag out of her knapsack and emptied its contents on the table. Wes laughed and sorted through the various face masks, fake noses, and ears. He found a pig's snout and pushed it across the table to Danny.

"Here you go," he said.

"Yeah, I don't think so."

"What's the matter? Pigs are actually really smart animals."

"So are crows, but I'm not going to wear a big orange beak either."

"Black," Nina said.

Danny gave her a puzzled look.

"Crows and ravens have black beaks," she said. "It's only in cartoons that they don't."

Wes nodded. "Like Heckle and Jeckle."

Danny looked at John. "Hey, Earth to John," he said. "Help me out here. We're not wearing costumes, right?"

John had drifted off, thinking about his brother as he did every Halloween.

"What can I say?" he told Danny. "It's Halloween and Halloween's all about the costumes."

He didn't feel like wearing one either—even just an animal's snout or ears—but he doubted it was for the same reasons the other guys didn't want to. Actually, he had no idea why they wouldn't want to. Danny was happy to show up at comic and SF conventions dressed as anything from a barbarian warrior to a Vulcan, and Wes loved any excuse to get formal, which was like wearing a costume so far as John was concerned. The first big paycheck Wes got years ago, he went out and bought a tuxedo. He had three or four of them by now.

"Unless you're Mexican," Wes said, "and then it's all about that whole Day of the Dead thing. You know, with all the skeletons, and where they hang out in graveyards and remember—" He broke off. "Oh crap," he said. "I'm sorry, John. I wasn't thinking."

John lifted a hand, like it didn't matter. After twenty-two years, it shouldn't. But every time the Halloween decorations started to go up in stores, and the sugar skulls appeared in his local Mexican grocery store, it would all come back to him.

He was fourteen and Tim was nine, and he and his friends weren't going to have some little kid tag along with them while they went out trick or treating. So Tim went out that night in his Batman outfit with the Cassidys who lived next door—Randy, Clarissa, and their father— because John and Tim's parents were working late.

No one could say exactly what happened, why Tim ran out into the street, darting out from between a couple of parked cars the way he did, right into the path of an oncoming car. The driver was devastated, but there was nothing he could have done. He was driving well under the speed limit, but Tim had appeared right in front of his car out of nowhere and there was no time to stop. Mr. Cassidy was overwhelmed with grief, and while John wanted to blame him for not keeping a more careful eye out for Tim, he knew the man couldn't have done anything, short of keeping all three kids on leashes.

No, the only person John blamed was himself. Tim should have been with him that night, end of story. The fact that he'd only been fourteen when Tim was killed made absolutely no difference. If John hadn't been so selfish, he'd still have his little brother.

John reached over and plucked a pair of ears and a bat snout from the pile on the table.

"Come on, guys," he said. "Let's try to get into the spirit of this. How often does Nina ask us to do something?"

"I don't know," Wes said. "Every five minutes?"

He was sitting too far for her to punch him, so she shook her fist at him instead.

"But John's right," he went on. He plucked the pig's snout from Danny's hands and put it on. "Oink, oink."

"Aw, I was going to take that one," Danny said.

"You can still have it."

Danny shook his head as Wes started to take the snout off.

"Not with your cooties all over it now," he said.

Nina rolled her eyes. "God, it's like they're ten years old. What was I thinking? If I was smart, I'd just go alone."

Danny gave her a hopeful look until he realized that John and Wes were frowning at him.

"Fine," he said. He picked up a dog's snout. "We're going, already. I never said we weren't."

"And no sulking," Wes said. "If you sulk, it doesn't count and you'll still owe Nina an outing."

"I'm not sulking. Look at me. Does this look like sulking?"

He pulled his lips into a huge fake grin which, combined with the dog's snout, made him look completely grotesque.

His friends picked up the spare costume parts and started throwing them at him.

There was a line outside the Solona Music Hall but Nina walked them past the motley array of men and women decked out as witches and ghosts and other personas that John didn't recognize. The doorman was wearing a long black cloak that couldn't quite close over his broad chest. He smiled at Nina from under his hood.

"Hey, Trevor," she said.

"Hey, yourself. Cool Hello Kitty outfit."

"Thanks. Can we go in?"

"Sure. The first band's just getting ready to start."

At ten-thirty? John thought. Here was the reason he didn't go out to shows much anymore. By the time the main act was coming on, he'd already have been asleep for a couple of hours.

"Are you going to be able to catch any of the show?" Nina asked the doorman.

He shook his head. "Only if this crowd thins out. But I should be able to hear the music just fine."

Nina smiled, then waved John and the others in ahead of her.

"C'mon, guys," she said. "The party awaits."

The Solona Music Hall could hold about twelve hundred people, but with the large mirrors that made up the walls on either side of the stage—a holdover from its burlesque days—there seemed to be three or four times that many people milling about inside. The large area in front of the stage was the most crowded, but each of the four levels that went up in tiers to the back wall were full of people as well. And unlike Casa Canelo's, the men here had taken as much care as the women with their costumes, though they weren't as skimpily attired.

"Okay, now I feel underdressed," Danny said. "I should have worn the Hellboy outfit I made for MediaCon last summer."

The others laughed.

"And who knew Wicca girls were so hot," Danny added.

"I wouldn't," Wes told him.

"Just behave," Nina said. "Please. It's my friends who are putting this on and I have to be able to face them again after tonight."

"Relax," John said. "We won't embarrass you."

"At least not on purpose," Danny said. "Hey, look at the girl in the leopard skin body stocking over by the bar. She's totally checking me out." He looked to the others for confirmation. "It's me she's checking out, right?" he asked. "Not John?"

"Go get her, Tiger," Wes said. "And remember." Nina and John joined in and they all said together, "Don't geek out on her."

Danny grinned. "As if."

"I need to find Sandy," Nina said when he walked away, "to see if she needs any last-minute help. Will you guys be okay?"

"Don't worry so much," Wes told her. "We'll be fine." She left as well, and Wes turned to John. "Looks like the band's about ready to start. You want to get closer to the stage?"

John shook his head. "You go ahead. I'm going to mingle."

"You'll need a drink in your hand if you're going to do that properly."

"Then my first stop's the bar," John said.

He watched until Wes was lost in the crowd, then checked on

Danny, who seemed to be actually just listening to whatever the women in the leopard skin outfit was saying to him instead of regaling her with gaming or comic book trivia.

There was a bar here on the ground floor in front of the stage, but John decided to go to the one on the third level, which didn't seem as busy. He ordered a beer from the Marilyn Monroe behind the bar, then found himself a place at the railing where he could look down at the crowd.

Though he hadn't worn a costume since the Halloween that Tim had died, he almost wished he was wearing one tonight. In his street clothes, with only the bat ears and snout, he felt a little out of place. *Everybody* was in costume here, and some of them were incredibly elaborate. On the next level down there was a guy in what appeared to be an actual suit of armor, carrying his helmet under his arm so that he could drink and talk. And then there was the group decked out like the cast from *Firefly,* which wasn't that hard to do for some of the characters. It was just the dedication of the group as a whole that impressed him.

He supposed that the only people here who hadn't made an effort were Danny, Wes, and himself. And maybe the woman with all the tattoos at the far end of the railing—unless her tattoos were an elaborate paint job done just for the evening. But she didn't need the tattoos to call attention to herself. It wasn't just that she was attractive—there were many attractive women here tonight—but that her features were so expressive. And he loved the way her looks seemed to completely change, whenever the light caught her at a different angle.

He found himself wishing he'd brought a little sketchbook so that he could do some drawings of her. As it was, he tried not to stare, but still study her enough so that he could hold an image of her in his mind until he got home.

It was easier once the band came on. Even up here, three tiers from the dance floor, people started to move. The tattooed woman got into the groove of the band's rhythm, a big smile on her face as she bobbed her head and danced in place, one hand on the railing, her gaze fixed on the stage below. The band was good, playing a kind of loud rockabilly that only seemed to have two speeds: fast and faster. They put John in a good mood and he even found himself dancing a little where he stood, though he wasn't exactly renowned for his dance floor moves. In fact, he couldn't remember the last time he'd been on a dance floor.

It wasn't that he didn't like music, or that the rhythm didn't affect him. There was just something about the jostling enthusiasm of the other dancers that always made him feel stupid and awkward.

At one point he was so caught up in the band's music that it was a few minutes before he glanced over at the woman again. The disappointment he felt when he realized she was gone surprised him. As did the happiness when he saw her wend her way back down from the washrooms on the fourth tier.

He almost laughed at himself. What? Like he was going to walk up and talk to her or something?

Nina appeared at his elbow when the band finished its set.

"What are you doing way up here?" she asked.

He shrugged. "You know me."

"I do. I was just hoping if we dragged you away from your studio and brought you to a place like this, you might actually hook up with someone. Or at least have some fun."

"I am having fun."

She shook her head. "Wes is flirting with a bunch of guys in drag. Danny is on the dance floor and I think he and Helen are actually hitting it off. But you . . ."

"Helen's the woman in the leopard skin outfit?"

"She is." She shook her head. "Maybe you should go to that party the waitress invited you to."

"Can't I enjoy the music without needing to try to pick someone up?"

"Sure, except you totally need to get laid."

He laughed. "You sound like Danny."

She punch his arm. "C'mon," she said. "You should try a little sex once in a while. It'll loosen you up."

"I have, and I like it. But I also like it to be with someone I might get to know for longer than just one night."

"I understand. Really, I do. But . . . isn't there one woman in here that you'd like to get to know a little better?"

He couldn't help himself. His gaze went to the tattooed woman

before he quickly looked back at Nina. But she picked up on it immediately.

"Well, well," she said. "I never pegged you for the Suicide Girls
type, but she's certainly attractive. Without the tattoos, I'd totally see
her being your type."

"I like the tattoos."

"So go talk to her."

He shook his head. "I wouldn't know what to say."

"Just be yourself. Women already like the look of you—Danny
wasn't off about that—so it's not like she isn't going to listen to what
you have to say."

"I don't know where you get this idea that I'm some kind of magnet for—"

"Are you going to talk to her, or do I have to do it for you? You
know that's going to be so high school." She mimicked a ditsy, girlish
voice and added, "So, my friend likes you. And you know, like, he's
wondering if you, you know, might like him, too?"

"Don't you dare."

"There's only one way to stop me."

And she'd do it, too, John knew. Nina wasn't the least bit shy. She
never had been.

"Okay," he said. "I'll talk to her. Are you happy now?"

She nodded and didn't move, arms folded across her chest.

"What?" he asked.

"I'm waiting for you to actually do it."

"Oh, for God's sake."

She went back to her ditsy voice. "So, my friend? He thinks you're
so awesome . . ."

John shook his head in exasperation, but, beer in hand, he started
down to the other end of the railing. He was aware of Nina trailing in
his wake, pretending complete nonchalance and disinterest, but knew
there was no point in asking her to go away. There was just enough
space for him to join the tattooed woman at the railing. He drank the
last inch of his beer to combat the dryness in his throat and took off
the bat's snout.

"So, um," he said to the woman. "That was a great first set."

She turned to him and studied him for a moment before she finally smiled. "Yeah, they were exactly what I was in the mood for tonight. Fast and loud."

"They certainly met both those criteria."

"Do you listen to a lot of rockabilly?" she asked.

He shook his head. "I don't really know much about it. About the closest I've got is a Stray Cats greatest hits collection."

"Oh, they're okay. But if you really want to understand what it's all about, you need to go back to the fifties and listen to cuts by, oh, Frankie Cochran, early Gene Vincent, and Elvis Presley, and the hundreds of great bands that no one's ever heard of anymore."

"I never thought of Elvis as rockabilly."

"But he was. Go back and listen to the Sun recordings. And that's another thing. In those days every label had its own sound. Dart. Imperial. Chess." She smiled and shook her head. "Listen to me go on."

"I take it you like all that music from the fifties and sixties."

She nodded. "What's not to like? Rockabilly. Surf guitar. Hot rod music. It's the best. Sometimes I wish that I'd grown up in those days, except then I remember how weird the rest of the world was. The civil rights movement was only just starting. They had the cold war hanging over them. And I sure wouldn't have been able to take shop in school. But the cars and the music—they were great."

"I'm beginning to wish I knew more about this music."

She smiled again. It was a great smile, John thought. The kind that lights up the whole face.

"You sound like you're trying to pick me up," she said.

He returned her smile. "What, just because I'm interested in what you've got to say?"

"That, and the fact that you've been shooting glances at me all night long."

So much for being surreptitious, John thought.

"You're a striking woman," he said. "I'd love to paint you some time."

"Okay, that's definitely a pickup line."

"No . . . I mean, it's just . . ."

Her eyebrows went up.

"I'm crap at this," he said. "Look, I'm sorry I bothered you."

He started to turn away, but at the same time as the woman put a hand on his arm to keep him from going, Nina appeared at his side.

"John really is an artist," she told the woman, "and a very good one. I'm Nina, by the way."

She reached out a hand.

"I'm Grace," the woman said as she took Nina's hand. "And you're his . . . girlfriend?"

Nina laughed. "God, no. But we've been friends since middle school."

"And you guys had, what? A bet to see if he could pick me up?"

John wished he could turn to jelly and just slide under the railing to the floor below.

"No, no," Nina said. "Nothing like that. I just knew he liked you, but he can get so damn shy that I threatened to come over and talk to you if he didn't."

"Nina," he managed. "You're not helping."

But Grace was laughing—and not at him, he realized.

"I think this is sweet," she said.

John sighed. Did he really want this woman with her tattoos and that touch of toughness about her to think that he was sweet?

"Welcome to embarrassment hell," he muttered.

Grace tapped him lightly on the shoulder with a closed fist.

"Don't be embarrassed," she said. "I meant 'sweet' in a good way." Then she held up her empty Negra Modelo bottle. "Aren't you going to ask if you can buy me a drink?"

"Would you like another one?"

"I would, thank you."

He turned to Nina.

"Nothing for me," she said. "I'll just stay here and keep Grace company until you get back—you know, tell her all your kinks and secrets."

"Nina . . ."

"I'm kidding. Go. We'll be right here, waiting for you. But don't be too long about it. You know how my mouth can just run on all by itself."

He glanced at Grace and was buoyed by the sympathy he saw behind the smile in her eyes.

"I'll be right back," he said.

The trouble was, Nina was right. Leave her alone with Grace long enough and she was liable to say anything. He wasn't sure if he should be ticked off or grateful that she'd intruded the way she had. But the end result was that he was talking to Grace, and she didn't seem to think that he was a total loser. Though that, considering his own ineptitude and Nina's embarrassing intervention, was more due to blind luck than anything.

Despite the press of the crowd, he managed to get to the bar, order two Modelos, and return to the railing in a reasonable five minutes. Grace smiled her thanks when he handed her one of the bottles and clinked it against his own before she had a sip.

"Grace is a mechanic," Nina informed him. "How cool is that? I wish I'd known her when the transmission went in the company's Honda, though I don't suppose it would have helped since she only works on old cars." She turned to Grace. "What did you call them again?"

"Hot rods. Customs. Do you have a car, John?"

"I'll leave you kids to get acquainted," Nina said before he could answer. "Have fun!"

And then she was off, sliding through the crowd with a practiced ease.

"Look, I'm sorry about how—" John began, but Grace was already shaking her head.

"Don't be," she told him. "I like her. She's so full of life."

"Oh, she's got energy to spare, and then some," John said.

"And I think it's great that the two of you have been friends for so long. I don't know anybody from my high school anymore, and I couldn't even call up one name from the kids in middle school."

"I can't remember us ever not being friends," he said. "Did she tell you about Wesdanina? The company that she and a couple of our other friends from middle school have?"

Grace laughed and nodded. "I can't believe how much she told me, *and* got out of me, in the little time you were gone."

"That's Nina."

"So why didn't you go in on the company yourself?"

He shrugged. "I wanted to see if I could make a go of my painting.

I do design work for them and a few other companies to pay the bills, but I guess I lost my enthusiasm for computers and media, and they never did."

"I never got into any of that stuff," she said. "I just never had the time. I started working on cars with my grandfather when I was in high school and I guess its kind of consumed my time ever since."

He nodded. "I was always drawing myself, but somehow I managed to waste many an hour in front of the computer and TV. It's funny how much time we have when we're kids."

"I don't suppose I need to ask which sort of art you prefer to do."

"Digital's useful, especially for commercial applications. But I like to work hands-on—the feel of the canvas giving under my brush, the grit of the pastel on my fingers. Of course it's way messier, but that might be part of its charm."

"I know all about messes," she said. She held up a hand, palm out. "The grease gets so deep into my pores I can never quite get it out."

"Seems clean to me."

"Yes, well . . ." She looked at her palm for a moment, then put her hand in her pocket. "You never told me what kind of car you drive."

"I don't have one."

"You don't?"

"I don't really need one. I live and work right downtown."

She smiled. "Nobody *needs* a car living downtown. But how could you not have one?"

"Do the plastic models I made when I was a kid count?"

"Not hardly."

"So what do you drive?"

A look of longing passed over her features.

This woman loves her cars, John thought.

"I've got a bunch of them that I keep in storage," she said, "but my street car's a '57 Fairlane."

"You're kidding. I made a model of one of those. I painted it black and red."

"No way."

"It's true. And I still have it. My buddy Danny was always going on about Corvettes back then, but the Fairlane was a much cooler car."

"You are so sucking up to me. *My* car's red and black, with chrome trim and whitewalls, and a V-eight under the hood. And I know. It's not environmentally conscious, but I swear that engine runs as clean as a hybrid."

He laughed. "You don't have to convince me."

"Sorry. I get a little defensive."

A second band had been setting up while they talked and the crash of their opening chord brought an end to further conversation. The new band was louder than the first act, and heavier. The thing that had been so good about the rockabilly band, John realized, was the infectious bounce that made it impossible not to tap your foot or nod your head in time to its lively beat. In comparison, the second band sounded like it was plodding its way through their first number.

Grace pulled a face and leaned closer to him.

"I hate this," she said in his ear. "Do you want to go outside until their set's over?"

John got a warm glow inside at the realization that she wanted to be with him instead of just leaving.

He nodded in agreement. They set their beer bottles on the end of the bar as they went by and took the stairs down to the exit. Grace's hand found his and she didn't let go until they had to get stamped at the door so they'd be able to get back in. They passed Danny and his new friend Helen, but they were in the thick of the crowd, so John just waved to his friend before he and Grace went outside.

"I wanted loud," Grace said when they were finally out on the street, "but that was like the sound track for dinosaurs mating."

"It certainly didn't have the bounce of that first band's rhythms."

"Amen, brother!"

There was still a crowd in front of the Solona Music Hall, but it was mostly people just out on the sidewalk for a smoke break. John looked up and down the street.

"Where do you want to go?" he asked Grace.

She shrugged. "Let's just walk for a while. We can come back in a bit when that band's finished its set."

She took his hand again and they started up Kelly Street, heading east. She made him laugh as she started making up stories about the owners of the parked cars that they walked by.

"And what would someone say about your Fairlane?" he asked.

"Obviously owned by a cool chick who just met a really nice guy."

"You think I'm a nice guy?"

She stopped and turned so that she was facing him.

"Nice guys are cool," she said.

Then she leaned in close, breasts pushing up against his chest, and kissed him.

John wasn't quite sure how they ended up sharing half a bottle of red wine at his apartment instead of going back to the Solona Music Hall. He didn't quite know how they ended up in his bed either, but by that point he was so head-over-heels for her that it didn't matter.

"Normally," he remembered her saying as they fell naked onto his bed, "I really don't do this kind of thing. But tonight . . . I just can't help myself."

"Same here," he said, smiling. "I'm glad we can't help ourselves."

He traced the tattoos on her stomach with a finger, trailing it down her torso. She grinned at him.

"I'll just bet you are," she said.

Then her mouth was on his again and they found other ways to express their appreciation for each other.

John couldn't remember when they fell asleep. But he remembered when he had to get up to take a leak. He remembered telling her about Tim when he got back into bed and how they were going to make love again, but then she was the one who had to use the toilet.

And then she was gone. Vanished from his bathroom like she'd never been there at all.

"So, obviously," Danny said, "you fell asleep again and she just collected her clothes and left."

"I guess. But I don't remember falling asleep again. I just remember hearing her use the toilet and then there was nothing. I got up and called her name, but when I got to the bathroom, she was gone."

"Dude, you totally fell asleep."

John had come by to deliver the new concept drawings for the Addison DVD that Danny had guilted him into doing. They sat in his office, Danny with his feet up on his desk, John slouched on the sofa. The walls of the office were festooned with posters of the sexier characters from video games—all female, of course. John looked away from some anime character with implausibly large breasts and eyes.

"So how did it feel to be talking to an actual woman last night?" he asked Danny.

"What?"

"That girl Helen. You two seemed to be hitting it off."

Danny nodded. "Yeah, she was cool. She used to be a gamer before she went all vegan and wicked."

"I think that's Wicca."

"Whatever. But you know, maybe there's something to be said for not eating meat. A lot of those Wicca girls last night were seriously hot."

"I noticed."

Danny shook his head. "No, you only noticed one thing, and you left the club with her."

"So are you going to see Helen again?"

"Sure, but you're changing the subject. What do you think the deal was with . . ."

"Grace."

"Yeah, Grace. Hey, maybe she was on some kind of twenty-four-hour pass from prison, and she had to get back to her cell."

John sighed.

"No, seriously," Danny said. "I mean, come on. All that ink."

"Lots of people have tattoos. And hers aren't jail tattoos."

"Yeah, but you don't know for sure that she isn't a felon, right?"

John swung his feet to the floor.

"I should get going," he said.

"I was just saying. I didn't mean anything by it."

"I know, Danny."

"So do you have a picture of her?" Danny asked. "Something we can show around?"

John stopped at the door and looked back. "What makes you think I have a picture of her?"

"Oh, come on, John. Like I don't know you? As soon as you start mooning over some girl, you're drawing her face everywhere. Send me a jpeg and I can show it to Helen and, you know, whoever."

John nodded. "Do you think Nina's back yet?"

"No idea. You should check her office."

"I will."

"And John?" Danny tapped the disk that John had brought in with his ideas for a revamp of the DVD menu art. "Thanks for this, man. You've put us back on schedule."

"You haven't even looked at it yet."

"How long have we been friends? I know you, John. It'll be great. Now go find the Tattooed Girl."

John shook his head and went down the hall to Nina's office. When he poked his head in, he saw her working at her keyboard, gaze locked to her monitor. He stood for a moment, then cleared his throat.

She looked up with a flash of irritation until she recognized him and smiled.

"Got a minute?" John asked.

"Always. What's up?"

"I was just wondering if you might have gotten a last name or a number when you were talking to Grace last night."

She gave him a surprised look. "Didn't you two leave together?"

"Yeah, but I didn't get either."

"First rule of dating," she said. "You get the name and number."

John shrugged. "I guess I'm just rusty." He waited a beat, then added, "Which reminds me. Thanks for your timely, if embarrassing, intervention last night."

"It doesn't sound like it was that much help if you came away without her phone number. Wait, she didn't give you a fake one did she, like for some pizza joint, like Danny's always getting?"

"No, everything was fabulous. It's just . . ."

Nina did something on her keyboard—"Ctrl - S" to save what she was working on, he assumed—and pushed her chair back from her desk.

"Okay, John," she said. "You know you can't leave without telling me all about it, right?"

Like Danny's office, hers also had a sofa. The big difference was that on her walls were tasteful posters from various downtown galleries and the Solona Art Gallery. The images were a little safe for John's tastes—a Renoir print, a Van Gogh, some from photo exhibits by photographers he didn't recognize—but at least they weren't adolescent fantasies.

He let Nina come around her desk and lead him to the sofa, where he went over his story for the second time that day.

"Wow," she said when he was done. "Hot sex on what wasn't even an actual first date. You're living large, John."

"I really liked her."

She patted his knee. "I know you did. You do. Since she didn't leave you her number, she'll probably call."

"What if she doesn't?"

She shook her head. "How many times do I have to tell you guys? Only put positive thoughts out into the universe."

"I know. But the way she just left. If it was you, what would make you take off like that? Was it because I told her about Tim?"

"You're overanalyzing this, John. She'll call."

"I shouldn't have talked about Tim."

Nina smiled. "The woman had tattoos up the yin-yang. She was probably pierced in places I don't even want to know."

John shook his head.

"Okay, but that doesn't change my point. A tough-looking woman like her? I really doubt she's so sensitive that your talking about your brother would send her running."

"It was funny about the tattoos," he said.

"Yeah, no kidding. You and a biker chick—who'd have thunk?"

"No, I mean, I noticed them, of course. But they weren't like biker tattoos, and anyway, after awhile I just didn't see them anymore. Then the light would change and they'd catch me by surprise all over again."

Nina studied him for a moment, then sighed.

"Trust me," she said. "She'll call."

But she didn't.

Not that day, and not the next either. The worst of it was, she was all he could think about. It was pathetic, really. He was a grown man, not some kid driven by raging hormones. But all he could do was drift from room to room around his apartment. If he did go out—mostly to wander aimlessly through the streets in his neighborhood—he always found an excuse to get back to the apartment in case she should call.

The only productive thing he'd gotten done in the past two days was the little job for Danny—that was if you discounted the half-dozen drawings he'd done of Grace from memory. They were good, but what was the point of them? They weren't going to bring her back or make sense of why she'd taken off, leaving no way for him to contact her. The only positive thing about the drawings was that when he was doing them, concentrating on lines and shadows and details, he felt connected to her and not so hollow.

He'd even gone down to the storage unit in the basement of his building where he'd taken down a box and dug out the plastic model of the '57 Fairlane he'd made back when he was a kid. He brought it upstairs and set it on his coffee table and would catch himself daydreaming in front of it, slowing rolling the model back and forth on the wood surface.

He played his Stray Cats album, then did a little research on the Internet and downloaded some other rockabilly music from a few online music stores. Some of the artists he bought just sounded too old-fashioned for him, but he found himself really liking more than a few, and he began to appreciate her love for twangy guitars and the infectious walking rhythms of the bass and drums. It was a simple music, especially some of the sax breaks. Lester Young or Sonny Rollins, these players weren't. But there was something endearing in the simplicity, and you couldn't shake the beat, once it got into you.

He knew he was becoming obsessed, but he couldn't seem to stop himself. He'd always laughed at movies where the lead characters fell head over heels in love when they first met, but it didn't seem quite so preposterous anymore. He knew it might just be some momentary infatuation, but he also knew he could never be sure unless he got to see her again.

His friends all had advice for him. Danny thought he should go door-to-door in the area around the Solona Music Hall with a small copy of one of his portraits to see if anyone recognized her, but that just seemed like slipping into stalker territory. Nina kept telling him to be patient.

"She probably just needs time to process what happened," she said. "You told me that she was surprised at herself for going home with a guy she'd just met, didn't you?"

"Except it's not like we had a horrible time. We weren't drunk and it wasn't just sex. There was way more talking and cuddling."

"She still needs to process it. I know I would, no matter how great the guy seemed to be."

But patience was hard, when every day without contact just seemed to pull her farther and farther away.

"I don't even know why I'm bothering," he told Wes. "She knows where I live. If she was interested, she knows where to find me. The fact that she hasn't should make it pretty plain that she's not."

It was the afternoon of the third day since Halloween and the two of them were having breakfast at a coffee shop around the corner from the Wesdanina offices.

Wes nodded. "I know the feeling. And it always seems that the guy you hook up with—"

John raised his eyebrows.

"Okay, the *person*," Wes said, "is usually married, and while it might have meant more to you, it was just a one-night stand to them." He pursed his lips. "Though she doesn't sound like she'd be the married type."

"What's that supposed to mean?"

Wes shrugged. "Well, I didn't see her, but from all Danny and Nina had to say, she looked kind of wild."

"Yeah, I guess she did. But wild people can be married, too."

John didn't think Grace had been married. And if she had, she wouldn't have come home with him. She seemed to have too much integrity for that. Except what did he know about her? Maybe that was the very reason she *wasn't* contacting him.

Eventually, he might have been able to put her out of his mind, except staring out the window one afternoon when he should have been working on a Wesdanina project, he remembered the "FoMoCo" tattoo on Grace's leg. When he'd asked her about it, she said it stood for the Ford Motor Company, and then she told him about her grandfather's Model A, and how working on it with him had started her love affair with cars, especially Fords.

"It doesn't matter how backed up I am at the shop," she'd said. "If someone brings in an old Ford, I'll always leave whatever I'm working on to talk to them."

Her street car was a Fairlane—the life-sized version of the plastic model he had on his coffee table—and she had another three Fords in storage, so she was seriously into the company's cars. Not only that, but she loved working on them, customizing other peoples' cars for them, or helping them get the parts they needed so they could do it themselves.

How many women mechanics could there be in the city with her specialization skills, who looked like her? Surely, she couldn't be that hard to find. Especially if he told whoever answered the phone that he had an old Ford he wanted to get fixed up. He'd deal with the little white lie once he got Grace on the line. Maybe she'd be mad, maybe she wouldn't, but at least he'd get the chance to talk to her.

He got out the Yellow Pages and thumbed through the flimsy pages to the "Automobile Repair & Service" section, looking for places that advertised vintage and custom specialization. He couldn't figure out why he hadn't thought of this before. Sure, there were lots of garages in town, but how many of them focused on vintage cars and had women mechanics?

A little Internet research informed him that, while it was hard to draw a line between street rods and real hot rods, a lot of the old-school hot-rodders felt that a real hot rod should be built of old Ford parts and stripped of everything unnecessary. For someone whose only experience with the mechanical workings of cars was the plastic models he'd built as a kid, John found the pictures of works-in-progress, and the discussions that mentioned things like frame rails and split wishbones, a little bewildering. But he gleaned enough information to feel comfortable about making his first call.

After all, he thought as he listened to the phone ring on the other end of the line, he wasn't presenting himself as an expert. He was presenting himself as a novice in need of an expert.

He started at the "A's" in the phone listings with Adamson's Garage. Their ad said "We'll chop, customize, and drop your ride!"

"Adamson's, Ted speaking. How can I help you?"

John explained how he'd brought an old Model A back from a scrapyard in California, that he wanted to fix it up, and how he was hoping they'd be able to work on it, get parts for him, and just generally advise him on the best way to go about the getting the job done.

"Well, Louie's our Ford man," Ted said, "and he's not in right now. But you know, you might have better luck talking to the guys at the hot rod club. I'm not trying to turn away business, but if you want to do a lot of the work yourself, their time's free. With us, you're paying the mechanic's hourly rate."

"Right," John said. "I appreciate your leveling with me. Maybe I'll try the club. You wouldn't have a number for them, would you?"

"No, sorry. I'm not into those old jalopies and rods the way Louie is."

"And he's your Ford expert?"

"Best in the city."

"Okay, thanks for your time. I'll probably drop by on the weekend if he's working."

Ted laughed. "Saturday afternoon, all the hot-rodders come hang out. You'll be right at home."

Except he wouldn't be going, John thought, because Louie wasn't Grace.

The conversations went pretty much the same for the next half-dozen places he tried. Some offered to do his frame welding. Some told them they could get any part he needed—apparently there was a whole secondary market for newly manufactured vintage parts. Some suggested he come in and talk to them, and bring pictures if he had any. At least two more told him he should contact the local hot rod club. None of them had a woman mechanic specializing in Fords.

He looked down at his pad where he'd been making notes and saw that he'd circled "hot rod club" a couple of times. Maybe that was the route to go. He looked up their number in the phone book, but there was no listing, so he did a search on the Web. Even though he'd refined his search to just "Santo del Vado Viejo" and "hot rod club," he still got a couple hundred hits, but the one he wanted was right at the top of the list.

He clicked on it. When the VV Hot Rod Club page came up, he found himself staring at a picture of Grace in a white T and jeans, sitting on the hood of some old customized Model A Ford. Under it was a caption that read:

> R.I.P.—Altagracia "Grace" Quintero
> We'll miss you, darlin'

Below that was a body of text that told how she'd been killed in mid-October while trying to stop some junkie gunman from robbing a Mexican grocery store.

John stared at the screen.

Killed in mid-October? But he'd met her on Halloween—two weeks after she was supposed to have been shot.

What kind of a sick joke was this?

Except the memorial seemed genuine, as did the dozens of comments appended to the initial article by her friends, acquaintances, and customers.

He scrolled up and down the page, stopping at each of the four pictures they had of her.

It was definitely the same woman he'd been with on Halloween.

Had the girl he'd met somehow stolen this other Grace's identity?

But how was that even possible? He couldn't imagine anyone duplicating all those tattoos. And for what reason?

He never read the paper or listened to the news, so he hadn't heard about the shooting. Now he went to *The Santo del Vado Viejo Star*'s website. A deep chill settled in him as he found confirmation in their archives.

He went back to the hot rod club's website, copied the URL into an e-mail, and sent it. Then he picked up the phone and called Nina.

"I've just sent you an url," he said when she picked up. "Could you go to the web page?"

"Sure. Just a sec."

He waited, listening to the click of her keyboard while he stared at the picture on his own screen.

"Oh, John," Nina said. "I'm so sorry. Now we know why you didn't hear from her."

"Look at when they say she died."

There was a moment's pause while Nina read through the text on her screen.

"That's impossible," she said when she was done. "It says here it happened two weeks before Halloween."

"But it's the same woman we met, right? At least she looks the same to me, and I know she has the exact same tattoos."

"I didn't get as close a look at the tattoos as you did," Nina said, "but yes, the woman in these pictures is definitely the same person we met at the Witches' Ball."

"Except we couldn't have, because she was already dead."

Nina didn't reply.

"So how could that happen?" John asked.

"They had to have made a mistake with the date," she finally said.

"It says the same thing on *The Santo del Vado Viejo Star* site."

"But it's not possible."

"No," John said, his gaze still locked on the image on his computer screen. "It's not. But at least I'm not the only one going crazy here."

"There has to be some logical explanation."

"Do you believe in ghosts?" John asked.

"I never did before."

"Me neither. And I'm not sure I do now. Like you said, there has to be some other explanation."

"But what?"

"I don't know, Nina. There just has to be. That was a real person I was with, not some ghost. That much I know, and one way or another, I'm going to find out what's going on."

"What are you going to do?" Nina asked.

He could hear the worry in her voice. He knew they'd all been worrying about how obsessed he'd become with finding Grace. An obsession like this was more Danny's style than his. Wes and Nina never seemed to have a problem hooking up with someone when they were interested in being in a relationship, and they were equally adept at disengaging themselves from their partner when the time seemed right, while John normally had an even more laid-back attitude to dating. He was always up front about wanting to keep things casual and had been ever since a disastrous relationship at university when his girlfriend Jenny had become so neurotically jealous that he'd had to break up with her, and then she'd stalked him for the remainder of his final year. All these years later, his nerves would still give an anxious little tic when he saw a tall woman with long, straight brown hair.

Danny was the one who was always ready to marry some girl he might have seen at a bus stop, or at a trade show. He'd talk about her for days and come up with outrageous schemes for how he might get to meet her. Or he'd spy a particularly attractive barrista in a café and spend all his waking hours obsessing over how gorgeous she was, getting the caffeine jitters from going into the café so often just for the chance to see her and exchange a few words.

John supposed how he felt for Grace could seem like that, but the difference was, they'd really connected. Or at least he'd thought they had. After her abrupt disappearance, he wasn't so certain, and he sure didn't want to turn into his own ex-girlfriend Jenny, chasing after someone who didn't want anything to do with him.

But now he was supposed to believe that he'd spent the past few days chasing a ghost? While that could certainly explain the way she'd simply disappeared from his bathroom, he didn't buy it.

He just couldn't bring himself to believe in ghosts.

"I don't know what I'm going to do," he told Nina. "I guess I'll try to find out more about this woman who got shot—as ghoulish as that sounds."

"It doesn't sound ghoulish at all," Nina said, the sympathy plain in her voice. "You're just trying to make sense out of something that doesn't make any sense at all."

"Tell me about it." He sighed, then added, "I'll talk to you later, Nina."

"Do you want me to come over?"

"No, I'm okay. It's just a shock, you know, and totally confusing."

"I understand. Of course it is. This is just such a totally bizarre situation, no matter how you look at it, but I'm sure if we sit down and go over all the—"

John broke in. "I'm sorry, Nina, but I really need to go. I know you want to help, but I need to process this for a while on my own before I can talk anymore about it. But I *will* call you later."

He hung up before she could say anything else and when his phone rang a moment later, he didn't answer. He could see from the caller ID that it was Nina calling him back, but he really did need to get his head around what he'd just learned.

He got up from his computer and walked into his bedroom, then stood there in the doorway to his bathroom.

Ghosts.

His perception of how the world worked had never included ghosts. He didn't even like horror movies, or ghost stories. They were either too gross or he just couldn't suspend his disbelief long enough to get into the characters and story. And really. If he ever had leaned toward believing in them, he'd have done everything he could think of to contact his brother Tim.

Now he didn't know what to think.

No, he thought, his gaze still locked on the view of his bathroom. He couldn't lie to himself. The moment he saw that memorial, his gut had known the truth. He'd only called Nina to get confirmation on what he already knew was true: they'd met Grace two weeks after she'd died. If there was any kind of sense to get out of that irrefutable fact, he didn't know where it was going to come from, but it wouldn't be from him and Nina rehashing the little they knew, over and over again.

He backed out of the doorway and returned to his living room where he stared down at his plastic model of the Fairlane and the sketches he'd done of Grace. He looked to where he'd left the phone receiver and it occurred to him that Nina wouldn't let anything as simple as a hang up dissuade her from coming over. Nina was the unstoppable force that could wear down both the rock and the hard place.

He got his jacket from the back of the couch and left his apartment. Once he was outside, the fresh autumn air helped to clear his head. It was overcast, but the air was dry. He walked with no destination in mind until he found himself a few blocks from his own apartment building, across the street from the big grey brick building on 26th Street called the Alverson Arms.

According to the *Santo del Vado Viejo Star*'s website, that was where she'd lived. And that meant . . .

His gaze tracked down the street.

The grocery store where she'd died was just down there, in the next block.

He had an urge to go into the store, just as he had an urge to stand in the foyer of her apartment building. Instead, he turned away and began walking again.

Though he hadn't planned it—he was just walking where his feet took him—many long blocks later he found himself in front of yet another important place in Grace's life.

There was a bus stop across the street from Sanchez Motors and he sat there for a while, watching the men who'd been her co-workers go about their business. He considered starting up a conversation with one of them, but they all looked busy, and pretty tough. None of them seemed to be the kind of person who'd have much patience for someone coming around to ask if any of them had also seen her ghost since she'd died, and did they maybe know how to contact her in the spirit-world, or wherever the hell it was that ghosts lived when they weren't haunting this world?

He bent down, elbows on his knees, face in his hands.

Shoot me now, he thought, before I start hearing voices, too.

When he did hear a voice, he started. But looking up, he saw it was only a Native American man—round-faced, with jet-black hair and shabby clothes. He appeared to be in his forties and looked a little like a street person, but he smelled like cedar smoke and something else that John couldn't identify until he remembered a trip he'd taken with Danny and the others to a powwow out on the Kikimi rez last year. A few of the participants had waved around smudge sticks made of sage. Wes had bought a couple from an old woman who had them for sale.

When the man continued to stand there, looking down at him, John said, "I'm sorry, what did you say?"

"I said don't let it get you down. Everything's on a wheel. We don't get to choose how it turns, but every chance you had once, eventually, it comes around again."

"I don't know what you're talking about," John told him.

"Sure you do. You've got traces of Ms. Gracie's spirit hanging all over you."

"What? Who are you?"

"My name's Norm and I'm a friend of Ms. Gracie. Did you know her before, or only after?"

"Before or after what?"

"She died."

All John could do was stare at him.

"Mind if I have a seat?" Norm added.

John managed to shake his head. Moments ago he'd been considering going up to one of those guys in the garage and asking them about Grace and ghosts. But now that he had someone sitting beside him, obviously ready to talk about either, he couldn't seem to find his voice.

It was one thing to talk about it with Nina—to *consider* the impossible idea—quite another to have that conversation with what looked like a street person.

"I'm guessing you only knew Ms. Gracie after she died," Norm said. "Because I think she would have told me if she'd met a nice-seeming fella like you. You like old cars?"

I can't be having this conversation, John thought.

He cleared his throat.

"What . . . what did you mean," he said, "you know, when you said her spirit's hanging all over me?"

"Not her spirit, just traces of it." He moved his hands around in the air. "Spirit's not like this one solid thing that lives inside you. Bits and pieces are always coming off and drifting around. When you have a strong relationship with someone, little bits of them hang on to you for a while."

"I only knew her for one night."

Norm nodded. "Halloween, I'm guessing. I saw her that night, too, and she was particularly present for a spirit."

John nodded. "Halloween, that's right. And then she just vanished."

Norm started to roll a cigarette. When he was done, he offered it to John.

"No, thanks. I don't smoke."

Norm studied him for a moment, then shrugged. He got the cigarette lit and held it up in the air to let smoke drift above them before he took a drag.

"Yeah," he said, "there's times spirits find it easier to cross over and I guess Halloween's one of them."

"I . . ." John had to clear his throat again. "I've got to say, I'm finding all of this very surreal."

Norm nodded. "My advice, you forget all about it. People think it's interesting and special to talk to the spirits. You see them all primed and ready to welcome them. Talk to me. Share your wisdom with me. But what they don't know is, it's not something you can just shut off. Unless you've studied on how to keep a filter on yourself, they just keep coming to you, thick and fast until you can't get a moment's peace and you think you're going to go nuts."

He took another drag from his cigarette and leaned back, looking up into the sky.

"So they're . . . they're all around us?" John asked.

"All the time. But mostly, we're not paying attention to them, and they're not paying attention to us, and that's the way I like to keep it."

John couldn't help himself. "Is she . . . is *she* here?"

Norm turned to look at him and shook his head. "It doesn't work like that."

"Then how does it work?"

"I don't know. I've spent most of my life trying to not find out."

"But you say the spirits are all around us . . ."

Norm shrugged. "There's not one kind of spirit. There's the ones that live in the cactus and arroyos and hills—out east, they call them the little manitous. I like that name. It means 'mystery,' and that's pretty much what a spirit is, right?"

"I suppose."

"Then there's the big guns—the thunders. The Kachina people and old man Coyote and the rest of them. And then you've got the dead who haven't gone on yet—what you'd call a ghost, I suppose."

Just a few hours ago, John couldn't have imagined having this conversation, or if he did, that he'd be taking it at face value. Or that he'd seriously ask, "Is it possible to contact them?"

"Well, I don't know how it would work for you white folks. I don't even know how it works for other tribes. But my people, we use sacred smoke and sweat lodges, dance ceremonies, or intermediaries like a shaman, or a holy aunt. You can go on a spirit quest, too." He grinned. "But that takes a lot of effort on your part. It's not like picking up the phone."

"So you're a . . . um, shaman, then?"

Norm shook his head. "No, I'm just an unlucky Indian who's tuned into their station and I can't turn it off."

"If this is all real—"

"Oh, it's real, all right."

"Then there's got to be a way I can contact her."

Norm nodded. "Easiest way is to wait for another one of those days like Halloween when the borders are thinnest."

"Are there other special days like that?"

"I don't know. You need to talk to someone who knows more about it than I do."

"I don't know anybody else who wouldn't laugh in my face, if I asked them."

Norm shrugged. "Then look it up in a book."

He finished his cigarette and ground it out under his heel, then leaned over to pick up the butt. Straightening up, he put it in his pocket.

"If I were you," he said, "I'd just let it go. Nothing good ever comes from messing around with the spiritworld. But if you do see Ms. Gracie again, tell her Norm says hello."

John got up from the bench before Norm could leave. "Wait. I've got a hundred more questions."

"Yeah, I'm sure you do," Norm said, "but all this talking about spirits is drawing their attention, and like I said, that's something I try to avoid."

"But—"

Norm shook his head.

"Good luck," he said, and he started to walk away.

John wanted to stop him from going, but he'd seen the look in the man's eyes—not exactly fear, but an anxiousness that couldn't be denied. He sat down again, mulling over what he'd learned so far.

Finally, he got up and went back home.

Nina was waiting on the stoop of his building when he got back. She sat on the top step reading a paperback, a latte in a take-out cup on the stone beside her. She looked up from the book when he approached, as though she could pick his footstep out of all the others going by his building. Knowing her, John thought she probably could.

Though she gave him a smile, he could see the worry for him present in her eyes.

"I'm sorry for bailing on you," he told her.

"Given the circumstances, understandable." She patted the step she was sitting on. "Sit down. You look beat."

"No, I'm just . . . I don't know what I am. I met this guy . . ."

"And?" she said when his voice trailed off.

He sat down beside her and told her what he'd learned.

"This is all such bullshit," he said when he was done.

Nina shook her head. "We've hung out with a ghost. After something like that, how can what this Norm guy told you be so suspect? Plus, it sounds to me as though it's the last thing he's interested in, so it's not like he's trying to sell you on it himself. Wasn't his advice to let it go?"

John nodded. "But I don't see how I can."

"Then you have to be prepared to accept that there's more to the world than what you've always been told."

"I don't know. I hear that kind of thing and my brain just wants to shut down."

"Not me. I'd like to meet Norm."

Of course she would, but Nina was much more open-minded about this sort of thing than John, Danny, or Wes. She'd always been that way—even when they were all kids. More recently, ever since she'd gotten involved with the local pagan community, it had become a way of life for her. But even though she was a believer, she'd never

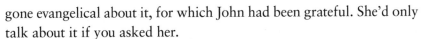

gone evangelical about it, for which John had been grateful. She'd only talk about it if you asked her.

Which was what John realized he had to do.

"So do you know anything about these special days Norm was talking about?" he asked.

She shrugged. "It's like he said—it's different for every belief system. With the Wicca, there are two days when the veils between the worlds are thinnest: Samhain and Beltane."

"And when are they?"

"We just had Samhain—that's the same as Halloween."

John nodded. "The Witches' Ball, right."

"Beltane is May Eve—the counterpart to Samhain. They divide the world into its two primary seasons: winter, or the dark part, and summer, which is the light. Samhain's about honoring death, so Beltane's about honoring life. It's the time when the sun's freed from his bondage to winter and can rule over the summer and life again." She smiled. "And I see your eyes glazing over."

"I'm sorry. It's just—you really believe all of this stuff, don't you? I mean, spirits and gods and everything."

"I always believed in spirits," she said, "though I've never seen any of them. But I can feel that the world is a bigger place than what I can see, or what we're told it is, and I've always sensed a secret life going on just beyond the one we all know."

She studied him for a moment, and he wasn't sure if it was to see if he was going to make a joke, or because she was trying to decide how much she wanted to tell him. Maybe it was a bit of both.

"Everybody's got an answer," she said after a moment. "The rationalists tell us that this world is all we get. The organized religions all have their own god to the exclusion of anybody else's, and seem to be more about what happens after we die than while we're actually living. And they're all so damn sure of themselves, aren't they? But I think our experience with God—with the world, or the spirit of the world—is more personal than scriptures and structure."

"Yet you take part in Wicca ceremonies, don't you?"

She nodded. "But that's an interesting thing. I was first attracted to them not because of how they celebrate the Goddess and her consort, but because they were people with similar attitudes to my own.

They're green—you know, big on recycling and leaving a small foot-print on the world. A lot of them are vegetarians. They're accepting, and definitely nonexclusionary." She smiled at him. "And they don't make fun of other people's beliefs."

"Come on," John said. "Danny's the one who's always making with the jokes."

"That's true. You and Wes just smile at them."

"So do you."

"Well, he can be so funny, can't he? Though I have to say I find it especially gratifying, not to mention a little ironic, that he's getting along so well with Helen—the woman he met at the ball."

"Tell me about it. He's been out with her twice now—both times to vegetarian restaurants. Willingly. I never thought I'd see that day come."

Nina nodded. "And I think we'll see a little less of the jokes for a while. Anyway, to get back to what we were talking about, I figured I might as well give their form of worship a try. And I have to tell you, I thought I was going to feel so self-conscious with their ceremonies. But that never happened. Instead, I felt right at home. Like things fi-nally made sense. And what's really interesting to me is that, while we do ceremonies as a group, I still feel that my interaction with the spir-its is very personal."

She paused a moment before adding, "Though not as personal, and definitely not as hands-on, as yours was."

John laughed, and he felt something loosen in his chest. It was weird how something as simple as a smile or a laugh could cut through heartache or stress, even if only for a moment.

"Okay," he said. "You've convinced me to never laugh at another one of Danny's jokes, and also to, you know, be a little more open-minded."

Nina smiled. "Considering your experience with Grace, you don't have much of a choice, do you?"

"Not much."

"It's such an astonishing thing, isn't it?" Nina went on. "To have irrefutable proof that our spirits—our souls—are more than just words."

John nodded. Their conversation was doing him some good, making him feel a bit more grounded for all its spacey subject matter.

"This is really helping me," he told her. "I shouldn't have taken off on you the way I did."

She shrugged. "Maybe you wouldn't have been able to listen without first having met Norm."

"Maybe. I probably owe him an apology, too. When I was on the phone with you, I think I just had a panic attack and had to take off."

"What happened to you—meeting Grace and then finding out she wasn't alive. That's not something anyone could plan for."

"I guess not." He looked across the street for a moment, before turning back to her. "I know it seems ghoulish, but I still so need to see her again. To talk to her."

"I think it's perfectly understandable."

"But how do I do it? Beltane's when again?"

"April 30."

"Which is almost six months away. That's the next time I can try to contact her? When the what did you call it—the veils between the world. That's when they're thinnest?"

Nina nodded. "But I don't know how you actually do it."

"Like I do."

"I could ask around for you."

"Would you?"

"Of course. And we could also go to the library and see what the literature has to say."

"That's what Norm told me. But how are you supposed to know which books are on the level and which are crap?"

Nina smiled. "Trial and error."

John got an image of the two of them standing in a graveyard in the middle of the night with candles and incense and some big leather book. Maybe surrounded by cloaked, chanting figures, their faces hidden under hoods.

"Great," he said.

Nina punched his arm.

"Come on," she said. "Buck up. Research can be fun."

"It's not the research I'm worried about. It's putting into practice the weird stuff we're going to find."

"That could be fun, too. Maybe it includes getting naked and dancing in the moonlight."

John groaned.

She gave his arm another punch. "I'm kidding."

"So when do we start?" he asked. "*Where* do we start?"

"Let me talk to some folks in the community, then we can take it from there."

Nina's pagan friends had plenty of theories, but nothing that anyone could guarantee would work, so that left the two of them spending evenings in the Solona Public Library, slogging through stacks of books. During the day, when he wasn't working on assignments to pay the bills, John trawled the Internet.

John hadn't expected researching the paranormal to be so boring. Part of the problem was that many of the writers, concerned with being taken seriously, wrote in such a dry, academic style that it would lull anyone to sleep. On the opposite side of the spectrum were the enthusiasts who wrote with such purple-prosed fervor that it made John feel embarrassed to be even reading the material.

In between were far too many books and websites that weren't quite one or the other, but they didn't have anything particularly useful to add to the search except references to more books, and links to ever more esoteric sites.

After a week of this, John went back to the area around Sanchez Motors, hoping to find Norm again. The tall figure in his shabby clothes wasn't hard to find, but he shook his head when John asked if there was anything else he could tell him.

"I've told you all I can," Norm said.

"Come on, man. I know you know more."

"Then let me put it this way: I've told you all I will."

"I really need to see her again."

He shook his head. "What you really need to do is forget all this crap. The spirits aren't looking out for us—they're only looking out for themselves. And by that I mean the spirits of the dead and most of the others you might meet. If they know you're paying attention to them, they start hanging around, in bigger and bigger clusters. The dead ones want to be saved. The rest want to hang around and comment on every thing you do, from how you take a bite into a burrito, to how you take a dump.

"Are you starting to get the picture now?"

John gave him a slow nod.

"And the thing that kills you in the end?" Norm said. "You can't make them go away. You can't touch them, you can't push them out of your life. You can't stick them in a box and mail them to someone who cares."

"I could touch Grace."

"Yeah. I noticed how *here* she was when I saw her that night, and I can't explain it. All I know for sure is that if you give the spirits a toehold in your life, they'll take the damn thing over."

"Okay," John said. "I get what you're saying. But I still need to talk to her. Just once."

"Your funeral. And I'm not going to help you."

"What about someone on the rez? Can you give me the name of someone who maybe would?"

He shook his head. "That's a whole other problem. You might not have noticed, but relationships between your people and mine aren't so good these days. The young bucks up there on the rez could easily take some serious offense to one more white wannabe looking for directions to the Red Road."

"I don't even know what that means."

"It's what the New Agers call our medicine ways. Like we've all got one, and only the one, view when we look beyond this world. Do you know how many tribes there are here on Turtle Island?"

John shook his head.

"Hundreds. Each with their own language and belief system. But the New Agers lump as all together. They like to talk about Native wisdom and Native beliefs like we're all one and the same. So you go up on the rez asking questions like this and they'll just kick your ass out of there."

"I went to a powwow there last year. No one treated me badly then."

"That's because they wanted you to buy their dreamcatchers and smudge sticks, and all the other so-called medicine crap."

"Do you really believe it's all crap?" John asked.

Norm shook his head. "Not for a minute. But no one's going to sell you real medicine for a couple of bucks, and they're never going to share the real thing anyway, because they're Indians and you're white, and until you make good on all the treaties you broke, they're not giving you anything."

"I had nothing to do with that," John said.

"But you're still reaping the benefits of what your forefathers stole from us."

John shook his head. "There's nothing *I* can do. I can't give you back your lands, or whatever it is that you want."

"You can't write to your congressman?"

This wasn't going at all the way John had imagined. He'd come here, thinking he might get turned down again. But he hadn't expected this verbal assault.

"I'm sorry things are the way they are," he said, "but nobody's going to listen to me anymore than they'd listen to you. I'm just an artist. It's not like I run some big oil company."

Norm nodded. "I know. You just pushed a couple of buttons. People look at a guy like me and they don't just see someone down on their luck. They see a drunken Indian—doesn't matter how long I've been on the wagon. They don't think I have any pride left in me, and if they did, they wouldn't care. Back in the day, they gave my people smallpox. Now I've got the new white man's disease: HIV. The one that they've reserved for queers and Indians and Africans and all the other people they've got no use for."

"Not everybody feels that way."

"Maybe not," Norm said. "But I don't see them doing much to help us either."

"I don't know what to say."

"Yeah, I get that way sometimes. Other times, you can't shut me up and I take it out on whoever's close enough to hear me." He waited a beat, then added, "So can you spare me a couple of bucks?"

He held up his hand to stop John as he started to dig in his pocket.

"Why are you giving me money?" he asked.

John shrugged. "Because a couple of dollars isn't going to hurt me and you look like you could use it."

"I've got a job," Norm said. He nodded with his head to the garage across the street. "Shorty pays me to sweep up and do odd jobs around the bays."

"Then why did you ask me for money?"

"To see what you'd do. To get your measure."

John took his empty hand out of his pocket. "Okay. Now what?"

"Now, nothing. Except what I told you before, and you need to believe it's true. Stay away from spirits. Forget you ever met Grace. Do that, and you'll be able to take up the pieces of your life again. It might take time, but you'll get over it. Keep pushing, and all you're stepping into is trouble. Deep serious trouble.

"It might come at you like a hammer in the night, it might come at you from a direction you'd never expect, but something's going to happen to you and your life'll be changed forever."

"I already feel like it's changed."

Norm shrugged.

"And I can't seem to let it go," John added.

Norm nodded. "Then you're screwed, man."

John had lunch at Casa Canelo with Wes the next day. A fine drizzle had been falling all morning, putting a slick sheen on the streets, turning the dirt alleyways into mud, and streaking the restaurant's windows. But inside where they were, it was warm and dry. Their waitress was Shannon, the same one they'd had Halloween night, but today her Catholic schoolgirl uniform had been traded in for a pair of black pants and a black T-shirt with a small Casa Canelo logo in white above her left breast. Her blond hair was tied back in a ponytail. John might not have taken her up on her party invitation on Halloween, but she was still flirting with him.

After they'd both asked for the lunch special—grilled chicken salad served in a large taco shell—and Shannon left to put in their order, Wes asked how the search was going.

"Do you really want to know," John asked, "or are you just humoring me?"

Wes was the only one of the four of them who hadn't actually seen Grace that night at the Solona Music Hall. But while he said that he believed what they'd seen, John knew that belief was tempered with a healthy dose of skepticism.

"Probably a bit of both," Wes said. "Don't get me wrong. Proof that there's something else after we die? How can it not be intriguing? But you know how it is. Or at least you did before Halloween."

"When it was only Nina into the weird and wacky."

Wes nodded and smiled. "Or something like that. Now we've got you chasing ghosts and Danny extolling pagan virtues—or at least extolling how they're packaged in a certain woman named Helen Taylor."

"Who's really nice."

"Agreed. But it does beg the question, what does she see in Danny?"

"You know she's into Halo right? She's got some incredible score."

"I do," Wes said. "And Danny's actually taken down all those anime posters in his office. Still, a junk-food gamer and a vegetarian pagan . . . it seems like an odd match to me, but God bless 'em. Danny's needed some kind of steadying influence to kick his ass out of his stalled adolescence. You, on the other hand . . ."

"Me?"

"Are falling right back into your adolescence," Wes said. "You've got your model cars out of storage and you're listening to rockabilly, which, I need to remind you, wasn't even popular when we were teens, so it's like you're reliving your dad's adolescence."

"I guess it could look that way, but I find it helps me—"

Wes cut him off. "I'm yanking your chain, John. I totally get it. You meet someone new and you want to experience the things that shaped them to become this really cool person that you've fallen for. But except for that private eye in *Laura,* most people pick someone who's actually alive."

"Don't I know it."

"So anyway," Wes said, "yeah, I am interested in how things are going. I haven't met a cute guy in weeks, so I need some vicarious romantic thrills—even when they're as lopsided as this relationship you've got going."

"One night's hardly a relationship."

"I know. Plus she's a ghost. But you're hardly acting like someone on the other side of a one-night stand. This obviously means something to you, and impossible as I think the chances are for you to come out of this happy, I'm totally rooting for you."

"I appreciate that," John said, "but honestly? I don't know how it could turn out to be anything but a disaster."

"That doesn't seem to stop you from wanting to see her again."

"I just need to talk to her."

"Right."

"To understand."

"I get it," Wes said. "But it's also worth remembering that sometimes things are as wonderful and perfect as they are because you only get to hang on to them for a moment." His gaze went to the bar where their waitress Shannon was sitting on a stool, chatting with the bartender. "And then, when you're off chasing after a dream, you miss out on what's happening right under your nose."

John followed Wes's gaze.

"I don't know anything about her," he said.

Wes nodded. "And from all I've heard, you didn't know anything about Grace, but that worked out pretty good except for the part where she vanished on you—and let me just add that there are guys out there who would consider that the perfect end to an evening."

"You don't think of gays as chauvinistic," John said.

Wes shrugged. "What can I say? We're still guys."

Over the next week, John put in long hours designing characters for a new Wesdanina project. It wasn't going well. While he usually had a knack for coming up with characters that were unique but still felt familiar—Wesdanina's string of successful animation projects was ample proof of his gift—the past few days were the exception. Everything he drew was uninspired. Worse, they seemed like bad copies of other animators' work.

When the phone rang, he was so relieved to be distracted by whomever it might be that he didn't bother to check caller ID. He simply picked up the receiver and said, "Hello?"

"I'd like to speak to John Burns, please," an unfamiliar voice said.

"I'm John. Who's this?"

"My name's Raul Delgado and I was wondering if I could interview you for a book I'm working on."

"For some kind of art book?"

Delgado laughed. "No, it's a little more esoteric than that. It's a collection of anecdotal experiences with the paranormal."

John's gaze went from his drawing board to the black-and-red plastic model of the Ford Fairlane that was still parked on his coffee table.

"Why would you be calling me?" he asked.

"I was given to understand that you've recently had such an experience."

"Who told you that? Is this some kind of joke?"

"If it is," Delgado said, "then I'm not in on it either." He paused for a moment, then added, "Do you have access to a computer?"

"Sure."

"Why don't you Google my name—that's D-E-L-G-A-D-O—and add 'author' to the search or you'll get a million hits."

John hesitated, then swung his chair around to his desk to where his laptop stood open. He typed the information into his search engine and the first of thousands of references filled his screen. He clicked on a review from *The Santo del Vado Viejo Star*'s site, which told him that his caller was a local author who specialized in books on folktales, mysteries, and the paranormal. This particular book was called *Milagros Country,* a collection of local religious miracles, and the reviewer had apparently liked it.

"Okay," John said. "Now the question is, how did you get my name?"

"My wife, Alma, and I were having lunch with Helen Taylor and her new boyfriend Danny Colvin, who's a friend of yours, I believe?"

"*Danny* told you about Grace?"

"It came up in our conversation—that kind of thing usually does when I meet new people and they find out what I do for a living."

John could hear the smile in his voice.

"And you didn't think it was weird? I mean, Danny telling you I was with a ghost?"

"Well, it *was* Halloween, the time when spirits can become corporeal, if they follow the rules."

"Rules? What rules?"

"The spirit has to be at the place of its death exactly at moonrise. Then they get to walk among us until the sun rises again. The unfortunate part of this is that they can't interact with people they knew before they died, because they don't recognize them."

"What about Beltane?" John asked. "The first day of May. Does it work then, too?"

"Walpurgis Night," Delgado said.

"What was that?"

"Walpurgis Night. April 30th. It's a lot like Halloween—in fact, it's directly opposite it on the calendar."

"I've never heard of it," John said.

"It's mostly a European thing, but it's another night when witches and spirits are supposed to roam the night. They call it Drudennacht in Germany, Vappu in Finland . . ."

"So *can* the spirits of the dead come back that night," John asked, "the way they can on Halloween?"

Delgado hesitated. "I've heard something to that effect," he said. "It is a 'between time,' when the veils between the worlds are at their thinnest, but I've never been able to confirm it."

John's thoughts were racing. He held on to what Delgado had said earlier—"the spirit has to be at the place of its death exactly at moonrise"—turning it over and over in his mind. Excitement rose in him, making him a little giddy. He *could* see Grace again.

"Mr. Burns?" Delgado asked. "Are you still there?"

"Yes, sorry. I'm just a little, um, distracted today."

"So would it be all right if we got together and—"

"How do you *know* all of this stuff?" John asked.

"Years of research—and sifting through the interviews I do with people such as yourself."

The hopeful cheerfulness John was feeling came down a notch or two.

"I don't know that I want to be in a book," he said.

"It could be an anonymous entry," Delgado said. When John

didn't respond, he added, "Or it doesn't even have to go in the book at all. But I'd still like to talk to you about your experience."

"Why?" John asked. "I mean, if it's not going to be in the book . . ."

"It will still add to the body of knowledge I've been acquiring over the years. The interview won't take up much of your time—no more than half an hour."

"Can I ask questions, too?"

"Of course you can," Delgado said. "I can't promise you answers, but I'll certainly share what I know."

"Or I could just buy a book."

Delgado laughed. "Which would help pay my rent. But the printed page will never take the place of a good conversation."

That was true, John thought. And he couldn't deny that Delgado's phone call was serendipitous, offering him contact with exactly the sort of guide he'd been looking for.

Did he want to meet with Delgado?

Without question.

They got together that afternoon at the Rosalinda House Café, since it turned out to be within walking distance from each of their apartments. When John opened the door he was welcomed by piano music playing on the café's sound system, slinky and cool, and such a rich smell of roasted coffee beans it almost had a physical presence. There were a half dozen customers scattered at various tables, but only one matched the image John had gotten from Raul Delgado's voice. That man was in his late forties or so, and sat at one of the window tables, looking a little like a beatnik professor in jeans and a rumpled tweed sports jacket. His hair was longish, his features dark, clean-shaven, and friendly. He was wearing wire-rimmed glasses and chewed on the end of a pencil while he concentrated on the papers spread across his table.

When John walked over, he saw it was a manuscript.

"Mr. Delgado?" he said.

Delgado looked up and smiled, waving him to the empty chair.

"Just Raul's fine," he said. "Thanks for agreeing to see me."

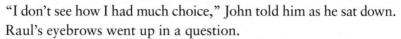

"I don't see how I had much choice," John told him as he sat down.

Raul's eyebrows went up in a question.

"Oh, I don't mean you forced me. I've just been beating my head against the wall for the past few weeks and your phone call's the first ray of hope I've come across in all of this mess."

"Do you want to talk about it?" Raul asked.

He gathered up his manuscript as he spoke, making a neat stack of the paper before he set it aside with the pencil on top.

"Mostly, I just want to ask you questions," John told him, "but I guess you won't have any context until I tell you what happened."

Raul nodded. "And as I said on the phone, I'll be happy to tell you anything I can. Only don't be disappointed if I don't have all the answers."

"I won't be. Truth is, I've already gotten more just from talking to you earlier than I did from days of poring through books and websites."

"Well, that's gratifying to hear," Raul said. He reached into the knapsack by his chair and pulled out a small digital recorder. "Do you mind if I tape our conversation? It's either that or I have to sit here and take notes, which I probably won't be able to read once I get back to my computer."

"I guess not . . ."

"Please, don't worry. Nothing will be used without your permission. I won't even play it for anyone else."

John gave a reluctant nod.

"Do you want to get yourself a drink before we start?" Raul asked.

"Sure. Can I get you anything?"

"No, I'm good."

By the time John got back to the table with his latte, Raul had set up the recorder and they were ready to begin. John felt awkward at first, and very aware of the machine lying there on the table, ready to save his every word for posterity. But once he got into his story, he forgot the recorder was there until he'd related his last meeting with Norm and Raul reached over to turn it off.

"So Grace was just there at the Witches' Ball when you met her?" Raul asked.

John nodded.

"And she didn't approach you."

"No. If it hadn't been for Nina, we would probably never have connected at all."

"It's interesting that she didn't approach you first," Raul said. "Usually spirits come back with a purpose. They have some sort of unfinished business, something they need to get done. But it sounds like Grace was simply using her time back in the world to enjoy herself."

"Why would she have any unfinished business with me? I'd never seen her before, and believe me, I'd have remembered." ·

Raul smiled. "She's that attractive."

"No, well, yes. But I meant the tattoos. They're not something you forget."

But then something Raul had said earlier on the phone came back to him.

"Except maybe I did know her before," he said. "Didn't you tell me that living people don't recognize spirits when they return? So maybe I knew her and just don't remember."

Raul gave a thoughtful nod. "Except then you wouldn't have recognized her as she really is."

John sighed. "God, this is so confusing."

"I know," Raul agreed. "The world around us can be bewildering enough without adding in the complications of everything that lies beyond the veils of what we think we know."

"Do you have a lot of firsthand experience with this sort of thing?" John asked, "or do you just document it?"

Raul didn't say anything for a moment. He looked past John with a far-off look in his eyes, before finally focusing on John again. He gave a shrug and a smile.

"I never know what to say when a stranger asks me that," he said, "so let me just say that I've seen a thing or two that some might consider impossible—enough to at least keep an open mind. I don't necessarily believe that Elvis is hiding out in a Wal-Mart or some old folks' home, but I wouldn't entirely rule out that he has returned. Or never went away." He smiled and added, "I'm a bit of conspiracy buff as well. Comes with the territory, I suppose, if you're ready to believe that those in authority are hiding evidence that would prove the existence of beings they say don't exist."

"You mean ghosts?"

Raul shrugged. "Space aliens and vampires, elves and goblins, animal people and who knows what all."

"And you believe they exist."

"Across the board? I have no idea. But I believe some of them do."

John shook his head. "Then why are you writing a book on ghosts? That seems a little tame compared to the rest of this stuff."

"Well, the thing with these otherworldly beings," Raul said, "is that they don't think the way we do. Some of them seem, and maybe are, similar to us, but most of them are so different that we can't begin to understand the reasons why they do the things they do. Ghosts, however, were once human. While they might have moved on, we can still understand their feelings and motivations, and of course I'm curious about what happens to them, because one day I'll be taking the same trip.

"So the answer to your question is that while I continue to be fascinated by the beings that inhabit the otherworlds of myth and folklore, the idea of the human spirit and what takes place after we die is of more immediate interest to me. Does that make sense?"

John nodded, though he hadn't considered it to such an extent. He was just interested in seeing Grace. And while there were any number of questions he could ask her about life after death and the afterworld, all he really wanted to know was if she felt the same way about him as he did about her, and if there was some way they could be together.

"You're an interesting man," Raul said.

John pulled himself out of his reverie to ask, "Why's that?"

"Well," Raul said, "people who've had an encounter such as yours usually manage to convince themselves that it never happened. If they do accept that it did, or that it seems as if it did, they'll try to come up with some logical reason to explain it. But you've simply accepted it at face value, and if anything, you seem quite determined to repeat the experience."

"You're forgetting. I didn't know Grace was a ghost until after I'd been with her. It wasn't like I was walking through some graveyard and saw her come rising up out of the ground."

"But still."

John nodded. "I just can't get her out of my head."

"It's a long time until April 30th," Raul said. "A whole winter."

"I can wait," John told him. "I have to."

"And if Walpurgis Night isn't like Halloween? If she doesn't come back?"

"Then I'll wait until next Halloween."

Raul nodded. "I know you wouldn't want me tagging along when you see Grace again, but would you be willing to contact me afterward and tell me what happened?"

"I don't see why not," John said.

Unless he figured out a way to go with Grace, wherever it was she went when she disappeared.

But he didn't tell Raul that. He didn't tell anyone. But he held on to the idea of it through that long winter and into the spring.

Grace

I think about what a nice guy John Burns is as I go into the bathroom. Well, except for leaving the lid up, I amend, as my butt almost hits the water in the bowl. I put the lid down and get back to considering his positive features, like I'm standing in a car lot, checking out a new set of wheels.

It doesn't hurt that he's handsome, but handsome guys don't always have much more to offer than the face that looks back at them from their mirror in the morning. They can be like some sporty little rice burner with nothing decent under the hood. John's got way more going on for him than just his looks. For one thing, he doesn't even seem to be aware that he's as good-looking as he is. Plus he's intelligent, a good listener, artistic, great in bed . . . and why the hell couldn't I have met him when I was alive?

This seriously sucks.

Sure, he's got some kind of guilt trip going on about his brother, but we all have issues. Like, sad to say, I'm dead. And just because a car's got a few dents, it doesn't you mean you write it off. Not if it's got those killer lines, the engine runs great, and you like everything else about it.

I trace the FoMoCo tattoo on my leg and smile to myself.

And if John's a car, I think, he's definitely a Ford. Something retro, like my two-tone Fairlane, but maybe more a white and turquoise than a red and black.

I finish my business and flush, then walk into the bedroom. I'm about to tell John that I've decided what kind of a car I think he is when I realize that everything's changed. The room is the same—I mean, it's got the same dimensions it did when I went into the bathroom—but the furniture has a different configuration and there's a dusty smell in the air. I remember appreciating how, even though we'd come here on the spur of the moment, so John didn't have a chance to spruce things up, the place had been clean, right down to the tiles in the bathroom.

It doesn't smell clean now. And there's a stillness so profound that my ears feel blocked.

Then I realize what's happened and I know where I am.

I'm back in that damned Alverson Arms world.

In the dawn light coming through a crack in the curtains—they were blinds before I went into the bathroom—I see my clothes scattered on the floor where I'd left them last night. My clothes, not John's. Because John doesn't exist here. I'm alone in his apartment. It's not even his apartment, not in this world.

My gaze drifts to the bed and my heart does a little jump inside my chest.

For one moment I think it's John, that somehow he came back with me, but then I realize it's one of the sleepers. He's lying there on his back, on top of the covers, arms crossed over his chest like he's in a coffin. His eyes are open, staring at the ceiling.

I clear my throat, but there's no response.

"Hello?" I try.

Still nothing.

I inch my way across the room until I'm standing right beside the bed. It's so weird seeing his eyes open when it's obvious that there's no one home.

I won't pretend this isn't creeping me out. I know I've had it described to me, but this is the first sleeper I've seen for myself.

"Hello?" I try again.

I'm not expecting the eyes to focus, nor the gaze to track across the room until it finds mine. But I can't seem to help myself and have to reach forward and wave my hand between his eyes and the ceiling.

"Where have you gone?" I wonder aloud.

If this was a horror movie, right about now the guy would suddenly sit up, or at least grab my hand, but it's not, and he doesn't. This is just my crappy afterlife where I have to deal with being cut off from, let's face it, pretty much the guy of my dreams, if I could even have imagined someone like John. A little straighter than the guys I usually date, sure, but kind of boho, too, with that whole artist thing going on.

Except he's *there* and I'm here and it'll be six months before I can go back and see him again, not that there's much chance of him wanting to see me. Let's look at it from his perspective: he has a great night, but the woman vanishes from his bathroom without a word of explanation, then doesn't show up again for six months. Yeah, *sure* he'll be waiting for me to come back into his life come May 1st.

"Maybe you're the smart one," I tell the silent guy lying on the bed. "What do you have to worry about?"

I start to turn away and damn if his hand doesn't shoot up from his chest and grab my arm, just like I'm in that stupid movie I was imagining moments ago. I squeal like a girl and jerk away, but that hand's locked on my arm and all I manage to accomplish is to almost dislocate my own shoulder. He pulls me closer and his gaze meets mine, flat and impenetrable.

I can't look away. There's nothing in that awful gaze—it's like looking into black oil—but there's *everything* there, too. Loss and hopelessness and despair.

And anger.

Dark, unbridled anger.

I try to pull away again, bracing myself with my foot on the side of the bed, but I might as well be trying to lift a V-8 with my bare hands. All it does is make my shoulder hurt.

You stink of life.

His lips don't move, but I hear his voice all the same. It's inside my head, cold and echoing, and is making me feel a little nauseous.

"Let me go," I tell him. "Get out of my head."

I'm not in your head. We're all in her *head.*

"What?"

The only relief is to give in.

"What are you talking about?"

And don't *wake me again. I am done with the pretense of living.*

The hand lets go of my arm and I fall back, arms pinwheeling to keep my balance. When I look at him, his arms are folded on his chest once more, his gaze unfocused, the voice in my head silent.

I stand there for a long moment, staring at him, my own arms covering my breasts. My legs are trembling. I'm breathing too fast and my pulse is still in overdrive. I feel relief, but I'm also a little pissed off with Henry and Conchita. They could have told me this could happen. They could have warned me that the sleepers can wake up all dark and scary.

I can still feel the unbreakable grip of his hand on my arm. I hated that feeling of helplessness. It was like that damn junkie in Luna's all over again, when I had no control over anything.

I don't know how long I stand there, feeling cold and numb. But finally my breathing steadies and my legs don't feel so shaky. I grab my clothes and back out of the room.

I get dressed in the hall outside the apartment, then walk through the building until I'm finally outside. The sky is clear, the sun is bright. There's a faint smell of creosote in the air. It's a relief to be out of the gloom, even though I'm blinking in the sudden light. I take a deep breath of the clean autumn air, then sit on the stoop outside the building, hugging my knees. I look across the street to the wall of mist, but now that I'm away from the creepy sleeper, I'm back to obsessing about John.

If what happened inside was like a scene from a horror movie, then I'm in a different one with John. A romantic comedy, maybe, except there's nothing funny yet. But we met cute, the way those couples always do, and now we've got the obligatory separation. Problem is, there's no way to get to the happy Hollywood ending, because at the end of the day, I'm dead and he's not, and that's not going to change.

The more I think about him, the more that sucks.

I don't know how I fell so fast and hard for this guy. All I know is that the ache I'm feeling for him isn't something that's going to go away any time soon.

"Okay, Henry," I say softly. "So you were right about this. Maybe it isn't such a good idea to go back."

It's true. I shouldn't have done it. If I'd just stayed here, I'd never have met John, and I wouldn't be feeling like this.

I rest my head on my knees and stare at the pavement and I guess I go away because when I hear a voice calling my name and I look up, it's midafternoon. I hear my name again. This time I look down the street to see Conchita approaching me. She lifts a hand when she sees that she's got my attention. I watch as she makes her way to me, a swagger in her walk, and I think at least somebody's happy.

She sits down on the stoop beside me.

"What're you doing here?" she asks.

"Feeling sorry for myself."

She gives a slow nod. "Yeah, the first time back after that little rush of freedom is always a bitch."

"I guess."

I can't believe I lost most of the day, just sitting here like a lump. Then I remember what the sleeping guy told me. *The only relief is to give in.* To the darkness, I'm guessing. The void. Just let yourself fall asleep and all your problems go away. All this pretense at living.

But then there was that crap about how we're all in somebody's head. Whose head? All he said was "her."

"You ever have one of the sleeping people talk to you?" I ask Conchita.

"A couple of times," she says, "but it's only when I've just gotten back from the other side. I think we carry something of the living world back with us and it kind of brings them back for a minute or two."

I nod, remembering the sleeper's first words. *You stink of life.*

"I hated the way his voice was in my head," I tell her. "He grabbed my arm, too, so I couldn't get away."

"Yeah, it's creepy, all right. But it never lasts long, so don't worry. It's not like you have to go through the same thing every time you stumble across one of them."

Which won't be happening to me, I think, because I have no intention of finding another sleeper to repeat the experience.

"What did they say to you?" I ask.

She shrugs. "I don't know. Crazy stuff."

"Why didn't you warn me?"

"I didn't think of it. It's only an issue right after you get back. The rest of the time you can use their bed as a trampoline and they still wouldn't wake up." She does that thing where she cocks her head with a question in her eyes. "Is that what's got you looking all bummed out?"

"No, I . . ." I laugh without any humor. "I met a guy . . ."

"Uh-oh. On the other side?"

I nod again.

She puts an arm around my shoulders.

"That never gets any easier," she says.

"So it's happened to you? You fell in love on the other side?"

She shakes her head. "I don't know that I believe in love. But I totally connected with a guy my second time over and it was cool until I vanished from the middle of his bed."

"What happened the next time you went over?"

"Well, first there was major drama for me as I had to get through the six months before I could cross over again. I obsessed over this guy. Then when I finally got to see him again he wasn't close to the picture I'd built up in my head. But he was still pretty cool in his own way, except he couldn't stop talking about the way I'd disappeared on him."

"What did you tell him?"

"What could I tell him? Oh, and by the way I'm dead?" She laughed. "No, I just pretended I was too out of it to remember—we did have a few drinks that night—but I was careful to have already said good-bye to him well before the sunrise brought me back here."

"Are you still seeing him when you go back?"

"No. The next time I didn't even try to look him up. The six-month gap was weird enough once. But a second time? What was I going to tell him the next time?"

"Yeah," I say. "That's pretty much the way I see it working out for me."

Conchita gives my shoulders a squeeze. "But it was great while you were with him."

"Oh yeah."

"So spill," she says when I fall silent.

"There's not much to tell."

"Liar."

"Okay, it was fabulous. Unbelievable. Is that what you want to hear?"

She nods. "And the details."

So we sit there on the stoop and I tell her about going back to the shop and meeting Norm and then how I met John at the Witches' Ball in the Solona Music Hall.

"It sounds like you've got more than just the hots for this guy," Conchita says when I'm done.

I nod. "If I'd ever taken the time to imagine the perfect guy, he'd pretty much fit the picture."

"After just one night."

"I know how stupid it sounds. Even if I wasn't dead, it still probably wouldn't have worked out."

"I don't think it sounds stupid," Conchita says with a wistfulness in her voice.

A few moments ago she was telling me that she didn't think she believed in love, but I'm guessing that's not really true.

She looks at the mist across the street and adds, "Maybe you should look him up next time."

"I don't know. It'd probably be a bad idea."

She gives a slow nod of agreement. "Probably."

"How about you?" I ask. "How was your night?"

She shrugs. "I didn't do much this time. Ate and peed like I always have to the moment I get there—can you believe how great it is to feel hungry and actually be able to taste food? And I don't know about you, but after I've had that first pee, I feel like I've just dropped some great weight that I didn't even know I was carrying around. After that . . . mostly I just walked around. I stood outside some clubs for a while and listened to music." She gives me a rueful smile. "I'm grown up inside my head, but I still just look like a kid, so I can't actually get in anywhere cool."

"That sucks."

"Yeah, it does," she says, but she's smiling. "So are you going to tell Henry?"

"About John? Why would I?"

Conchita laughs. "Not about John. About that guy from your old life who recognized you."

"You mean Norm."

"Yeah, him. Henry's always saying that nobody can recognize us and I just believed him. And since I've never actually seen anybody I knew from before, it's not something I could ever check out for myself."

"I don't think it really counts," I tell her. "Norm's got second sight or something like that. Before I got shot, he was always talking about spirits this and medicine that, so I guess you could say he's got the edge on most people."

"Sure," Conchita says, "but if you tell Henry about him, he'll get all wired into researching that, and off our case about not helping him put together a head count."

I know what she means. I've only been there a few times, but whenever I go to the library, Henry does seem fixated on leading the conversation around to how he'd really like to get a census of the Alverson Arms world.

"I'll do what I can," I tell her, "but Henry seems a bit like a bull-dog."

Conchita grins. "All the more reason to throw him a different bone."

She gets up from the stoop and I follow suit. I look back at the building and shiver, remembering the sleeper hand grabbing me and his weird voice in my head. Then I follow Conchita down the street, heading back to 26th Street. She chats about her own trip, making me laugh with some of her observations, but the chill never quite leaves me.

I go over to the library the next day and tell Henry about Norm. Just as Conchita thought, he's all over it, like a gearhead being asked to plan out a new custom job with an unlimited budget. We sit in that big room on the second floor, the autumn sunshine pouring in through the windows, while he has me retell my conversation with Norm more often than I feel is necessary, but I've come to see that's just the way Henry is. He takes notes the whole time, nodding to himself as though this new information is opening all kinds of doors in his head.

It's different for me. The more I get into all of this, the more confused I feel. But Henry acts as though it's going to explain everything.

"Norm's not exactly a regular guy," I warn him, "so he's more the exception than the rule."

"Sometimes it's the exceptions that define the rules."

"I suppose. It's funny. I always thought this stuff he used to go on about was just crazy." I smile. "Except it turns out it's not."

Henry nods. "I didn't have much patience for this sort of thing myself, back when I was alive."

"And when I did see other people I knew," I go on, "it happened like you said it would. They totally didn't recognize me. In the store where I got shot they had a little memorial set up with a picture of me and everything, but Estefan looked me right in the face and there wasn't even a flicker of recognition."

"It's unnerving, isn't it?" Henry says.

I can see he's thinking about the time he went back and his mother didn't know him. But while I didn't like the feeling when it happened to me, I know it's not going to stop me from going back.

"Speaking of telling people things," I say, "why didn't you tell me that the sleepers can wake up and talk in your head?"

"What?"

So then I have to go through what happened when I walked out of John's bathroom, back into the Alverson Arms world.

"I had no idea," he says when I'm done.

"Well, apparently Conchita knew."

Henry nods, but I can see he's still worrying at what I told him about my experience.

"He said we were all in somebody's head?" he asks.

"*Her* head is how he put it. What do you suppose he meant by that?"

"I don't have a clue." Then he smiles. "Did you ever have those very earnest existential conversations in college along the lines of what if the world was just a dream that someone was having?"

I shake my head. "I barely managed to squeak through high school." Then I think about what he just said and add, "Do you think that's possible?"

"Before I died, I didn't think life after death was possible."

"Well, duh. But now that you know?"

"I have no idea. In the world on the other side? Probably not. But this place where we find ourselves? Who knows? Maybe that explains everything."

"So for argument's sake," I say, "let's just say it's true."

"Okay," he asks. "Then what?"

"Who's dreaming?

He shrugs. "That's the million-dollar question."

I find it hard to take seriously—this concept that we're trapped here in somebody's dream—but I can't stop thinking about it. And though I try not to, I can't stop obsessing about John either. The odd thing is, that's not who I am. I'm not the type of woman who reads the fashion magazines, poring over the articles on how to get, or keep, or please, a man. I've been in relationships before, and I enjoyed them, but I never felt so passionate about someone before.

I suppose I've just never been in love, except I even have trouble with that. I've never believed in love at first sight, unless it's for a car, and they don't come with emotional baggage. But people? How can I be in love with someone I met only once? It wasn't just that the sex was so good. Everything felt good. Better than good.

"It's part of going back to the other side," Conchita tells me. "Everything's more intense over there. We feel like we're alive here, but it's not until we cross back over that we realize how much this life is just an imitation of the one we had to leave behind."

"I know," I say, remembering how unbelievably good the tamales and latte were. And that first Modelo at the Solona Music Hall? Heaven.

"And trust me," she adds, "I know all about obsessing over a guy. After the six months I put in, I could write a book about it."

I know she's saying this to make me feel better, but I only feel worse.

Does the fact that everything's super-intense over there mean that what I'm feeling isn't real?

What if I want it to be real?

I don't know if I do or I don't.

There are too many questions, and there's too much time in which to think about them, so I decide to do what I always do when I need to distract myself: I work on a car.

Near the corner of Guadalupe and 25th, just down from the park, I find myself a junked 1948 Ford coupe, rusted, dented, and up on blocks in the alley behind a long adobe building. It looks like someone's scrap yard find, except he never got to restore it. At least not in this world. On the other side, it might be street worthy, and he's driving it to meets and shows.

It doesn't matter. All that's important is that it's exactly what I'm looking for.

I ask around, but that car's just here, no one's laid claim to it. So I do. I'm going to play with it. Maybe I'll hot rod it—go all "Big Daddy" Roth, even—or maybe I'll just do a custom, but one thing's for sure: I'll get it up and running again. I'll find the lines.

Considering how I don't have access to my tools and the parts at the shop, it's a project that's going to take a lot of ingenuity and plain hard work. In other words, it'll keep me busy for at least the next six months. But it's going to be a classic when I'm done, though I guess the Classic Car Club of America would argue the term. It still bugs me that there's not a single Ford on their "Approved List of Classic Cars, 1925 through 1948." The morons.

I clear everything out of the alley except for the coupe: garbage bins, a stove without an oven door, a pile of wood scraps, and a whole bunch of car parts that are rusting in an untidy tangle near the coupe. I guess this alley used to be some gearhead's makeshift garage, back in the day. Now it's going to be mine.

Using two-by-fours from the scrap wood, I frame in that section of the alley, then use tarps to close off the ends and put up a roof. The roof tarp I rig up with a series of pulleys that I got from some unused clotheslines. It takes me a few tries to get it to run smoothly, but once I've got it working, I've got myself a poor man's garage. When the weather's nice, I can roll back the roof to catch the light, unrolling it when it rains or the deep summer sun's beating down. I've got power from an extension cord that I'm running through the back door of the building, which turns out to have been some kind of grocery store, way back in the whenever. I plug my cord into an outlet in its back hall and use it for my compressor, and the heaters I'm going to need once the rains come in November and February.

Conchita finds me under the coupe one afternoon while I'm still assessing the car. I'm lying on a dolly that I made out of a piece of one-inch plywood and the wheels from an office chair, checking the chassis for rust damage. I'll do a more thorough job once I remove the body, but I haven't got the winches set up yet to lift it from the frame. As it is, I can tell that a few of the braces that run from the side rails to the center cross-member are badly twisted, and I'm going to have to replace the center box and rear transmission mount.

"I've been thinking," Conchita says when I slide out from under the car to find her sitting on a cinder block, waiting for me to emerge. "I'd like to help you do this."

I study her for a moment.

"It's hard, dirty work," I tell her.

"I don't care. It's something different, isn't it? I've been here long enough and I'm so bored that I'll try anything that's different."

"I thought you liked it here."

She smiles. "No, what I said was that it's better here than it was when I was alive. But even though it's better, it still gets old. And you know, two days of real living out of a year doesn't really cut it."

I nod. I understand that all too well. It's part of the reason I decided to work on this old coupe. I need *something*—not just to get my mind off all the big questions, but to fill my days. I'm not built for drifting from one day to the next the way Edna and so many of the other people here do. Vida used to say I just don't know how to relax—like that was a negative. She loved working on tats, but she loved being away from the parlor, too—partying, or just hanging out.

"Do you ever think about what we're missing by being stuck here?" I ask.

"All the time. But then, when I think of the people who don't end up here, well, who's to say they're not stuck in some other little weird world that's maybe worse?"

"I guess we won't ever know, will we?"

She shakes her head.

"It's sure not what I expected from the afterlife," I tell her. "I thought I'd be seeing my mother and abuelo again. I mean, I had issues with the Church, but it's not like I didn't still believe in God and everything." I smile. "I think maybe those issues had more to do with my mother."

"I never gave a lot of thought to it myself," she says. "Not while I was alive. If you did ask me, I'd probably say that death was either the end, or the beginning of something else. But this"—she waves a hand around us—"it's not oblivion in a hole in the dirt, but it doesn't really seem like the Heaven or Hell everybody talks about. Though it could be Limbo, I guess."

"But being here tells us that the spirit does survive when we die."

She nods. "It's funny," she says. "I used to think about killing myself—back when things got really bad, and before someone made the choice for me. I thought even oblivion would be better than some of the crap I was going through." She smiles without any humor. "But until I got here, I guess I just never understood that wherever you go, you take yourself with you. That's the way it is when you're alive, and it doesn't change after you're dead."

"Maybe it's different for those who don't get stuck here."

"Maybe. But I doubt it. It seems to me that our baggage stays with us until we deal with it. So ever since I got stuck here, I've been trying to make up for how I just let things happen to me when I was alive— do you know what I mean?"

"I think so. Though my life wasn't like that."

"I can tell. You were all gung-ho from the moment you got here."

I wipe some grease on my jeans and look at my hands. They finally look familiar again.

"I think you have me confused with somebody else," I say. "All I remember being is really scared and confused."

"You weren't that bad."

Conchita stands up and looks in the direction of the Alverson Arms. We can see just the top floor above the buildings and mesquite trees that crowd the alley where we're standing.

"Maybe Henry's right," she says, "and all of this has to do with the Alverson Arms." She looks at me and grins. "Maybe there's a switch somewhere inside it that turns the effect on or off. Or one of those wheel thingies you see in movies that open and close submarine doors, or the valves in some big old factory."

"A hatch ring."

"Right. A hatch ring. The thing is, we could turn it the other way and we'd all go to wherever it was we were supposed to go."

I give a slow nod. "Except, just saying that was the case, do we have the right to make that decision for everybody here?"

Work on the car goes slowly, but I was expecting that. I'm not in any hurry anyway, and I love every minute of it, even when parts of it take me twice as long as normal to do. I do have a few tools—things I've scavenged from garages and sheds around the area, as well as a handful of my old tools that I had in a storage locker at the Alverson Arms. It's more than some of those original hot-rodders had back in the late forties when they first starting chopping and customizing their machines.

What I don't have, I can jury-rig a replacement for, and at least I've got my old cutting and welding torches, and my rivet gun—retired years ago, but still in good working order. The rivet gun runs off a compressor and I've got electricity for that, but I spent one whole afternoon going door-to-door with Conchita looking for spare CO_2 canisters to run the torches. We found a surprising number of them and in some of the oddest places, considering the Alverson Arms world is just a few city blocks without a garage or hardware store on any of its streets. Like the six of them standing all in a row on a work shelf in the back of the library.

Conchita comes and helps out every day, though half the time she sits on the lawn chairs we found in someone's backyard and chats while I work. She also loves to play DJ with the boom box we brought from my apartment, and she's actually starting to put on some of my rockabilly and surf guitar disks without me having to ask her to. I like her company, and of course having that third hand is a huge help. I still can't get over how much older she seems than her age, but then I have to remember that while her body stopped aging, her mind didn't.

Once I build a winch and pulley system out of ropes and the last of the scrap wood, things go a little easier. I use it to lift the engine out and put it on a table we built out of two-by-fours and a door. The engine's pretty much a mess and I can't decide if I'm going to rebuild it, or just take one out of another car. There are plenty to choose from. But I decide to work on the rest of the car before I make that decision.

"You don't think you can actually get that thing to run again?" Conchita says, looking down at the mess of rust, rotted tubing, and wires that was once a working engine.

"So long as there aren't any cracks in the manifold or block, why not?" I reply. "If you've got the time and inclination, you can get almost anything back into working order again."

"But look at it."

"I know." I wave a hand toward the wreck of a car we just pulled the engine from. "But look at the car itself. Remember, I didn't say it was going to be an easy job."

She rolls her eyes, but she sticks with me all the same.

Removing the body from the chassis is a little trickier with just the two of us, but through trial and error, we get it done. Then it's time to get to the real business, rebuilding from the bottom up.

I start in on that coupe the way we did when I first started working on cars with Abuelo. Back then we didn't order the things we needed from a company selling retro parts made in China or Korea or some place like that. We searched them out in junkyards and at swap meets, and if we couldn't get a part, we customized something from another model, or even another make. And if *that* didn't work out, we made the part from scratch.

I know it's not for everybody, but I love working with metal. Cutting and welding, the sparks flying, bouncing off your face mask—it's like a little fireworks show every time your blade hits the metal. Gene Vincent or Link Wray rocking on the boom box. And everything else goes away. The mystery of this world, my feelings for John. *Everything.*

But I'm not obsessive. I don't only work on the car.

Sometimes I play cards with Edna and her friend Ruth, downstairs in Edna's kitchen. I love all the old stories they have about the neighborhood, and even though I don't actually know any of the people they talk about, after a month or so, they're as familiar to me as characters on a TV show I might have watched on a regular basis.

I drop in on Henry at the library and listen to his latest theories. I meet his friend David, who's decided to teach himself piano since he got here and spends six or seven hours a day practicing. When the two of them are together, they get into these passionate discussions about quantum physics and string theory and I have no clue what they're talking about, but for some reason, I enjoy it all the same.

From time to time, I run into Frankie, the paranoid junkie, but he almost always crosses the street and slinks off into an alley when he sees me coming.

I visit with Kit over on John Street—the woman I met on my first trip to the library. She used to work for this agency that brought aid to impoverished countries around the world and, like Edna and Ruth, she's full of the most amazing stories. She'll pull out photo albums, or sometimes show me these grainy home movies of all the fantastic places she's been.

A lot of the time Conchita and I will hang out with Irwin, the guy who took over the record store. He's a small, slender man in his thirties with big opinions and a fashion sense that makes it seem like the New Wave of the seventies never went away. The first time I go into the store, he looks at me with a cooler-than-thou lift of his eyebrows and says, "You've got a lot of tattoos."

"I know."

He smiles. "Yeah, I guess you would." He waits a beat before he adds, "Anything you'd like to hear?"

"Got any Super Stocks?"

He grins. "Hot rods and surf guitar. I think I do."

It's become a game with Conchita and me. We try to come up with bands or songs that he won't know, but while he might not always have a sample of the actual tunes, the guy's like a walking encyclopedia of music, and we rarely stump him. The times we do, maybe a week will go by, but eventually he'll come up with a 45 by the artist we were asking about, or some old hissy-sounding cassette with a version of the song by somebody else. He does a lot of scavenging through the various houses and apartments in the area, but he's not looking for tools or car parts or CO_2 canisters like me. Instead, he's tracking down recordings—vinyl and cassettes, reel-to-reels, eight-tracks and CDs—and squirreling them away in this store of his which doesn't sell its merchandise.

Sometimes people drop by where Conchita and I are working. Everyone seems to be fascinated by the project—I think it's mostly the idea that anyone would take on such a long-term, physical project. Even Henry makes a rare excursion from the library to check us out, wheeling into the alley in his chair, its battery-driven motor humming. He's the one who made sense of all the interest, even from people who couldn't care less about somebody fixing up an old car.

"Nobody does this kind of thing," he says, "because if someone dies in this spot on the other side, everything you've done is going to disappear. It'll be replaced by whatever's there on the other side when the guy dies."

"Thanks for the vote of confidence."

"I'm not saying people are hoping for it," he tells me, "but it does bring out a kind of morbid curiosity. You know. Will she get it done before that happens?"

That's when he tells me that he keeps a second set of all the notes and maps he's made over the years in a house a couple of blocks from the library.

Why am I not surprised?

It would have taken me a couple of days in the shop, but after a week and a half I finally get the center section of the chassis perfectly repaired to factory specs. I made a new center box and transmission mount, straightened the side braces, then riveted all of it in place, along with a new motor mount. I like using rivets on a frame. They're strong and they look perfectly stock. And since I'd ground all the welds to a perfect finish, by the time the job's done, there's no way to know that the center section of this chassis has ever been repaired.

Next up, we tackle the suspension, axles, and brake lines. I decide on a straight axle in the front, dropped just a little to lower the front of the vehicle. It goes slow and steady, but I'm not impatient. Like I've said, if there's one thing we've got here in this place, it's time.

When the weather gets cooler, we run the heaters, but the cold doesn't bother us the way it would have when we were alive. I find myself both appreciating that and hating how it reminds me of where I am and what happened to me.

As work on the car progresses, a welcome calm comes over me. I also come to a decision about John, and Conchita spends the rest of the winter trying to change my mind.

But while working on the car calms me, and I've made peace with the idea that I should never see John again, I can't let go of the mystery of why we're all stuck in this afterlife limbo. I become preoccupied with it as much as Henry is, though our approaches are different. When I'm not working on the car, I talk to people, trying to find a common link between us, beyond the obvious one of having died in the neighborhood of the Alverson Arms.

I don't have any more luck than Henry and come back to the same place he did. It's got to be something about that greystone apartment building I call home because it's at the dead center of everything we've got here.

By midwinter we've stripped out the interior of the coupe—and I mean everything; dash, steering wheel, headliner, carpet, the doors are off and the seats are out. We remove the hood and trunk lid, bumpers, grill, everything that's not part of the actual body, all in preparation to take the metal back to a bare surface.

That's how we spend our mornings. Afternoons, we go through the Alverson Arms looking for whatever it is in the building that makes this world exist. We have no idea what we're looking for—maybe it's as simple as Conchita's theory of an on-off switch, or a hatch ring. Maybe it's some nerdy little guy sitting in a hidden control room full of monitor screens, manipulating switches. We try to keep an open mind and be prepared for anything, though I wonder sometimes if we'll even recognize it, should we find it.

We work our way methodically from the basement—I think this is the only building in Solona that has one—starting with the storage lockers and furnace room, then go up through the rest of the building, apartment by apartment. When we get to Edna's apartment, she just laughs and tells us to go ahead and knock ourselves out.

It turns out that Edna and I are the only people living in the building.

"Nobody feels comfortable squatting here," Conchita explains. "I don't know why. It just doesn't feel right."

That isn't much help, but it's all she can tell me. She won't take anything from any of the units in the building either. It turns out that no one will, even though there's good stuff in some of these apartments and we all scavenge what we can, where we find it—so long as no one else has claimed the house or apartment as their living space.

Finally, all we have left is the top floor, and that's where we're stopped. The old elevator needs a special key to open on that floor. The stairs going to it stop at a small foyer with a pair of large oak doors that are locked. Conchita has a go at picking the lock, but she can't get it open.

"Where'd you learn how to do that?" I ask.

She shrugs. "In juvie. You can get stuck in some weird foster homes where they lock you in, so it's been handy to know. I don't like being locked up."

I never have been, but I can imagine the feeling and know I wouldn't like it any more than she does.

I turn away from her and give the doors a last considering look. It'll take a tire iron to force our way in, but I decide to ask Edna about it first.

I find her sitting in her living room, listening to R & B on her little radio. I've never been able to figure out how she gets radio reception, but I can't get my Internet connection. It's all just data in the air, right? And if whatever magic it is that sustains this place lets her get radio transmissions, why can't I get on the Web?

But I'm not here about that.

Edna's on her own today. When I tap on her doorjamb, she smiles and waves me in.

"Where's Ruth?" I ask.

"Oh, you know that woman. She's always got something on the go. Have yourself a seat, girl. You look tired. Let me get you some lemonade."

I shake my head as she starts to lift her bulk from the sofa, but I do take a seat on the easy chair across from her. I don't exactly feel tired—it doesn't work like that here—but I am feeling a little . . . I suppose thin would be the best way to put it. Like I'm being stretched, only on the inside, and not in a good way. It's not my mind being stretched and more open, it's a disconcerting physical feeling that sits inside my chest. I try not to pay attention to it, but it's always there.

"I was just wondering," I say, "do you know what's on the top floor?"

She shrugs. "Beats me. I've never been up there. I think it's a penthouse."

"You need a special key to get the elevator to go up to it. You wouldn't know where that is, would you?"

She shakes her head. "Did you look in the janitor's workshop in the basement?"

I nod. Conchita and I have already tried every key we could find in there on both the elevator and the oak doors.

"Then you've got me," Edna says.

So we're down to the tire iron.

I fetch it and some other tools from the alley where we're working on the car, then Conchita and I go back upstairs to the foyer in front of the oak doors. I hate to wreck these doors. They're solid, built with real craftsmanship—not the hollow crap most stores sell now. The texture is soft and smooth, and the grain in the wood is like a piece of art. But I also want in.

"Maybe this isn't such a good idea," Conchita says.

I fit one end of the tire iron into the crack between the doors. I jiggle it in as deep as I can, right where the lock is.

I smile. "Why? Do you think it's booby-trapped?"

"No. Maybe. I don't know. It just doesn't feel right."

I turn and take in her worried look. I wonder if she's having a real premonition, or if this is more of that indefinable unease she and the others have about living in the Arms, or taking anything from its apartments.

"You don't have to stay," I tell her.

But she tells me she does.

I make sure I've got the edge of the tire iron in deep enough, put my shoulder to it and . . . nothing. So I try it again, with about as much success. The wood doesn't even splinter.

I don't understand.

I'm not as strong as a guy, but I'm stronger than most women. It comes with the territory, doing the kind of work I do. I've got the leverage of the tire iron working for me. I don't expect to pop the door open immediately, but there should be some give. The wood should splinter. *Something.*

We tried the doors before, of course, but while we couldn't get in, they still had a bit of give to them. I check again. That hasn't changed. They move slightly when I rattle the knob. I point a flashlight into the crack. I can see the brass fittings of the lock. It's most likely a deadbolt.

Okay, if the tire iron doesn't work, it's time for plan B.

I fit a hacksaw into the crack. It goes in easily and I start to saw, but I can't get the blade to bite.

I learned a long time ago from working with uncooperative bolts that getting frustrated or impatient doesn't make the job go any more quickly. You just dab some solvent on the rust and go away and work on something else while you wait for the magic to work.

Magic, I think.

I step back from the door and trade the hacksaw for a chisel and hammer.

"Stand back," I tell Conchita.

"What are you going to do?"

I don't bother to answer. I set the chisel at an angle in the wood alongside the lock face and give it a couple of good whacks with the hammer. The crack of metal on metal is loud in our ears, but the chisel doesn't even chip the wood. I give the chisel a couple more whacks but I might as well be hitting the door with an oil rag. I replace the tools in my bag, then hoist it and the tire iron.

"Well, we're not getting in this way," I say.

Conchita steps up to the door and runs her hand along the door where the chisel should have bit into the wood.

"There's not a mark there," she says. "I didn't know wood could be that hard."

"It isn't."

"But it doesn't feel like metal."

"It's not. We would have heard it clang if it was."

"Then what is it?"

"Magic," I say.

I'm convinced now that whatever we're looking for must be on the top floor. But since we can't access it, I find myself going through the other apartments again. I'm about to leave one when I stop and look at the newspaper that's lying on the coffee table. The headline reads: "RACE RIOTS RAGE IN WATTS." Under it is a grainy black-and-white photo of crowds rampaging through the LA streets, trashing storefronts. Smoke spirals up from the buildings.

"What is it?" Conchita asks.

"This newspaper."

She gives it a quick look. "I don't get it. This happened, like, forever ago, didn't it?"

I nod. "But I've seen it before. A whole bunch of times."

She still looks blank.

"In other apartments," I explain.

"I still don't get it."

I put my finger on the date. August 15, 1965.

"That's when it must have happened," I say. "If the Alverson Arms is the center of this little world, then that's the day it was born. Why else would the same paper be in so many apartments?"

But we check again, just to be sure, and can't find a newspaper with a more current date anywhere in the building except for my apartment and Edna's.

"We have to tell Henry," Conchita says.

I nod, but I can't stop thinking about the penthouse. "I really want to know what's on that top floor."

"Maybe we can get into it the next time we cross over—you know, when we're on the other side. Then, when we return, we'll already be inside."

"And maybe trapped for six months."

"Maybe longer that that," she says, "because if we can't get back to the place where we died on Halloween, we'll just be stuck in there forever."

"Great."

"Except I don't have a better idea," she says, "do you?"

I shake my head. I'm not going to be seeing John, and I certainly don't want to meet someone new, so a project like this would be good.

"We could meet there just before sunrise," Conchita says.

"It's a plan," I tell her.

It turns out that even people who acted like they had no real curiosity about how or why we're all here are interested in what we've discovered with the newspapers. There's endless talk and speculation, though some are cooler about it than others.

"Nineteen sixty-five," Irwin repeats. "That was a great year for music. Dylan went electric, the Byrds put out *Mr. Tambourine Man,* The Beatles gave us *Rubber Soul,* The Velvet Underground formed."

"Anything special about August 15th in particular that you can remember?" I ask.

"Um . . . the Beatles played Shea Stadium?"

"I was thinking of something more along the lines of something that happened around here—on this block."

Irwin shrugs. "How would I know? I was just a little kid and we hadn't even moved to the city yet."

"And yet you can tell me when The Beatles played some gig."

"Well, sure. That's historic."

All I can do is shake my head and laugh. I guess everybody's idea of what's historic isn't necessarily the same.

Kit, the woman who lives on John Street, gives a slow nod of her head when I ask her.

"There was that terrible war in Vietnam," she says. "Every night they'd show us clips about it on the news—all those poor boys who died."

We talk some more, but she doesn't remember anything that will help.

"I didn't do whatever it is you think I did," paranoid Frankie says, his gaze shifting back and forth, never quite meeting mine.

"I didn't say you did anything."

"Then why are you giving me the third degree?"

"I'm not. I'm just trying to—"

"Pin something on me. Yeah, I know. But I wasn't even born then, okay?"

"Forget it."

I don't talk to him very often, but I should have known this would be hopeless.

"I don't care what Conchita says," he tells me. "I still think you're a narc."

I just walk away.

"I remember that time," Edna says, holding a copy of the paper that I brought to her from one of the other apartments. "We were all so scared the riots were going to spread across the country. And it sure didn't seem like it was going to help the cause much."

Sitting beside her, Ruth nods in agreement.

"Cause?" I ask.

"The civil rights movement, girl. White people were scared enough of us as it was. All we could think was, how is this going to set us back? At least that's what us older folks were thinking. My boys, and the kids their age . . . they'd all been listening to Malcolm X and thought the revolution had come."

David, when I can tear him away from his piano to talk to me, is like a lot of us—too young to remember the sixties. And since he'd only just moved into the neighorhood when he died, he doesn't know a lot of the local history.

"But if something major took place," he says, "and I'm speaking now of something on a scale that can duplicate such a relatively large section of the city into its own little afterworld existence as has happened here, you'd expect it to continue to resonate throughout the neighborhood for years later. The fact that it doesn't—that no one remembers such an event—tells me that however this place originated, it was due to something done in secret. That being the case, I doubt we'll ever know what it was."

Yeah, I know. He always talks like that.

"Do you think somebody here knows?" I ask.

He nods. "But if they've kept it a secret for this long, why would they tell us now? Perhaps our very existence here depends on it being kept a secret."

"So you don't think we should be trying to find out."

"Yes, I do. I think it makes for a stimulating intellectual exercise, but not one on which we should concentrate all of our time and effort. Being here seems to me a chance to grow as individuals, to stretch ourselves in ways we either couldn't or didn't while we were alive. I, for one, don't wish to waste this opportunity we've been given."

But if David's more interested in practicing scales on his piano than tracking down the origins of the Alverson Arms world, my news puts Henry in nerd heaven.

"This was some great detective work," he tells me. "Knowing the exact date could lead us right to the cause behind all of this."

I don't bother to bring up David's argument about how we shouldn't be focusing all of our time on this particular riddle. I'm sure that he and Henry have discussed the pros and cons any number of times already, and I don't really feel like getting into it myself, even though I half agree with David.

Henry smoothes the newspaper lying on the desk in front of him. He treats it like it's some kind of rare and holy artifact, even though I've told him there are dozens of copies back at the Alverson Arms.

"They were all inside the apartments?" he asks. "None of them were still in the halls in front of the doors?"

I smile. "It's not a hotel, Henry. Papers are delivered to the mailboxes in the foyer, and yes," I add before I can ask. "Everybody seems to have collected their copy."

He nods thoughtfully, fingertip tapping the headline above the photo of the Watts riot.

"So," he says, "it had to have happened sometime during the day of the fifteenth—probably later in the day."

I nod. "Whatever happened, happened *after* they were delivered."

"And since the library came here a couple of years later, somewhere we should be able to find a mention of what caused it to happen." He pauses, then adds, "We just have to be able to recognize it."

I know that feeling from when Conchita and I went through the Alverson Arms.

"Well, I'll leave you to it," I tell him. "I'm going back to work on my car."

"I could use some help."

I shake my head and get up from my seat. "Sorry. Paperwork's not really my thing."

"That car's not ever going to take you anywhere," he says.

I pause in the doorway to look back at him.

"You're wrong about that," I tell him. "Every day it takes me away from this place."

He gives me a thoughtful look, then slowly nods to let me know he gets what I mean. I turn away again and walk toward the stairs, my footsteps echoing in the vast cavern of the library.

By the time May Eve rolls around, nobody's any closer to figuring anything out, least of all me. But Conchita and I have finished the bodywork on the coupe. We did an inch chop on the roof. With the drop in the front axle, the slope gives the whole car the exact line I was looking for. We've reassembled the body and it's been primed, ready for the paint job, but first I have to decide on a color—and repair the nozzle of my spray gun. There was a reason it ended up in my storage unit.

I'm also still not sure what I'm going to do with the interior. Back in my other life I usually got the seats stitched at Vintiques Custom Upholstery, over on the east end of 112th Street. I'm thinking I might try to do it myself, stretch and stitch new covers on the original seats, but I've never done it before and I'm not entirely sure where to begin.

But all of those are questions for another day. Right now it's May Eve—a beautiful spring afternoon, warm and sunny. Conchita and I are standing outside Luna's Food Market, saying our good-byes as we get ready to cross back over to the world of the living.

"I'll see you at the Arms an hour or so before sunrise," Conchita says before she heads off to the park beside the library where she died.

"I'll be there," I tell her.

I watch her figure dwindle as she continues down the street. When she turns the corner, I step into the store to wait for the moon to rise.

Nobody almost stumbles over me when I appear in the grocery store this time, and while I see a flicker of recognition in Estefan's face, I know it's only because he has a great memory and I was in here six month ago. He doesn't know *me*.

I'm starving again, and also have to pee like crazy—it's weird how you're totally in your body again, once you cross over. As I buy a couple of tamales, I see they still have the memorial to me behind the cash register. There are even fresh flowers on either side of the picture.

Seeing it, knowing that they're still thinking of me, makes me feel awkward and weird. When you're on the other side, you forget that people might still be mourning you here.

I make my purchase and get out quickly, needing to find a washroom, but then I stop dead in my tracks. My hunger and need to pee vanish, swallowed by my surprise.

I see the car first, parked at the curb, an exact duplicate of my old '57 Fairlane, right down to the black and red paint job, and the whitewalls with their red trim. And what a paint job. Under the glow of a recent waxing, the paint looks a foot deep, like you could almost reach right into it.

Then I see the guy leaning against its fender.

All I can do is stand there with what I'm sure is the world's most stunned expression on my face.

I've spent the past six months carefully putting my feelings for John in a box, burying that box deep, then covering it up with layer after layer of harmless memories and other mental debris until I was sure that I could pass him on the street and not feel much more than a small twinge of regret that things had to work out this way.

But one look at him and my pulse jumps into quick time and I feel such a rush of affection I just want to hold him, and be held, and neither of us to ever let go. He grins and I know he feels the same.

"What . . . what are you *doing* here?" I ask, the words stumbling and thick in my mouth.

"Looking for you."

"But . . . but . . ."

"I wasn't sure it was true," he says. "You know, that you'd actually be here. Not one hundred percent." He pauses for a long moment, then adds, "Is this too weird for you? God, it's so great to see you, but if it's too weird . . . I don't want to come off like some creepy stalker guy . . ."

I'm not sure which of us makes the first move, but the next thing I know we're holding on to each other, and it feels amazing. I've never felt like my body so perfectly fits with another.

We stand there for a long time, oblivious to the other people on the sidewalk who have to detour around the small island we've made with our embrace.

"I . . . I was trying to put you out of my mind," I say into his shoulder.

"How'd that work out for you?"

I push back a little so that I can see his face. He's smiling, but there's a touch of worry in his eyes.

"I thought I had it beat," I say, "until I saw you standing there."

"I didn't even try to forget you—not even when I learned the truth."

"And . . . and you're okay with it?"

He chuckles but without any real humor.

"Not really," he says, "but you take what you can get, right?"

"I guess."

Finally we step apart, but I find I can't let go of his hand. My gaze goes to the car.

"This looks just like my Fairlane," I say.

"That's because it is." My surprise must show on my face, because he adds, "I bought it from your friend Shorty because I thought you might like to have something familiar to drive around in these times that you come back."

"You bought the Fairlane just so I can drive it twice a year?"

He looks a little sheepish. "I guess it's kind of crazy."

"Well, yeah," I tell him, "but also incredibly sweet."

I know right then that I'll never be able to fit the way I feel about him into a box again. I can't figure how I ever managed to do so in the first place.

"I'm surprised Shorty let you have it," I say.

"I lied. I told him we were old friends and that I really wanted to have the car in memory of you. He hemmed and hawed, said he felt the same about it, but you left him a bunch of cars, didn't you?"

I nod.

"So he finally let me have it. I also gave him a painting I did of you."

"You've been doing paintings of me?"

He shrugs. I can see that talking about it makes him feel a little self-conscious so I change the subject.

"The car looks great," I say. "You've really been taking care of it."

"I don't drive it much," he says. "Just enough to keep it from getting lot rot. And before you ask, I give it a good hosing down whenever I've taken it out into the desert."

"I wasn't going to ask." I pause for just a moment, then add, "Well, not right away."

"To tell you the truth," he says, "I've kind of picked up the old car bug from you. I've rented a nice big garage, over on Mission Street, and store the Fairlane in one half under a tarp."

I can tell he's dying to tell me what he's got in the other half, but he wants me to ask. So I do.

"That's where I'm working on this old '42 Willy's pickup that I also bought from Shorty."

"A Willy's, not a Ford?"

He smiles. "Yeah, I knew you'd say that, but I just fell in love with it."

"You don't have to apologize," I tell him. "I love those old Willy's coupes and trucks, too. I almost bought a Willy's jeep a few years ago, but when I took it out for a test drive the engine caught fire, so I ended up passing on it. I already had enough old cars that needed work, and that one wanted a serious overhaul. But I did like its lines."

"Well, this pickup I got is in rough shape," he says, "and I don't know much about working on cars, but I'm learning, and loving every minute of it. Shorty's been giving me advice and he's a great source for parts."

"I'll bet he is."

That was so Shorty. He'd sell some junker on the cheap, then make his money selling parts to the buyer. He wasn't cheating anybody, and his advice was free, but all those little side projects he had going with the buyers added up to a nice little chunk of change at the end of the year.

"So can I see it?" I ask.

"Sure." He hands me a set of keys. "Do you want to drive?"

"I would *love* to drive," I tell him, "but I really need to pee first."

He gets a look on his face and I remember how I bailed on him six months ago, right after using pretty much the exact same words.

"No, that's not going to happen," I assure him. "It's just, when we come back to this world, our bodies kick into overdrive. We're starving, we need to pee. All our appetites get bigger."

He grins. "*All* of them?"

"Down, boy. We can get to that later. But first—"

"You need to pee. Right."

"I promise you, I won't vanish again. We've got all night."

He nods. "Until sunrise."

How does he *know* all of this stuff?

"Actually, I've got to meet a friend about an hour before that," I say, "but I'm all yours until then." I smile and add, "And you are *so* going to have to tell me how you figured all of this out."

"But first you have to pee."

"I just hope I make it to the coffee shop across the street."

I give him a kiss and push him gently away when it starts to linger. I don't want it to end any more than he does, but I also don't want to pee my pants right here on the street. The desire I see in his eyes makes my pulse go into overdrive.

"Hold that thought," I tell him, then, taking advantage of a break in the traffic, I dart across the street.

John

John watched Grace cross the street and step into the coffee shop, appreciating the fit of her jeans and the way her long dark hair bounced against her back. Once she was out of sight, he wondered if he'd actually see her come back out, or if she would simply vanish from his life again the way she had from his apartment six months ago.

When she first stepped out of Luna's Food Market, he'd tried to be cool and not make too much of an ass of himself, but it was hard, especially considering that, for all his plans over these past few months, he hadn't been entirely convinced that she actually would return.

But she had, and seeing her again, he was sure he'd stood there with the look of a country hick getting his first glimpse of a skyscraper.

But it had been impossible to contain the sheer thrill of her being here. It was still hard, standing here waiting for her. He wanted to call Nina and the others and tell them: "See, I'm not out of my mind. She came back. There really is more to the world than we assume there is."

To be fair, they had believed that he'd had a paranormal experience—after all, both Nina and Danny had also seen Grace at the

Witches' Ball—and they'd all been friends for so long that they could see through one another's B.S. The others just couldn't accept as John had—or had at least hoped—that he'd be seeing her again. And they really didn't understand his sudden and continued interest in old cars and retro music.

Meeting Grace had opened doors for him into avenues of interest he hadn't realized he could care about as much as he did, but whenever John tried to explain it, his friends would give him knowing looks and tell him to try to keep some perspective. They'd questioned his buying Grace's old Fairlane, and they'd really begun to worry when he got the Willy's pickup and told them that he planned to fix it up on his own.

"I could see it if you were actually spending time with her," Wes told him. "That's the way it always goes: you meet somebody new and you want to experience all the things that give them a buzz. But come on, already. She's not here for you to impress with your sudden car know-how, and then there's the fact that you live right downtown. None of us have ever needed to own a vehicle—we've got the company Honda for whenever we've needed to drive somewhere, but you've rarely borrowed it."

"And your point is?"

"Now you've got two."

But while they worried, they couldn't find fault with the change in John's overall mood. He'd always been melancholy by nature, even as a teenager—or at least he had been ever since his brother Tim had died. It showed in his quiet demeanor, in the moody introspection of his art, even in the designs he did for Wesdanina. No matter how goofy or frivolous his animated characters might be, they always carried an echoing undercurrent of that same melancholy he did. It wasn't excessive, but it did give them more than the superficial layer too many animated characters had and probably explained the special appeal they held for viewers. They certainly helped bring Wesdanina contracts that they might not have otherwise got.

In the months since he'd met Grace, John could still tap into that part of himself for his character designs, but he smiled more easily now, and often caught himself cheerfully humming some old Ventures tune, or singing along with a Gene Vincent song as it ran through his head. Though he'd known he might never see Grace again, it didn't change his appreciation for the things to which she'd introduced him. The cars, with their classic lines and the dangerous rumble of their motors. The old music, with its twangy guitars and great harmonies.

Meeting Grace hadn't changed him so much as it made him look beyond the small world he'd made of his life to see the endless potential that lay outside its confines. He felt like he was starting to live for the first time and he saw the irony that it had taken falling for a dead woman to make him appreciate life.

Though when he was with her, she certainly didn't seem like a ghost.

He was leaning with his arms on the roof of the Fairlane when she came out of the coffee shop again, two coffees in hand. He straightened up and was surprised to see a look on her face that told him she'd been as unsure of his still being here, waiting for her, as he'd been of her coming back through the door.

She crossed the street and gave him a quick kiss, then handed him a coffee.

"You didn't think I'd be coming back, did you?" she said.

"I wondered."

"I kind of thought I was dreaming, too, but here you are." She ran her hand along the roof of the Fairlane. "And here's my old car." She pulled the keys he'd given her out of the front pocket of her jeans. "Are we still going to see your truck?"

"We'll do anything you want."

"*Anything?*"

He smiled. "It's your night, Grace."

"*Our* night," she said.

She gave him another kiss, then opened the driver's door and slipped behind the wheel. Still smiling, John circled around to the passenger side and got in as well. Grace started up the Fairlane and grinned at the sound of the motor.

"Sweet," she said, then turned to him. "Now I need directions, because I don't have a clue where we're going."

John started to feel a little anxious as he directed her to the garage. He hadn't gotten into working on this old Willy's to impress her—he genuinely loved what he was doing—but now that she was here on the way to see the pickup, he realized he wanted her approval, and he wasn't sure he was going to get it.

He tried not to worry, to appreciate instead that she had returned, and how it felt so right to be sitting here beside her on the bench seat of her Fairlane, but it was like trying to tell yourself not to think of a certain word, because then that was all that was in your head.

With the traffic on Mission Street, it was five minutes before he had Grace pull the Fairlane up in front of a pair of garage doors and shut off the engine. They got out of the car. John dropped their empty coffee cups into a trash container by the doors, then opened the door on the right. It groaned and rattled as it went up.

"I need to fix that sometime," John said.

He stepped into the darkness. When he switched on a light, Grace joined him inside. The Willy's pickup sat in the right half of the garage, surrounded by clutter: tools, tires, the dismantled panels of the pickup's bed. A workbench ran along one half of the back wall. Beside it was a door, then a tall shelving unit and another door. A tarp lay pooled on the cement in the other half of the garage where the Fairlane was usually parked.

"Hmm," Grace said and John immediately took it the wrong way.

"I know it's not a professional work space like you're used to . . ." he began, then broke off as she laughed. "What?" he asked.

"It's nothing. After being in your apartment, I had this picture of you in my head as a really tidy guy, but this place is just as messy as you'd expect any gearhead's garage to be."

"And that's—"

"A good thing," she said and slipped her arm around his waist. "I'm not exactly the poster girl for tidiness. I'm not saying I love a mess, but it's good to know that you can make one."

"You should see me when I'm painting."

She gave his waist a squeeze then stepped forward to look at the Willy's. John closed the garage door while she walked all around the vehicle, tracing the lines of the hood with her fingers, tapping the fenders, peering underneath the chassis.

"It looks rough with all that surface rust," she said, "but I don't see any holes and the frame seems solid as a rock."

John nodded. "Physically and mechanically it's actually pretty sound. It only has what Shorty calls 'emotional difficulties.' You know, the engine's got good compression, but it leaks a bit. The tranny and axle assemblies are tight, but they leak, too. The T-case whines, but it works fine."

"That's so Shorty," Grace said.

She popped the hood to look at the engine.

"It's not original," John said.

"Looks like a Chevy 350 V-8."

He nodded. "A 1978—at least that's what D.K. told me."

Grace glanced up from the engine and grinned. "You're getting to know all my old friends, aren't you?"

"Just the ones at Sanchez Motors. Hey, what does 'D.K.' stand for anyway?"

"The Draggin' King—he loves to race old hot rods."

"They're a great bunch of guys."

"Yeah. I miss them."

"I'm sorry. I didn't mean—"

She waved a hand before he could finish.

"It's cool," she said. "I don't expect everybody else's life to stop just because mine did. And I like the idea of you getting to know them."

She stepped away from the pickup and looked around the garage. When she saw the CDs stacked beside a boom box on the workbench, she walked over to them and went through the titles. Stray Cats. Robert Gordon. The Torquays. A Starbucks compilation of surf guitar. The Reverb Syndicate. Greatest hits collections by The Ventures, Los Straitjackets, and Gene Vincent. She turned and smiled at him.

"Old cars and twangy guitar music," she said. "It looks like you've thrown yourself into my world."

He shook his head. "It's not as obsessive as it might seem. It's just that meeting you also introduced me to things I didn't realize I'd enjoy as much as I do."

But she wasn't finished with teasing him.

"The next thing you know," she said, "you'll start getting tattoos."

He shook his head again. "No, I'd just look silly. I don't have the beautiful canvas that you have to work with."

She laughed. "And now you're back to the pickup lines that you really don't need anymore."

"Except it's true."

She held his gaze for a long moment, then pointed to the door at the other end of the long workbench filled with tools and car parts.

"What's back here?" she asked.

"I don't know what it was originally," John said. "Some kind of closet or extra storage space, I guess. I cleaned it up and set up a little cot in it."

Her eyebrows went up in a question.

"It's for when I forget the time," he explained, "and it's too late to catch the bus back home. There's only street parking around my apartment and I don't trust the area enough to leave the Fairlane out overnight."

"You've got a cot in there?" Grace repeated.

John nodded.

She came up to him and took his hand. "Why don't you show me how it works."

"That was perfect," she said later, her head cradled on his bare chest.

It was a little cramped on the narrow cot, but John reveled in the press of her body against his. He traced the outline of one of her many tattoos with a finger.

"And not just," she added, looking up into his face, "because everything's more intense on this side."

"So what's it like, where you go when over there?" he asked.

"It's hard to explain."

"Maybe I shouldn't be asking."

"No, it's cool. I don't know what dying is like for anybody else, but it's seriously weird for anybody who dies within a few blocks of the Alverson Arms—you know that big greystone apartment building on 26th Street, just down from where you picked me up in front of Luna's?"

John nodded. "What do you mean it's weird for anyone who dies around it?"

She sat up then and told him about getting shot in Luna's Food

Market and waking up in the Alverson Arms world, how no one there knew how or why they'd ended up in that little pocket afterworld, but that it had to have something to do with that tall greystone building she'd called home when she was still alive. She went on to explain how they'd gone through the whole building, looking for she wasn't exactly sure what, but all they'd found was a pretty good indication of the date it had happened: August 15, 1965. So now she was hoping to figure things out from this side.

"Remember I told you I had to see somebody about an hour before dawn?" she said.

He nodded.

"Well, that's when I'm meeting Conchita outside the Alverson and we're going to try to get into the penthouse while we're on this side."

"Can I help?"

"I don't think so. You can come with me, but I don't think you should be inside the penthouse at dawn because then you'll just be stuck in there on your own while we're whisked back to the Alverson Arms world." She cocked her head and looked at him. "I can't believe you're so okay with all of this weird crap."

"I've had six months to get used to the idea, though I have to admit that until you walked out the door of that grocery store, I still wasn't sure it was real."

She took his hand.

"I know," she said. "It took me awhile to get used to the idea, and I was over there living it. But now you need to tell me: how'd you come to be waiting for me outside of Luna's? How did you work all of this out on your own?"

"I didn't," he said. "I had help."

He told her about finding her obituary on the VV Hot Rod Club website, meeting her friend Norm, and all the help that Nina and Raul Delgado had given him.

"I wouldn't have known where to start," she said when he was done. "I don't know that I'd even have been able to take it seriously."

He nodded. "Like I said, I had doubts all along the way, but I knew I'd met you—and so had Nina. And my friend Danny had seen you, too, when we were leaving the club. And . . ." He hesitated a moment before he went on. "If you *could* come back, even if just for a couple of days a year . . . I just couldn't miss the chance of seeing you again."

"You're a pretty amazing guy."

"You're pretty amazing, too. I never felt connected to someone so hard and fast before in my life. I couldn't let that go."

"I wish I'd met you when I was alive," she said.

"Same here."

She leaned against him, sighing with contentment when he put his arm around her.

They fell into an easy silence for a long moment. It was hard for John. He didn't want the moment to end, but he could see the sun rising in his mind's eye and this time, an hour before it came up, she'd be gone again for another six months.

"I didn't think dying would be like that," he said.

"I know. Me neither."

"It makes me really wonder about my brother Tim . . . where he is. If he's stuck in some place like you are, but where he doesn't even get a couple of days to come back."

"Maybe no one told him," she said, then she sighed. "Abuelo, my grandfather, died just a few weeks before I did. I was so sure that I'd get to see him again when my own time came."

"Yeah, I was kind of hoping to see Tim again myself."

He played with her hair as he spoke, curling it around a finger.

"You know, a funny thing happened since I last saw you," he went on. "I know I wasn't to blame for his death, but all the same, I carried the weight of what happened to him. Which, after a while, gets pretty morbid, I guess, but I couldn't shake it. Over these past few months, though, I haven't been comparing everything I'm doing with what he never got to do."

"You didn't forget about him because of me, I hope," Grace said.

"No. But after meeting you, I've tried new things, and between the cars and the music and thinking about you, the weight of Tim got lighter inside me. Don't get me wrong: I don't miss him any less. I just feel less guilty about my own life. Is that weird?"

Grace shook her head against his chest.

"What I think," she said, "is that you just finally tapped into the way it's meant to be. We're supposed to carry on. That's what they'd want. At least I know it's what *I* want the people who cared for me to do."

They were quiet again, each of them thinking of loved ones lost. Then John broke the silence once more.

"Well, I know one way I can see *you* again," he said.

Grace sat up and turned to face him, her eyes flashing. She banged him in the chest with a fist.

"Don't you *dare* go killing yourself around the Alverson!" she told him.

"Whoa. I wasn't saying I would. I was just saying . . ."

"Well, don't," she said, her eyes still flashing. "Promise me you won't. You have no idea what it's like over there. Nothing tastes right or feels right. You can't sleep, and maybe because you can't sleep, every day you start to feel a little thinner than you did the day before. We wouldn't have anything like *this* over there. We'd just be passing the time together."

"Okay."

"Promise."

"I promise."

"You better mean it," she told him. "You have so much to live for."

Without her? John thought. He wasn't so sure about that.

He could tell from the look on her face that she knew exactly what he was thinking, and he wondered if he'd screwed it all up.

"And we can still have something," she said. "We have two days a year—unless that's not good enough for you. And I'd totally understand if you saw other people."

There was a knock on the outside garage door before he could answer. Grace glanced in its direction.

"Are you expecting anybody?" she asked.

John shook his head. "Let's just ignore them and hope they go away."

"But what if it's important?"

"What could be that important?" John began, but then he remembered. "Crap, the Fairlane's parked outside. Maybe something's happened to it."

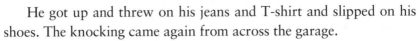

He got up and threw on his jeans and T-shirt and slipped on his shoes. The knocking came again from across the garage.

"Hang on!" John called to whoever was out there, then added in a quieter voice to Grace, "I'll be right back."

He hoped somebody hadn't run into the Fairlane. He'd kept it in perfect shape ever since he'd bought it and hated the idea of something happening to it tonight, the first time Grace could get back and see how he was keeping it for her. But when he rolled up the garage door he found Nina standing outside.

"I *knew* you'd be here," she said, "and then I saw the car, so I knew I was right."

"Nina, what are you doing here?"

"I've come to cheer you up," she told him.

"I'm feeling pretty cheerful."

"Oh, come on. You can't fool me. I know how much you were counting on her coming back tonight. But just because she didn't, it doesn't mean you have to hole up in this place for the rest of the night."

"Nina . . ."

"It's okay. You don't have to thank me. The guys are waiting for us at Danny's place—Helen's going to be there, too. We'll just sit around and . . ."

Her voice trailed off as she looked past his shoulder. John turned to see Grace crossing the garage floor in her bare feet and a T-shirt, her long bare legs covered in tattoos. She stood beside John, slipped an arm around his waist, and smiled.

"Hey, Nina," she said. "It's nice to see you again."

For a long moment all Nina could do was stare at her, blinking as though Grace's presence was a speck of dust in her eye and if she just did it enough, Grace would go away. Finally, she gave a little shake of her head and a handful of words finally spilled out of her.

"Oh my God," she said. "You're real. I mean you're here. You actually came back."

"I did."

"I . . ."

John stifled a laugh to see Nina lost for words. He couldn't remember the last time that had happened.

Grace put out her free hand and patted Nina on the shoulder.

"See," she said. "In the flesh and everything."

Nina gave a slow nod.

"You should come in," John said.

Nina gave another nod. When she stepped into the garage, John rolled the rattling door closed behind her. He walked her to a lawn chair he had set up in the space between the Willy's and where the Fairlane would normally be parked. Once she was off her feet, he grabbed a bench and brought it over. He and Grace sat facing Nina, close enough so that their thighs were against each other.

"Are you going to be okay?" John asked.

"I'm getting there," Nina said.

Her gaze lifted from the cement floor up to Grace's face, obviously taking in all the tattoos on Grace's legs and arms. John and Grace smiled at each other as they saw her realize just how many there were.

"See something you like?" Grace teased.

Nina flushed. "What? Oh, no. I mean, you've got great legs, but it's just . . ."

"So many tattoos. They're under this T-shirt, too. You think it's too much, don't you?"

Nina quickly shook her head. "It's none of my business. But I just, well, I can't help wondering, don't you worry about how they'll look when you get older and you're not all sleek and gorgeous the way you are now?"

"I'm dead, Nina," Grace said. "I'm not going to get any older."

"Oh, God. I didn't mean . . ."

"It's okay. I know what you meant. When I was alive, it just wasn't an issue for me. But you have to understand. I got these tattoos for me. Other people see them, sure, but that's not the point. My ink's like a diary and I don't care what anybody thinks about it, and if someone doesn't like me because of them, well, why should it bother me? I don't want to be friends with anyone so narrow-minded."

Nina nodded. "Sure, I understand. I was just curious. I guess it's something I always want to ask when I see someone with so many tattoos, but I never had the opportunity before."

"Don't worry about it. I know the tats are the first thing people see when they meet me. The keepers are the people who see past them." She turned and smiled at John before she looked back. "I've heard how you've been helping John," she added. "You're very resourceful."

"Hardly. He did all of this on his own."

"I meant working out this whole coming-back-from-the-dead business." Grace smiled.

"Oh, right."

"You don't approve of the cars, do you?" Grace said, making a motion with her arm to take in the garage and the Willy's.

"It's . . ." Nina gave John an apologetic look. "Okay, I'm going to be honest with you, because I hate it when people don't just say what they mean."

"I do, too," Grace said.

Nina looked from her to John. "God knows I love you, John—we all do—but we can't help but worry about how deep you're getting into all of this . . . you know, car stuff and everything."

"You didn't hear me trying to talk you out of hanging out with your pagan friends."

Nina smiled. "Okay, that's fair. But this seems different. It's like you're, I don't know. Using these old cars to try to capture the buzz you get when you can't be with Grace."

"Except it's really not like that," he said. "It was more like stumbling across something I always liked, except I didn't know that I did until I got to experience it. It's hard to explain, but it came to me as this sudden realization that there's more in the world than I was aware of and I just knew I wanted to explore it." He paused, then added, "I can't be the only person to go through something like this."

Grace nodded. "I've seen it before—lots of times."

"But hot rods?" Nina asked. "In this day and age?"

"It doesn't just happen with old cars," Grace told her, "but I can promise you that people turn into gearheads all the time. It's like a midlife crisis, except it can happen at any age, and then it's all about customs and hot rods instead of fancy little sports cars and cute blondes half the guy's age." She laughed. "It happened to me when I was a teenager, still in high school, and my grandfather asked me to help him with this old '32 Ford he was working on in his garage. He just meant that he needed someone to help him hold a couple of things—that third hand comes in so handy, you know? It wasn't like he was trying to turn me into a gearhead, but it happened all the same. I just fell in love with it. The fact that it was doing something with my abuelo was part of it, sure, but the oil and smell of gas got into my blood, and fast."

"And besides," John put in, "I like it, so where's the harm?"

Nina shrugged. "None, I guess. So . . . I give up. Play with your old cars."

John's eyebrows went up. "*You* give up? Did someone replace the Nina I know with a pod person?"

"Ha ha."

John got up from the bench.

"I've got a little fridge in the corner," he said. "Does anybody want a beer or a pop?"

"I would kill for a beer," Gracie said.

John nodded. "What about you, Nina?"

Nina shook her head and gave Gracie's outfit another once-over. John knew she recognized it as one of his old T-shirts, though he didn't think he'd ever looked as good in it.

"I don't think you guys need any company right now," she said.

"But you just got here," Grace said.

Nina smiled and stood up. "Where it turns out no one's got the blues and needs to be distracted. At least not by me. You kids have fun and play safe."

They followed her as she walked to the door. John rolled it open again and touched Nina's arm before she could step out.

"Thanks," he said. "I know you're just looking out for me."

She gave him a hug, hesitated, then hugged Grace, too.

"You don't feel even remotely like a ghost," she said when she stepped back.

"It creeps me out, too," Grace assured her.

"It creeps *you* out?"

"Well, think about it. I never signed up to join any spook squad. I was just minding my own business, trying to buy a pack of smokes, and the next thing I know, I'm waking up in Ghost Town with some big black woman telling me I'm dead. And the worst thing about it? She's right."

"I'm sorry," Nina said. "Of course that would be awful."

Grace shrugged. "It's not like you had anything to do with it."

Nina looked from her to John. She had that sympathetic look on her face like when Danny was crushing on some girl he'd never even met—wanting the best for her friend, but not seeing much hope for it going anywhere.

"I hope you guys can work something out," she said. "Maybe it's impossible, but you just being here already seems impossible, Grace, so who knows what you might be able to figure out."

"Thanks," Grace said.

"Do you need a lift home?" John asked.

Nina shook her head. "I'm good," she told them. "You have little enough time together as it is tonight, so make the most of it."

They watched her walk off down the street, then stepped back into the garage. John rolled the door back down. The clang it made when it tapped against the concrete floor seemed to shut all the unhappy realities of their situation outside. It was just the two of them again, living outside the boundaries of normal time and space, protected in a nest of old cars, rockabilly music, and the feelings they held for each other.

"What do you want to do?" he asked Grace.

"Have that beer you promised me," she said. She grinned and took his hand. "And then get back to what we were doing."

The night was going by too fast for John. He had months of conversation stored up that he wanted to share with Grace. He wanted to hold her and love her. He wanted to take her to all his favorite places and go to all of hers. He wanted to listen to her voice and watch her move and memorize each of her tattoos. He wanted to make a quilt of the comfortable silences that fell between them and wrap it around them to keep them safe from the world beyond the garage doors and the approach of dawn.

But time was an army of minutes and seconds on the march and there was no stopping it.

He looked across the hood of the pickup at Grace. She was bent over the engine with an intense look on her face, trying to loosen a bolt. The muscles of her arms stood out in strong definition, the tattoos pulled tight.

"It's no use," she said, straightening up. "We need to put some oil on that sucker and let it do its magic."

She smiled when she saw John just leaning there with his arms on the other side of the car, looking at her.

"What?" she added.

"I just love having you here," he said.

"I love being here. Hand me the oilcan, would you?"

He brought the can over and watched her drip oil on the stubborn bolt.

"You know what I'd like to do?" she said, looking up at him again.

"Me, too, but unless you have some Viagra stashed away in your jeans, it's not going to happen for a little while yet."

Grace laughed. "I was thinking more of taking a drive out into the desert. We still have a few hours before I hook up with Conchita. All I've seen for the past six months is the few blocks around the Alverson Arms, and for a girl like me who loves the wide open spaces, being stuck in the city for that long's been driving me crazy."

"That's doable," John said. "More doable than what I was thinking."

"Well, who knows what'll come up once we're out there in the hills and under the stars."

John never drove in the desert at night except as a means of getting from point A to point B. It was just something you did when you had to. It certainly wasn't something you paid a lot of attention to since everything beyond the reach of the car's headlights was scrub and cacti, and too dark to really see properly anyway. Since he was usually a passenger, he would focus his attention on whatever music they had playing, and whoever was with him in the car.

But tonight it was an entirely different experience, fresh and exhilarating. They had the top down, the wind in their hair, the stars bright above in a sky that had cleared into an expanse so wide it was impossible to take in all at once. And then there was Grace's enthusiasm, which was impossible to ignore.

The Cadillac Angels were on the stereo, and except for the faint hum of their tires on the asphalt, they seemed to float just above the highway. But at the same time John felt like they were completely grounded in the vast landscape that stretched off into the distance, dark and mysterious on either side of the pavement. Grace didn't drive the way he expected either. He'd thought she'd have a heavy foot on the gas pedal, and he'd been preparing himself for a wild ride. But once they got on the highway, she drove at a steady clip, just over the speed limit, her fingers tapping on the steering wheel to the rhythm of the music.

Half an hour from the city she pulled off the highway into a truck stop, but instead of stopping, she took a dirt road that led off from the truck stop's parking lot up into the hills. The road was relatively smooth, the Fairlane's suspension easily riding its few bumps. Finally, she pulled up along the side of the road onto a bluff and shut off the engine. They listened to the pinging of the engine and the slow return of the desert's night sounds that they had disturbed into silence with their arrival. Tall saguaro cacti stood all around them, reaching for the sky. The Kikimi called them the aunts and uncles, he remembered Nina telling him once, because they were inhabited by the spirits of their ancestors who had lived a worthy life.

"It's gorgeous out here," John said.

Grace nodded.

"I don't know how I ever ended up living in the Alverson Arms," she said. "The first time Abuelo took me out this way, I just fell in love with the land—the land and the cacti, the hawks that circle overheard, the coyotes howling at night—everything. I was determined to get a place somewhere out here. I thought I'd turn into some mechanic-slash-desert rat and spend all my time working on my cars and exploring the desert. But I let myself get . . . I don't know. Distracted, I guess. And now it's too late."

Because some junkie with a gun had stolen that option from her, John thought, and there was nothing either of them could do about it now.

Grace shifted in her seat so she could look at him.

"This isn't going to work, you know," she said. "You can't have a meaningful relationship with someone who's only around two nights out of the year. You need to find someone who can always be there for you."

"I don't want anybody else."

"I get that. You don't know how much I get that. But we can't do this. It's not right."

"Why don't you let me decide what's right for me," John said.

She shook her head. "We can never be together like we want to be—and don't even start with the jokes about how you can always kill yourself outside the Alverson Arms. If you come over to where I am, it won't be the same. I promise you that."

"I understand, but—"

"I don't know that you do. God knows I don't want it to be this way, but we can't have any sort of meaningful relationship."

"Except two nights a year."

"How could that ever be enough?"

He reached out and took her hand. "Because we don't have any other choice."

"That's not true. We can choose to end it."

"Is that what you want?"

"No, but I'm dead. I don't get to decide what I can or can't have anymore. But you're still alive."

He nodded. "And I'm going to live my life—as fully and completely as I can. But twice a year I'm going to be parking this Fairlane outside of Luna's Food Market, whether you want me to or not. If you'd rather not see me, I'll just leave you the car."

"You're impossible."

"No, just smitten."

"Nobody says 'smitten' anymore."

"Except we both did."

Grace looked like she didn't know if she was going to laugh or cry.

"God, I'm going to miss you," she said.

She snuggled up to him and laid her head on his shoulder, burrowing a little deeper when he put his arm around her. They let their gaze take in the vast panorama of desert and night sky, listened to the murmur of the wind in the weeds and dry grasses. Somewhere, in the near distance, a coyote howled. Closer at hand—probably from around the truck stop, John thought—dogs responded with a cluster of barks.

"I don't feel dead when I'm here," Grace said suddenly. "Especially when I'm with you. I don't feel dead when I'm over there either, but there I just feel weird. Here it's like nothing ever happened. Like I never got shot."

"You don't feel dead to me either."

She laughed softly. "I should hope not. How gross would that be?"

"Too." John waited a long moment, then added, "Sunrise is going to come too soon."

"I know. I've been thinking that all night."

She took the hand that was on her shoulder and turned it so that she could look at his watch.

"And speaking of which," she said, "it's time for me to go meet up with Conchita."

"Do you have to do this?"

"I need to understand why this is happening to me."

"I get that. It's just . . . if you find a way to undo it . . ."

"I can't undo it," she said. "I'm always going to be dead."

"I meant, being stuck in that other place."

She nodded. "What about it?"

"If you fix whatever has you trapped, you'll go on, right? To wherever you were supposed to go when you died."

"That's my guess."

"And you won't be coming back—not even twice a year."

Grace didn't say anything for a long moment. She leaned her head back and looked up into the night sky. Finally she turned to him.

"Then things will be the way they were supposed to be," she said, "and whatever time we've had together will be a gift we got to share."

Before he could respond, she pulled away from him and started up the car.

"I don't like it any better than you," she said as she backed the car up so that she could turn around. "But I know it's not natural—what's happening to me and everybody else in the Alverson Arms world."

With the car turned around, she started down the dirt road that would take them back to the highway.

Conchita was waiting in front of the Alverson Arms when they pulled up to the curb in front of the building—at least John assumed that's who the young, somewhat scruffy girl standing there was. Grace turned off the Fairlane's engine and reached under the seat.

"Ah," she said. "You even kept my stuff."

She pulled a tire iron from under the seat, then got out of the car and stepped out onto the pavement. John waited a long moment, then opened the passenger door and joined her.

"Are you really going to need that?" he asked.

Grace shrugged. "Only if Conchita can't work her magic lock-picking skills on the door."

He glanced at the small figure waiting for Grace by the front door of the building.

"She can do magic?" he asked.

Grace shook her head. "No, just the kind of lock-picking that seems like it."

They stood there for a moment, looking at each other.

"I guess this is good-bye," he said.

She put her free hand on his arm.

"Don't think badly of me because I need to do this," she told him. "It doesn't mean I care any less for you."

"I know that. I know it's something you've got to do—something you probably *have* to do."

"That's the way it feels to me."

"I'll still be in front of Luna's next Halloween."

For a moment he thought she was going to argue about it again, but she only sighed.

"And if I can," she said, "I'll be there to meet you."

She stepped closer, her free arm lifting to encircle his neck, and he enfolded her in a tight embrace. She tilted her head up so that his mouth could meet hers. When they finally stepped apart, they were both a little breathless. Grace put a finger to his lips as he started to speak. She placed the car keys in his hand.

"I'm crap at good-byes," she said.

"I just wanted to tell you that I love you."

She nodded. "Me, too. More than pretty much anything else I can think of."

She gave a him a last quick kiss, then walked away to join Conchita. She carried the tire iron by her side and didn't look back.

John watched as they both went up the steps of the building. Grace still didn't look back, but her companion waved to him before they went inside. John lifted his hand in response. He bounced the car keys in his hand a couple of times, then walked around to the driver's side, but he didn't get in. Instead, he leaned on the roof and stared at the building.

He knew he should leave, but the thought that Grace could still come stepping back through that door before the sun rose kept him standing there on the pavement, waiting. Hoping. If she didn't . . .

He wondered if he'd be able to tell. Would there be some flash of light from the top floor where they'd gone, some tremor coming up through his soles from the pavement to cause a lurch in his heart? Would he even feel her absence in the world?

He doubted it, but only because he was already feeling her absence.

He continued to stand beside the Fairlane until the light grew around him, long shadows creeping down the street as the sun finally topped the horizon. He looked back at the Alverson Arms, up to the penthouse floor. He felt no different, but he knew she was gone now.

He waited a few moments longer, then opened the car door and got inside. The Fairlane started up immediately. Since there was still no traffic, he made a U-turn and headed down 26th Street.

"Your light was still on," he said when Nina opened the door of her apartment.

She was dressed in sweats, a TV remote in her hand. Behind her he could see the screen of her TV set throwing an ever-changing flicker of light and shadow on the living room wall. The sound was muted.

"I thought you might come by," she said.

"Yeah, I'm not quite ready to go home and be by myself."

She gave him a sad smile and put a hand on his arm.

"So's she gone again?" she asked.

He nodded. "And now it'll be another six months before I can see her."

"You should come in."

He nodded again and let her lead him inside. She steered him to the far end of the sofa. A mug of tea steamed on the side table at the other end of the sofa where she usually sat.

"The water's still hot," she said. "Do you want a coffee or some tea?"

"Tea would be great."

"Sit," she told him as he started to get up. "It'll just take a moment."

He watched the silent screen as she went into the kitchen. An old *Star Trek* episode was playing.

"Haven't you seen this, like, a million times?" he asked.

"More like a zillion," she said, coming back into the living room with his tea. "It's comfort TV for me."

"Maybe I should get a TV to see me through the next six months."

Nina laughed. "That would make Danny so happy."

John laughed with her. "Yeah, that's my big goal in life. It's all about making Danny happy."

"He worries, too," Nina said. "We all do. Not about your keeping up with technology, of course, but—"

"I know. I appreciate it. But maybe you can see that I'm not so crazy now. She did come back. As for the rest of it . . . come on. You know, people change as they get older. They discover different interests and it's not the end of the world. You weren't always Wiccan."

"No, I get it. It's just . . . I hate to see you sad, and all this business with the cars and music seemed like an escape from a real life."

"I feel more like I've escaped *to* a real life. Like I was just idling in neutral before."

"In a lot of ways, I guess you were."

The conversation died and they watched the silent TV for a while, sipping their tea.

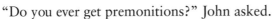

"Do you ever get premonitions?" John asked.

Nina turned from the TV to look at him. "Like what?"

"I have this feeling I'm never going to see Grace again—at least not until I die."

Worry blossomed in her features. "Oh, John, don't tell me you can even be thinking of—"

"No," he broke in. "I'm not thinking of killing myself. Why is that the first thing anybody thinks of? I just mean . . . now we know some part of us continues on—our soul, our spirit, something with our personality stamped on. So I'll get to see her again then. And maybe Timmy, too."

"You'll see her before that," Nina told him. "You'll see her in six months. You only feel this way because she's gone again. My friend Sandy had this long-distance relationship where she and her boyfriend only saw each other every second month or so. She felt just like that every time they had to say good-bye."

"Except they could probably talk on the phone."

"Racking up huge phone bills, but, yeah."

John gave a slow nod.

"I guess that's what it is," he said.

He smiled to show Nina that he wasn't going to brood on it, but while he could school his features, he couldn't get rid of the fear that was snaking around inside his head.

John meant to call Raul the next day. The man had been so helpful when John was first trying to figure everything out, and they'd stayed in touch, but by the time he got up late in the afternoon, he didn't really want to talk to anyone about Grace. He had another six months of being without her ahead of him and he'd just as soon get on with his life as it was going to be, concentrating on things he could do on his own and with his friends, rather than focus too much on what he couldn't have.

Maybe later, when he got into a rhythm of ordinary life, but not right now when the loss was still a raw and open wound.

But it *was* better than the first time. Today he knew for certain how she felt about him and that, fears aside, he'd be seeing her again, whereas six months ago he'd been questioning his sanity. He found it easier to get back to work on his current Wesdanina project—a proposal they were putting together for a series of animated ads to promote a new cell phone company—and he had the Willy's in his garage. Nina had spoken to Wes and Danny, so neither of them pressed him for details about seeing Grace again, and even Nina was being good about not bringing it up every time they talked.

It wasn't until two weeks later that John remembered Raul, and that was only because he went into the Rosalinda House Café to get a latte where he saw Raul sitting at a table in the back with a woman he didn't recognize. He considered backing out the door before Raul looked up, but he made himself go up to the counter, get his latte, and then bring it over to Raul's table.

"John!" Raul said. "I was wondering how you were doing."

John looked, but he could see no trace of reproach in Raul's dark features.

"Let me introduce you to my wife, Alma," Raul went on. "Alma, this is John Burns."

She had a Latin cast to her features—a lighter shade of brown than Raul, which seemed even paler set against the long jet-black hair that framed her face. She seemed a little younger than Raul and very fit. When she shook his hand, her grip was firm and he caught a glimpse of a large tattoo under the sleeve of her jean jacket—a pattern of swirling Oaxaca colors, but the quick view he got didn't allow him to see the detail. Alma noticed his interest and pulled back the sleeve of her jacket to show him that the colors were actually a collage of flying dogs and cats and flowers, all rendered in the style of Zapotec folk art.

"Nice," he said, having gained an appreciation for this sort of art from knowing Grace. He found he was much quicker to notice people's ink since he'd met her.

"Alma plays with the VV Rollergirls," Raul said, as though her tattoos needed an explanation.

John pulled out a chair to join them and smiled. "I don't see the connection."

Alma laughed. "Don't mind him. He thinks Roller Derby is all fishnets and tattoos and girls banging into each other while on roller skates."

"My friend Danny's the same. He's forever trying to get me to come to one of your games."

"If by Danny," Alma said, "you mean Helen's boyfriend, then you must be *that* John Burns."

John glanced at Raul. "Oh God, what have you told her?"

Alma touched his hand, reclaiming his attention. "Nothing bad. I think it's wonderfully romantic."

"And you don't think it's weird?"

She laughed. "You *have* spoken to my husband, haven't you?"

"Oh, yes. But I didn't think he'd . . . you know . . ."

"You don't have to worry," she said. "Whatever he tells me stays between the two of us. I would never betray that trust."

"Right. Um, thanks."

John tried not to show his discomfort that Raul had spoken to anyone about his situation, but she looked from him to her husband, then said to John, "Would you excuse me for a moment? I need to phone my friend Lacey to make sure the team's still on for an extra practice this afternoon. We're playing Tucson's Saddletramps tonight and they're such a killer team, we need every spare moment we can sneak in."

She took her cell phone from her purse. Leaving the purse on the table, she opened the phone and started to punch in a number as she wove her way through the tables to go outside.

"I don't keep any secrets from my wife," Raul said.

"No, of course not. I just . . . it's weird when a stranger knows this kind of thing about you—you know, that I'm dating a dead woman."

Raul smiled. "It sounds bad, when you put it like that. But she's not dead when you're with her." He waited a beat, then added, "I assume you were with her on Walpurgis Night?"

John nodded. "I meant to call, but then . . . I guess I just wasn't ready to talk about it. I'm sorry. I didn't mean to shut you out—not after you've been such a help."

"You don't have to apologize. It's not like I'm your parole officer."

"I know. It's just . . ."

Raul waved a hand. "Don't worry about it. But now that you're here, I'm curious. Did you ask her if the two of you had known each other before she died?"

John blinked in surprise.

"I never even thought to ask her," he said, "but I don't think so. We both talked about wishing we'd met before she was shot."

"I know this is your life," Raul said. "These are your emotions, and I don't mean to pry into them like some tabloid writer, but I can't deny how fascinating your circumstances are. Whenever I think of you, I just want to know more."

"It's weird all right."

"No, it's not just that. I don't know if I've ever heard of a ghost falling in love with someone after they've already died. It goes the other way, of course. A man falling for a long-dead movie star, or something like that, but ghosts usually haunt people and places that they had some connection to when they were alive."

John hadn't put the time into studying the supernatural as Raul had, but with Nina's help, he'd taken a crash course once he'd found out that Grace had died in the weeks prior to the Witches' Ball.

"I don't have your experience," he said, "but I haven't heard of it either."

"Then why did she single you out?"

John didn't correct him. Grace hadn't singled him out so much as Nina had blackmailed him into going up to talk to her, then stepped in when he'd been about to walk away.

"Do you believe in soul mates?" he asked instead. "That there could be someone out there in the world who you're meant to be with?"

Raul looked out the café window to where his wife still stood, talking on her cell phone.

"Definitely," he said.

"Well, maybe that's what this is," John said. "Maybe Grace and I were supposed to be together, but circumstances being the way they are, these two nights a year are all we get."

"It sounds like a fairy tale."

"I wish it was. I wish I could keep silent for a year, or sew a cloak out of nettles—do *something* to make things work out better for us."

"Don't rule any possibilities out," Raul said. "This is all unknown territory. None of us know what the rules are."

"Or if there even are rules."

"There are rules. We might not know what they are, but there's always cause and effect. Nothing happens in a vacuum."

"I don't know . . ."

Raul gave him a considering look.

"Is there something you aren't telling me?" he asked.

"Nothing that makes any sense."

"Try me."

"What do you know about premonitions?"

Raul shrugged. "They're a feeling of anticipation, or anxiety about, some future event. Often they're a forewarning of danger." John supposed Raul saw something in his face, because then he added, "Though sometimes they're just that: a feeling. A sensation that only feels real because we're already fearful or anxious about something."

"Well, that fits what's happening to me."

"Which is?"

"I have this feeling that I'm never going to see her again."

"Because . . . ?" Raul asked when he didn't go on.

"There's no good reason. She's as crazy about me as I am about her, but . . ."

He shared a brief version of what Grace had told him about what she called the Alverson Arms world, and how she and her friend Conchita had determined that it all had something to do with that old greystone building. How just before dawn, they'd planned to break into the penthouse apartment, because they couldn't breach it in the other world, but they felt the answer was in there.

Raul slowly shook his head. "I've never heard of anything like this."

"Welcome to my life."

"But your premonition, it could still just be natural anxiety. It happens to ordinary people in this world who are just starting a relationship."

"I know," John said. "But what if they did get into that penthouse and found a way to stop what's happening to them? What if they broke the spell, or whatever it is, and they've gone on to where they were supposed to go when they died? Then I won't see her again, will I?"

Raul didn't say anything for a long moment. His gaze went to his wife again, before he returned his attention to John.

"I don't know," he said finally. "That's not something anyone can know for certain."

Grace

"So was that him?" Conchita asks when we step inside the foyer of the Alverson Arms.

We used my key, which still works, to get into the building. The tire iron I'm holding oh-so-casually by my side is for that more problematic door up on the top floor. I'm hoping that on this side we can force our way in where we couldn't even scratch the wood on the same door back in the Alverson Arms world.

"That was John," I say.

We keep our voices low so that no one will get curious enough to open their door to see who's out here in the halls at this time of night. I feel a little strange walking by Edna's door because for the past year her apartment's been as familiar to me as my own, but here, in *this* world, I have no idea who lives in it.

"He's got a cool car," Conchita says.

"Yeah, I know. It used to be mine."

"Really?" Conchita shoots me a quick glance. "How'd he get it?"

"He tracked it down and bought it."

Conchita shakes her head. "Okay, that's a little stalker creepy, don't you think?"

"No, I think it's sweet."

"I guess. But I've got to tell you, you surprised me tonight, so I have to ask. After everything you said about not seeing him again, what made you decide to go look him up?"

I smile, remembering.

"I didn't," I tell her. "When I stepped outside of Luna's at moonrise, there he was. *With* the car. I thought it was pretty amazing, really, how he figured everything out . . . that I could come back, where I'd appear."

I shake my head. I still think it's amazing.

"He'd been waiting six months for me to return," I add.

"Whoa. He was waiting outside of Luna's that whole time?"

I laugh. "No, he was waiting for April 30th—the same way we were. Then when it finally came around, he parked out front of Luna's in the late afternoon and waited for moonrise."

"He's totally a stalker," Conchita says, but she's smiling.

"I know. I really, really like him. And he's planning to wait *another* six months before we can be together again, even though I told him he should just get on with his life."

"Now I'm jealous. I wish *I* had a stalker."

"I think he's a one-of-a-kind."

Something happens inside me when we get to my floor. I can't help it. I leave the stairwell and walk down the hall to stand in front of the door to my apartment. I lay my hand on its wooden panel. I could be in there, sleeping . . . if I hadn't gone down to Luna's that night. I could still be alive and everything would be different.

"Grace?" Conchita whispers. "What's going on?"

"Nothing," I tell her, keeping my own voice low. "I was just wondering who lives here now."

I have a key. If the new tenants didn't get the lock changed, I could probably get in. I could go inside and stand over their bed and watch them sleep. And wouldn't that freak them out if they woke up to find some tattooed chick standing there at the side of their bed, looking down at them, a tire iron dangling from her hand. Maybe it would shake them up—make them appreciate what they've got *while* they've still got it. Maybe I'd be doing them a favor . . .

"Grace?" Conchita asks.

I don't realize I've taken a step back from the door and lifted the tire iron until she speaks. I lower my hand.

"What's happening?" she asks.

I shake my head. "Nothing. It doesn't matter."

"This is your apartment," she says.

"Yeah."

She touches my arm. "I didn't think. This must be really weird for you."

"Yeah, but I'm fine now."

"But . . ."

"No, really. I'm good at compartmentalizing the crap in my life. It's like driving a car—you never forget how."

"Unless you have Alzheimer's or dementia."

"And you worry about me when all you can talk about is stalkers and dementia."

Conchita sighs. "Sorry. I guess I didn't have such a good night."

"What did you do?" I ask as we head back to the stairwell.

"Nothing different from what I'd do back on the other side. All I did was wander around this same neighborhood—the same few blocks. I walked all night. I looked at all the people going about their lives, and I felt totally disconnected. It's like that back home, but here, that feeling's way more intense."

"Because everything's more intense."

She nods. "Even how we feel about a guy."

"I know what you're saying," I tell her. "I keep it in mind."

"But," she says.

"But then I look at him, and he's feeling it as intensely as I am, and he's still alive. So there's something happening. I'm not just making the whole thing up."

"I didn't think you were."

"I know," I say. "I just worry that I am."

We reach the top floor and the doors to the penthouse that we couldn't get through in the Alverson Arms world. I look up at the night sky through the skylight. It's lighter, but how much lighter, I can't really tell. It's not like the dark out in the desert where John and I sat in the Fairlane and watched the stars. With all the light pollution, the sky is always brighter in the city.

Conchita pushes back a sleeve and checks the time.

"Nice watch," I say.

She shrugs. "I borrowed it from some guy at a bus stop who's never going to miss it. It won't come back with us. Nothing ever does."

"I didn't know that was another one of your skills."

She grins. "I'm just full of surprises."

"So how are we doing?"

"I synchronized the watch to a TV in a store window and checked the paper for times. We've got about ten minutes until the sun comes up."

I nod. "Gentlemen, start your engines."

"What?"

"Sorry. Race car talk. It just means it's time to get going."

I turn back to face the doors, stick the narrow end of the tire iron into the space between them.

"You sure you don't want me to try to pick the lock first?" Conchita asks.

I shake my head. "No. I feel the need to inflict a little damage on something."

I put my shoulder into it, and the wood splinters. The door pops open. I slip inside, still holding the tire iron. Conchita comes in behind me and closes the doors as best she can. Because of the damage I did forcing them open, they won't quite come together again.

We listen to see if the noise of our breaking in was noticed. As we listen, I look around.

We're in a large, dimly lit room that's choked with furniture and has the cloying smell of an old lady's perfume with an underlay of dust. I couldn't live with this much furniture stuffed in one room. Wherever I look there's some clunky piece: sofas and easy chairs, a half-dozen floor lamps, straight-back chairs, end tables and side tables and a small writing desk with yet another chair. One wall is full of bookcases that hold a bewildering array of knickknacks as well as books. Cobwebs cluster in the corners and the carpet underfoot sends up a little puff of dust with every step we take farther in the room.

It's so quiet our breathing sounds loud. We seem to be alone, but there's a hallway running off the room on either side. At the end of the one on the right I can see a kitchen. To the left I can see a number of closed doors. Who knows how many people could be sleeping behind them?

My grip on the tire iron tightens. I don't want to actually use it on anybody. I just want it as a threat until the sun rises and we're taken back to the Alverson Arms world.

Conchita steps closer to me, her mouth near my ear.

"What do we do now?" she whispers.

"We wait for the sun."

She nods.

"This place is a pigsty," she says, still keeping her voice low.

"No kidding."

But it surprises me a little. The Alverson Arms isn't the most prime piece of real estate in Solona, though I guess at one time it was. Now, except for the library, you'd be hard-pressed to find anything that fits the bill. But even run-down the way the Arms is, you'd think somebody'd be renting this top floor. I paid 750 a month for my one bedroom. With all the space up here they could probably get a couple grand—if it wasn't so grotty.

I go over to the window and look out. Conchita follows me. The window faces west, but I can see the long shadows growing as the sun starts to top the eastern horizon.

I'm not really interested in exploring too much, not on this side. That can wait until we cross over. Right now, I'm focused on being in this apartment when that happens.

Conchita gives up a sudden little gasp, but I don't have to ask her why because the hand holding the tire iron is suddenly not holding anything. I turn to her and she lifts her wrist to show me that her "borrowed" watch is gone.

"That was creepy," she says. "It just kind of slid away."

I'm still feeling a little weird from how the tire iron disappeared on me—I hold up my hand and flex my fingers—but I'm grinning.

"We did it," I say in a normal voice. "We're in."

I turn around to see that everything's changed. The clutter of furniture is still there, but while it still smells like an old lady, the dust and dirt is all gone. It's a pretty good trick, one I wish I'd known back when I was alive and my apartment needed a major cleaning. But I suppose being dead enters into the equation, and I could easily pass on that.

Conchita turns to me. "Where do we start looking for . . . what did you call it? The hatch ring?"

I'm not so sure that's what we're looking for, exactly. Hatch ring, switch, a button, who knows what it'll look like? Then I hear a rustle of clothing, and when I turn around, I realize we didn't need to look for it.

It found us.

She's the oldest person I've ever seen, so worn away that she's only skin stretched tight over bones. Her white hair's up in a tight bun and she's dressed in some old-fashioned sixties blouse and skirt, but she could be wearing the best designer's work and she'd still look awful. She looks like a famine victim—or one of the Jews from Auschwitz. No, it's worse. She looks like something you'd find in a coffin that you'd dug up from some old graveyard, except she's not dead.

Bad as she looks, her eyes are worse. They're pale and too bright and blaze with anger.

"How did you get in here?" she wants to know.

I can't stop staring at her. She has no lips, so every movement of her mouth is like watching an animated skull. I'm not surprised that the room smells like an old lady's perfume. I just can't figure out why it doesn't smell like something died in here, too.

"I asked you a question," she says, that furious gaze whipping back and forth from Conchita to me.

Conchita edges closer to me.

"We came in through the door," I say.

"Impossible."

"Not here—from the other side."

The slash mouth shapes a frown that's just an ugly line under the sunken memory of her nose.

"That's still not possible," she says. "No one can see the penthouse floor. It's guarded and hidden from every living eye."

I think about that for a moment. Is that the reason I never heard a peep about something weird going on with the Alverson Arms? I mean, back when I was alive. Is that why the penthouse isn't rented out? Did this skeletal woman do something so that people aren't even aware that it's here?

But then, Conchita and I aren't really people.

"Yeah," I say, "except we're dead."

She shakes her head and this horrible image comes into my head of it falling right off.

"No," she says. "Only Justin would be able to see it."

"Who's Justin?"

"My boy who died in that damned war overseas. But he's coming home to me. I can't leave until he comes back."

"What war are we talking about?" I ask.

"You shouldn't be here."

"We got that. Except here we are."

"What *are* you?" she asks. "Some sort of sideshow performer?"

Again with the bad-mouthing my tats. This gets way too old sometimes.

"Look, lady," I say.

She shakes her head again. "Get out of here!"

"Not until we get some—"

She lifts a bony arm with a claw of a hand at the end and makes a dismissing motion. I want to smile—I mean, what's she going to do? Throw us out? She looks like she'd have trouble crossing the room.

But something picks us up and flings us toward the door. I flinch, expecting to hit it, but we go right through. We don't hit anything until we're on the other side. I bang into the railing. Conchita starts to fall down the stairs, but I grab her jacket. It's all I can do to haul her back onto the landing.

We sit there with the breath knocked out of us, staring at the closed door. The closed *undamaged* door.

"How . . . how did she do that?" Conchita asks.

I'm still trying to process that myself.

"Damned if I know," I say after a long moment.

Conchita nods. "I didn't know white people could be brujas."

I turn to look at her. Is that what just happened? I don't know that I can buy into witches and magic, though that old lady sure looked like the worst nightmare version of an evil bruja. I never really believed in ghosts either, but here I am in some ghost-town version of Santo del Vado Viejo all the same.

"I remember when I was a little girl," Conchita says, "my abuela told me that a dead bruja is more powerful and more dangerous than a living bruja."

"What does that even mean?"

"I don't know. But she said that a bruja has no limit to her magic except that she has to take complete responsibility for her actions and she has to be willing to submit to the consequences. So maybe that's why that old woman looks the way she does—whatever magic she's doing is coming back on her."

"I'm not sure I even believe in witches."

"Says the dead woman."

"You know what I mean," I say.

Conchita nods. "Except sometimes things exist whether we want them to or not. That bruja in there waved her hand and we were blown right through the door without our touching it."

I rub my shoulder where I'd banged up against the banister and look at the door, an untouched and untouchable barrier.

"I guess," I say. "So did your abuela have any advice for how to protect yourself against brujería?"

"It's not all bad. It just depends on the person using it."

"Sure, but if the person you're up against is an evil old hag, is there anything you can do?"

"Call on los santos," Conchita says.

I smile. "They didn't listen to me when I was alive. What makes you think they'd listen to me now?"

"Maybe *your* magic's stronger now that you're dead."

"I don't have any magic, Conchita. Trust me on that."

"I know that."

"So how can we protect ourselves?"

"I don't know. Abuela just said that los santos and a holy cross are shields against evil brujas." She smiles. "And a man named Juan."

"What man named Juan?"

"It doesn't matter. That's just how they used to do it. When people knew about an evil bruja, they'd send out a man who was named Juan to capture her—any man named Juan. They're supposed to have special powers and could turn the bruja's magic back onto her."

"That doesn't make sense," I say. "Why do they have to be named Juan?"

Conchita shrugs. "Maybe it's because of the priest Juan Diego who was the first to see Our Lady of Guadalupe."

"I wonder if it would work with a guy named John," I say, though then there's the whole problem of him being alive, and you have to be dead to get into this ghost-town world we're stuck in.

Conchita gives me a thin smile that tells me she knows just what I'm thinking.

"It's not the same thing," she says. She pauses a moment, then adds, "What's most important with all this is that you have to have faith that it will work. You don't look for proof, you believe because you have faith."

"You're just supposed to believe?"

"Or not," she says. "But without faith, it's only stuff."

"Faith," I repeat. "Seems like believing in something without having proof that it's true would just weaken you."

She smiles. "Actually, it's supposed to be what makes you strong."

"How do you know all this stuff?"

"I don't. I'm just repeating things my abuela told me."

"So how did she know?"

"She was very superstitious. She saw signs in everything." Conchita sighs. "I used to laugh at her because of it, but then she died and I started getting into trouble, and now I'll never get to tell her I'm sorry."

She falls silent and I don't know what to say, so I just cover her hand with mine. When she leans against me, I put my arm around her shoulders and stare at the door in front of me.

Abuelo never talked to me about witches and their brujería; he only talked about cars and sports, and if he had a few too many tequilas, politics. I knew he had some beef with the Church, but he never talked about it at all.

To Mama, everything not blessed by the pope was witchcraft. Needless to say, that included hot rods, ink, and rockabilly.

Papa didn't stay around long enough to tell stories to either Tony or me.

As for me, I don't know anything about any of this: that los santos have magic, not just our prayers; that a bruja can leave her mark so strongly on the world that her handiwork reaches past death.

I also don't know exactly how I feel about the old lady on the other side of the door—besides nervous.

I should be pissed off. She's what's keeping me from being with my family in the afterlife—if that's how it works, though considering the fact that I'm here in the Alverson Arms world, after being shot twice in the chest, I'm pretty sure that some part of us goes on.

But maybe I should be grateful. If I hadn't come here, I'd never have met Conchita, and truth to tell, she's been as good a friend to me as Vida ever was. And if I hadn't met Conchita, who knows when I'd have found out about the two days a year that we can go back and walk among the living? I might never have met John.

It's all very confusing.

Finally, I get to my feet. I work my shoulder where I banged into the railing—that's going to bruise—then reach down and give Conchita a hand up.

"We should go," I say, "before the bruja changes her mind and comes out to turn us into donkeys or something."

"They can only transform themselves," Conchita says as we start down the stairs.

I glance back at the door.

"Well, if that's true," I say, "you'd think she'd transform herself into something that didn't look like it just crawled out of a grave."

Conchita laughs, but she makes the sign of the cross. After a moment, I do the same.

Henry spreads out a map of Santo del Vado Viejo on the table and uses a red marker to outline the borders of Solana, the part of town that the Alverson Arms world came from. It's the middle of May and we're in what Conchita likes to call Henry's "war room" because every time she does, she gets a rise out of him. Today it's just Henry and me in here. Light pours in from the windows and I'd rather be out there in the sun than in here with all the books and papers, but Henry had sent David to ask me to come by the library. Apparently, he's figured a few things out and wants to run them by me.

Henry puts down the pen and looks up at me.

"I need to back up a bit here," he says. "How much do you know of the history of this area?"

I shrug. "I don't know. Not much."

He nods. "Okay, that's not a problem. Can I assume you've heard of the Hohokam?"

"Vaguely. They're like some old Indian tribe, right?"

"Our Kikimi are descended from them and Puebloan peoples."

"You're not going to tell me that the Alverson Arms is built on some ancient Indian burial ground, are you?"

He laughs. "Hardly. I just want to give you some perspective. The Kikimi, or their ancestors, have lived here along the San Pedro River for some ten thousand years. Then the Spanish came with their land grants and pushed the native population back into the mountains where their rez is now."

"Okay, I sort of know all of that," I say. "What's your point?"

"Well, you know what happened next. It's what always happens. Businessmen from the east came for the copper in the mountains and the timber. They set up a train depot in the foothills—"

"Linden," I say. "I've been there. They have a vintage car show out there every spring. That, and the one at the Mountain View Motel, are the two big ones we have around here."

Henry nods. "The businessmen built Linden, and while they were at it, they took over Solona from the Spanish landowners and the rest of Santo del Vado Viejo grew up around it."

"Everybody knows that."

"Did you know that Hugo Alverson was one of those mining and timber barons?"

"And he would be . . . I don't know, the guy who built the Alverson Arms?"

"And the library," Henry says, "and also a big greystone foundry that's now the San Pedro Shopping Mall."

I frown, trying to picture the mall. Wednesday nights people will often have impromptu car shows in the parking lot.

"I don't remember any greystone building there," I say.

"That's because the foundry was destroyed in an explosion in the thirties. Anyway, all of that's just background. What's relevant to what we need to know is that his great-granddaughter was Abigail Alverson."

"I'm still not getting the point."

"She's the old woman you met in the penthouse. She has to be. Abigail Alverson lived there right up to where my records end and she had a son named Justin who died in Vietnam. She never left the apartment after that—apparently she was very active on the social scene—and then all mention of her stops."

"So she moved away."

"Possibly. But don't you get it? When she got the news about her son, she had a very public meltdown. There was all sorts of speculation in the society columns right after her son died, but then nothing. It's like she ceased to exist. Or . . ." He grins. "She found a way to no longer be noticed."

I hear the old woman's voice in my memory.

No one can see the penthouse floor. It's guarded and hidden from every living eye.

And that was true for me, too, until I died and came here.

"So you're going with the bruja theory, too," I say.

"The what?"

"Magic, witchcraft."

"Do you have a better explanation?"

I shake my head. "I don't have anything."

We sit for a while at the table, staring at the map, neither of us speaking.

"But we know a woman is responsible for what's happened to us," Henry finally says. "Remember the sleeper you talked to said *her,* not *him.* Can you think of a better candidate than Abigail Alverson?"

"Okay," I tell him. "Say she's the old lady in the penthouse. Say she's the cause of it all and we have it all figured out. Now what?"

"I don't understand."

"What are you going to do next?"

Henry shrugs. "Talk to her, I guess."

I shake my head. "You're forgetting. You can't get into the penthouse, and even if you could, she's got all this mojo that'll just throw you out again."

"Oh, right."

"Why's she doing this anyway?" I say.

Henry gives me a surprised look. "I think it should be obvious. From what you've told me, it's all about a mother's love. She's waiting for her son to come back and can't let go until he does."

"But he won't."

Henry nods. "No. Or it seems unlikely. He died overseas and he probably went on to wherever we normally go when we've died. So that means Abigail is going to sit up there in her penthouse waiting forever."

"I don't get it. Why's this so important to her?"

"You don't understand that a mother's love could be so strong?"

I think of how Mama doted on Tony. More often than not, I was just an embarrassment. The daughter who didn't attend church and would probably never get married. Who covered herself with tattoos and worked in a garage like a man. She'd asked me more than once if I was gay.

But none of that's Henry's business. His mother, from what he's told me, had her heart broken when he died, so he'd understand Alverson better than I ever could.

"I wonder where she got all this magic mojo power?" I ask instead.

Henry shrugs. "There've always been curanderos and brujos in this area. She must have convinced one of them to teach her what she needed to know."

"Too bad we don't have any around right now. They could tell us how to protect ourselves from her."

"You can always do what Conchita said: arm yourself with a cross or maybe the retablo of some powerful saint. Or better yet, a relic."

"Where are we supposed to find the relic of a saint?"

Henry shrugs.

"And what saint?" I ask. "God, there are so many."

Henry gives me another shrug. "San Pedro? The river's named after him so he has a strong connection to this area."

"If you're talking powerful saints," I say, "I think the more likely candidate would be the one that gave the city its name."

That's what Santo del Vado Viejo means: Saint of the Old Ford. The story is that, during a terrible storm which turned the San Pedro into a raging torrent that tore families apart, the saint appeared and helped reunite the families by ferrying them across in a little wooden boat that was miraculously unaffected by the wild water. When the storm was over, neither the boat nor the saint was ever seen again. But what proved he'd been a saint was that anyone who'd ridden in the boat with him was cured of any sort of ailment they might have had, from warts to blindness and, it was said, one man who regained a missing leg.

There's a monument to him downtown that's always swimming in flowers, photos, milagros—the prayers of the faithful and the curious—but to this date, no one actually knows his name.

"That's just a folktale," Henry says. "It's not like he created a new ford—there's been one here since ancient times—and if there was ever someone who helped people as happened in the story, I doubt he was a saint. If there has to be some religious connection, it was probably a priest from the mission and he wouldn't have been able to cure anybody."

"So you accept magic and witchcraft but not folktales?"

"Just because one impossible thing is true," he begins, "that doesn't mean every—"

"We're dead, aren't we?" I say breaking in with Conchita's argument to me earlier. "But here we are all the same."

I know he wants to debate it some more, but I also know that he realizes it doesn't matter. We already know things that shouldn't exist can be real—we're the proof of that—so where do you draw the line between impossible and possible?

"Maybe Conchita knows," I add.

"Maybe."

"But it doesn't really matter. It's not like we'll be going up to Abigail's door again, anyway."

"Unless," Henry says, "we want to end this."

I can see he's serious. That he really wants it. Maybe I'd feel the same way, if I wasn't able to see John twice a year.

"I've had this discussion before," I tell him. "With Conchita. How can we decide something like that for everybody? A lot of people like the way things have turned out for them."

"Have you specifically asked them?"

I shake my head.

I want to say, "And I'm not about to," but now he's got me curious. Sure, people like Edna and Ruth seem happy, but *are* they really?

And then it occurs to me that I shouldn't need to find the image of a saint. I've already got one on my skin—a portrait of my namesake, Our Lady of Altagracia. Except that didn't stop Abigail Alverson's mojo from throwing me through the door alongside Conchita.

Maybe Our Lady of Altagracia's not powerful enough.

Or maybe I was supposed to invoke her first.

I try to go back to my old life, but it's not the same. It can't be. Before May 1st rolled around and I found John waiting for me outside of Luna's, all I was trying to do was forget him. I wanted any thought of him *out* of my head.

How quickly things change. Now I just want to savor my memories as I count the days until another six months are up and I can see him again.

But it makes the time go slow.

Conchita and I finish up our work on that old '48 Ford in the high heat of summer. When we take it out for a drive along 26th Street, the engine's purring and every inch of the paint and chrome gleams in the bright sun. It's like it just rolled out of the showroom—well, so long as you don't look under the hood. I didn't feel like getting the original engine back into working order, so we popped in a Y-block that we pulled out of a '57 parked behind an adobe house on Ironwood Street.

It's funny. People gather on the sidewalk and cheer as we go by. We didn't tell anybody about the test drive, but I guess the unusual sound of a car motor coming down the street brings them out.

Looking at Conchita beaming in the shotgun seat beside me, waving at the friends and strangers who've come to see our inaugural run, makes me think of Vida. She'd be like Conchita, soaking up all the attention. Me, oh, I won't deny that I feel the glow of satisfaction with a job well done, but mostly I find it a little embarrassing to be the center of attention like this. At the car shows, I was always happier talking engines with the guys while Vida was the one posing for the photographers in one of her endless vintage outfits.

I also have to admit that my heart wasn't really into finishing the job. Working half an hour with John on the Willy's when I'd crossed over back in the spring still seems far more real than all the hours Conchita and I've put into this Ford. But at least the project kept me busy while the time passed.

The longer I'm here, the harder it is to engage. I can't help but feel that I'm pretending at life and I find myself doing what I told Henry I wouldn't, asking people what being here is like for them. Would they rather have gone on, even though no one knows what's waiting for us behind that last veil? If it was possible for them to go on now, would they?

I only get to ask a few before I notice a change in them. Like, take Edna. She was content before I brought it up, but now I find her restless. She'll be out walking in the summer heat, where before she'd be content playing cards at her kitchen table, listening to the R&B coming out of her tinny radio speaker, or sitting in her living room, gossiping with Ruth. Kit, who's a voracious reader, will be sitting on her lawn chair like she always does, but now the book's closed on her lap. When I talk to her, she keeps drifting off into her own thoughts. I'll find Irwin in the record store staring out the window, nothing playing on the stereo.

So I stop talking about it, because these people are my friends and just because I'm miserable with all the crap I've got going through my head, it doesn't mean they should be, too. But I can't help wonder: did they *really* never consider this before?

Getting through the next few months makes for the longest summer I can ever remember. Like somebody once said, "The trouble with doing nothing is you never know when you're finished." Night falls, morning comes. It gets hot, then hotter.

I play cards with Edna and Ruth, when we can get Edna to concentrate.

I hang out in the library with Henry, and David if he isn't practicing his piano scales.

I go to the record store and whenever Irwin gets too spaced out with his thoughts, I play DJ, looking for the music that will bring him back. It's usually British Invasion stuff, but not the bands that most people would think of first. Beatles or Stones? Not much reaction. But throw on something like "Honey I Need" by The Pretty Things and he'll usually sit up and take notice.

I think about John. A lot.

Conchita's with me most of the time. She, along with Henry and David, are the only ones I can talk to about why we're here and where we might have ended up if Abigail Alverson hadn't worked her mojo on the area. Or if we'd died someplace else.

Without them going all weird on me, I mean.

Except I notice that Conchita's more contemplative these days. She doesn't space out like Edna or Irwin, and she's still up for anything that might be fun, but a lot of times our conversations get serious—talking about the big ticket ideas like the meaning of life, or fate and karma—and they can go on for hours at a time.

I think of Shorty listening in on us and what he'd make of it. Me, who never had much patience for conversations that didn't center around cars or music. And Vida . . . well, she'd just roll her eyes and say something like, "It's life. You're supposed to live it, not talk about it."

Still, even here in the Alverson Arms world, time doesn't stand still. Eventually, the nights get cooler, the daytime highs barely crack 80, and the clear summer skies give way to clouds teasing rain that never actually comes. And then it's Halloween and Conchita's knocking on my door wearing a skeleton mask and carrying a paper bag.

"Are you going trick or treating?" I ask her.

"Depends on the treat," she says. She takes off the mask and laughs. "But this stuff won't come over with me, anyway," she adds.

"And you couldn't bring your treats back."

"That, too. Are you going to see John tonight?"

I smile. "I'd hate to be the person who tried to stop me."

"Consider me warned. And you're sure you don't want to try to get in to see the old lady again?"

I shake my head. "What's the point? All she has to do is wave her hand and her mojo kicks us out."

"I don't know. I've been making pictures of every saint I could think of."

She walks over to the dining room table and starts to pull them out of her paper bag. There are dozens of portraits, all painted in bright primary colors and decorated with bleeding hearts and crosses. They're more like the things you'd find in a kid's coloring book, but hanging around with Norm and watching him draw gave me an appreciation for the finer points of art that I might not have had otherwise. I can see the energy in Conchita's portraits—the emotion with which they were drawn.

"These are really good," I say. "When have you been making them?"

Because I don't remember her working on them.

She shrugs like it's no big deal, but I can tell she's pleased.

"Just last night," she says. "I started to think, if we did want to go by the old lady's apartment, they could be useful."

"Except we can't bring anything over."

"I know. I thought of that. I figured we could slip them under the door this afternoon, then they'd be there, waiting for us when the sun comes up."

I lay down the painting of San Pedro that I've been holding.

"I'll go with you if you really feel you need to do this," I tell her, "but I have to be honest. I'd much rather spend the time with John. We're only going to have the few hours we can grab before the sun rises and there's so much I want to do."

Conchita makes a kissing noise and I laugh.

"Oh, we'll be doing that, too," I say, "but I also want to get to know him better in a nonbiblical sense."

Conchita shakes her head. "It's always a disappointment."

"Not in this case."

We're both in a good mood, looking forward to when we can actually *feel* again. To be able to really taste what we eat and drink. By the time she leaves me at the corner of Camino Vajilo and 26th Street,

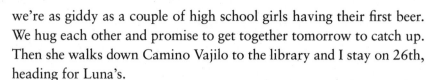

we're as giddy as a couple of high school girls having their first beer. We hug each other and promise to get together tomorrow to catch up. Then she walks down Camino Vajilo to the library and I stay on 26th, heading for Luna's.

It's only my third time crossing over, but I feel like an old pro now. I don't fret and worry. I just wait calmly at the place where I died. Eventually I get that weird feeling that's like the color blue with its sharp static charge, and I'm back. I have the sense of real weight—of *substance*—and take a deep smell of the spices and fresh tamales that fill the air with their heady scent. Juanes is on the stereo tonight, but I don't recognize the tune. He must have a new album out.

There was no one in the aisle when I arrived. Except for Estefan and his daughter Rosie, there's no one else in the store as I walk up to the counter and order my tamales. Rosie smiles at me, then goes back to the magazine she's reading, her head bobbing to the music. Estefan gets my tamales, but before he hands them over he gives me a curious look.

"I know you," he says. "You were here last Halloween."

"You have a good memory."

"<And again once in the spring,>" he adds, switching to Spanish.

I nod in agreement, eager to get my tamales and leave the store so that I can see John and have my pee. It's weird talking to Estefan with him not knowing who I am and that picture of me still on the shelf behind him. There are marigolds in the vase and new votive candles on either side. Sugar skulls and fresh *pan de muerte* litter the counter.

"<But I never see you come in,>" Estefan says.

Rosie looks up from her magazine, curious now.

"<You were busy,>" I tell him.

Estefan spreads his arms expansively and I watch my tamales go farther away from me. I'm so hungry I just want to grab them out of his hand and wolf them down.

"<Look at us,>" he says. "<Do we look busy?>"

"Pop," Rosie says, "don't give her a hard time. Sorry," she adds to me.

But Estefan's as unrepentant as he's ever been.

"<I'm just saying. You're not here, then *poof,* you're here.>"

"<Maybe I'm a ghost.>"

He starts to make the sign of the cross, then he catches himself and lays my tamales on the counter instead.

"<Some jokes are not so funny to everyone,>" he says.

"Pop!"

"<I know,>" I tell him. "<I'm sorry. I forgot about your friend. I meant no disrespect.>"

I see Rosie look at my picture, then at me.

"You remind me of her," she says.

I shrug and switch back to English. "We're both Mexican . . . we both have a lot of ink."

"No, it's more than that . . ."

"Well, I never met her," I say, unless you count any time I've looked in a mirror. "And I don't mean to be rude, but I'm running a little late. Can I pay for my tamales?"

"<Of course, of course,>" Estefan says.

I can feel them looking at me as I head out the door. I'm going to have to think of something else the next time I cross over. Maybe I can slip out the back door . . .

My thoughts trail off when I realize the Fairlane's not parked outside, waiting for me.

Worse than that, neither is John.

I swallow my bite of tamale, but I have trouble getting it down. My throat's suddenly too dry.

He's just late, I tell myself.

I go across the street and use the coffee shop's washroom. When I come out, I'm carrying two coffees. But the Fairlane's still not there, and neither is John.

And then I see Nina.

She darts across the street and before I can say or ask anything, she steps up and gives me a fierce hug. I give her an awkward one back, holding the coffees and tamales away from her so that I won't spill anything on her.

"It's so weird," she says, stepping back. "I mean, I saw you the last time, so I know this whole thing's for real, but it's still kind of freaky—in a good way, of course." She looks past me and adds, "Where's John? I was sure he'd be here with you."

"I was about to ask you the same thing. I guess he's running late."

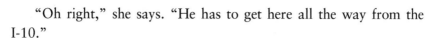

"Oh right," she says. "He has to get here all the way from the I-10."

"What are you talking about?"

She gives me a puzzled look. "Where he totaled the car . . ."

Her voice trails off at the look on my face.

"Oh, God," she says. "You don't know, do you?"

"Don't know what? What do you mean he totaled the car?"

But I do know. It's like my heart is running way faster than the rest of me. My chest is already tight and hurting.

"There was this eighteen-wheeler," she says. "It was coming the other way when the driver lost control. It jackknifed, then jumped the median and the whole back of the truck came down and . . . and crushed John's car. He was just coming over a hill when it happened and he never had a chance to get out of the way."

I stand there and stare numbly at her.

"John's . . . dead?" I finally manage.

"I'm so sorry, Grace. I thought you knew. I thought you guys'd be together . . ."

"I don't believe you," I say. "It can't be true."

But I know it is. I don't know Nina very well, but I think I know her well enough to know that she wouldn't make up something like this. And it's only something like this that would have stopped John from coming to meet me.

Dead.

How can he be dead?

I'm supposed to be the only dead person in this relationship.

I realize that Nina's talking to me, but I shake my head and walk away. She calls out, then starts to follow, but I pick up my speed until I lose her voice.

I feel sick. My mouth tastes like ashes and I can hardly breathe.

I drop my unfinished tamales and the coffees in a garbage bin.

It's this world. It's this damn world that makes you feel everything so much stronger. Your hunger. Your love.

Your broken heart.

My broken heart.

I look back and see Nina standing on the sidewalk, on the other side of the street I just crossed. She's about to come after me, but I shake my head. She holds my gaze for a long moment, then she finally nods. I wait until she heads back toward Luna's before I turn around myself. I start walking again because if I stop now I know I'll just collapse. I'll curl up in a ball on the sidewalk and lie there until the sun finally rises to take me away again.

I want to cry, but though my eyes burn, the tears won't come. It's like the desert that lies outside the city has crept in on the wind to claim me. Its dry breath fills my throat, my eyes. My heart.

I feel like there's a vast and empty expanse of badlands that stretches away inside me. A no-man's-land of rock and dirt and cacti scrabbling to survive. Turkey buzzards circle high above me in a sky so bright it hurts. I'm walking down a street in Solona, the night falling steadily around me, but inside the pain beats on me like the burn of a relentless sun. I can't see anything for blocks. There's only the white, blinding light as I stare into that unforgiving sun inside me.

After awhile, I don't want to say it eases, but the intensity lessens because I guess we can only bear so much pain before our bodies start to adjust to their new parameters. I remember Abuelo once saying that the human animal can adjust to anything. I never believed it before, but I do now. The loss hurts more than ever, but it's no longer a white heat. It's a yearning as big as that landscape I can feel inside me, that keeps spreading and spreading.

I can't bear it, but I have to. Just until the sun rises and I can cross back. When I get back to the Alverson Arms world, I'll welcome the numbness. I'll go to my apartment and lie down on my bed and I'll do like the other sleepers do: I'll just fall away and never feel anything again.

But then some of the things Nina said come back to me.

Where's John? I was sure he'd be here with you . . .

I guess he has to get here all the way from the I-10 . . .

Where he totaled the car . . .

I thought you knew . . .

I thought you guys'd be together . . .

John knows about May Eve and Halloween, the nights that the dead can come back—and not just from the Alverson Arms world. The dead can come back from wherever they go. But it'll take him time to come into town to meet me in front of Luna's. He must be on his way now.

We *can* be together.

I just have to get out there and find him.

I make myself focus on my surroundings. Once I orient myself, I set off for Sanchez Motors. As I leave central Solona, the streets begin to widen and the houses get farther apart, with dirt alleys running in behind them. The dusty yards get bigger, with mesquite and palo verde trees standing guard over junked cars, doghouses, and home-made shrines to the Virgin and various saints. Prickly pear and ocotillo grow alongside adobe buildings with white flaked paint and doors and sills painted blue. Occasionally, a saguaro rears up into the night sky.

The garage is dark when I get there, but a couple of dim spotlights on either side of the building are enough to light the lot. I recognize one of the cars parked against the building to the right of the garage. It's an old Ford of mine. Not the Fairlane. No, that's just scrap metal now. I try to make myself stop before I picture the crumpled metal . . . the body inside . . .

I bury that unwelcome image deep in the desert that the news of John's death opened up inside me and focus on the car. It's a '56 Ford Victoria with a beat-up body, but everything else had been in top run-ning order before I died, and since it's parked here instead of with the junked vehicles in back, I figure it's still in working order.

I need a car to get out to I-10. I could have hot-wired any of the vehicles parked along the curb on my way here, but this car was mine once and taking it doesn't feel so much like stealing.

Happily, it's still got plates.

I try the door and it's unlocked. Well, who'd steal a piece of junk like this?

I check the usual places to hide a key. When I can't find one, I bend down under the steering wheel to get the wires I need. But be-fore I can start it up, the passenger door opens. I look up to find Norm peering at me.

"Ms. Gracie?"

"Hey, Norm." I bend back down to get at the wires.

"You need to stop coming back," he says.

"I'm kind of busy here," I tell him.

"You keep coming back, some witch man is going to get hold of you and suck all your spirit away."

"A witch man. Right. I think there's an old lady who's already got that all sewn up."

"I'm being serious, Ms. Gracie."

"So am I."

That only stops him for a moment.

"And that's not all you've got to worry about," he goes on. "Other ghosts are going to try to drag you down into the mess they made of their lives when they were still alive. They'll be asking you to help fix things for them, even though there's nothing that can be done. But they'll get mad when you won't, or can't, help them, and they won't let it go. You get drawn into that kind of thing and you'll never find the path you need to take."

I sit back up again and look him in the eye.

"A path," I say.

He nods. "It's like the wheel of life. You die here and the path takes you someplace else, takes you to where you need to be next."

"Yeah, well, I don't get a path," I tell him. "All I get is a prison that's about six blocks square, with a free pass out twice a year."

"I don't understand."

"Welcome to the club. And here's something else: I just found out that my boyfriend's dead. So things being the way they are, I think I'll be coming back twice a year, and I'll be hanging out with his ghost, and there's not a damn thing you or anybody else is going to do about it. Not some witch man. Not some old lady waiting for her dead son. Not you or your ghosts."

"But—"

"And like I said, I'm kind of busy right now."

"But you need to find your path, Ms. Gracie."

He's starting to tick me off, which is weird. Back when I was alive, I always had patience for what everybody else thought was just made-up crap. But now that I know it's all real, listening to him is driving me crazy. And it doesn't help that all I can picture in my mind is John's ghost, walking alone along the I-10, trying to get here to see me.

"Why are you even talking to me?" I ask Norm. "I thought when you did, all the ghosts and monsters start paying attention to you."

"They do."

"So go away already."

"I'm worried about you."

"Well, you don't have to be. I'm dead—that's pretty much the end of the road in terms of bad things happening."

If you don't count your boyfriend dying on you, I add to myself.

"But that's just it, Ms. Gracie. If you don't get on the right path soon, more bad things *will* start happening to you. Things you can't imagine. Your spirit's a precious thing—don't let it be spent by things that are just going to use it, then throw what's left of you away."

I meet his gaze. He's sober and serious. I think about the old lady, Abigail Alverson, and the sleeper I met in John's bed when dawn pulled me back across the barrier between the worlds. He'd said:

We're all in her *head.*

The only relief is to give in.

Maybe that's what he meant. Maybe she was using us somehow to keep the Alverson Arms world going, like we're the gas and oil that keeps the engine running. But there's nothing I can do about that until I get back and right now I've got a different priority.

"Okay," I say. "I'll work on that. But now you need to go. *I* need to go."

He nods. "To get back on your path. Good."

"Right," I lie, just to get rid of him. "So if you'll just shut the door, I'll get this thing started and be on my way."

"A car can't take you where you need to go," he says.

"This one can."

I ignore the question in his eyes. Bending back down under the wheel, I find the wires I need and spark them together. The engine turns over, coughs a couple of times, but then it runs smooth. When I straighten up, Norm's still in the passenger door, looking at me. Something occurs to me, something I've always wanted to ask him.

"If you could live your life over again," I say, "would you want to change anything?"

"Oh, Ms. Gracie," he tells me, "I don't want to live my life over again. I just want to keep moving on to whatever's coming next. I think I overstayed my welcome here a long time ago. People like you and Jenny . . . people who treated me like I was a real person . . . you're few and far between."

"Don't be so eager to cross over, Norm. Take it from me, it's no picnic on the other side."

He nods. "Everything in its time. That's why I'm trying to tell you that you need to stay on your path."

In the back of my head I can feel a clock ticking. I can imagine John's ghost trudging along the freeway, trying to get to Luna's to see me.

"I will," I tell him. "I am. Now you need to step back, or get in, but either way, close that door."

"I can't go with you, you know that."

I shift into first and goose the gas pedal, keeping my other foot on the brake. The car lurches. It wants to get moving as much as I do.

"Good-bye, Norm," I say.

I pull out of the parking spot, leaving him standing there, the passenger door swinging. I reach over and tug it shut before I drive onto the street. In the rearview, I see Norm standing there, shaking his head.

I know he just wants the best for me, but I don't have the patience for what he was trying to tell me. He has no idea what this has been like for me. Let him die like I did. Let him die *where* I did and wake up to find himself trapped in a few blocks for eternity. Then he can talk to me about his paths and wheels.

Once I leave Sanchez Motors, I turn east onto a side street, heading for a connection to the I-10. I should have been at the on-ramp in minutes, but I forgot that, this being Halloween, the annual All Souls Procession is in full swing. The procession closes down Camino Presidio, all the way from 4th Street here in Solona to City Hall on the other side of the dry riverbed that becomes the San Pedro River for a few weeks each year.

Presidio is filled with thousands of people, lining the street, or walking and dancing as part of the procession. The air resonates with singing and shouting, and the rhythm of percussion, banged out on everything from simple tin cans and sticks to native skin drums and marching band instruments. Most people are in costume, with skeletons being the order of the day: skull masks, or skulls painted right on their faces. Rising up above the crowd are sculptures carried by the participants—fanciful skeletons, both human and animal—while walking on stilts are the catrin—dandy skeletons based on the art of José Guadalupe Posada.

The procession is to honor the dead, but over the years it's grown from simply celebrating friends and relatives who have died to ideas that have died, pets that have died, Death itself that has died . . . but all of it underlaid with a hope for tomorrow. For a lot of people, it's just a big party, and is that such a bad thing? With the world the way it is, everyone can use a little happiness shared with their neighbors.

I could sure use some, but I have somewhere else I need to be tonight.

I back into an alley and turn the car around. With the crowds and all the congestion, I can't get within two blocks of Presidio, so I have to go south on Mission Street until I can circle around the procession. I don't realize how close I am to San Miguel Cemetery until its large white public cross suddenly comes up on the right.

I drive past the cars parked alongside the road until I find a place I can pull over. I might not have had time to join the raucous celebration on Presidio, but I can't see driving by the resting place of my grandparents without stopping just for a moment to pay my respects. I haven't been here since Abuelo's funeral.

Throughout the graveyard I can see the flickering lights of lanterns and votive candles. Garlands of flowers twist around the front gates and papier-mâché skulls look down at me from the posts as I walk between them. Families are gathered around the graves having picnics of *pan de muerto,* dark sugar cones, and hot chocolate. Mariachi music plays from transistor radios, the thin music carrying in the still air.

I wonder if any of the people I see among the graves are like me: the dead come back for a visit.

Maybe they don't bother because nobody would recognize them anyway.

It's not something that ever would have occurred to me when I used to come here with Abuelo to pay our respects to Abuela. We'd rake the dirt around her grave and leave fresh flowers by her stone. At the end of October, Abuelo would put a fresh coat of white paint on the stone, though he didn't spend the night at her graveside as many families do.

I feel a twinge of guilt at the thought of how their graves will have been neglected, even though there was no way that I could come back to tend them. But when I make my way to the corner of the cemetery where they are, I find a surprise waiting for me. Someone has taken the time to paint the stones and rake the dirt free of debris and stones. There are marigold petals scattered in front of both stones with a pair of votive candles flickering in their glass containers on top.

I wonder who did it, because unlike the other parts of the grave-yard, there's no one here now. It's just me, and their graves.

I have to admit that I half-expected to find my grandparents here, my abuelo and abuela, holding hands, waiting for me. But they're not. And I wouldn't know what to say to them if they were.

"I miss you" seems so inadequate.

After a few moments, I focus on the grave on the far side of Abuelo's. I already know whose it is as I walk slowly over to it and go down on both knees in the dry dust, but that doesn't make it feel any less strange to be kneeling here, looking at this more recent grave.

My name's on the headstone.

The dates of my birth and death.

The words "She will be missed."

I guess Tony didn't bother to come home for my funeral either. If he'd arranged it, I would have been in the graveyard by Mama's local parish where she's buried. This must be Shorty's work. He and Vida are the only ones I ever got around to telling that I wanted to be laid to rest in San Miguel with Abuelo. It must have been Shorty who cleaned up my grandparents' graves.

He'd seen to mine as well. There's a votive candle on my stone with an image of Our Lady of Altagracia on the glass.

With my finger, I trace the words of my name etched in the stone, then stand up and brush the dirt from my jeans. When I turn around, somebody gasps.

Vida.

I haven't seen her in forever, but she looks pretty much the same as she did the last time I saw her. Her hair's longer, but it's still dyed blond, and she's as voluptuous as ever. Shorty once told her she had good childbearing hips and I remember holding my breath. It could have gone either way, but she laughed instead of slapping him.

"I'm sorry," she says now. "You took me by surprise. I thought you were someone else—someone who . . . who couldn't be here . . ."

It takes me a moment to figure out that she thought she saw me. My ghost. And that's exactly what I am, but she doesn't realize it, and I can't tell her.

"Did you know Grace?" she asks when I don't say anything.

I nod. "From a long time ago. I only just found out that she'd died."

"It was terrible. Just a stupid, stupid waste."

I nod again. My guilt's back. Why did I never try to see Vida? Of everyone I knew, surely she would have seen past whatever disguise death has put on me to see the friend she knew.

Except she doesn't recognize me right now.

"Were you good friends?" I ask.

"We were best friends. I feel so responsible for what happened to her."

"I thought she was shot in a grocery store."

"Sure, but she wouldn't have *been* there on her own if I'd just pushed a little harder."

"I don't understand."

"You know her abuelo died a couple of weeks before she did, right?" she asks.

My gaze goes to Abuelo's stone.

"Yeah, I'd heard," I say.

"Well, she was pretty broken up about it," Vida says, "as you can imagine, but instead of just dealing with it like she always did with a problem, she went inside herself. She'd go to work, but she hardly talked to anybody while she was there, and then it was straight home. No going out, no socializing, nothing. She even took up smoking again and she'd been so happy to have finally managed to give it up."

As soon as she says it, I wish I had a smoke. It's not something that ever occurs to me in the Alverson Arms world, which is kind of funny, because it's not like I'm going to die of lung cancer anymore.

"So what could you have done?" I ask.

She shrugs. "I don't know. *Something.* I could have gone over to her place more. I could have got her out. She didn't even enjoy *driving* anymore."

"I remember."

Vida gives me an odd look.

"Who'd you say you were?" she asks.

"Just an old friend."

"There's something familiar about you."

"I get that a lot," I say.

"Really?"

I don't need the suspicion in her eyes to know what she's thinking. With all my tats, it's unlikely that I'd be mistaken for very many people. But what can I say to her? I'm sick of lying, but the truth is too complicated and even if she did believe me, it would just freak her out.

"I'm sorry," I say. "I'd love to stay and talk, but I have to go meet my boyfriend."

She grabs my arm as I turn away.

"You're pretending to be Grace, aren't you?" she says.

Okay, *this* I wasn't expecting.

I look down at her hand and tug my arm away.

"Don't be crazy," I tell her.

She shakes her head.

"I don't know what you're up to," she says, "but it's not going to work. Yeah, you've got a bunch of tats, and maybe you even know something about cars, but nobody will believe you're her."

"I don't expect them to," I say, "because I'm not up to anything. Except to see my boyfriend."

"No, there's something going on here."

"Let it go," I say.

"Why? What are you hiding?"

"I'm not—"

"You know what night this is, don't you? Her ghost could be watching us right now, watching *you.* You won't get away with whatever you're trying to pull."

It comes out before I even realize I'm saying it: "Oh, for God's sake. When did you ever believe in that kind of thing?"

She takes a step back.

"You don't know anything about me," she says, but I can see a troubled look come into her eyes.

I want to tell her about the first time we got drunk in Jimmy Valez's garage. How she stole a lipstick from Jerry's over on Guadalupe, then felt so guilty, she had to sneak it back. How we spent the whole night once looking for Butch, her first and only dog, because after she lost him, she couldn't bear to replace him with another. No other dog *could* replace him, she said. She wasn't like her mother with her mother's endless parade of Chihuahuas.

I could tell her a hundred things that no one else could know, only I don't. But she sees something all the same. In my face. In my eyes. I don't know.

She makes the sign of the cross between us.

"Get away from me, evil spirit," she says. "Get away from the grave of my friend."

I want to laugh and ask her how she knows I'm evil, except my heart breaks to have Vida say such hurtful things to me. Why don't you recognize me? I want to yell at her. Instead, I turn around and re-trace my route through the cemetery. I know she's watching me and I wonder what she thinks when I get into that old '56 Vicky, because I know she'll recognize it. I bend under the steering wheel and spark the wires together. The Vicky starts up right away.

I look back into the cemetery. I can see Vida still standing where I left her, but she's too far away for me to read her expression.

Coming here was such a bad idea, I think as I pull back out onto Mission Street. This whole crossing over has been a disaster, right from the beginning.

I weave through a few cross-streets until I can finally get onto the I-10.

I *so* need to see John right now.

I keep one eye on the traffic, the other on the sides of the road, look-ing for that familiar figure walking back to Santo del Vado Viejo to meet up with me in front of Luna's. The traffic's light, so I don't need to concentrate on it the way you usually have to on the interstate, but mile follows mile and I don't see him, don't feel him.

Then I come over this one hill and I have to pull over to the shoulder.

This is it.

This is the place.

I don't know how I know it, but this is where John died.

I get out of the car and walk to the front of the Vicky. Leaning on the hood, I look down the hill. I can imagine John cresting the hill behind me, the eighteen-wheeler jackknifing, and there's nothing he can do about all those tons of metal coming down on the Fairlane.

My imagination is too good. The image of it is too real and I can't get it out of my head.

I push away from the car and start to walk along the shoulder of the highway. My boots scuff the dirt and gravel, sending the odd stone skittering out onto the asphalt. I get maybe a hundred yards away from my car when a voice calls out to me.

"Hey, dead girl."

I turn to see a man sitting on a nearby boulder. My night vision's good—the benefit of being dead, I guess—but though I can make out his features, I don't recognize him. He's just some old white guy, skin like leather, a shapeless hat on his head, thin grey-brown hair touching his shoulders. There's an old beat-up Army-issue backpack in the dirt at his feet. Cradled on his lap is a 4 X 5 field camera. I recognize it from photo shoots that Vida's done at the car shows. Some of the guys that come to them are vintage everything.

I cross the stretch of dirt and cacti from the car to where he's sitting.

"Hey, yourself," I say. "Who are you?"

He grins. "Shouldn't that be 'Who were you?' seeing as I'm as dead as you?"

"How do you know that?"

"How do you not when you look at me?"

"If that's some special superpower that ghosts have, I didn't get it."

He laughs.

"So what are you doing here?" I ask.

He shrugs. "It's Halloween and like a lot of other dead folks, I can't let go of the old life. I just have to keep coming back."

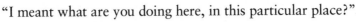

"I meant what are you doing here, in this particular place?"

He points to a cliff set back from the highway.

"I was trying to get a shot of the headlights coming up the interstate," he says, "and then I fell off those rocks and broke my fool neck." He shakes his head. "Man, I've hiked these hills since this was still just a two-lane blacktop, so you'd think I'd know better. But all it takes is one mistake."

I nod, thinking, I know all about mistakes. Like going for cigarettes and stepping into an armed robbery.

"How about you?" he asks.

"I'm just looking for my boyfriend's ghost. He died here a few months ago."

"Was he driving a black-and-red '50s Fairlane?"

I can't hide my surprise. "Yeah. How did you know?"

"I saw it happen. A big tractor trailer fell on his car. That was a sweet ride he had. A real vintage piece. But man, what a mess. The truck was hauling tomatoes and when that trailer of his burst open, it looked like the whole interstate was covered in blood."

"How could you have seen it happen?"

"I don't wander far," he says. "Even tonight, when I've got me real flesh and bone, what do I do? I hang around here."

"Did you see him tonight?" I ask. "The man who was in the car?"

He shakes his head. "No, he's not like us. He didn't stick around."

"What do you mean?"

"You know. He went on. Last thing I saw of him was him walking out of the wreckage—right down the middle of the highway—and then he was gone. I guess he went on to the big wherever instead of hanging on like you and me. But I'll tell you, he had a grin on his face like he was going someplace special. I almost felt like following him, but you learn pretty quick that one man's Paradise is another man's Hell."

"He thought he was going to see me," I say, more to myself than to this old desert rat. "He thought we were going to be together."

"Hey, no offense. I wasn't saying being with you would be Hell."

I give a slow nod and start to turn away.

"You can make that same choice yourself," he says. "Any time you want. None of us old haunts *have* to stay here."

I shake my head. "Yeah, well I don't have that choice."

"We all have that choice. Call it God, fate, the way the universe works. We chose to stay, but we can also choose to move on, just like we can choose to come back once a year and walk around with flesh on our bones."

"We get two of those free pass days," I tell him.

"Yeah?"

I nod. "Beltane's the other one—May Eve."

"Damn. I never knew that. Are you sure?"

I nod again.

"I have to go," I say, and this time he doesn't call me back.

I return to the car and give a last look down the stretch of interstate where John died. Abuelo always said, and I've believed it, too, that we make our own luck. But now I'm not so sure. Ever since Abuelo died, I've had one thing go wrong after the other. Even meeting John—now it feels like that was just setting me up for the way I'm feeling right now.

Until the old guy sitting over on the rocks told me that John had moved on, I've been holding myself together with looking for him. I was sure he was out here, somewhere along the interstate, making his way back to Luna's to meet up with me. But now . . . now I've got nothing. Just that big empty landscape inside me, stretching out into forever.

I don't know what to do, where to go. There are still hours until dawn and I don't know how I'm going to get through them.

Well, at least I can return the car to Sanchez Motors.

I turn away from the depressing view, but before I can get into the car, a police cruiser pulls off the interstate and parks behind the Vicky. The state trooper takes one look at me and his hand goes to the butt of his gun.

"Everything all right, miss?" he asks.

He's talking to me, but his gaze is everywhere, checking out the car, my tats, the ditch. I sneak a peek at where the old guy was sitting, but he's gone.

"Yeah," I say. "My boyfriend died here a few months ago. I was just stopping to pay my respects."

"My condolences."

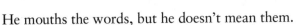

He mouths the words, but he doesn't mean them.

"Is this your car, miss?" he adds.

Do you see anybody else around here? I want to say. But I just nod.

"I'd like to see your license and registration."

"Why?" I ask.

"Just routine."

Routine, my ass. This is starting to seriously tick me off. But I pull out my wallet and then I realize I have a problem. When he runs my license through the system, my name's going to come up as deceased. But it's too late now. He already has his left hand out, reaching for my license. The right is still on his gun.

Well, what's the worst that can happen? Come the rising sun, I'll just vanish from wherever I am and end up back in the Alverson Arms world. Except . . . does that still work if you're not in the corresponding area in this world? What if the sun comes up and I'm stuck in some jail cell in the middle of nowhere?

I'd be free of the Alverson Arms world.

"Miss?" the state trooper says.

"My registration's at home," I say. "I didn't think I'd be coming out. But here's my license."

I hand it to him, then lean against the side of the Vicky, my arms folded across my chest.

"I'll just be a moment," he says.

I watch him return to his cruiser and input my driver's license number into his computer. I can see the exact moment when he reads what I know it's going to say, but he tries to play it cool. He gets out of the cruiser and comes back to where I'm waiting. It's not until he's too close for me to get away that he loses his smile.

"Hands on the roof of the car," he says.

"Why?"

He's good at his job, I'll give him that. Before I know what he's doing, he's got me turned around. He kicks my feet out and I have to put out my hands or go face-first into the roof of the car. He read me my rights as he pats me down, then it's hands behind my back and he slips a pair of handcuffs on me. He marches me back to the cruiser. Opening the back door, he pushes down on my head and forces me inside. With my hands behind my back, I sprawl across the backseat. By the time I'm sitting up, he's behind the wheel.

I don't even rate lights or a siren. He drives down the interstate until we come to a place where he can turn and take us back into town. I lean my head against the back of the seat and try to prepare myself for the interrogation to come. My only consolation is thinking about how they're going to deal with my disappearing from their locked cell when the sun rises.

If I disappear.

When we get to the station, I refuse to talk. They're like Vida. They think I'm trying to steal the identity of a dead woman and there's not much I can do to convince them otherwise, so why bother trying? They put me in a holding cell with some tough-looking women, but my tats and scowl make sure that they're not immediately in my face.

"<What're you in for>?" one of them asks me in Spanish.

She looks like a gangbanger's girlfriend with lots of ink, black hair teased to twice its size, tight capri pants, stiletto sandals, and a short midriff T-shirt that says "What are you looking at?" where it stretches across her breasts. I don't want to jump to conclusions, but she's probably a hooker.

"<Being dead,>" I tell her.

"<What?>"

I lick my lips and grin. "<It's the Days of the Dead—when we spirits can come back.>"

"<Yeah, right. You got some more of that crack you're smokin'?>"

"<What makes you think I'm high?>" I take a step toward her. "<What makes you think I'm not here to collect your soul?>"

She knows I'm bullshitting her, but she still makes the sign of the cross. And leaves me alone.

D.K.'s cousin Carlos told me that when you're on the inside you only get the one chance to make an impression. "If you're not stronger or tougher than the other inmates," he said, "then act crazier. Nobody wants to go up against a crazy person because you never know what they're going to do. They could bite off your nose, they could piss on your food. You could beat the crap out of them, but crazies don't feel the pain and it just makes them worse. So most people give them their space, you know what I'm saying?"

I didn't then, but I do now, because no one else tries to talk to me. Instead, I get to sit here on a bench by myself and think about how everything in my life's gone to hell. I want to concentrate on something other than the endless dead landscape that just stretches bigger and bigger inside me, but I can't stop thinking about John, and that keeps spiraling me down and down and down.

Dawn takes a few weeks to come.

When it finally does, I stand up in relief to face the corner of the holding cell. I lift my hand to the security camera and give whoever's watching the finger.

And then the Alverson Arms world pulls me back and I'm standing in the aisle of Luna's Food Market on 26th Street, giving the finger to nobody, with the shocked cries of my cellmates a fading echo in my ears. But now that I'm here in the place where I died, I let my hand drop. All my cockiness dies away as it comes back to me in a rush: I'm never going to see John again.

But that's not the worst of it. The worst is that the pain isn't so close and hard anymore. I hated it. I hated that bleak landscape that stretched away inside me. I hated the hollow ache where my heart used to be. But at least I was feeling *something*. This damned world won't let me actually feel my pain.

I'm not sure how I get outside, but when Conchita finds me I'm in front of Luna's, sitting on the pavement and hugging my knees, just like I was the first time we met. She sits cross-legged in front of me, just as she did that time, but now she takes my hands. She holds them for a long time before she finally asks what's wrong.

"Oh, Grace" is all she can say when I tell her. "I'm so sorry."

I nod, but I don't say anything. I feel like I've run out of words.

"I want to say it'll be okay . . ." Conchita starts.

Her voice trails off because we both know it won't. It'll just be more of the same.

Forever.

All because of Abigail Alverson—that damned witch in her penthouse apartment.

And then I know what I have to do. I have to put an end to the hold she has over me. She can keep her little world. She can keep whoever wants to stay here. But she can't have me anymore.

"I'm coming with you," Conchita says when I tell her.

I shake my head. "This isn't an adventure," I say. "This is the end. I'm getting out of here, one way or the other. Except for you, there's nothing for me here and I'm sorry, but that's just not enough anymore."

"I'm still coming."

I start to shake my head again, but she cuts me off.

"There's nothing for me here either, and you know it. You're the only friend I've ever had. What am I supposed to do when you're gone?"

"I'm not your only friend. What about Irwin and Henry and—"

"It's not the same. Everybody treats me like a kid except for you."

"You said you were happy here."

"No, I said it was better than where I came from."

I give a slow nod of my head, remembering now, and get to my feet. I offer her a hand up.

"Okay," I tell her. "Here's what I figure we'll need."

I'm a little late when I get to the short hallway in front of Abigail's apartment, but Conchita's not here yet, so no one has to know. I set down the box I'm carrying, but it slips the last couple of inches and lands with a clunk and clatter on the floor. I hold my breath, worrying that the witch might have heard me, but then I have to laugh at myself. She's a witch. If she's paying any attention, she knew I was on my way as soon as I started up the stairs. Banging this box around isn't going to make any difference, one way or another.

What's in the box? What isn't?

I've spent the last couple of hours scrounging about to find the things I figure I'll need to do my own protective mojo, so it's full of crucifixes, votive candles, cans of paint, painting supplies, some tools, and a retablo of San Juan that I noticed a few weeks ago in one of the apartments. I have no idea if it's enough, or even what the right way to go about using any of it might be. All we can do is play it by ear. But I do know that now that I'm standing in front of the door, I just want to get right to trying these things out like Conchita and I figured might work, only I have to give her a little more time to get here.

Fifteen minutes crawl by as I fiddle with the contents of the box, or sit there staring at the door. But finally I have to admit it: Conchita's not coming.

I'm disappointed, but I get it. If this doesn't work, it could be anything from a letdown to a complete disaster. And if it *does* work, well, who knows where we'll actually end up? We could end up somewhere a thousand times worse and find ourselves begging God or the universe to let us come back to this damned place.

But I wish I could have said good-bye to her. I know I tried to argue Conchita out of getting involved, but I was actually happy when she insisted on coming along. She's the best thing about this place. I'm fond of some of the others—like Edna, and Henry and Irvin—but Conchita's more like the soul sister I never knew I had. I've spent more time with her in the past year than I have with anybody else in my life except for Abuelo and Vida.

So it sucks that I didn't get to say good-bye. But I'm not going to go looking for her. If I do that, she'll just think I'm trying to guilt her into joining me and I don't want to put any pressure on her.

It's probably better this way, anyway. Now if I mess it up, nobody gets hurt but me.

I get up from where I was sitting against the banister and start to rummage through the box. The first thing I do is lay out the crucifixes along either side of the door. I light a votive candle and place it by the right doorjamb, then put the retablo of San Juan by the left with another candle. Using a screwdriver, I pry open a can of dark blue paint, then pour some into the roller tray. Taking the cellophane off a fresh roller, I roll it back and forth in the tray until it's loaded with paint, then I stand up. I wish I had some holy water, but I think what's important here is faith, not rituals. This isn't like some movie dealing with a vampire, where it doesn't matter what you believe—the crosses and the holy water and the garlic will work all the same. According to Conchita, that's just the articles of faith used as a gimmick.

The crosses I've brought, the one I'm painting, the tattoo of Our Lady of Altagracia on my shoulder—these aren't the fail-safes of fiction. They're here to help me connect to my faith—a faith, I have to admit, that I'm not sure I have. Or at least I don't think I have enough of it.

I sure didn't before I died, and whatever I did have, Mama chased away. But now . . . now that I know that the spirit carries on, well, I'm guessing there's a lot more to the Church than I was willing to accept before I ended up here.

But if los santos and God are real, well, why should they listen to me now? Why should they care about anything I might—

I catch myself. I can't go there.

I shape the stations of the cross with my free hand, then paint a long vertical line from the top of the door to the bottom. Refreshing the roller, I finish the cross with a shorter second stroke. I take off my jacket and lay my palm against the tattoo on my shoulder.

"Look," I say to Our Lady of Altagracia. "I know I'm not exactly the poster child for the Church or anything, but if you can hear this, if you can see this, you know I never intentionally hurt anybody. I've always tried to do the right thing. Now I just want what I was supposed to get when I died. I don't know if it's good or bad, but it's got to be *something* different from this."

I sigh, my gaze fixed on the cross.

"I know we're not supposed to ask things for ourselves," I go on, "and for sure we're not supposed to ask for proof, because that's what faith is about, right? So yeah, I want out of here, and I won't deny I'm hoping to see John and Abuelo and Mama. But mostly I'm asking for your help because this isn't right. This place, that bruja trapping us all in it. It's . . ."

I look for the word.

"Isn't it an . . . affront to how it's supposed to be?"

I don't get any kind of response, but I'm not really disappointed. Maybe my saint's just thinking over what I said. Maybe God's on another line and he'll get back to me. I think what was important was that I say it aloud. That I'm honest and show how I'm willing to face whatever's coming next, whether it's being stuck here, getting to go on into the mystery of what's supposed to come next, or having to deal with the freakshow witch on the other side of this door.

I pick up a paintbrush and start to paint smaller crosses in the quarters of space around the large one. When I'm done with them, I paint smaller crosses in the quarters of those crosses.

"Hey, Abigail Alverson," I say while I'm painting. "I know you're in there and I'm pretty sure you can hear me. I'm sorry about your kid and everything, but you know, other people have had that and worse happen to them, and they deal. They don't screw it up for everyone around them. Right now, you're being no better than one of those psycho guys who has to kill his wife and family before he can kill himself, when really, all he should do is go off into some field by himself and stick the barrel of the shotgun in his mouth.

"But no, he's got to bring them with him. Maybe he thinks he can keep tormenting them in the afterlife the way you're doing with us."

There's a feeling in the air now as though an electrical charge is building up, like when you see the dark clouds rolling in over the desert from the mountains and you know there's a storm coming. But instead of having it happen out in some wide open space, all that energy is concentrated in this one little hallway. The door and walls in front of me are starting to glow—except for where I've painted the crosses. There's a pressure in my ears.

"Okay," I say. "So maybe that's a little harsh, but come on. Even you waiting for your kid to come back makes it all about you, not him. Your boy died overseas in the war. Don't you think he'd want to go on from there? Do you really still think he should have to come home to Mommy first?"

I keep painting my crosses while I'm talking and they stand out, deep blue and stark against the glow of the walls and door. The paint hisses a bit when I apply it.

"Because he's not coming back. No more than John is, or my family, or anybody who's gone on. They've all gone to where we should be going. Because, like it or not, that's how it's *supposed* to be."

The door seems a little translucent, like it's there and not there at the same time. Dark blue lines appear, jumping from the points of my crosses to join each other and spray a network of crisscrossing lines from one side of the wall to the other, floor to ceiling.

For a long moment all I can do is stare at them, amazed that this is working. Or at least that *something*'s working.

"I've got to tell you," I go on finally, "I feel sorry for Justin, growing up with you. I'm sure you loved him—I guess you still love him—but I'm thinking, if you were anything back then like you are now, you must have choked him with that love. Man, he must have jumped at the chance to join up because it meant he was getting away from you."

The wall and door suddenly vanish and I'm staring into Abigail's apartment. She stands right where the door used to be, inches from the network of lines connecting my crosses, and still looks like the walking dead. I remember what Conchita said.

A bruja has no limit to her magic except that she has to take complete responsibility for her actions and she has to be willing to submit to the consequences. So maybe that's why that old woman looks the way she does: whatever magic she's doing is coming back on her.

But if most of her looks like the walking dead, her eyes are alive and burning with anger—hot and dangerous in that cadaverous face.

"How dare you," she says. "How *dare* you talk about my son in such a way."

It's all I can do to hold my ground and not back up against the banister.

"Jeez, I don't know," I tell her. "What gives you the right to fuck around with *our* lives?"

"You foul-mouthed harridan. You have no idea the sacrifices I have made."

"I'm guessing goats and chickens under a full moon. Maybe a couple of babies, too."

"I would never harm an infant."

"Screw you, lady. There's a baby that was found in the back of a Dumpster that's always going to be what it is now. Newborn and dead, but unable to move on."

"I didn't kill it."

"No, you're just torturing it by keeping it here."

"You have no idea what—"

"You think your son wants that? Justin's dead, too, but I'm guessing he can probably see what a horror show you've put together in his name. And you know what? Even if he could come back here, I doubt he'd ever want to."

"Don't you dare presume to tell me what my Justin will or won't do."

"Yeah, well, let me go and you won't have to listen to me anymore."

"I can do better than that," she says.

She does the brushing off thing with her bony hand and I flinch, waiting to be sent ass-over-heels down the stairs. But nothing happens.

Thank you, Our Lady of Altagracia, I think. If I ever get to a place where I can do it, I'll light a dozen candles in your name.

Abigail looks like she's about to have a stroke, she's so pissed. Veins bulge and pulse in her temples. Narrowing her eyes, she makes another brushing off motion with her hand, but this time more forcefully. That doesn't affect me either.

We stare at each other for a long moment until, just like that, she goes calm.

"I take so little energy from you," she says. "Just enough to keep myself here for Justin."

I clear my throat. I won't pretend I'm not still anxious, but I know I have to do my best to hide it from her.

"Yeah," I say. "So what? That still doesn't make it right."

"No, but it does make me powerful. Especially when I can draw on every one of you, all at once, and take as much as I wish."

Oh, crap. I had no idea how this works. But if she can feed on everybody trapped in this sorry little world, all of them at the same time, unprotected, unsuspecting, juicing her mojo . . .

I am so screwed.

I brace myself for whatever she's going to throw at me next because I know it's going to be bad.

She reaches her hands out and clenches them into fists, like she's grabbing some invisible thing. I feel a worrying all over my skin, trying to burrow inside me, but if she's trying to suck anything more out of me, Our Lady's stopping her, because the sensation stops. I feel a momentary relief, but the old lady just gives me a knife-slash smile and grabs at the air again, reforming her fists.

This time it starts like when you're sanding metal—you know, how you can feel the little specks bouncing off your arms and your face mask?

Thousands of tiny sharp bits of her mojo are pinging against my bare skin and right through my clothes. As each of those invisible little specks hits me, they burrow under my skin like millions of tiny deer ticks. Then I feel them coming together inside me to form . . . I don't know what. Something dark and oily that itches, then hurts. *Really* hurts.

It's all I can do not to tear at my skin with my nails.

She's still smiling—that slash of dark humor on her skeletal face makes my stomach lurch—and then I know this is just the start.

I honestly don't know what would have happened if we hadn't been interrupted. Maybe whatever her mojo was putting inside me would have eaten its way out, right through my skin. Maybe I would have exploded, splattering bits of me all over the walls.

But there's a noise from behind me and the feeling ebbs just a little. Abigail's gaze leaves mine and goes past me. I turn to look.

I guess I'm expecting zombies to be shambling up the stairs, given how Abigail looks like the queen of them, but what I see is even more surprising. I think the whole population of this weird Alverson Arms world is crowded into the stairwell below me. This has to be Conchita's doing and it sure explains why she wasn't here to meet me earlier.

But she's here now, standing right at the front of the crowd, with Edna and Ruth directly behind her. Everybody else fills the stairwell behind them: Kit, Irwin and David, the two of them supporting Henry between them—they must have carried him up the stairs—and so many others. Some I've never seen before, most I've at least glimpsed at one time or another. I even see paranoid Frankie and I wonder how Conchita ever managed to convince him to show up.

Conchita is holding up a sheaf of her saint drawings. Edna has a Bible, Ruth a crucifix. But the religious artifacts vary from the Catholic to Edna's Baptist Bible to someone holding up a Koran. Henry's got a copy of Darwin's *The Origin of Species,* Irwin's got a vinyl copy of the first Beatles album. I guess people brought whatever they believe in— the relics and objects that give them faith.

If that's what it takes, maybe I should have brought something with a Ford Motor Company logo. But while I have faith in an old Ford, it's not Faith. The Beatles might have spiritual importance to Irwin, or Darwin's book to Henry, but at the end of the day, an old car's an old car, and I don't feel a spiritual connection to it.

And sadly, while I know it should be different, I don't have much faith in the Church either. Not like Ruth does in her Baptist roots, or Conchita in the Catholic Church and its saints.

But Abigail has whatever conviction I lack, and she has it in spades. She believes in her mojo. She believes this pathetic little world she's created is going to bring her son back to her. Hell, maybe it will. She made it, didn't she? If she can do that, why *shouldn't* she be able to make her son return to his old home on 26th Street?

When I turn back to look at her, I can see that she knows that what little faith I might have mustered is already faltering. She's got that awful smile slashed across her face again.

"You couldn't have known," she says to the crowd below, "but you really should have chosen someone with more conviction to lead your confrontation. But as it is . . ."

And there you have it. My heart sinks. Sure, Conchita's managed to round up all of these people to join this little rebellion of ours, but since it depends on me, it doesn't mean a damn thing. I'm the weak link, and because of me, we're all screwed.

Abigail lifts her hands again. It looks like all she's doing is grabbing fistfuls of air again, except I know what's really happening. I'm ready to feel her mojo burrowing under my skin again and I brace myself for it. But behind me is the little ragtag army that Conchita has raised. They haven't experienced the witch's power firsthand yet.

Yelps of pain and surprise rise up in a chorus from them and that just pisses me off.

Abigail Alverson has no right to do this to them.

I'm the one who decided to stand up to her, and I'll be damned if the rest of them are going to suffer just because of me.

"You want conviction?" I ask Abigail.

I reach down into the box of paint cans and tools I brought with me and grab an X-Acto blade.

"What are you doing?" Abigail wants to know when I click the blade out of its casing with my thumb.

The push of her mojo grows stronger, twisting and clawing its way still deeper inside me. It's like oil fresh out of the can, thick and black and slow, but at the same time there's a sharpness to it that's as keen as the edge of the X-Acto blade in my hand.

I know that these crosses I made are all that's holding Abigail back from just brushing us off the way she did to Conchita and me last May. The crosses and Bibles and Korans and crucifixes and whatever else everybody in the stairwell is carrying—mostly, it comes down to our faith. But all of this still isn't enough. Some of her mojo is still getting through.

"Maybe I *am* the weak link," I tell her. "Maybe I don't have the faith of a saint or a martyr."

But I'm thinking, if I'm the meeting point, the center of the prism that's supposed to focus all this energy against her, then I need something powerful to help me do just that. The thing is, I've only got one thing to offer up.

"But this is something I share with the saints and martyrs," I say.

"Grace, no!" Conchita cries from behind when she realizes what I'm about to do.

Abigail doesn't waste time saying a thing. She just increases the pressure of her mojo.

But they're both too late.

I run the blade of the X-Acto knife across my bicep, right over my tat of Our Lady of Altagracia. I don't cut too deeply, but it's deep enough to spurt blood. There's no pain—maybe that'll come in a moment. Dropping the knife, I wipe my palm across the wound, then I step up to the blue cross I painted on what's now an invisible door. I smear red, bloody streaks onto it, up and down, then left to right. Making a second cross on top of the first.

The red blood turns purple against the blue, hissing and sparking like I'm using a welding torch. I feel like I'm filling with light and I know I'm on the right track now. The light burns away whatever crap it is that Abigail's trying to shove inside me, all her greasy mojo, heavy and slow, but it still cuts as sharp as a fistful of razor blades.

It really is all about the blood, I realize, my head filling with a wave of understanding that seems to come from somewhere outside of me.

Blood.

The blood of saints and martyrs.

The blood of Christ.

The literal blood that sustains our lives, and the blood of the lamb that sustains our souls.

I'm not saying I'm a saint or a martyr. But like anybody else, I've got blood, and no matter what a person believes or doesn't believe, that blood is sacred. It's what keeps us alive. It's the gateway to life and connects us to every living being. To the seas and the land, to the whole damn planet.

Which is another way of saying that it connects us to God.

Against the sacrifice of blood, a bruja's ugly little powers turn to dust. Because the sacrifice of blood is the more potent magic. But more to the point, all of us, each and every one of us, are magic.

I remember telling Conchita that I had no magic, but as I cut myself and smear my blood on the blue cross, I realize that isn't true. Not only do we all have magic, it's all around us as well. We just don't pay attention to it. Every time we make something out of nothing, that's an act of magic. It doesn't matter if it's a painting or a garden, or an abuelo telling his grandchildren some tall tale. Every time we fix something that's broken, whether it's a car engine or a broken heart, that's an act of magic.

And what makes it magic is that we *choose* to create or help, just as we can choose to harm. But it's so easy to destroy and so much harder to make things better. That's why doing the right thing makes you stronger.

If we can only remember what we are and what we can do, nobody can bind us or control us.

Especially not now, when we've stepped beyond the confines of the living world to a place where mind and spirit are all that matter.

I meet Abigail's gaze and I see something else in her eyes besides the blind anger. It takes me a moment to realize that it's fear. Because now she knows that I know exactly what we've been dueling with here.

"You have no idea what you've done," she tries to convince me.

Not exactly. But does it really matter? The itch is gone from my skin. The mojo's not crawling around inside me anymore. I don't feel like I'm filled with light anymore, but the memory of it lingers, making me feel strong and pure. Though it doesn't stop my arm from bleeding.

I grab a clean rag from the box by my feet and try to tie it one-handedly around my bloody arm. Before I make a total mess of it, Conchita shows up at my side and does it for me.

"Someone should lock you away before you really hurt yourself," she says, but she's grinning.

She ties the rag tight around the wound, then tucks the loose ends into the folds.

"This has to stop," Abigail says.

I turn from smiling at Conchita to look at the witch.

"Get real," I tell her.

"If you continue to cut me away from the energy I need," Abigail says, "this small semblance of a world will fail and blow away like dust."

"Yeah, so what?"

"Are you sure everyone thinks as you do?"

I jerk a thumb over my shoulder. "They're here, aren't they?"

"Damn straight we are!" I hear Henry yell up from the stairs behind me.

"Many of the inhabitants are here," Abigail agrees. "I'd say at least half."

"Half . . ." I start, then I realize where she's going with this.

Crap. We're back to that argument again: How can some people decide what's right for everybody?

"So, what are you saying?" I ask.

"It's simple," she says. "You've won. I will let you go—any of you who wish to go. But allow those who wish to remain the freedom of their choice. Allow them to sustain me, and so this world."

"Just like that."

She nods.

"Why are we supposed to trust you?"

She draws herself up, standing with her back straight, her eyes flashing. God, but she's an ugly piece of work.

"If I give you my word," she says in a stiff voice, "I cannot break it. Not without . . . dire consequences to myself."

"Yeah, right."

"Actually, she is right," Conchita says. "My abuela said that a bruja can't break her word. She can do any number of despicable things, but if she gives her word and then breaks it, all her magics come apart."

I look at Abigail.

"Which means," I say, "whatever's keeping you alive stops working its mojo."

I don't frame it as a question, but she nods all the same.

"So, what happens?" I ask. "You turn to dust like you were supposed to fifty years ago?"

"I," she says, "and this place I've brought into existence."

I turn to Conchita. "Are you sure you're remembering your abuela's stories right?"

She nods. "Her stories are all I have left of her."

I look down the stairs to where the rest are listening, waiting. I don't have to ask them what they think. I can see in their eyes, and from the way that they stand, that they're leaving the decision up to me. Edna gives me a thumbs-up and smiles.

"Okay," I say, turning back to Abigail. "I guess we've got a deal."

"Then take down the protective crosses."

"Um . . . I have no idea how to do that."

She shakes her head. "You simply will their power to wane."

"Right."

I stare at the main cross, two messy slashes of blue with the purple cross made from my blood inside it. I put my hand on the bandage on my arm that covers both the wound and my tat of Our Lady of Altagracia, my namesake.

Thank you for all your help, I think, directing my thoughts to her. Thank you for letting me help these people who trusted in me.

I imagine the protection Our Lady lent me fading, and damned if that isn't all that it takes. The transparent walls and door become solid again. They're plaster and wood with crosses of blue paint and blood on them. From behind me I hear a kind of collective gasp from the people on the stairs and I get what they're feeling because the whole thing's kind of freaking me out, too.

I can't believe I'm still standing here.

I can't believe we actually pulled this off.

The door opens with a loud creak and though I know we've won,

I still flinch when Abigail's actually standing there in front of me, in the flesh—or at least whatever flesh she's got left on that ghastly body of hers. But more to the point, the doors are open, the crosses gone. There's no protection between us anymore.

"We must bind our agreement," she says. "Your blood to mine."

She uses the fingernails of her left hand to slash across her right palm, then offers it out to me. There's still blood on my own palm.

I hesitate for a moment, then take her hand.

As soon as our palms touch, there's this huge dark rush in my head, like I've had a car blanket thrown over my head. I get this horrible, dropping feeling of vertigo and the air seems like it's filled with static electricity.

I try to pull away but her grip is like a vise.

Easy, her voice says in my head. *We are only binding our agreement. Your saint's light is as discomforting to me.*

Um . . . right.

I try to say the words aloud, but my lips don't work and the words just bang around inside my head. But she seems to hear me all the same.

Any who choose to leave, may leave, she goes on. *I will hinder no one's departure. But any who choose to stay, you will respect their decision.*

Though that doesn't mean I can't try to convince them, right?

She hesitates, then concurs. *So do we have an agreement?*

And you won't hurt any of us.

Agreed.

Then sure. We've got a deal.

So on our blood, let it be done.

Except I have a thought.

Wait a minute, I add. I close my fingers around her palm before she can let go of my hand. *What about any new people that show up here? They get the same choice, too, right?*

The darkness in my head turns into Abigail's cadaverous face. It's like she's just inches from me, her eyes blazing.

We have an agreement, she says. *Don't presume to change it now.*

I want to crawl away to some place deep inside me where she can't reach, but I don't think there is such a place. And crawling away's not going to help anybody else who might happen to die in the vicinity of the Alverson Arms building. So I gather up the tatters of my courage.

I'm not changing it, I tell her. *This is just how it's supposed be.*

Then you should have thought of that earlier.

You want to go head-to-head again? I ask.

She's pissing me off and that swallows my fear. But all my little threat does is turn her own anger to steel.

Don't think for a moment, she says, *that you or your saint have any real power over me. You caught me by surprise—once. It won't happen again.*

But I remember the insight I had when I took her down earlier. How doing the right thing makes you stronger.

You're not scaring me, I tell her. *I know I'm in the right.*

She laughs.

Oh, but you should be scared, she says, her voice touched with a cold humor.

A moment ago it seemed like her face was directly in front of me. Now she's all I can see—like there's nothing in the world except for her.

Right, wrong—they mean nothing here, she goes on. *This is my creation. Here, there is only power, and I have enough in the tip of my little finger to turn your soul to ash and blow it so far and wide that your saint will never find enough to put you together again.*

I . . .

You will do nothing, Abigail informs me like it's a done deal. *You will take your small victory. You will walk the few blocks west on 26th Street to where the mists will now be your door to freedom. I will leave that passage open until the last of you who have chosen to leave are gone. Then I will close it, and it will stay closed forever.*

"Now *go!*"

She says the last words aloud and lets go of my hand. I stagger back, disoriented to suddenly be outside of my head and back in front of her apartment.

"Grace?" Conchita asks. "Are you okay? What just happened?"

I can't respond. I can't even look at her. All I can do is hold Abigail's hateful gaze.

"You bitch," I say to her.

She smiles. "And you are still foul-mouthed, but it changes nothing. We have our bargain."

Then she steps back, the door slams in my face, and I'm staring at the crosses instead of Abigail's awful features.

"What's going on?" Conchita asks.

I give my head a shake and muster up a smile for her.

"Nothing," I say. "She was just inside my head and it creeped me out." I give Conchita a light tap on the shoulder with my fist. "Don't look so worried. We won, right?"

"No, you won. You did this for us."

"No way. If we hadn't all been in on this together, she would have blown me right out of the building with that mojo of hers."

I turn to face the crowd in the stairwell. They've been so quiet that I hardly recognize them. Like, take Henry. When did he ever not have something to say? But he's there with the rest of them, looking up at me, expectant.

"Did you hear that?" I ask them. "We beat the old witch because we all stood up to her together. And now we're free!"

A big cheer rises from them, fists pumping the air.

I put my arm over Conchita's shoulder.

"Let's get the hell out of here," I say.

There's no mass exodus for the passage that Abigail opened for us at the south end of 26th Street. Even with the choice of whether we go on or stay having been put in our own hands now, even knowing that the old witch is feeding off us every moment that we're here, no one seems in much of a hurry to leave.

I can't explain it. But any time of the day or night you'll find one or more people there at the end of the street, staring into the mist. Some of them stand together and talk about what might be on the other side. Some keep to themselves, studying the grey wall, keeping their thoughts to themselves. When people do go, it's usually a private moment. No one sees them leave. One day they're just not around anymore and you realize that they must have gone into the mist.

That's how Kit went. One day she's sitting out in front of her house on El Canto Street, the next her lawn chair's still there, but no one sees her again. There's a book on the chair, her place marked about two thirds in. She didn't even stay long enough to find out how it ends.

Edna and Ruth went together.

Irwin slipped off on his own, but he left us a note in the record store.

Frankie was one of the first to go, but I think the only reason he went was because Conchita told him there were no cops on the other side of the mist. If he stepped through, he'd never have to be looking over his shoulder again.

By the end of November, I think only about a third of the Alverson Arms world residents are left—those that are mobile, I mean. None of the sleepers have woken up and I guess they're what's giving Abigail the main juice to keep this place up and running.

Conchita and I are at the gateway with Henry. David's long gone, but Henry wanted to get his notes in order before he left, God knows why. It's not like anyone's going to use them. We all know what this place is and how we came to be here. We all know how we can get out.

Henry probably would have chosen a private exit, but there's a curb in front of the mist and crap on the sidewalk, and no way his electric wheelchair can deal with either. He needs help getting up the curb.

"You want us to give you some privacy?" I ask after we've muscled his chair up from the road.

"For what?" he asks. "I'm just going into the mist. It's not rocket science and it's sure not anything I need to do with no one watching."

"We're going to miss you," I tell him.

I am, too.

He nods.

"When are you going?" he asks.

I shrug. "Soon."

He studies me for a long moment and I realize he knows exactly why I'm staying.

"Sometimes you need to look out for yourself," he says.

"I know."

"Okay, then . . ."

None of us say anything for a long moment. Finally, I give him a hug. Conchita gives him a hug. Then we stand back with our arms around each other and watch him roll his chair into the mist.

I've seen this a couple of times now, but I never get over how anti-climactic it is. There are no bright lights. No choirs of angels. No distant rumble of thunder. Not even a static charge in the air like there is when Abigail's working her mojo.

It's just, one moment the person's here, the next they're not.

And the only other thing that's different is how we feel, those of us left behind.

It's going to be weird not having Henry hanging around in the library, making his notes, coming up with his theories. Almost as weird as how empty Edna's apartment is whenever I walk by its door.

"What did he mean?" Conchita asks.

I turn to look at her and play dumb. "About what?"

"About you needing to look out for yourself. You're not staying on just for me, are you? Because I'm ready to go any time. We can go right now."

I shake my head. "No, it's me. I'm not ready to go."

I don't add "But you should go," even though I think she should. The problem is, I can't tell her that without telling her why I have to stay, and then I know she really won't go.

I don't want to be alone, but she deserves more than this. I keep thinking that any day now she'll be ready to go ahead on her own. She won't know it, but I just won't be following.

Conchita steps back to look at me.

"You're not planning to go at all, are you?" she says.

"I . . ."

So much for keeping her out of the loop.

"I know you're not scared about what might be coming next," she says. "I don't think you're scared of anything."

"You're wrong. Lots of things scare me."

She ignores that.

"So what is it? What aren't you telling me?"

"It's nothing."

"I thought we were friends," she says.

"Come on, Conchita. Don't do this."

"Don't do what? Get mad because you're keeping secrets from me?" She cocks her head. "What did that old witch tell you when she grabbed your hand?"

"Tell me?"

"Oh, come on. Now I know you're playing stupid. You don't think I already know she was talking to you in your head?"

We've had all our usual conversations in the weeks since we faced Abigail. We've talked about stuff we've done, people we knew, just goofed around like we always do. We've had our serious discussions, too: What's waiting on the other side of the mist? Is life really a wheel like Norm told me the last time I saw him? How weird it was meeting Vida at my own grave. How strange Conchita finds it to be so much older than the kid she appears to be. How much I miss John.

But we've never talked about that last moment I had with Abigail. Conchita never asked and it wasn't something I wanted to share.

But now?

Because Conchita's right. We *are* friends. We shouldn't have secrets between us.

So I tell her.

We sit on the curb across the street and she doesn't say anything for a long time after I'm done. She just stares into the mist and picks absently at a loose thread on the seam of her jeans. But finally she sighs and turns to look at me.

"And when were you going to let me in on all of this?" she asks.

When I hesitate, she shakes her head.

"Goddamn it, Grace!" she says. "You weren't going to tell me at all, were you? You were just going to be all noble and self-sacrificing about it."

"It wasn't like that."

"Then what was it like?"

There's no give in her today. She's going to make me come out and say it, and I can't blame her. If our roles were reversed I'd have done the same.

"Okay," I say. "I was keeping it from you because I didn't want you to be stuck here, too."

Because that's how I'd worked it out. My agreement with Abigail said the passage would stay open until the last of us who'd chosen to go through it left. So I figured, if I didn't leave, then the passage would stay open for any new people who would find themselves trapped here. My being here would keep it open forever.

"It doesn't have to be like that," Conchita says. "We could just leave a message. We could spray paint it on the wall of some building."

"And if that building changes because somebody on the other side dies in it?"

"Then we'll paint the message on a whole bunch of buildings."

I nod.

"And if Abigail comes along and gets rid of every message we leave?" I ask.

"You've already done this, haven't you?" she says. "You've figured out everything that could be done, then scratched them off the list, one by one."

"Pretty much," I say. "I've gone at it front, back, and sideways and I can't see another way. Someone has to stay here to tell the new arrivals the real score and show them the way out."

"Do you really think she'll let us do that?"

I don't have to ask who Conchita means by she. There's only one witch here with all the mojo. One Abigail Alverson.

"She has to," I say. "Unless she breaks her word."

"And then all of this is gone anyway."

I nod. "And it won't be our problem anymore."

I stand up and offer her a hand up. Once she's standing, she brushes dirt off the seat of her jeans, looks up and down the street, then gives me a grin.

"So what do you want to do?" she asks. "Rebuild another old car?"

One thing I've learned after being here for this long is that the few blocks around the Alverson Arms are a lot safer that I ever would have guessed. I'm not saying nobody ever loses their temper or that there aren't any fights. I can remember guys getting into it outside the Solona Music Hall back when I was still alive, the fistfights sometimes escalating into knifings, especially when some psychobilly or metal

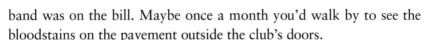

band was on the bill. Maybe once a month you'd walk by to see the bloodstains on the pavement outside the club's doors.

But most people in this area die by accident, it seems, or of natural causes, and even then there aren't a whole lot of those. Conchita's murder and the way I died are pretty much the exception to the rule.

The whole time I've been here, there have only been three arrivals and they were all old folks who'd died in their sleep. And apparently not one of them had any interest in being here because they never got out of their beds. They turned into sleepers and the only way we ever knew that they'd arrived was because the buildings they died in changed when they crossed over.

It's quiet in the weeks after Henry leaves, and Conchita and I have our talk. We miss Henry and Irwin. We still go to the library and play music in Irwin's store, but it's not the same. The hollow feeling we always carry around on this side of life is stronger since everybody's gone. Lots of times I'll end up standing at the end of El Encanto Street, staring into the mist, thinking about John. When Conchita finds me there, she doesn't say anything. She just takes me by the arm and leads me home.

I live across the hall from her now, up above the record store, because the Alverson Arms gives me the same creeps it gave everyone else. Plus there doesn't seem to be much point living there with Edna gone, and knowing that old bag is up on the top floor.

It's another couple of weeks before we get someone new. One day Marshall's Vacuums & Electronics is just like it always is, full of quaint-looking old radios and cleaners that must have seemed very modern back in the sixties. The next morning it's changed into a gallery I remember from when I was alive. Conchita and I go inside to find a man sprawled in the middle of the retail space, his head set at an impossible angle from his shoulders. There are broken pots and jars and sculptures scattered all around him, pottery shards and too many pieces of little clay Mexican dandy skeletons to be able to count. A tiny skull here, some arms and legs over there.

We walk carefully, trying not to step on any of them.

The man's Mexican, in his mid-forties, brown-skinned, dark-haired, and in pretty good shape for a guy his age. He's wearing a white shirt and jeans and doesn't have any ink. At least none that I can see. There's a ladder on the floor, running off at an angle from where he's lying, and a broken lightbulb crushed in his bleeding hand. We look up and see the empty socket of the light fixture.

"We should clean this up," Conchita says, "so it's not such a mess when he comes around."

"I suppose."

She studies me for a moment. "I know that look. What are you thinking?"

I shrug. "I don't know. How much easier it would be to just take him down to the passageway and toss him into the mist? Then he wouldn't have to go through all the crap we did, trying to adjust, and we wouldn't have to argue with him."

Conchita lifts her eyebrows.

"Yeah, yeah," I say. "I know. Free choice and all that. And it would piss Abigail off. I'm just saying it would be easier to push him through and be done with it. I know I said I'm staying here to pass the message on, but that doesn't mean I'm actually looking forward to doing it. Remember how well *I* took the news?"

"But we're not really going to . . ."

Conchita's voice trails off as I shake my head.

"No, of course not," I say. "Let's see if we can find a broom."

There's a door in the back wall of the gallery. I'm about to see what's on the other side of it when I realize something.

"Look at this," I say.

I kneel beside the body and point at his neck. His head is no longer at that awkward angle it was at when we first found him. Conchita opens the fingers of the hand clutching the lightbulb. Although there's still blood on the floor among the broken shards of glass from the bulb, there's none on his skin anymore. And there are no cuts.

Conchita sits back on her haunches and looks at me.

"That's just weird," she says.

"No kidding."

We stay there and look at him for a while, then finally get up and look for a broom and some cleaning supplies.

It never rains, but it pours. Miguel, the guy we found in the gallery with a broken neck, slipped off into the mists a week after he arrived. Three days later, we hear a crash and run outside to find a mid-sixties Plymouth pickup across the street, smashed into the corner the Alverson Arms. It hit so hard that it doesn't have a front end anymore. The engine's sitting in the cab.

Conchita comes to a stop in the middle of the street.

"I don't want to see this," she says. "Miguel and his broken neck was bad enough."

I nod, but someone has to deal with this. I leave her standing there and continue on to the truck.

We already know that the truck wouldn't be here if someone hadn't died in it. And by the mess of the vehicle crushed up against the Arms, it's not going to be pretty inside that cab. But when I get close enough to look inside, its even worse than I imagined. There's a whole family on that long bench seat—father, mother, a boy who looks around twelve in between them, and an infant in the mother's arms. Blood and crushed body parts are splattered everywhere.

I have to turn away and take a steadying breath before I can look again. I'm not even aware that I'm doing it, but I make the sign of the cross. When I do realize what I'm doing, I'm not surprised. I've been having a lot of one-way conversations with Our Lady of Altagracia and I haven't forgotten how something bigger than me helped me stand up to Abigail Alverson.

When I look back into the cab this time, I try to focus just on studying the metal. How it's twisted, where it's holding the victims, what we need to do to get them out. Because I know this much: I wouldn't wish waking up inside this horror show on anyone, especially not a kid.

"Is . . . is it bad?" Conchita asks.

I look over to where she's still standing in the middle of the street. I really wish we didn't have to do this.

I nod. "It's bad. We need to get them out of there before they come around."

"I was afraid you'd say that."

It's awful work. We hook up the Ford coupe Conchita and I rebuilt and use it to drag the pickup away from the greystone wall of the Arms. The front of the Plymouth is like an accordion but there's not a damn mark on the wall. Once we have room to maneuver, we remove the hood with torches and bolt cutters and whatever else we can find to tear back the metal. Then I get underneath and cut away all the bolts holding the engine to the frame and we lift it out with the pulley we made when we were working on the Ford.

That occupies us for most of the day, but I'm relieved to have it done. There's no way to tell how long it'll take for someone to come around. It took me three days, but others have woken up into this new world almost immediately after they've died. I think it has something to do with the severity of your injuries, but I'm not Henry and I don't really care to make a study of it. I just want to make sure none of these victims wakes up with an engine on their lap.

The victims.

The whole time we're working they're in our face and it's impossible to ignore the carnage. The only reason we can keep at it is because of how the Alverson Arms world dampens your feelings. This is a time I'm grateful for it.

But the shock and horror still gets through. You're cutting cables and just happen to look in the cab and you see that baby crushed against its mother before you can avoid it.

We look away, back at our work.

We keep at it.

Blow torch on the door panels.

Hook a rope from the door frame to the Ford and pull the door off.

Another rope to the steering wheel, and it's gone, too.

And finally we can pull the bodies out.

We lay them out in a row on the sidewalk and that's when I notice how Conchita's just shivering, her eyes big, gaze fixed on the smallest corpse.

The bodies are a mess, but we are, too. Covered in the victims' blood.

I step closer to Conchita and put an arm around her shoulder. She presses her face against me and I steer her away from the awful scene.

"Let's go get cleaned up," I say. "There's nothing more we can do for them now until they wake up."

She nods.

"Will they all wake up at the same time?" she asks.

"God, I never thought of that. What if . . ."

I let my voice trail off, but Conchita finishes my thought for me.

"What if the baby wakes up first?" she says.

"I guess we'll have to keep watch over them," I say. "But first we'll go grab a shower and some clean clothes."

The man wakes up first. He's white, maybe thirty, dressed in old jeans, scuffed cowboy boots, and a T-shirt with a beer logo on the front. I see his eyelids flutter and I'm by his side and helping him sit up as soon as he opens his eyes and tries to get up on his own. As I do that, I keep myself between him and his family and point him so that he's looking down the street, away from the accident. There's blood on the ground from where he was lying, but none on his clothes.

"God," he says. "I had the worst dream . . ."

He runs a hand through his short brown hair. His eyes are a startling blue, but their focus is lost. They look off into the distance until his gaze finds Conchita and settles on her.

"Who . . . ?"

And then I can see the memory come back to him—the last thing he saw. The wall coming up so fast, maybe. Or maybe he was looking at his family in that last instant.

He starts to turn toward them, but I put my arms around him and don't let him. He's strong, and I know this won't last.

"Before you do anything else," I tell him, "you need to listen to me." I start with a lie: "Everything's okay. It's weird, but you and your family are okay. It just looks worse than it is."

This time, when he twists out of my grip and turns, I can't stop him. His face goes white, seeing them laid out there on the pavement.

His wife, his son, his baby girl. My heart breaks for him, but he's not feeling the love. Hell, why would he?

He moans, reaches out a hand.

"They're going to be okay," I tell him, keeping with the lie for now. "They're going to wake up, just like you."

"Oh, God, oh God . . ."

"Seriously, man. You need to pull yourself together. You need to be there for them when they wake up."

"Wake up, wake up? What do you mean wake up?"

I sigh. There's no easy way to explain and I guess I understand how Edna could be so matter-of-fact with me when I first woke up myself. How do you even *start* to explain this?

"Do you remember driving into the wall?" I ask.

"Oh God . . ."

"Stay with me. That was the worst of it. Now you're here—past all the hurt and pain."

"Here? Where's here?"

"It's hard to say exactly. It's kind of a station stop on the way to where we all go after we . . . you know . . . pass on."

He looks at me and I see in his eyes how maybe we've gotten past the shock stage. But then he scrambles to his feet and stands between us and his family, fists clenched at his sides.

"Who are you people?" he wants to know. "Why did you bring us here? What did you *do* to us?"

I try to look nonthreatening, but we're in the middle of a rare, late autumn heat wave. It's hot today and I'm wearing a sleeveless T. All he can see is my ink. All he sees is some gangbanger's chica, and the little punkette that Conchita is.

"Take it easy," I say.

Conchita nods. "We didn't have anything to do with you coming here."

"How do I know that?"

"I guess you'll have to take that on faith," I say.

"This is bullshit."

"I know what you're feeling."

He glares at me. "You have *no* idea what I'm feeling. But if you don't give me some answers right now, you're going to wish you never messed with us."

I wish I could muster up the serenity I imagine Our Lady of Altagracia would in this situation, but I guess I'm just not wired that way. I don't have the honey in me.

"Look, tough guy," I say. "We've just spent the last two days cutting you and your family out of that truck so you wouldn't wake up inside with the engine in your lap and glass sticking out of your face. Then we spent another three days watching over you so that when you did wake up, you'd have somebody on hand to help you deal with this. For all we know, you were drunk and killed yourself and your family with your shitty driving."

"I wasn't—"

"I don't care if you were or you weren't. The point is, we didn't *know*. Just like you don't know the first thing about us. Now I'm not looking for a big thank-you here, but the least you could do is be a little fricking polite."

He stares at me for a long time. I can see his confusion fighting with his temper, but then he finally gives a slow nod.

"You're right," he says. "I . . . there was this kid. He just came out of nowhere and I swerved to miss him—" He turns to look at the truck. "Christ, I did miss him, right?"

"He's not here, so you can assume he's safe."

He puts his face in his hands. "God, God. We were just coming into town for some ice cream . . ."

Conchita and I look at each other. I shrug, figuring the best we can do right now is let him work through this.

After a few moments, he pulls himself together again. He looks back and forth between us, then settles his gaze on me.

"So, what're you saying? That we're . . . dead?"

"Yeah, sorry about that."

"And you—" His gaze flicks between us again.

"We're both dead, too."

He holds his hands out in front of himself and looks at them. He wiggles his fingers, rubs them together, then shakes his head.

"I don't feel any different . . ."

I don't know what else he might have added because just then the baby cries behind him.

"Rachel!"

He kneels on the pavement and scoops the baby into his arms. Cradling her against his chest, he makes comforting sounds that his eyes give lie to. But the kid can't see that. She just knows that Daddy's there, so everything's okay.

The boy comes around next, quickly followed by his mother.

Conchita and I sit on the curb and give them their space. Eventually, they approach us, the whole family. Baby in her mother's arms, the boy holding his father's hand. The boy's trying to be brave, but his lower lip trembles. I watch the woman's eyes as she takes us in and makes her judgment on us. I don't think we come off well, but she manages a polite smile.

Who knows what her husband told her? Conchita and I waited out of hearing range and all we heard of their conversation was the murmur of their voices, not what they were saying.

"Hello," she says. "From what Danny told me, you and he might have gotten off on the wrong foot."

I shake my head. "No. We're good."

"My name's Vicki," she says.

I introduce Conchita to her and give her my own name.

"Now, I'm not sure what's going on here," she says, "or what you think you can get from us, but we're not rich people. We don't really have anything. We're up to our ears in debt and that's not going to get better any time soon, not with a new baby in the house, so—"

I hold up a hand to cut her off. "We don't want anything from you."

She gives me a puzzled look before she says, "Then just let us go home."

"Did Danny tell you what we told him?" I ask.

She nods. "Some ridiculous story about—"

I hold up my hand again, then point to their Plymouth.

"Look at that pickup," I say. "Do you think anybody walked away from that in one piece? We had to cut you out of the cab."

"I don't understand. Please. We just want to go home."

"There's no way back," I tell her. "Do you think we'd be here if there was? All we get now is two choices: stay here, or go on to where we were supposed to before we got sidetracked to this place."

"Why are you doing this to us?"

I shake my head. "I already told your husband. We've got nothing to do with any of this."

I look at him. He studies the ground, unable, or unwilling, to meet my gaze.

"We're not like some people," his wife says. "We're not afraid to go to the police."

I nod. She thinks she's still in the real Santo del Vado Viejo where the gangbangers use the threat of further violence to keep their victims from talking to the cops.

"Good luck with that," I tell her and turn to Conchita. "Come on. I think we're done here for now."

We cross the road, heading for the record store. The sun's high in the sky so there are hardly any shadows. I'm looking forward to being inside where it's cooler.

"Hey!" Vicki calls after us. "You can't just walk away from us."

We ignore her and keep going.

"I forgot about how we'd have to deal with this," I say to Conchita as we step up onto the opposite sidewalk. "I guess it's because of how Miguel just took it all in stride."

Though his death had been as unfair as any—I mean, come on; breaking your neck while you're changing a lightbulb?—he'd been so serene about everything, including our explaining where he was and why he'd ended up here.

Conchita nods. "Those people are never going to listen to us."

"Maybe, maybe not. But I can't blame them. I look at them and all I see is me yelling at Edna when I first woke up in what I thought was my apartment."

"Goddamn it!" the woman yells from behind us. "You come back here."

We pause at the door of the record store. Conchita shows me her hand, middle finger extended.

"Can I?" she asks.

I shrug and open the door. She lifts her hand above her head, then we're inside, the door shutting behind us. Conchita engages the lock.

"Just in case she gets crazier," she says.

She waits by the front window looking out to where the woman still stands across the street, yelling something that we can't hear. I go behind the counter and look through the records for something to cheer us up, but nothing looks right.

"We need her to go on," I say, "if only to shut her up."

Conchita laughs, but I can see in her eyes that she's feeling the woman's confusion and pain the same as I am.

We ignore them for two weeks—or rather we walk away from them every time Vicki starts yelling at us, or Danny threatens us. It happens sooner or later in every conversation we have with them. I understand what they're going through, but we don't have to listen to it. And I hate the way their son looks at us with his scared eyes. But I'm proud of myself for developing some patience and Conchita's laid off with the vulgar hand signals since they weren't helping any.

And eventually they do come around—with no real effort on our part, because by the time they want to talk again without yelling or threats, we haven't spoken to them for almost a week. I figure something happened. Maybe they found Henry's notes in his war room at the library. Maybe they stumbled upon one of the sleepers. Maybe they met up with the old witch herself. They don't say, and we don't ask.

But Vicki comes up to where we're sitting in lawn chairs in front of Kit's old place and we just go through the whole business again. We point the way down El Encanto Street where the mist looks the same as it does at the end of every other street around the Alverson Arms, except when you step into it there, you don't come back.

"Where do you end up?" Vicki asks.

Her voice is civilized, or maybe she's just tired. I can tell that when she looks at us now, she sees two people, not a couple of girls who probably hang around with gangbangers, so that's at least an improvement.

"We honestly don't know," I tell her.

"Wherever we were supposed to go before the bruja trapped us here," Conchita offers.

"Bruja . . ."

"The witch," I say. "Abigail Alverson."

"We tried to talk to her," Vicki says, "but she wouldn't answer the door. And we couldn't get in. It's the only door we've tried that won't open."

"You don't want to meet her," Conchita says.

"If you say so."

There's a world of difference between the Vicki talking to us now and the one we knew before. That one had a chip on her shoulder the size of an oil pan.

"So, this place we go to," she saying. "Maybe it's good, maybe it's bad . . ."

I nod. "Though it's got to be better than this."

"I still feel like I'm alive," she says.

"I know. Except nothing has the same intensity, does it? We don't eat or sleep or drink . . . or at least we don't have to."

She shivers.

"I take it you tried sleeping," I say.

She nods. "It was like I had a switch inside me and someone just turned me off."

I hesitate a moment, then say, "There're people in some of these buildings who never come back. I don't think they even have a switch anymore."

She shivers again, sitting here with us on a lawn chair in the hot sun.

"I know," she says in a quiet voice. "We . . . we came across some . . ."

Conchita puts a hand on her arm.

"Don't worry," she says. "It's not like some horror movie where they lunge out of their bed to grab you."

Unless you disturb them coming back from the land of the living, I think. But that's something we haven't told Vicki and her family—the get-out-of-jail cards you get twice a year. We figured that would just complicate matters. Because until you actually go back and see for yourself, you're sure it'll be different for you. How can the people you loved *not* recognize you?

"Why do you stay here?" Vicki asks. "Why don't either of you go on?"

"It's like we told you. We're the last ones left who made the bargain with Abigail. If we go, the gate closes and everybody else who shows up will be stuck here forever."

"I couldn't do that," she says.

That's when I'm sure they're leaving.

"You don't have to," I tell her.

She shakes her head. "It's just . . . how long have you been here?"

"It's been four, five years for me," Conchita says.

"I'm a year plus," I add.

"How can you stand it? It's so desolate."

"It used to be different," I say. "There used to be a lot more people to hang out with."

Conchita nods. "And we rebuilt that Ford we used to drag your truck."

She waves a lazy hand in the direction of the Arms. I'm not sure if Vicki would know a Ford from a Chev, but she nods.

"We really got off on the wrong foot, didn't we?" she says.

I shrug. "You should have heard how I was with Edna when she tried to tell me I was dead. I thought it was just a bad dream I was having and that she'd broken into my apartment."

I'm not sure Vicki even hears what I'm saying. She's looking at me, but I can tell her thoughts are somewhere else.

"We're leaving tonight," she says. "We have to. The baby's so unhappy. She doesn't understand and . . ." She shakes her head. "What am I saying? None of us really understand what's happening to us."

I don't know what to say, and neither does Conchita. After a few moments of staring across the street, Vicki gets up and says good-bye. We watch her walk up El Encanto until she turns onto 26th.

We never see her or her family again.

A few weeks later somebody dies in one of the old adobe houses down on 25th Street near Guadalupe Park. I know because I'm walking by when the place changes. I stop and look, remembering the old lady who lived there when I was alive. Her name was Wanda Lopez, and the only reason I know that, or her, is because she was the landlady of a guy I was dating for a time. Johnny Baker.

Word was, Lopez used to run with one of the biker gangs that worked the drug trade over the border and used the money she made to buy up old buildings in the barrio off Mission Street. I don't know if that's true, but she sure owned a bunch of them, including the crappy place that Johnny rented from her. She was one of those real confrontational people—you know, where everything's an issue—and didn't trust, or much like, anybody. Her dirt yard was fenced off and a half-dozen pitbull and mastiff mongrels had the run of it.

The place looks the same as I remember except there aren't any dogs. It's just a squat, single-story adobe with a beat-up Oldsmobile and a GMC van in even worse shape parked out front. Prickly pear, palo verde, and mesquite trees grow along the side fences. The paint's peeling on the house and a trash can lays on its side under the big window to the left of the door. But there's a shiny new satellite dish on the roof. I wonder if it brings in a signal the way Edna's radio did, or just dead air like the wireless card on my laptop.

I stand there looking at the house for a long time. I think of going to get Conchita—she's back at the record shop, listening to music and reading—but then I climb over the fence and scuff my way across the dirt yard. The front door is unlocked, so I swing it open. I hesitate another moment and consider calling out. Instead I cross the threshold and look around.

There's a big flat screen in the living room and a mess of old Mexican movies scattered on the floor in front of the DVD and tape players with titles like *La Mujer Murcielago* and *El Grito de la Muerte*, and dozens of Santo and Blue Demon films. Who knew the old lady was into those old luchadores movies where the masked wrestlers are like superheroes fighting not only each other, but werewolves, vampires, and killer mummies?

Conchita's going to get a kick out of those, I think, as I walk down a short hall. I find a bathroom—cleaner than I expected; a bedroom that's being used as an office—tidier than I expected; and then finally the bedroom with the body. I thought, what with her reputation in the neighborhood, that she would have been shot, or chopped up with a machete or something, but she's lying peacefully on her bed like she died of natural causes.

She already has the look of a sleeper, settled in and *gone,* but I know it's only because she's so recently crossed over. I can't remember the last time I saw her, but she seems pretty much the same. She's still got that thick, greying hair and those strong, chiseled features that might have given her a hard look when she was younger, but now allow the face character. I think she must have some Indian in her—not like the Kikimi around here with their broad faces, but from south of the border. Aztec, maybe. She's still lean to the point of skinny, too, her dark skin roadmarked with wrinkles.

Then she sits up and my pulse jumps into overtime. I'd have calmed down when I saw that her eyes are human and brown, not the dark holes that reach into infinity the way a sleeper's seem to, except she's immediately on my case.

"<How the hell'd you get past the dogs?>" she asks in Spanish.

Some things never change, I think, remembering how she'd always been the hardcase with Johnny. But before I can tell her that there aren't any dogs out there anymore, she pulls a big pistol out from under her pillow and points it at my head. I don't know much about guns, but this thing looks monstrously huge in her skinny little hand. I find myself wondering if she'll break her wrist from the recoil when she fires it.

"<It doesn't matter,>" she says. "<You won't be stealing anything from this old lady.>"

"<I wasn't . . . .>"

"<You've got till the count of three to tell me what the hell you're doing in here.>"

"<You might as well put that down,>" I tell her. "<I've already been shot dead once. It didn't take.>"

The gun never wavers in her hand.

"<You're going to need to explain that,>" she says.

I'm surprised that having a pistol pointed at me doesn't freak me out, considering what happened the last time. Maybe it's because, like I said, I've already been shot once and we all know how that turned out. Not good, but not like you'd expect when you're still alive.

"<I know you,>" she says before I can tell her what I meant. "<You used to be one of my deadbeat tenants.>"

I shake my head. "<I only dated one of them. Johnny Baker. My name's Grace Quintero.>"

"<I don't care who you are. I just want to know what you meant about being shot dead, and what you're doing in my house.>"

"<Do you feel like putting down that gun first?>"

"<No.>"

I sigh. "<Fine. Do you mind if I sit down?>"

"<Yes. Stop stalling.>" She gives the gun a little wiggle. "<The next time you open your mouth, tell me something I want to hear.>"

I don't know if it's what she wants to hear, but I start off telling her that she's dead and then go from there straight into where she is and how the Alverson Arms world came to exist in the first place. She's a good listener. Maybe that's why I end up telling her way more than I meant to. Or maybe I just needed a fresh set of ears to hear my story. But I find myself talking about Abuelo and John. I tell her about Norm's wheel of life and the path he says I'm supposed to be on, and how I feel more connected to the Church now that I'm dead than I ever did when I was alive—or at least I feel connected to the Our Lady of Altagracia, my namesake.

And I tell her about our mission—the reason why Conchita and I stay on.

Sometime during our conversation she laid her gun down on the nightstand and I sat on the end of her bed.

She shakes her head as I finish up.

"<Bullshit,>" she says.

I shrug.

"<You can believe it or not,>" I tell her, "<but like Edna first told me when I got here, that's not going to change the fact that you're dead and you're stuck here in this weird little world. Unless you take that walk down El Encanto Street.>"

"<Oh, I've got no trouble believing I'm dead,>" she says. "<I'm old enough now that every night I go to sleep, I don't really expect to wake up again. And if this is the afterlife, well, hell. It seems nice and quiet to me. I don't hear any noise out there at all.>"

"<Then what—>"

"<It's all this noble crap about how you and your friend are staying on so's you can help out all the other poor souls that end up here.>"

I get up from the bed and glare at her. "<It's not crap.>"

"<No, not completely. I'm sure you're doing it for all the right reasons. But I'm guessing you found all those reasons because you're too scared to go on yourself.>"

I can't believe what I'm hearing.

"<What?>" I say. "<We talk for a couple of hours and all of a sudden you know everything about me?>"

She shakes her head. "<I don't know dick about you, honey. Just what you've told me.>"

"<I didn't tell you that.>"

"<You didn't have to. I didn't live as long as I did, and do as well as I did, by being a poor judge of character. I can read between the lines, girl. I heard the things you didn't think you were telling me.>"

"<Oh, yeah? Like what?>"

She shrugs. "<There's no point in getting into it. You're not interested in listening to anything I've got to say. Not now. Maybe never.>"

She's right.

"<But take this thought with you,>" she adds as I turn to leave. "<Most times we only see things for the way we are. But we're good at lying to ourselves. Sometimes we need somebody who's not living in our skin to point out how things really are.>"

"<Screw you,>" I tell her, "<and your damn platitudes.>"

"<What you need to ask yourself,>" she says, "<is does your friend really want to stay here, too, or are you holding her . . . >"

I don't hear her finish because I'm already out the door and stomping down the hallway. But I don't have to hear her out to know where she was going with that last thought.

I get outside and stand there in her dirt yard, blinking in the bright light. I see there's the rusted frame of an old one-speed bicycle in the prickly pear. The sun's still high overhead, though I feel like I've been in there for hours.

I can still sense the presence of the old lady in the house behind me. The weight of her words seems to be pressing against me.

The worst thing about this is she's right. I don't want to be here, but in the end, I'm too scared of what might come next on the other side of the mists.

Helping people's just an excuse to stay.

Conchita finds me standing at the end of El Encanto Street, staring at the stretch of grey mist that all of our friends have already stepped through. I'm imagining, not how I remember the street looking as it continued westward, but the desert that lay far beyond. The mountains rising up above them. The wide, open roads that I've cruised so many times I know them like the back of my hand.

I won't be seeing them again.

No, that's not true. I can go back and see them twice a year. But it's not the same. It's not the same at all.

"What's going on?" Conchita asks.

"I'm just thinking."

"About stepping through? You weren't going to leave me, were you?"

I shake my head. "Never. It's just . . . there's this new arrival—an old lady in one of those adobes on Twenty-fifth. She got me wondering: Am I doing this for the dead still to come, or for me?"

"For you? What do you mean?"

I turn to look at her. "She thinks that the reason I stay on to help other people isn't to be the good guy, but because I'm too scared to go on myself."

I expect her to laugh, or to say something like, "You? You're not scared of anything," the way she has before.

But, "Are you?" she asks.

I look away down 24th Street and study a heat shimmer on the far side of the library. I could be that shimmer. My skin's got that hot, sweaty flush you get when you've been caught out in a lie.

"Grace?" she says. "Look, I didn't mean . . ."

"It's okay," I tell her.

I make myself meet her gaze. I feel so much love for this sister I never knew I had, that I had to die to be able to meet.

"I am scared," I tell her. "Big-time scared. I don't know where people like Henry or Edna got the peace of mind to just step through. All I can worry about is all the stuff we've talked about, and a whole bunch we didn't. What happens? Are we still ourselves, or do we just kind of drift apart into some kind of unconnected energy? Do I lose you? Do I really never see mi abuelo or John again? Do I not get to make peace with my mother? Or worse, what if I do see them again, but they don't know me, just like the people back in Santo del Vado Viejo don't know us on Halloween and May Eve?"

"That's not something anybody knows," she says.

"I get that. But if I could just get some hint, some sign . . ."

Conchita smiles, without humor, but with great affection.

"That's the point behind faith," she says. "It's not something you can prove."

"Yeah, yeah . . ."

"I know you hate to hear this, but you either have it, or you don't."

"And you do?"

She nods.

"You can still believe in a God that would let you be stabbed to death when you're only seventeen? You had your whole life ahead of you!"

"I don't put my faith in God," she says. "I put it in the saints and martyrs and Our Lady. I put it in *their* faith."

"So where does God fit into this?"

"I don't know. Maybe that's something we'll find out when we cross over. I just believe that los santos and Our Lady care for me and will look out for me." I guess she sees a dubious look on my face. "They were only human, Grace. They couldn't be everywhere. They weren't there for me when that guy came at me with his knife. But I know they'll look out for me now." She pauses, then adds, "They brought us together, didn't they? They gave me a big sister."

I look at the wall of mist.

"So you'd go through it?" I ask.

She nods. "As long as I went with you."

"I don't know. How can you be sure Heaven's waiting for us on the other side?"

"I'm not," she says. "I just know wherever we go, we'll be there together. I believe my abuela will be there, along with John and your family. So what do you say?"

She holds out her hand to me.

"What about the people who are going to show up here after we're gone?" I ask.

"What about them?"

"Well, maybe I'm using them for an excuse, but you know, we can't just leave them to their fate." I have to laugh as I say that. "God, could I sound more melodramatic?"

"I know what you mean."

"So, what about them?"

"I'll tell you what I think," she says. "I know the bruja thinks she made this place, that it's going to exist until she gets her son back, but I think it's become something else since then. I think it's become a place for some people to come so they can work through things before they move on to whatever comes next."

"What did you need to work through?"

"The fact that I hated everybody and everything." She smiles. "Oh, don't look so surprised. Yeah, it was terrible that I got killed the way I did, but the truth is I was a little shit who didn't appreciate the first thing about how crappy I made the lives of everybody around me. My abuela was a goddamned saint to put up with me the way she did."

"And me?" I ask. "What did I need to work through?"

She shrugs. "I don't know. That's something you've got to figure out for yourself. Maybe it was your relationship with your namesake, Our Lady of Altagracia. You know, to figure out where you really stood on your faith without considering the guilt your mother laid on you about it, or for that matter, your abuelo's disinterest in talking about that kind of thing."

"Everybody's a philosopher today."

She gives me another shrug.

"So I guess we didn't do any favors for Miguel and that family that died in their pickup. We shouldn't have talked them into going."

"I don't think they would have gone on if they weren't ready."

"And if we leave, what about those who come here after us? They won't get the choice."

"Which is how it was before you got here," she says. "And maybe that's the way it's supposed to be. And maybe when people here are ready, someone else will come along like you did and make a change."

"So it's all laid out for us. Everything's predetermined."

She shakes her head. "No, we get to choose. You chose to confront the bruja. You get to choose whether we stay here or go on."

"And what about you? Don't you get a choice?"

She grins. "Sure I do. I choose to be with you."

Damn kid's got an answer for everything. I wonder how long she's been working this all out and keeping it to herself. Though she's not a kid, I have to remind myself. Not really. She just looks like one.

I find I've brought my hand up to my tattoo of Our Lady of Altagracia. I feel the ridge of the scab from where I cut it. I keep the palm of my hand there as I think about what Conchita's just said.

"Maybe you're right," I say finally. "I had—have—a lot of issues with the Church. It's not just my mother and Abuelo. It's not even turning on the evening news and finding one more story about freaky priests, because I know they're not all like that. It's how I'd look at what the world was like and think, what kind of a house of God would let this crap go on?

"I guess the saint—Our Lady of Altagracia—seemed apart from that. Like if she were here, she wouldn't stand by and let that kind of thing go on. She'd be like Mother Teresa."

Conchita nods to show she's listening.

"So I get what you're saying about the saints and martyrs," I say. "I just don't see how their faith can give me faith. Especially when I'm so ambivalent about it all in the first place." I sigh and shake my head. "I understand old cars. I understand the people who are into old cars, and the whole rockabilly and ink culture that seems to go hand-in-hand with it. After that . . ." I give her a helpless look. "Unless God's looking for a good mechanic, I don't know that there's a place for me on the other side. To tell you the truth, if there's a Heaven and Hell, then there's probably a guy in a red suit with a tail and horns who's already got a reservation waiting for me."

"You know that's not how it's going to be."

"Do I?"

She nods.

"But I don't," I tell her.

"Then accept that I know."

"Because you have faith."

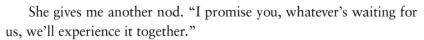

She gives me another nod. "I promise you, whatever's waiting for us, we'll experience it together."

"Again with the faith," I say.

She holds her hand out again.

I look around me. The heat wave broke a few days ago, but it's still warm with the sun high in the sky.

Faith, I think.

"There's no reason to stay," I say. "Is there?"

"Unless you choose to."

"Except for one thing."

She rolls her eyes, but I've got this idea, and now that I've got it, I know I have to give it a go. It probably won't work, but it's like when you're improvising parts on some old car. You still have to try.

"Grace," Conchita starts.

"I know," I say. "We're done here—I get that. But I think I might have figured out how we can go but also make sure that nobody else gets stuck here."

"Unless they're supposed to—"

I hold up my hand. "If that's the case, then that's how it'll be. But first I need to try this one thing."

"Which is?"

I shake my head. I don't want to say the words aloud. Who knows what Abigail can or can't hear?

"You'll see," I tell Conchita. "Wait here."

That's how I find myself on the top floor of the Alverson Arms building again, standing in front of Abigail's door. Alone. The door is still covered with the blue crosses I painted—and the largest one still has the cross of my blood on it. The unlit votive candles stand on either side of the door. The retablo of San Juan has fallen down and I set it upright again.

I know that none of this stuff will protect me today. Whatever mojo they had got burned away. But I'm not here for a confrontation. I'm here for conversation.

I lean against the banister, arms folded across my chest.

"So we're going," I say. "But before we leave, I just wanted to tell you something that maybe you don't know."

There's no response, but I know she's listening.

"That passage you made at the end of El Encanto Street? Turns out the passage goes both ways. Oh, I don't mean spirits are crossing over from the other side to this one, but if you stand close enough to the mists, you can talk to them. It's not easy. There's a lot of, oh, I don't know. It's like static. You miss words, or part of what they're saying gets garbled.

"Anyway, I've been talking to the ghost of a young soldier boy and I promised him before I left that I'd pass along a message for him. His name's Justin Alverson and he wants to know when his mother's going to finally join him on the other side because he's been waiting for her for a long, long time."

This is all bullshit, of course. But hope and yearning are funny things. Henry told me that Abigail's here because of a mother's love for her son. If that's true, even if she sees through the load of B.S. I'm shoveling here, she's still going to be curious. She's still going to want to check it out.

I wait a couple of minutes, but there's no response. Finally, I straighten up from where I was leaning against the banister.

"Okay," I say. "I did my bit and passed on Justin's message. I guess the rest is up to you."

I start for the stairs, stop when I hear the door creak open, and there she is, the horror-show bruja herself.

"Liar," she says.

I shake my head.

"I've got nothing to lose or gain here," I tell her. "I'm just passing along a message, and now Conchita and I are out of here."

"My Justin would never speak to someone like you. If he was that close by, he would talk to me. He would come to me."

"And you've been standing there at the end of El Encanto how many times?"

She frowns at me. We both know the answer to that: never.

"You're up to something," she says.

"Of course I am. I'm up to leaving. But tell me this: What makes you think spirits can cross over to this little world you've made? The only way to get into it is to die, and he was already dead."

"There was always a way in for him."

I nod. "But there he is, waiting on the other side for you."

"You're lying. I know you are."

"There's an easy way for you to find out for yourself."

She shakes her head. "No, you've got something planned."

"I do. Like I already told you, we're leaving."

"No, there's more to it than that."

I lift a hand. "I'm not here to argue. I just came to pass along the message like I promised Justin I would."

"I don't believe you."

"Doesn't matter," I tell her. "I'll be seeing you."

I turn then and start down the stairs. The skin at the nape of my neck prickles in anticipation of . . . something. I know she promised not to hurt me, but hell, she's a crazy woman. Who knows what she'll do?

But nothing hits me. No mojo comes along and pushes me down the stairs.

Instead, I hear her footsteps on the risers behind me.

I don't turn to look. I just keep descending the stairs. When I get to the ground floor, I walk through the lobby and out onto the street. I can sense her hesitate outside of the Alverson Arms. Looking across the street, I catch her reflection in the Laundromat's front window, standing on the steps, and I wonder when was the last time she actually stepped outside of the building?

Then I'm walking west on 26th and I can't see her anymore.

I make the turn onto El Encanto and make a point of not checking that she's still following. But when I finally catch up to where Conchita's waiting for me at the end of the street, I can tell by the widening of her eyes that the old witch is still coming.

"What?" Conchita begins, but I put a finger to my lips.

We stand there together until Abigail is abreast of us. She studies the mist for a long moment, then turns to Conchita.

"I suppose you've been talking to my son as well?" she asks her.

"No, it was just me," I say before Conchita can say anything. "She doesn't even know about this. Nobody does."

Abigail fixes that piercing glare of hers on me.

"I've been patient with you," she says. "Don't think I haven't seen you ferrying new arrivals out of my influence. But I tell you now, if you've lied about this, if you're playing some infantile game with me, you will regret it. I promised not to harm you, but there are other ways to torment a person that leave no mark. Consider eternity in a box in the ground. No light, no distractions. You might attempt to fall into the long sleep, but I won't let you. You'll stay awake and aware until I will it to be different."

I shrug with a nonchalance I'm not feeling. My every nerve is on edge. My heart is racing way too fast. But I tell myself to be patient. I'm only going to get one shot at this and I can't screw it up.

I clear my throat.

"Just go listen," I tell her. "Hear for yourself."

She holds my gaze, like she's trying to get inside my head. I don't know if she can without physical contact, but I'm not taking any chances. I remember the picture Henry showed me of her son—the death notice in the paper—and let it fill my mind.

"I know you're lying," Abigail says.

But she turns to the mist all the same. She steps close. Closer.

It's now or never.

But before I can lunge forward to push the old witch into the mist, Conchita grabs my arm. I try to break free, but she just says, "Look!"

I don't get what she wants me to see. I want to tell her that she's screwed up everything. I see my future—forever in that coffin Abigail threatened me with.

"Look at her face," Conchita says. "I don't know what you told her, but she's hearing something."

Then I do look. It's true. Not only is Abigail listening to something in the mist, she's leaning closer to it. She's smiling—not that freak-show smile just before she does something horrible to you, but one that almost makes her look human.

She turns to look at us.

"Thank you," she says in a soft voice I've never heard her use before.

And then she steps through, into the mist, and she's gone.

"Holy crap," I say. "He was really there."

"You told her Justin was waiting for her?"

I nod. "I don't believe it. I was just trying to get her close enough to push her through."

Conchita shakes her head. "I didn't think even you'd be that stupid."

"What's stupid? It worked, didn't it?"

"No," she says. "But I think los santos were looking out for you all the same."

"Maybe yes, maybe no." I look around. "How come the world's still here?"

"Maybe this kind of a place is easier to make than it is to unmake."

I give a slow nod. But really, it doesn't matter. I'm done with talking, done with thinking. I remember the presence I felt when we faced down Abigail back in the Alverson Arms. The light that seemed to fill me.

I feel that light waiting for us now, too.

"So," Conchita says and holds out her hand. "My sister . . . full of grace. Are you finally ready?"

She smiles.

I give her a slow nod. Taking her hand, I let her lead me to where the mist waits for us.

As we get closer I think I smell creosote—the smell the desert gets after it rains. I think I hear the rumble of an engine that reminds me of how my Fairlane used to sound when it was idling. I imagine John leaning against it, the way he was when I came out of Luna's what seems like a million years ago. Maybe Abuelo and Mama are standing nearby and they're actually getting along. And maybe there'll be another old lady there, too—Conchita's grandmother.

Or maybe not. Maybe it's all just in my imagination. But it doesn't matter any more now.

I hold Conchita's hand tight in my own and we step into the damp grey mist.